MW00415806

The InBetween

PRAISE FOR PREVIOUS NOVELS
by DICK WYBROW

Hell inc.

One of the best comedic adventure stories I've ever read!
-- *James Jones*

Wow! What a book! I laughed constantly. Funny and well written to boot.
-- *Scott Luttrell*

Not since reading Hitchhiker's Guide have I so laughed out loud. This is can't-put-down good.
-- *Bobbi Shockley*

The Swordsmen (Fifty Shades of Gray Matter)

"Loved this book... Fabulous!" -- *Natasha Schmidt*

"Too funny. Laughing just thinking about it!" -- *LadyP*

"Brilliant." -- *Jack White*

The Mentor

"This truly is a masterpiece." -- *Corey Foley*

"No question, The Mentor is a powerful thriller -- but it's also funny."
-- *Brad Meltzer, New York Times bestselling author*

Copyright © Dick Wybrow 2019
www.dickwybrow.com

Edited by Red Adept
Cover by Warren Design

This is a work of fiction. Names, characters, places and incidents either are the product of the author's imagination or are used fictitiously. Any resemble to actual persons, living or dead, is entirely coincidental.

All rights reserved

Without limiting the rights under copyright reserved above, no part of this publication may be reproduced, stored in or introduced into a retrieval system, or transmitted, in any form or by any means (electronic, mechanical, photocopying, recording or otherwise), without the prior written permission of the copyright owner of this book.

To my mother...

who taught me that life is wonderful, but it's also fleeting.

Especially, when I put my feet on the coffee table.

The InBetween

by Dick Wybrow

Prologue

She wished she could dream, but the dead never sleep. Then she remembered—dreams could be deadly.

The Butterfly reached out to brush the hair from his eyes then stopped, not wanting to wake him. But no touch from her would ever again stir him. She remembered how a soft caress of her fingertips could make him quiver.

But like small, dry berries in a deep basket, her memories—little bits at a time—were slipping out through the cracks.

How long had she been here? Back in this room. Their home. What used to be their home. It was only his now.

At first, when she lost the light, she wandered. That tiny room with the strange bed. The scratchy gray blanket with the hole that would always snag one of her toes. The pillow filled with sand.

Then after that, the city and its pulsing sky, so much different than she remembered. Every step felt like walking at the top of a high rise, her toes and heels shrinking back from the ledge. Every step threatened to take her off the side, to forever fall.

She was the Butterfly. Weak and vulnerable. Delicate. Prey.

In the city, the Butterfly had spent days hiding in the Dumpster of an abandoned restaurant. The lock had rusted shut, so no one could get in. Of course, the living were no longer a threat to her.

The dead? They were another story.

She'd seen others like her but shunned them. Given them wide berths, eyes cast down. This skill, if it was a skill, was something she had learned in the handful of months before losing the light.

The Dumpster had come after she'd been pursued. However, a frail Butterfly is a tiny snack, and she'd quickly been forgotten. But they were out there, the hunters.

It wasn't supposed to be like this. Her flirtations with religion, albeit never fully embraced, had promised a plan, even for her, after the light was taken away. Movies and books gave some version of the good take the stairway to heaven; for the bad there's a subway to hell.

But this was neither of those things; this was someplace between them.

Finally, she found somewhere safe. That is, found it again and rediscovered something she'd forgotten ever existed in the world: warmth. At least the hint of it. A flickering glass bulb in a long-forgotten closet. She could almost feel something.

Crossing the threshold of their home again, a breath had caught in her throat at the sight of him.

Her Stephen.

Her husband.

No, wait.

Not husband. That hasn't happened yet. Not yet. And, well, not ever now.

It didn't matter. She'd found him again. This was where she belonged, even if he could no longer see her. Hear her. Feel her.

She watched the young man as he ate, when he slept, as he worked late into the night, always on the phone.

She watched when he showered. That was a bit tortuous. Her hand would pass straight through his body. Who knew you could feel sexual frustration after you died? She didn't remember Dante ever passing that one along.

On the table near his computer desk was the digital picture frame. She remembered buying it for him one Christmas. Or birthday. Or did he buy it for her?

When she'd first seen the screen, it was the two of them, a selfie they'd taken during a stolen moment in DC. So much promise back then. The look in both their eyes reflected the fire, the thrill of youth! Unaware of the challenges on their road ahead but ready for the adventure of a life full of love and success and joy.

Her fire was out. But she wasn't gone. Not gone yet.

Ten seconds later, the next picture. Outside a surf shop in Daytona Beach. She was laughing. Huge smile, teeth parted. He could do that to her like no one else could.

When the next came up, it was the video they'd taken on a chartered fishing boat off San Onofre. SoCal! She'd been reeling in something big, pulling the line hard. A look of determination on her face mixed with that moment before a fit of laughter. She watched as the camera rhythmically jerked. He'd been cheering her on—Go! Go! Go!—something the speaker-less frame showed only in pantomime.

Stephen had set the frame's hashtag to her name so that pictures of her in his photo library would display. She knew he missed her as she missed him.

That brief warm flicker turned to fear. How long would she be allowed to stay with him? Would she slowly fade or flick off like a bad circuit? Gone. Off.

If only she could let him know she was right here! Sitting next to him as he ate. Stroking his hair as he worked the phone. Grinding against him as he stroked himself.

A live boy and a dead girl. The ultimate star-crossed lovers!

That same expression had been how her mother had described herself and the Butterfly's dad. But if there had been a good memory of her father, she couldn't recall it. And not merely because, in this place, her memory frayed at its edges like a flag snapping in the breeze at the beach, the saltwater and wind stripping away the threads.

In those early years, people would say how the Butterfly was just like her dad, but they didn't know him. No one did until the end. Then everyone knew.

But she wasn't like him. She was smart and determined and could even be ruthless. But it only made her successful at whatever she did. When she competed, she always won. Nearly every time.

He had been violent and crazy and dangerous and deadly.

As a child, she had been a weak little Butterfly, and her mother had saved her. Hidden her from her father.

But there had been one last encounter. An impossible visit when his voice was dry as autumn leaves.

Stephen's laugh broke her spell. He'd answered his phone, but she hadn't noticed.

Always working. He'll be governor one day!

This tone was… different though. He was smiling. But that one, that had been her smile. The one for her. Who was he talking to? She tried to listen to his words, but that sound in her brain, that awful fucking crackle and hum!

Why was her father's voice in her head? Wasn't it enough he'd blackened her life? Surely she'd earned freedom from him now, in this place!

She shook herself violently—Get out!—and when she stopped, her eyes drifted toward the picture frame again. Stephen and her at a Cubs game. They both had on tiny plastic baseball hats that had once been filled with ice cream.

Another picture. They'd gone skiing. She'd forgotten that one!

The crunching racket in her mind grew softer.

The next picture, a café. She's mugging at the camera for Stephen.

Another: trying on a big, floppy hat in a small store in a small town during a road trip.

Each picture, every tiny serving of happiness, pushed her father's voice farther and farther from her mind.

Then the digital device played the first few frames of a video clip, dark and grainy.

Behind her, Stephen laughed again. She became annoyed. Still on the phone. Who was he talking to? Why was he smiling like that?

Her eyes fell back to the frame, and as she watched, she drew closer to it, pulling away from Stephen and pressing her nose right up against the frame.

What is this?

The aspect was high, from a corner in a parking lot. The pool of streetlight and a handful of cars parked neatly. Except one.

The car looked familiar. It was—

The clip stopped, and then she was frozen in time at a hotel pool, outside and in a bathing suit she'd always hated.

Then another picture and another. How many did he have on the computer linked to the frame? Another, then another, but the smiles now felt less real. As her head began to spin, the crackle returned, growing louder again.

Picture, picture, another fucking picture!

She put a fist to the side of her head, trying to push the ache away, stop the noise. Seconds ticked by like hours, and the agony, the crackle, was being driven into her skull like some cruel, hateful symphony.

When she opened her eyes, a video clip was playing, but not the right one!

There she was, back on the boat off the San Onofre coast, the camera moving and shaking but farther through the clip now. She was pulling the fish onto the deck. Puny thing. An embarrassed laugh.

More pictures, more pictures, more pictures, more pictures.

Nothing she could do but wait, and her teeth hurt even though she didn't have teeth anymore. But her teeth, her jaw—

There!

The dark clip was back. She blinked to get a good focus on the frame.

It was CCTV footage. She knew this clip! It was...

Dammit, why can't I remember?

Looking closer at the car, she saw that it was a late-model Audi. Oh no.

Not just any late-model Audi. She knew this car.

No, no! I don't want to see this.

But she couldn't turn away.

She squinted to see. Yes, the front end was crunched inward, jagged, about the size of a little boy. Could she see a stain, or was she imagining that?

The frame would show just a few more seconds before it went back through the library once more. She didn't she think could take that again.

Her eyes locked on the upper-left corner of the frame. She remembered now. Her breath felt trapped in her chest as she prayed for the clip to play just a few seconds longer. And right before it switched, she'd seen him.

Just a fraction of a second, but she'd seen him.

The Butterfly crumpled to the floor and let the chaos in her head wash over her. She didn't need to see any more. She'd seen it at the first trial. Then, as she waited for the second, it would run on the news. The others in their jumpsuits would laugh and jeer and point fingers, ignoring her tearful requests that they turn the channel to anything, something else, any fucking thing! This only made them laugh harder.

She knew how it played out.

Even in just that half second, the tiny, black-and-white grainy image of Stephen looked almost heroic.

The rest of the clip played in her mind. Stephen running to the car. The time in the upper corner said sometime after midnight but not yet dawn. His arms pumping against his sides, coming to her.

But by that time, there was nothing he could do.

Later, her Audi would be towed to a police impound yard. She never saw the car again. It probably got crushed. Turned into bottle caps or cheap pliers that get forgotten in kitchen drawers or maybe cock rings.

Who knows? Who cares?

The last few moments of the clip would show Stephen gently pulling her from the car. A rag doll, she'd refused to awaken. He held her, his shoulders bobbing in huge, heaving sobs as she slept. As she dreamed her deadly dream.

Stephen had wanted to be her hero.

But she could not be saved.
And now there was nothing left to save.

Chapter One

"You get all his dough?" said a large, hairy man with a nose busted more times than the tenth commandment (note: that's the covety one).

"Sure, Hamish, I got what he had under the bed and in his sock, but—"

"You check everywhere?" The man grunted as he folded the dead man in half.

"Yeah, sure, I checked everywhere." The big man's partner was a young, scrawny kid with cold sores that had festered to such a degree that they no longer required the attention of a medical professional but rather a member of the clergy. "You worried we killed him, and he had the cash? He was screaming bloody murder, so he woulda told us if he had someth—"

"No, no," Hamish said through clenched teeth. "But this is a Collect & Close, you idjit. On C&Cs, we get fifteen percent of whatever we recover following the close of the postantecedent dead guy's account."

The kid chewed his lip and instantly regretted it, as he'd bitten into a blister. It hurt like hell, and his eyes watered, but he knew not to say anything about it. Hamish had long lectured about the young man's generation being "pussified." There was no need to give the big bastard any more ammunition during those long drives like the body dump ahead.

"See, I don't know that legal stuff like you do, Ham."

"I coulda sit the bar."

"I know it."

"I chose not to. Lawyers are scum," said the organized-crime heavy and freelance hitman.

"You got principles. I hear ya."

"And I got fifteen percent insteada the usual ten. On account of this was the closure of this knucklehead's account."

"Right."

"So while I grab a smoke, check his shorts and do a thorough cavity search to be sure he ain't hidden away a roll of quarters or something."

The skinny kid looked down at the man stuffed awkwardly into a suitcase, gingerly moistened two fingers with his blistered mouth, and, not for the first time on the job, wished he'd paid more attention in math class.

I watched as the man hovering over the methhead screamed yet again as the kid jammed two fingers up his dead body's ass.

"Stop it, stop it!" the ghost shouted and had been shouting for the last ten minutes. Me, I waited. Before I said anything to a potential new client, it was best to sit tight until they were adequately distraught yet not full-on furious.

Bad things can happen when somebody's out of control, even here in the InBetween.

The man, who I later learned was named Allister Hale, once again swung his ghostly fists at the skinny kid, crying tears that would never fall.

"Leave me alone, leave me..." he screamed, "... alone!"

He then attempted to kick the head of the kid, who was now two knuckles deep in the dead man's rectum. However, without a solid form—i.e., body—at his command, Allister swooshed right through and dropped flat on his back.

For a few seconds, the kid stopped twiddling his fingers, and his eyes cut left and right. A fleeting moment later, he was back at it, fingers now searching in the dead guy's mouth.

Same fingers, by the way.

Not that it should matter, but respect for the dead and all, right?

Blechy.

Here lay Allister, now finally under the numbing spell of that familiar concoction of remorse, defeatism, and sadness. His ghostly image warbled with small, breathy sobs as he lay next to his own body, which had been busted up, cut up, smashed, and twisted to fit into a large rollaway suitcase.

This was my window of opportunity: right after the righteous indignation and self-pity screamfest but before the seething, angry plotting for revenge (which, you're dead, total waste of time, in my humble opinion).

"My name is Painter Mann," I said as I had many, many times before. "And I'm here to help you."

Allister the ghost looked toward me then back at the skinny kid, who, somewhat over-eager I would say, was back in the dead guy's colon. The spook simply waited, staring at me for a moment, then back to the junior crook.

"I'm not talking to him," I said. "I'm talking to you."

Allister stared at me like someone who'd just heard the punch line of a joke but somehow missed the setup.

I'm a kind person, but I suppose I was hurrying the guy along a bit, looking for an easy win after a recent case that hadn't worked out. Not because I hadn't cleared that woman. I had. But something went wrong. All the work for nothing. She was stuck in the InBetween despite my efforts.

Whatever. It happens.

"Listen, I'm sorry to be the one to tell you this," I said. "But you're dead, man."

The guy's eyes went out of focus for a moment, and he said, "Yeah, got that. Kid went pretty deep, didn't even take his rings off. And I never felt a thing."

"Oh, okay, that makes sense now."

Allister's eyes cleared a little, and he looked at me squarely for the first time. "What? What makes sense?"

I pointed at the boy, now struggling to get three fingers inside the guy's backside.

"I think he mighta lost a ring."

Allister closed his eyes slowly and turned away. He then stood and began to shuffle to the other side of the room. I wanted to let the guy grieve but didn't want to lose the client of an open-and-shut case.

A nice easy tick in my box.

Speaking to him in a soothing tone, I told him he wasn't alone and that I was there to help him. I was a friend and all that blah blah blah stuff.

He introduced himself and asked me if I was an angel. Smiling, I said as I spread my arms wide, "You call me whatever you feel you need to, Allister."

Note: I am no angel.

At least not yet.

Allister walked toward me, absentmindedly dragging his ghostly arm through an upturned wooden end table—the thick blood on two of its legs now dark and drying. He looked up at me with dead eyes.

That is, you know, empty. He was dead, so any expression was gonna be dead. He could be shiny, happy Allister, and he'd still have dead eyes.

Just trying to be clear there.

Then Allister brought his hand up and tapped at my chest, which sent small waves of nausea through me, and I grabbed his wrist to stop it. His eyes grew wide (but still dead, btw), and he began to go into a low-boil panic until I let go and set him straight.

"No touchee, Allister! That's a part of Rule #1!"

"Why?" he said and looked at his hand.

I reached up and flicked his ear, and since I was taking back the spoonful of energy he'd leached from me with the chest taps, he went a bit weak in the knees and then fell to the floor in a heap. A half minute later, he was back on his feet.

"Okay, got it," he said, raised his hands, and took a big step backward. "Rule number one firmly established, Mr. Mann."

"Ugh, don't call me that. Everyone calls me Painter. Mister Man sounds like a pejorative Kathy Bates used in that movie where she clubs James Caan's ankles."

"Misery?"

"No, no, but it does bother me a little," I said and waited for the laugh. It didn't come. Whatever. I'm about fifty-fifty on that joke. Good ice breaker when it works.

If I was being honest, I began to like Allister a little less. Time to get to business.

"Okay, partner, here's how it works," I said and walked toward the suitcase stuffed full of Allister. The big guy had returned, so now he and the shitfingers kid were struggling to get the zipper on the luggage closed.

"How what works, Painter?" Allister said, trying not to look at them. "I'm dead, right?"

"No, it—"

"I'm not dead?!"

"What? Yes, yes, you're dead," I said and brushed away his interruption. "But I can help you. I'm here to help you cross over to the Next."

"Why?"

"Because this here is not the end. Around here, we call this 'the InBetween.' Like a train station between life and the afterlife. Or the salad that follows the appetizer, yet before the main meal."

"Okay."

"Or the yellow light between the green and the red."

"I get it!"

I smiled. "I could go on and on. I got hundreds of them."

Allister responded as about twenty percent of my new clientele do in the early stages. "But no, wait! I want to go back. I wasn't done yet! I want—"

"Oh, hell no, you don't want to go back!" I said and walked toward him, slowly pitching my head side to side. "You can't, for one, but if you could, would you? Look at yourself!"

We both watched as the two killers caught the bridge of his dead nose in the zipper. With a meaty fist, the big guy smashed it in and, after a couple sharp tugs, finished zipping the suitcase closed.

"Dude, you don't want to go back into that. You got at least eleven savagely broken bones, a smashed nose, and costume jewelry up your ass," I said, letting my hand hover above his shoulder—this way he could feel it, but it didn't send him reeling. "Time to move on."

Despite not having a body anymore, Allister's eyes began to water. He said, "How? How do I do that?"

I jumped in with my pitch. "Okay, here's the deal. Because those guys killed you, the world's ever so slightly out of balance. You died before you would have normally, naturally."

"I don't underst—"

"You don't have to, but here's the gist: if I can determine who killed you, as your personal private detective, then you, my client, can merrily zip on to the next place. The afterlife."

"But, but…" Allister said as the two men stood, the skinny one grabbing the handle of the suitcase. "But we know who did it! Those two goons did it," he said, his voice beginning to quake.

"Yes, yes—"

The ghost standing next to me shouted, "They murdered me!"

"Ah, ha," I said, putting up a finger. "You know that, and I know that. But does your family, huh? Do your coworkers? Does your, uh, wife?"

"I'm not married."

"Girlf—"

"I don't have…" Allister said and added, holding onto some strange notion of earthly pride, "I mean, I'm between relationships at the moment."

Ah well, at least there'd be fewer people to miss him.

"Either way. You don't want those thugs to get away with it, do you?" I said, giving him my power face and talking quickly. "Listen, you've got a limited window here. We expose who has murderously, uh, killed you, and then huzzah! the balance is back and you slip off to the next world."

Allister considered this. Then: "What do you get out of it?"

"The knowledge of a job well done."

"Job? What job?"

I stood back and spread my arms again. "I'm the world's best private investigator."

He didn't look convinced.

"Okay, at the very least, I'm the world's best dead private investigator. The InBetween can be a bit monotonous, but in my profession, death has some significant vocational advantages."

"A dead P.I."

"The best," I said and smiled. Then I added in full disclosure, "And I suppose, if we wanted to put all the cards on the table, since I'm the only dead private investigator, I'm technically worst, too." He nodded slowly. "But since dying, I've made a point to try and put a positive spin on things."

He didn't look convinced. Feeling I was losing him, I decided it was time for Plan B.

"Come on, Allister, do what's right for you here, man," I said and slowly tapped my foot on the floor.

The new ghost said, "No. No, maybe I should hang around here for a while. Get my bearings before—"

At that moment, the air crackled, suddenly heavy with electricity and, passing through the far corner of the room, a massive beast of scales and claws, all rippling and sinewy muscle and blood-stained teeth. The creature was easily three times our combined size. Its fists were gore covered, while its thick, spiked tail dragged across the slate wood floor with a thup-thup-thup.

And as quickly as it appeared, it was gone.

"Whew," I said, my breath ragged. "Allister, my friend, we got lucky."

"Wha—what was—?"

"Hmm. I suppose since you're new, he couldn't smell you yet," I said, then I clasped my hands together. "But in a few minutes, you'll have been here long enough, and that will change."

A lie, sure. But it was for his own good.

Slowly, Allister began to nod. He said, "Okay, okay. Wow, that… thing—I should go, then?"

"Good idea," I said.

He was nodding furiously now. "So how do we even the, uh, balance?"

I slipped through a wall, briefly leaving him behind, then turned back and stuck my head through and said to him, "Do you have a LinkedIn page?"

Chapter Two

Bernard Grimsby had never set out to be a mail carrier in Madison, Wisconsin.

A relatively moot point, certainly. No one has ever set out to be a mail carrier in Madison, Wisconsin.

Still, the hours were relatively good, there was fresh air, and he got to peek into people's windows without any overwhelming fear of incarceration.

If he were honest with himself (which, as a rule, he avoided), that was really the best part.

In fact, at one point, he'd even laid out a little map with all the best homes along his route for doing a little peepin' tomcat. He'd printed it off, got it laminated at one of those grocery store do-it-your-self stations, and then pinned it to the inside of the visor in his US Postal Service–issued Grumman LLV mail truck, which was a good decade past its recommended final service date.

He didn't mind if the Grumman was old and looked, if you were to remove the official markings, a little like what a prolific child molester might drive. After a dozen years with the Madison post office, it was his and no one else's.

It smelled like him. The seat was molded nearly perfectly to his thick body, and it was even losing paint in places similar to where he was losing hair.

Out of a mini fridge behind the mail truck's only seat, Grimsby pulled a short, fat Schlitz, because if anything, he was a local boy. He pulled out the milk-bottle charm that hung around his neck and used it to pop open the beer.

The cap went tinkling to the floor then ricocheted under the seat, joining dozens of others.

"Bar is open, boys," he mumbled to himself and brought the cold bottle up to his dry lips. Today had been one of those days during which his eyes kept returning to the green LED readout of the AM/FM standard issue radio. Eleven o'clock had sure taken its time to get here.

He'd made a rule, ten years earlier, that the Grimsby Grumman Saloon didn't open until eleven. That is, on weekdays. Weekends were all his, so on those two glorious days, it was a twenty-four-hour establishment.

Since that he started most mornings before seven, noon was damn near nighttime. And in truth, eleven a.m. was actually noon on the east coast.

That's the American east coast. And Grimsby, by golly, he was an American.

So eleven a.m. was a good, American-centric kickoff time.

Tipping the cold brew back, he saw two women coming up the street with a stroller. He knew both of them and had by chance seen one, Mrs. Talbert, in her underwear through the bedroom window three years earlier.

That "chance" had come from standing on an overturned wheelbarrow at the side of the house, getting a grip of the eaves, and arching up as high as he could on his tiptoes. Sure, she was in her late fifties and had some weight on her, but still, that was the thrill.

The forbidden peek!

Over the next few months, he actually caught her on several more occasions in various states of undress and then realized she was now purposely removing clothes and hanging out near windows for the mailman to catch her. That was when he began heading straight up the path, slipping the mail through the slot, then turning on a heel and leaving.

It was less of a thrill if she was into it.

This was one of Bernard's very few stabs at living on the edge. He was a full-on coward, so any attempts at living on any sort of edge would have to be known to him and him only.

He would be a maverick in Bernardtown, population: one.

And he didn't know if getting drunk while employed in the public-service sector and peeking in houses could earn him any time in prison, but he knew, absolutely knew, he'd not last locked up in jail.

Years earlier, he'd gotten trapped in an elevator for fifteen minutes, and when the firemen finally pried the doors open, Bernard was discovered trying to knock himself out by shoving a sock down his own throat. He'd not actually been wearing socks, so the first twelve of those fifteen minutes he'd spent trying to wrestle it off the foot of one of the two elderly men trapped in the elevator with him.

He'd been charged with assault, but the judge let him off with a warning and fined him $4.80, awarded to the old guy for a new pair of socks.

After that, he'd routinely only taken the stairs and refused to enter buildings with more than three floors.

Bernard belched—a long, wet one that sent a pleasant spray cascading through the midmorning sun onto the black steering wheel ("Oh, a rainbow!")—and once the two ladies with the baby buggy rounded the corner, he reached down and grabbed another cold offering of premium American lager.

"Just one more," Bernard said to himself. "A chance to enjoy the sunny day, the light breeze, and—"

As the mail carrier brought the bottle to his lips, he felt a slight spray of beer as something flashed before his eyes, pierced the Schlitz logo dead center, then a long spike buried deep into his nasal cavity and entered his brain.

Bernard died before he could finish his sentence and his beer. Instead of falling forward, his body slumped upright on the only stool in Grimbsy's Grumman Saloon, and his arms fell to his sides.

The smashed beer bottle, held together by its label, lay pinned to the middle of his face with a rusted railroad spike.

His breathing failed, and the penultimate thing he heard was the final beat of his heart.

Then, as he faded to black, a voiced said, "Oh shit, that's much better."

Chapter Three

I strode into my home office with a purpose and found one of my "Temps," eighty-three-year-old Harrison, swirling a viscous brown liquid around a plastic bowl with a spork.

"Harry!"

My octogenarian employee brightened and sat up in his bed, and a smile broke across his face.

"Paint! How ya doin', son?"

"Good, man," I said and poked my head into Harry's bathroom, saw no one, and stepped back in. A few moments later, Allister shuffled into the room facing the wrong direction.

I walked over to look at Harry's dinner and bent down, giving it a theatrical sniff so he could hear me. I couldn't actually smell it, but in truth, the way it looked, I was somewhat thankful at that point. The sense of smell isn't lost on the dead; it just takes a much stronger odor to illicit it.

Tapping my lips once with a finger, I motioned for Allister to wait by a large, well-worn sofa chair.

"Whatcha eatin', man? That don't look too good."

"It ain't," Harry said and tossed the plate onto an end table, spilling some of the liquid onto the phone. To me, it looked a bit like skin. "They tell me it's meatloaf."

I laughed. "Where's the loaf?"

"Well, things ain't as regular as they used to be, but if all works in my favor, that'll happen in about two to three hours."

Both Harry and I howled at his joke, but Allister simply stared. The formerly alive tax accountant and shitty gambler raised his hand. I told him to put it down.

Harry's eyes darted around the room. "You got a case, Paint? Is he here?"

"Yeah, Harry, sorry. I shoulda warned you."

"Nah, don't bother me none."

For a moment, I watched as Allister, with both feet planted on the ground, slid very slowly across the room. I put my hand up to my mouth and asked him, "Y'all right, man?"

"I can't seem to… it's just, I feel like I'm standing on an air hockey board. Not moving my feet but—"

"Yeah, don't worry about it," I said, walked over, and gently extended a hand to stop the guy from drifting. "I'd say you will get used to it, but you're not gonna be here that long, Allister." I pointed to the sofa chair. "Why don't you take a seat?"

Harry sat up in his bed and leaned forward, clutching a thin blanket, straining to hear. A moment later, Allister fell through the chair.

"Ooof!"

Harry burst out laughing, looking up at the ceiling. "He fell for it, didn't he, Paint?" The old man rolled into another fit of laughter.

"Yeah, it's kinda mean, but—" I explained as I walked over and helped the dead man off the floor, "—it makes Harry laugh, so…"

Allister stumbled to his feet. "What happened?"

"Yeah, solid isn't so solid for you anymore. It's mainly about perception and stuff like that," I said. "I've discovered how some of it works. Other stuff the Professor has clued me in on. Floors, the ground, stairs—for the most part, you're cool. After that, it gets dicey. Frankly, I don't understand it."

The tax accountant snapped his arm away from my grip. "How can you work in an environment you don't understand?"

"Do you know how gravity works? Electromagnetic fields? Microwave ovens? Why Jimmy Fallon got The Tonight Show?"

Allister shrugged. "Right, okay. I got it."

"Don't worry about it. You're going home soon."

"Home?" Allister's eyebrows jumped.

Harry chimed in, "Not your old home, son, your new one."

Allister noticed the old man sitting in the hospital bed wasn't exactly looking at him. The ex-accountant asked my Temp, "Wait, are you dead?"

"Nearly."

"Can you see me?"

"No, son, you're dead. You ain't got no body for me to see!"

"But you can hear me."

"Yes."

"How?"

"Because I'm nearly dead," Harry said then scrunched his face up. "Thought we covered that part."

Allister began to drift across the floor again, albeit more slowly this time. "Doesn't that, I dunno, frighten you?"

"Dying? Aw, hell no," Harry said. "I'm goddamn tired and sick of the food here. And the only reason any of the family show up is to jockey for position in my will." The old man rubbed his hands together with a big, dentured grin. "Me? I'm ready for the next big adventure."

I was going to miss Harry when that happened. And he was a good Temp, which is important, because the dead can't do admin.

One of the toughest parts of being in the InBetween is you can't take notes. That can be a challenge for someone in my profession. And since, here, I was the only one in my profession, that particular problem was potentially mine and mine alone.

If I'm ever working on a complicated case, trying to figure out who might have offed some nice, freaked-out lady, there's nowhere I can write anything down.

We've all seen those movies where the police detectives are all in a room, and they've got maps and pins pushed into photographs, and sometimes, for visual flair, they'll use various-colored strings to indicate which clues might be connected.

Yeah, none of that for me. No maps, no pins, no photos, no strings. Well, mostly no strings. However, the rare ones around here don't do me any favors, trust me.

So me, I gotta be like that old TV magician from the seventies, the Amazing Kreskin.

Kreskin, he was known as a mentalist that could "read" people's minds or even implant ideas through the power of suggestion. If you'd heard of the guy, you may not know that he also had a fantastic memory.

Thankfully, he was able to teach me a few tricks when I first got started. He wasn't dead. And he wasn't near dead like Harry. But ol' Kreskin could somehow drift his consciousness between the two worlds.

Like I said, I don't understand it, and to be honest, I don't think A.K. (as he asked me to call him) really knew either. But I think that sort of thing made him a couple bucks over the years.

So if I come across a bunch of names or dates, in my mind, I'll often attach images to each of them—sometimes a succession of images—to remember them. It's helped in recent times, but I didn't do this originally. That's probably why I don't remember much about when I was alive.

Thankfully, in Allister's case, I had the name of his killer and now just needed Harry's help. He was my latest in a long line of Temps. His wife Margaret was also in the home and another Temp of mine. She was probably going to go before Harry but was still up for the occasional recon mission.

Harry is basically bedridden, so he's my computer guy.

"You got your laptop, old-timer?"

Moving his sheets around for a moment, he revealed a slick black Dell. He opened the lid and stiffened a little when the screen came alive. Smiling, I took a step back and let him change the webpage.

Still, I couldn't help but give the guy a little grief. "I hope they pay that young lady well."

"Oh, come on, leave it be! We got work to do, don—"

"She's very flexible."

The old man reddened. "It's her website. She runs the damn thing. The other ones there are her, you know, servants."

"Slaves, Harry," I said, unable to stop smiling. "I believe that particular community uses the term slaves."

Allister Hale sided up to us. "What's 'pegging'?"

"None of this matters!" the old guy shouted, which prompted a shuffling from the hall. A moment later, a nurse with graying hair tucked up into a cap opened the door slowly and peeked in.

"You all right, sir?"

"Yes, Denise." Harry gave her a kind wave and a fake smile. "I'm fine."

"She's a pretty one," I said, knowing only Harry and Allister could hear me.

The old man said quietly, "Don't start with me, boy."

Nurse Denise frowned. "Are you sure you're okay, Mr. Knudsen?"

I leaned toward Harry's ear. "Maybe she'll make you one of her servants, Harry."

"WE'RE ALL good in here," Harry shouted at first, then calmed and gave her a big toothy grin. "All is fine. Playing some online poker."

The nurse twisted up her lips and said, "Is that what you all call it?" She closed the door.

Harry wiped his face and exhaled a deep breath. "Jesus, Paint, you can't rile me up like that. I got a bum heart." He clicked to the main Google page. "You'll have to find some other stiff with hacker skills to be one of your Temps, you keep at it."

"You ain't a hacker, Harry," I said. "I love ya, man. But black hat you ain't. Hell of a research man, though."

The old man looked in my general direction. His face, usually playful, went a bit slack. "I'm serious, though. You do gotta find some new recruits. There's a reason why you call us Temps."

"I'm lining up a couple," I said, trying not to think too much about losing Harry. I really did like the guy. "I think Mr. Abrams is getting close to being ready to hear me."

Harry scoffed. "That guy? Nah, I think he was a Nazi or something."

"He's Jewish, man."

A shrug. "Self-loathing is a powerful thing." Harry spun the screen toward us. "Okay, where we logging this guy?"

Allister Hale the tax accountant, in fact, did not have a LinkedIn page. Nor did he have much of a Facebook presence or anything else useful. We'd have to give him the Basic Package.

"What's your name, son?" Harry asked as he navigated to the Wikipedia authors' page.

"Why? Wait, what are you guys doing? I thought we were going to get those thugs busted. What's about to happen?"

I turned to my client, not completely surprised by his sudden panic. Facing losing the only reality you've ever known can be terrifying. But I don't have any idea what comes after the InBetween. Don't know anything about the Next.

So it's possible terror is entirely appropriate. Either way, I had a case to clear.

"Allister Hale, Minneapolis tax accountant—"

"I'm not from here. They'd sent me on a business trip," he said and stared off. "A setup, obviously. I'm from Atlanta."

"Allister Hale, Atlanta tax accountant—"

"Actually, I live in Kennesaw, Georgia. But I was born in Richmond."

I nodded, pursing my lips. "Right. Alabama?"

"No." Allister frowned. "Virginia."

I heard Harry thump the delete button in a couple rapid taps, then type in the corresponding letters.

"Okay, so here's how it works, or rather how we believe it works," I said, looking into his twitchy, ghostly eyes. "If you die au natural like ol' Harry is going to in the coming days—"

"Sooner the better," the old guy said, typing.

"—despite the staffing issues it will cause me, it's pretty much the Express Train to the afterworld for people like him. Do not pass Go, do not collect two hundred dollars."

Al nodded, blinking quickly. "Okay, natural causes, you go straight to Heaven."

"Yeah, wherever," I said and shrugged. "But like I told you before, if your life energy is interrupted by murder, then the balance is off. And the one thing that's clear is the universe doesn't like unbalance."

"By universe, you mean God."

"No, I don't," I said. "I just know that the unbalance is ungood, and the system in place wants to right itself."

Allister frowned. "Animals kill animals all the time. You're saying that's unnatural?"

"Don't confuse murder and killing. Two entirely different things."

Apparently, that clicked something in the accountant's mind. "Okay. How do you, uh, re-balance?"

"The killer needs to be revealed."

Allister frowned again. "You said that before, but do you know who killed me?"

"Al—"

"I mean, the bookie was a manager at this seedy bar in Marietta, but the big boss, I think he was a South American guy or something—"

"No, no," I said and put a soft hand just above his shoulder. "Trigger man. The actual guy."

"But, but, I don't know that g—!"

"Wait, wait, calm down," I said. "I do. It was the big guy with the boxer's ears. His name was Hamish Blank, common spelling."

Tap-tap-tappity-tap.

"So, okay, now we can get a message to the police, right? Tell someone who might be investigating—"

I shook my head. "Nope. Tried that in the past. Sent emails to the police, found out the names of the detectives on the case, had some of my Temps go speak with them. In the end, it was too much time and effort, and in most cases, we got nowhere with the cops."

"So how do you—?"

"We fire up your wiki."

"What?"

"Create a Wikipedia page with your name and a few details and then identify your killer—in your case, Hamish Blank." I looked over at Harry.

My old temp asked, "What kinda name is Hamish, for cryin' out loud?"

"Family name, I bet. English. It's like ham and an 'ish.'"

"Gotcha."

Tappity-tap.

Allister looked at me with a wrinkled brow. "That's it?"

"Yes, for the most part, that's it," I said and gave him a big smile. "Once the world is made aware of the identity of your killer, you're off to paradise, man!"

"How long does that ta—"

And, in a wink of light, Allister Hale was gone.

I said, "Not long."

Chapter Four

Death has been very good to me.

Not the actual dying part; whew, that was shit from what I can remember. There was a lot of screaming, begging, bleeding, and, inevitably, a cold, hard wind that blew through me like a sexual shudder.

But after that, it's been quite rewarding.

Granted, I don't sleep anymore, so there's a lot of monotony. More than most people can stand. In fact, I think that's what finally pushes some of those who get stuck in the InBetween to just go away. They haven't been cleared as far as I know. Just not around anymore.

The more fortunate ones get cleared, like Allister. Many times, cops get there, but it can take a while. That's where I come in. But it's not like someone can stop by my office or call me up. I have to get clients on my own.

They're out there, but not as many as you might think. Within a hundred miles, there will be a few of them wandering in the dark. Each spook still carries an energy, or juice as we like to call it here because it sounds cooler. You wander around long enough, and you're sort of drawn to each other. Like some sort of weak gravity or magnetism.

That's how I find them.

The simplest way is just walking around and looking for some wide-eyed spook jabbering to themselves. I'm not sure why so many of them get talking to themselves, but if you keep an ear out, on occasion, you'll hear something like:

"—so how was I supposed to know? Me, I just wanted a pack of smokes, and hell, I thought that was the shit that, you know, was going to get me in the end, but nope, there's this guy, big stupid-looking prick with a twelve gauge, tapping on the six-inch plexiglass as he's pointing to something on the back wall, what, I'm just going to spin on a dime and walk out? No, you get shot in the back that way, but hell, I got shot in the face instead, so goddamn closed casket for me, not that anyone would even turn up unless there was a good spread, which…"

And so on.

It can be slow going to find leads that way.

And since here is mainly just a shell or dimension that's been folded over the everyday reality, you could just be hearing some muttering guy in the real world.

Depending on the light, it can actually be hard to tell spooks from livies just on sight. There are subtle hints like the way their clothes or body will shimmer a little, but certain types of light can hide that.

There are easier ways to pick 'em out though.

One is to look at their feet. Spooks have a memory of walking, so they take steps, but it won't exactly match up. In fact, if they're really engrossed in thought, their legs could be pulling one way and their body sliding in an entirely different direction.

Also, the newly dead will almost always appear in the manner in which they were killed. Ax to the head, still sticking out. Or a big hole where the face used to be after a shotgun makeover.

After long enough in the InBetween, from what I can work out, spooks will start looking like the person they saw in the mirror every day.

You would think then it's somehow changeable. So I should be able to "wear" something different every day, but I look down, and it's a gray hoodie and blue jeans. Same getup always. I spent a whole week one time just trying to conjure up a T-shirt.

Nope, every day I'm dressed like I'm permanently walking to hockey practice.

The only one I've ever even heard of that can change himself at all is Gary. I met Gary a long while back after he was killed by, he thinks, his super. He was in a rent-controlled apartment in downtown Minneapolis and had refused to move out despite pleadings from the building's owner. The guy had wanted to double the rent on the place.

Went to bed one night and woke up dead with his head in the oven, going full-on Sylvia Plath. Gary says the police did a half-assed job and quickly wrote him off as a suicide. It's kinda hard not to see his point since the oven was electric.

But Gary has helped me out on occasion, as he'd done with suitcase-sized tax accountant Allister Hale. I'd seen him a few minutes earlier and asked him to hang around in case the potential client needed a bit of convincing.

Gary's monster is terrifying, and, more importantly, he's always up for a quick drive-by adventure.

It takes him a bit of effort, so he's usually just walking around as plain ol' Gary. If I were him, I'd make myself look like a movie star or athlete or some famous person in history. Or even, just for the laughs, Patrick Swayze.

I'd been standing in Harry's room for the last twenty minutes, listening to a couple of his family members ask how he's doing, if he's being treated well, and if he has any plans for the BMW. It was time to think about heading out and finding another client.

However, for the last five minutes, a little girl—I think maybe a kid or stepkid of one of Harry's clan—had been creeping me out a little.

She was probably about seven. And she'd pretty much been staring right at me the entire time.

At first, I thought she was doing that dim kid stare, where they can lock onto a wall or something in middle distance, looking like the Dark Lord is feeding them evil instructions and they're just trying to take it all down.

But each time I moved, she tracked me.

And to make it more unsettling, it seemed that if she did actually see me—which she obviously couldn't—she wasn't pointing it out to anyone else. She didn't exactly look scared, and she wasn't desperately pointing a tiny kid finger, screaming, "Stranger danger!"

She was eyeballing me, and it was just creepy. She was spooking me out.

I looked over at Harry, who was patting some crying woman's hand as she inquired about Harry's timeshare in southern California. He looked as though if they stayed much longer, he'd actually order up a visit from the Grim Reaper in an Uber.

Walking over to the bed next to him, I whispered in his ear. "Harry, that pint-sized granddaughter or godniece or step-whatever looks like she's staring at me! It's weirding me out!"

With his free hand, he waved me off, stuck in his own personal hell, and I crossed to the opposite side of the room.

Yep, those little beady eyes locked on me the whole way.

I stuck my tongue out at her but got no reaction. Maybe it was a coincidence. Maybe it was all in my head.

"Stop staring at me," I said to her.

She looked away.

This, you would have thought, should have made me feel marginally better. Nope. At that point, I got a major case of the willies.

And remember, I'm the fucking ghost in this scenario!

As I stewed about what my next move should be, finally, the family started making sounds like their visit was coming to an end. A heavy woman pulled a winter coat over her shoulders, wiping her damp face with its sleeve. Next to her was a man who was going bald young and had massive snow gloves on that made it look like he had gorilla hands.

They piled out the door, dragging the little girl behind them.

I stared at her to see if she would look back, but nothing. She trailed behind the two adults until a big monkey hand hurried her into the hallway. After the door shut, I had some questions.

"Harry, what the hell was that about?"

"That's my son and his wife, they—"

"No, no, the little girl, she—"

He quickly waved me off as the door cracked open once again. From the hallway, I could hear the woman's voice. She sounded like she was admonishing the kid.

"No, no, he's tired. You had your chance to say hello."

"But I just want to give Pop-pop a quick hug."

"Fine, fine," the woman said, caving. "Fine! Go quick. We'll be waiting at the elevators."

The door creaked open wider, and Harry smiled wide, extending his arms. I think he was touched that someone so young would care about an old, dying man.

Apparently, not so much caring, and she walked right past Harry and stopped about three feet from me. She looked up and crossed her arms.

She said, "I want to hire you to find out who killed my stepdad."

Chapter Five

She was finding it hard to concentrate.

"Thank you, Mr. Jorgensen," the clerk said to her and handed Jan Jorgensen's credit card back. "If you want to wait down at the end of the counter, your drink will be ready in just a minute."

Jorgensen nodded and twisted his face into an expression that might pass for a smile. Or the early stages of a stroke.

Even after all this time inside the man, Chandra found that it wasn't a simple task to control the more nuanced mannerisms. Smiles, winks, or basic finger snaps were often cumbersome and awkward moments. Thankfully, those gestures were rarely required.

Except, of course, his morning stops at Starcups, a massive Seattle-based beverage chain that routinely burned its coffee and had no similarities at all to Starbucks.

A far bigger headache, literally, was the constant, inane chatter that surrounded him the entire time he was in the shop from both the living and the recently dead.

She wasn't sure why so many of those trapped in the InBetween gravitated to this particular chain of coffee stores, but in each of the ones she'd searched in the greater Chicago area over the past several weeks, there they were, sometimes by the dozens.

Just chattering away to themselves and nearly drowning out the voices of the living. But she wasn't there for conversation.

Jorgensen grabbed his froth-topped coffee and went over to the condiment bar. A couple packets of sugar, some cinnamon on top, a little chocolate, a little nutmeg. Anyone waiting to use the flavor station next would have wondered if there were now more condiments than coffee in the man's cup.

Didn't matter. She wasn't planning on drinking the vile swill.

She stood there, eyes focused on the reflection in the window, not even looking down at what she was having the man's hands do. She simply watched.

Across the room, surrounded by three others, the handsome young congressman sipped his chai tea as if he had no problems in the world.

Chapter Six

The Uber driver looked in his rearview mirror for the fourth time. It was only about twenty minutes until he got to her destination, but he was obviously mulling over dumping the old woman out right then and there.

"Are you okay, madam?" the driver asked for the third time since she'd climbed in at the Denny's restaurant. Generally, it was a routine pick-up spot. Except for the fact the restaurant had been closed for more than three months.

"I'm fine. Mind yer business."

"Are you sure? Who are you talking to?"

"Nobody. I'm old!" Mags said to the man then brushed him aside with a swipe of her wrinkled hand. She turned back to me or at least where I'd told her I was sitting. "I know I shoulda told ya."

"Yeah, that would have been a good idea," I said, staring at my fingers, shifting in my seat as if I'd mistakenly sat on a plateful of dice. The big ones, too. Like Dungeons-and-Dragons big. Big and pointy. Whatever. I was kinda pissed. "At least I'd have been prepared for it."

"She's cool. Don't sweat it."

"She's six!"

"Nine."

"Whatever!" I threw a hand up and was mildly disappointed I was the only one to see the exasperated gesture. "Can you explain to me how she can see me? I mean… for the most part, livies can't see anyone in the InBetween."

Mags squinted in my direction. "I can sorta see you."

"No you can't," I said. "That's just some spotting from your cataracts or something."

"Harsh."

I stared out the window, wishing I could feel the sun just for a moment. Then I mumbled, "I'm sorry. That was uncool."

"De nada."

"Ma'am," the driver said, his voice a little higher this time. "Are you sure you don't want me to drop you off, maybe at a hospital or something?"

"No, I just busted out of a hospital. Home, really." She shrugged. "Same diff."

He then flipped on an AM station that was playing something foreign, with string instruments that sounded as if they were weeping.

"So tell me about this stepdad, then."

"He's dead."

"Check. I totally got that from when your granddaughter said, 'Hey, can you find out who killed my stepdad?'"

"Yeah." Mags put a thumb into her mouth and pressed a denture up a little higher. "Those two you saw, they aren't her parents. That's my boy and his horrible family. My daughter, her momma, doesn't go out much. She's been holed up in her house since Boyd died."

"Killed, right? He was killed."

"Seems so," Mags said and pulled a hard candy out of her purse, picked a little lint off of it, then popped it into her mouth. "But it's not so clear-cut. Cloudy."

"How cloudy?"

"Monsoon cloudy."

This was new territory for me. A living client? Still, I'd told her I'd give it a try. Mainly because I was freaked out as all hell because a little girl, a little live girl, was asking me to do it.

"Did Boyd have any enemies that you know of?"

"How would I know, Paint? He was my son-in-law, but I didn't know him too well. He'd only been married to my oldest for about two years."

"What did he do?"

"He's on TV," Mags said. Then, "Or was. He called out the lottery numbers. You know, the guys with all the balls. Everybody tuned in and watched him grab his balls."

I sighed. "I think you say stuff like that on purpose to get a reaction."

Mags cracked the hard candy between her chompers but never cracked a smile.

The Nissan Leaf took a hard turn and accelerated quickly down the street. If it had been an internal combustion engine, it would have roared, likely the desired effect. Instead, the car just went a bit faster.

"Madam," the driver said, little bits of spittle hitting the rearview mirror. "Are you on the phone or do you have an earbud in or something? I mean—"

"Yes, shh," Mags turned her head slightly and tapped her hearing aid. "Can you please not eavesdrop on my conversation?"

The driver shrank, gave her a nervous smile in the mirror, then let out a breath that should not have fit in his tiny body. The next turn he took was much more even. The car nearly glided around the corner on a pocket of air.

"You're a bit cavalier about me of late," I said, my hands gripping the seat next to her.

"I'm dying. That has a way of loosening you up a bit."

"Apparently," I said and grunted as we took the next corner. "This guy never heard of an interstate? I'm having a tough time holding on here."

Mags turned toward me as if she'd just remembered her cat had casually mentioned that it might kill her as she slept.

"Right! How are you even doing that? Aside from the stuff under your feet, I thought you slipped through solid things."

"I'm about to," I said. Mags looked down and noticed two slight indentations in the seat. "It takes a bit of stored up energy to—to cross…"

"You're holding on?"

"Sort of." If I'd been alive, there would have been sweat pouring down my face.

"Why bother? You could skate from one place to another faster than a cab." She looked up at the driver, who was humming to himself, smiling. Mags called up to him. "Can you speed up? It's, you know, a matter of life and death."

The Uber driver looked in his rearview mirror again, an eyebrow cocked. "Madam, I would think at your age, every day is a matter of life and death."

"Sure," she said and met his stare. "But not solely for me."

He took a tiny swallow and pushed harder on the accelerator.

I said, "I prefer to be in a car. This here, um, this area isn't a great neighborhood."

"What does that even mean to someone like you? Why should a ghost have to worry about a bad neighborhood?"

"No, not the way—"

Mags waited for a moment, shifted in her seat a couple of times. She said, "Not what way, Paint? Whaddya mean?"

She looked at the seat next to her. The two slight divots were gone.

"Paint?" she said, wiping a withered hand across her sweater. "Stop the car!"

The driver slammed the brakes.

"Jesus H. Christ, you lunatic! I didn't say go all Flintstones full stop! That's what you get when you hire immigrants."

"Ma'am," the driver looked in the mirror, lips flat, eyes unblinking. "I'm from Canada."

"That… still makes you an immigrant."

His eyes went to the left. To the right. He blinked. "Not... really."

"Yes. Yes, really. By the very definition of the word."

The driver shrugged and slowly began to move forward again. "We'll just have to agree to disagree."

Mags watched him for a moment then mumbled, "I don't think I'm entirely safe in this vehicle." She twisted in her seat and looked out both windows. The sun was beginning to drop below the horizon, and above them, a bat was swooping down, grazing on the bugs encircling the streetlight.

She looked behind them and saw nothing.

"Is this a bad neighborhood?"

The driver shrugged. "I'm brown, and you're white," he said. "Our definitions of a bad neighborhood may not be similar."

Mags nodded, unsure why she was so worried about a guy who was already dead.

"Do people get shot around here? Stabbed?"

"Not that I know of. But," the driver said, then looked up at her in the mirror again. "This area? I know it sounds, um, childish, but around here, this part of town, people say is... spookhuis."

"I don't know what that is."

He briefly turned in his seat to face her.

"Haunted."

Chapter Seven

There is no sleeping in the InBetween, but there are times you feel like you're in a dream. Or a nightmare. That invariably happens when you run far too low on juice. It feels like you've been up for days, and you're confused, wishing for just a few minutes of sleep that will never come. You almost feel warm and safe.

Which, I knew by now, meant that I was fucked. It was time to get outta sight, and I had to do it quickly.

My vision was filled with hazy clusters, pinpricks of light. I blinked a few times then forced myself to stand up from the crouching position I'd folded myself into, arms wrapped around my legs.

The only thing that saved me from a full beating was that, when I'd felt a hand thrust into my chest, instinctively I'd put my feet down, ankles angled outward. That saved my ass.

I'd had some momentum from the vehicle and was able to hold on briefly by my fingertips, and then my "skating" kept me moving for another block or two. It was enough to give me a little bit of space between me and whoever had clocked me. But that meant my attacker was close.

And, high off the rush of the juice they'd stolen from me—like sudden bloodlust—they'd come looking for the rest.

Maybe it was a random mugging—a reverse drive-by in this case—but something in my brain laughed at me, pointing its finger. Usually, my intuition isn't such a dick, but in the InBetween, all bets are off. I'd been dead for a while, so by now, for all I knew, the damn thing might have become sentient and was now in Fiji burning through Tinder.

I headed for an alleyway, which, when you're alive, would be the last place you'd go to be safe. But as a ghost, I'd be the scariest thing in there.

But not for long,

As I passed into the darkened, narrow lane, I heard two angry voices. Despite not actually having a mouth, I felt it suddenly go desert dry.

"How the fuck—"

"He's here somewhere! No way he had enough juice to run too far."

I wasn't sure how far back they were, but no question, once they saw the alleyway, I wouldn't be the only spook down there. They were right—I had nowhere near enough energy to get out of there. Not yet. Best thing I could do was hide, which was what they would be expecting.

And if these bozos who'd pulled me from the car knew what to look for, I was fucked.

"There! Real faint, but you can see his trail."

Yep. I was fucked.

* * *

"Paint!" Mags called again. She'd asked the driver to wait at the curb, hoping her ghost friend might catch up. After all, they were on a case, heading to an interrogation. But the driver had gotten a notification about another nearby fare, and she, despite some halfhearted arguing, had had to get out.

As the car pulled away, far too quickly for a residential street, the old, dying woman stood in front of her ex-son-in-law's townhouse, wondering what to do next.

"Paint!"

She froze when the porch light came on. A dark figure in a dull white T-shirt and gray sweatpants pushed opened a rusted screen door.

"Who's that?" He raised his hand to block the light from his eyes. She said nothing, unsure what to say, and it took him a moment to recognize her. "Margaret? That you?"

"Hiya, Hank."

He took a couple strides down the concrete steps and let the bent metal door fall back onto its jamb.

"What are you doing here?" he said. "I mean, nice to see ya, I guess. I thought you woulda been, you know…"

"No, not yet," she said, putting on a smile and walking forward. "Soon enough. I'll be out of everyone's hair soon enough."

Hank eyeballed her and rubbed his hand across his mouth. He had more hair on his knuckles than he had on his head.

"This one of those things where you wanna clear up accounts before you check out? Tell me what a prick I am?"

"No," she said and took a couple shaky steps toward him. "I don't got too many days left. No use wasting time by telling you anything you already know."

He laughed and slowly shook his head. "I wish your daughter was a little more like you. We woulda probably still been married."

"You mean dyin'?"

The middle-aged man raised his hands, turned, and took a couple steps back up toward his home. "I ain't getting into it with you, Mags. I know better than that." He stopped at the concrete landing, pulled back the screen door again, then looked back at her. "Why you here?"

Stalling, she shrugged. "Why shouldn't I be?"

Hank pushed open the door to his home and let the screen slam shut behind him. A lamp in the living room put the man in silhouette—just a dark figure standing against the light.

He said, "Come on up and speak your piece."

The eighty-two-year-old woman took a few steps across broken concrete, then grabbed the rusted handrail and maneuvered the four stairs. Her face gave nothing away. Or at least, she hoped it didn't.

Hank added, "And let's make this the last time you and me ever talk. How about that?"

"That sounds like the best offer I've had in weeks," she said, grabbing the metal handle of the screen door then looking over her shoulder into the darkness behind her.

Where are you, Paint?

* * *

Here's the rub about being dead and all that.

You're not all dead, I suppose is the best way to explain it. I mean, yeah, your meat is rotting in a grave or cremated into a powder that Hannibal Lecter would pay top dollar for to make into pancakes. But whatever that thing was that is you, that hangs around.

It seems you are not the fleshy bits so much, maybe. I dunno. But you are, as the old song says: pure energy.

At our very essence we aren't really meat, so maybe we shouldn't be going on and on about it. I suppose, in some way the vegans were on the right track. But they get just as dead as the rest of us. And, heads up—in the InBetween, they still don't shut up about veganism. I think they're still trying to convince themselves they were right. Who knows? Maybe they were. Doesn't really matter anymore here.

But back to "pure energy."

Each day in the InBetween, just by movin' around, you generate energy. The Professor is the smartest person I know around here, and she explained it to me like this: picture you're a bottle blond in a tight red dress walking through a redneck country bar just trying to get to the jukebox. There's a lot of "hey baby!" and, caught in their orbit, subsequent forces that will interact with you. If you've built up enough momentum to whip past it, that pull between you and the "hey baby!" force can gin up some juice.

I'm not a science whiz, but that doesn't clear things up much for me. And it also makes me wonder what sort of life the Professor might have lived before coming here a long, long time ago.

So moving builds you up a bit of energy. Moving over vast distances quickly gets you more. I've learned that by using what I call "skating," I can generate juice faster than most. I'll go for skates that are hundreds of miles, longer, and along the way tap the brakes now and again, and that gets me even more of a charge. Like a dynamo on a car. So yeah, basically I've died and turned into a Prius.

Another way to get energy or juice is to steal it from other spooks.

It's like being mugged for your cash, but the only real currency here is juice. So as a-hole muggers beat on you, they quickly drain your energy.

And they can take damn near all of it.

So much so that you can't even move. You are an undead statue. From what I've been told, it's Hell in Purgatory.

Lately in the InBetween, the bad people were getting more organized and stronger. I'd seen the rise of the Ghost Mob in recent months, and it scared me.

We've got no government. No authority. No police. But the worst spooks in the world were getting organized? There soon would be no one to stop them. But why would you even make plans in the InBetween? There's nothing to gain. Sure, you can drain juice from other spooks, but to what end? Why bother?

It seems even after they're dead, shitty people just really dug being shitty.

I'm a good person but not stupid enough to take them on. I could if I had superhero powers. I'd often wondered if I could conjure them up like Gary can with his monsters.

However, I'm sure if I ever did, I wouldn't be one of the cool heroes, more like that kid from the Wonder Twins who could only turn into water. But you wouldn't get far battling baddies as a rip current or a lemon-infused Pellegrino. And even if you could become the "form of an Ice Segway!", what's the point?

"He's gotta be somewhere around here."

I had to focus because I could feel the thugs closing in. The problem was when you use juice to do something—like run through an alley—you can leave the faintest of trails. A sort of spiritual exhaust. Eventually, it dissipates.

But it means you sometimes can track someone if you know what to look for.

If you're that someone being tracked, you gotta find somewhere to sit still long enough for the trail to go cold. Trouble is spooks can see spooks as much as livies can see livies. Hiding spots, though, are inverse.

Livies can't see terrified, sniveling cowards in the dark. For spooks, we're energy, right? It's the opposite.

With the ghost thugs after me, I had to find a nearby source that radiated enough energy to confuse them. Sort of get myself lost in the noise. Thankfully, this isn't common knowledge, so I had a chance.

One of the best hiding options is a fat, old-school cabinet television.

They radiate heat, electromagnetic fields, and light. There's also—and I'm only just starting to understand this bit—emotional leftovers. Stuff that hangs around maybe from the owner but also, it seems, embedded into the broadcast from writers, producers, actors—all sorts of emotional energy or pain or joy.

I asked the Professor about it, but she had no idea what I was talking about. I'm working on a theory.

Anyway, so the big-ass TVs. All that noise can hide you for a while. But you can't hang out inside it too long, or it'll do your head in.

"He made a big damn arch over here…"

"And here, goddamn it!"

"He's trying to hide his tracks."

These guys were apparently just looking to steal my energy and leave me for, well, dead. If they got it from me, I might end up lying in one spot for days or weeks until the most subtle, the smallest of movements, begin to gather enough energy to let me move a finger. Then a hand. After a couple of days—or longer—of waving at the air, I could finally gather enough energy to stand up and get out of there.

I'd never been mugged and had no interest in breaking that streak. I was the world's only dead private detective and had a job to do. Can't help anyone if I'm lying around like a throw rug.

The first few apartments all had flat-screen televisions, the middle-income bastards. That won't do much to hide you unless you're about an inch thick.

I headed to the basement apartments.

There I found a beautiful, beastly nineties Sony Trinitron TV. The sort that when movers come over and see you've got one, they spin on a dime to let the gig go to someone else.

They were high tech in their day, but they weigh a good two hundred pounds. In this subterranean apartment, the guy watching it easily doubled that weight.

Quickly, I planted myself in the middle of the set, my knees to my chest, and squeezed into a ball. Ol' boy on the couch, he was passed out. A dozen tall red cans were scattered around the front of his furniture, each crumpled at the center.

On the end table, a half dozen more of them said he was out for the night.

Thankfully, he'd passed out with the television still on, which, given the size of the old Trinitrons, had a lot to do with why he was so broke and living in a basement without windows. I bet when he eventually did click it off, buildings downtown actually got brighter.

"Bee-dee-bee-dee-bee-dee, what's up, Buck?"

Can't say much for the guy's taste in television, but it didn't matter. Looking back to the stairs, I could see my trail dispersing by the second.

That was, until I saw a face poke through the wall. It moved toward me.

"Look at that!"

Another spook slipped into the room, and both dead men had their eyes trained on me. I looked to the left and right without moving my head.

Sure, I could make a run for it, but this low on juice, I had no chance.

A third spook entered the room, coming right for me.

He said, "Oh, I always loved that princess or queen woman on there."

"Shit yeah!"

"All sorts of dominatrix fantasies about that chick. The leather and—"

"All right, no one wants to hear about you pullin' your preteen pud, for chrissake," a third spook said. "Where the fuck did he go?"

The other two looked toward me, then looked at the third.

"He musta had some extra stores of energy saved up. Or help, maybe?"

All I had to do was sit still, not move. But the energy from the massive TV tube was beginning to make my head swirl more by the second. The strangest sensation: I was actually feeling nauseous.

A dead guy getting sick.

I just had to hold on and let the thugs move onto another target.

"Come on, let's do another sweep around. You two take the neighboring buildings. I wanna do a last check of this one."

The first spook in the room slid over to the television, putting his hand up toward my face. For a moment, it was if we'd locked eyes.

"All that leather…"

"Come on!"

The other ghosts began to slip from the room. This one, though, was moving closer to me, the expression on his face changing slightly. All I could do was hold still in the storm of light.

"Hey!"

Within inches of my face, he spun back around to one of the others who'd slipped back into the room. The guy in front of me frowned. "What?"

"Boss ain't gonna be happy we screwed this up."

"There'll be other chances."

The two started heading for opposite corners.

One of them cursed under his breath then said, "Painter can't hide from us forever."

Chapter Eight

Hank Clark set a glass of lemonade down for Margaret and put a beer in front of himself. After his ex-mother-in-law had arrived unannounced, he'd taken a moment to clear the kitchen table and chairs, pushing stacks of newspapers, days of them, to the floor. Pen marks had scored up the classifieds, some until they weren't readable anymore.

She took a small sip of her lemonade then winced. "It's a bit sweet."

"Sorry, it's all I got."

"Hmm," she said and sniffed at it. "Maybe a little whiskey would cut all the sugar."

Hank eyeballed her for a moment then stood.

Mags was stalling, but she didn't know the first thing about investigating. She wasn't any sort of detective.

Well, she thought, officially Paint really isn't either.

Less than a minute later, Hank had returned with her lemonade. It was slightly darker than when he'd left. Mags took a sip. It was far too strong, but she smiled widely anyhow, knowing she had no chance of finishing it and remaining upright.

"Perfect."

"Great," Hank said and took a pull off his drink, dropping a body built by beer and cigarettes into the only other kitchen chair. "Why ya here, Mags?"

"Can't an old woman see her son-in-law?"

"Former son-in-law."

Mags held up a finger. "Blood is blood."

"We ain't blood, Mags. Not no more."

"Sure we are," she said and took another small sip, which over the next few seconds made it feel as though her left ear had dropped a half inch. "Once it's all mixed together, you can't unmix it. All swirly and intermingled."

He rubbed his chin, went to reach for the beer, then pulled away. "I'm gonna ask you again, nicely, because you were always nice to me."

"Thank you."

"Can't say that was true of the rest of your kids. Especially crazy Beth," he said, referring to his ex-wife's sister. "She still kicking around? I kinda hoped she'd have joined a death cult by now, put on a pair of purple sneakers and started scanning the skies for comets."

The old woman rolled her eyes. "She's still my daughter. I don't like you talking ill of her. She's family."

"What about when I was family?" he said and finally reached for his bottle of beer. "You still feel that way when I had the entire brood talking shit about me? Like some goddamn witches' coven, blaming me for everything that went wrong in their lives, peeking in my windows in the middle of the divorce."

Mags shrugged. "It was a difficult time."

"Yeah, for me, too. Except they had a family to go to. I had nobody."

The old woman met his eyes. "That's not entirely true. In fact, I think that's what spurred the entire process in the first place."

Hank took a swig. "You don't know what you're talking about. You think you do, but you really don't. It wasn't like that."

"Neither here nor there."

"No, I mean it," he said. "I can take all the others thinking shit about me, even my ex, I don't care. But you gotta know all that stuff she said about me. I was a good husband. I tried my best."

"I don't doubt that."

"Nobody ever told me your daughters were bat-shit crazy."

Mags was buying time, hoping, praying Painter would get there before she was kicked out. But she wasn't going to just let Hank shit-talk her family.

"Kin is kin, Hank," she said evenly. "That's my family you're talking about, and I didn't come here to hear you—"

"Then why did you come here?" Hank said, his voice rising. Mags knew he had a temper and didn't want to push things. "I didn't ask ya!"

"No, no. I intruded on your time, so—"

"Yes, you did," Hank said. He took a swig of his beer and slammed it down on the table. A small spurt of liquid erupted from its opening. "Screw it. You gotta go, Mags. Thanks for the company."

The old woman avoided his eyes, pointing at her drink. "I haven't finished my lemonade, and you were kind enough to make it special for me."

The hard expression on his face collapsed, and his voice softened. "I know. I'm sorry. I just… listen, just go back to the home, okay? We got nothing to say to each other."

"But that's why I came here. I do."

"Then what, Mags?" he said, his eyes watering slightly. "What? What the hell do you want from me?"

"Just—just give me a minute."

"You got your minute and a few extra," Hank said, his voice getting louder. "Come on now, I'm done fooling around. You can take the glass. Just call your convalescent home van to come get you—"

"I'm here, Mags. I'm so sorry."

The old woman yelped and smiled so widely that Hank thought she was having a stroke.

She said, "Oh, Jesus. Thank god."

*   *   *

"I'm sorry, I'm so sorry," I said, still feeling awful from my run-in. Mags scanned the room, her gaze crossing through me several times. She's so strong I forget she's old. And dying. "Trust me, that wasn't of my doing. I'll tell you later."

"Okay, I trust you."

Hank froze, looked from corner to corner of the room, and said, "Trust me? What are you talking about, Mags? You having a seizure or something?"

My eighty-two-year-old Temp did that thing where she straightened up as if she was locking a steel rod into place. She gave the guy sitting across from her a sharp look. Hank looked a bit like his daughter Katie.

"No, no seizure. But I have some questions for you before I go," she said, then added. "Don't I?"

"Yes, you do."

*   *   *

"YES, I do," Mags said and stood, then reached down and took a swig of her lemonade and whiskey. She plunked the glass back down, noticed that a moisture ring was beginning to form, then lifted the glass, grabbed a coaster from the floor, and put it back down again.

"Thank you," Hank mumbled.

"I want to know…" she started and then stared off for a moment. "Where were you the night that Boyd died?"

Hank stared at her for a moment, his mouth hanging open. Then he slammed it shut, and his face grew dark. "You know where I was."

"Why… I mean, ah ha, right, if you're so worried to answer the questions, that might mean—"

Hank growled, rolling his hands into fists. "Jesus, I answered all these damn questions with the police!"

"So you'll talk to them about it but not your own family?"

"Former family," he said, his fingers flexing, clutching. "They cleared me, for chrissake. Is that why you're here? You think I had something to do with Ally's new husband?"

"Did you?"

"NO!" Hank said, then his lips battled each other briefly, and he added, "Not really."

"Good enough for me," Mags said, shrinking, then paused, tilted her head, and added, "Uh, no. That is, in fact, not good enough for me, apparently. It seems I want to know…"

Hank exhaled. "What? What the hell do you want to know, Mags?"

"Listen, it's not me," she said slowly. She took her seat again. "Ally has been so sad since… that day. So sad."

"Like I care? I'm sorry, but I should care?"

"You should, because it's breaking Katie's heart. She sees her momma hurting, and it's breaking her heart, Hank."

Hank's eyes began to water. He blinked hard and slugged his beer. "Well, I don't know much about that because she don't talk to me." He said, then softened. "How is my Katie?"

"Truth? I think she misses her daddy."

"Don't… don't do that. I tried everything."

"You're right. I'm not here for that," Mags said. "That's between you and Katie."

"Then why are you here?"

"I want to know… if you disliked Boyd."

Hank shrugged. He looked at his own reflection in the dark mirror of his dead television and said, "Yeah, sure. Why wouldn't I? He had my family."

"Right. I get that."

"That was between me and Katie's mom," he said. "But he seemed like he was good to my Katie, so in a way… you know… I was fine with that. Didn't seem like a creep."

"He wasn't."

"Well, if he was, I woulda killed him."

Margaret looked at him and let out a breath, raising her eyebrows.

Hank said, "But I didn't. You know that."

"But somebody shot him, right?"

Hank stared at Mags, eyes beginning to droop. He then looked away and said, "Cops cleared me. I didn't kill the guy. He deserved it, but I didn't kill him."

"You said that."

"I was telling the truth."

Mags seemed to consider this for a moment then forced a small smile. She nodded, pulled a phone from her purse, and opened the app to call for a ride.

"It seems I am happy with your answers and also believe that it's time for me to go."

Hank blinked. He then motioned to the door with an open hand. She would have to show herself out.

"Okay," she said and took the last belt of her drink then stuck her tongue out. "Wuff, strong stuff. I'll sleep well tonight."

"You're welcome."

She walked toward the screen door, opened it, and turned back.

"Last time we'll see each other, I reckon."

"Yes. I hope you're… well, nice seeing you, Mags."

The old woman smiled, but there wasn't much joy behind it. "You best be telling me the truth, Hank."

He raised his arms and let them fall to his sides. "Why'd you all of a sudden get some bee in your bonnet about this? If you're lookin' for answers, go darken someone else's doorstep. I got none."

"Doesn't matter," she said, pushing through the door. "What I know of it, if you're lying to me, I can haunt the hell out of you after I die."

"Oh, Jesus."

"Take care, Hank."

And with that, she was out the door.

Looking down to her phone, she saw that the taxi was just two minutes away. Thankfully, it didn't appear to be the skittish fellow who'd first driven her to Hank's house. Margaret looked around, up at the streetlight with the tiny, fluttering bugs swirling around it, then down again.

"Paint?" she whispered. "You out here?"

No reply.

She smiled and said, "Good hunting, detective."

Pulling aside a thin, dirty curtain, Katie's dad could see the woman get into a car and speed off.

For more than a minute, he just stared out into the street. Then Hank walked to where he'd been sitting, reached toward his beer, but then pulled his hand back. Dipping his fingers into the inner pocket of his jacket, he pulled out a cell phone.

He poked at the screen then held it to his ear.

"You around?" Hank said into the handset. "Seems that shit about Boyd ain't over."

Chapter Nine

I stood there drumming my fingers in the air as I watched Hank click off his phone and pocket it. He was doing that quick dart-from-room-to-room thing that people do just before they leave their house.

It was frustrating because I was still pretty wiped out from my encounter with the Three Stooges. It would take a little while to drum up some energy and get my strength back.

And I certainly didn't have the mental energy to try to work out who they were and why they'd been looking for me specifically.

Hank patted his two front pockets, his eyes cut from side to side, then he stepped back into the kitchen.

The cost of my wee detour on the way to his house meant that if he was driving anywhere, I couldn't follow. It costs far too much juice to hold onto something based in the living world. I could skate after him, but it still takes a bit of energy to get that going. And I didn't have it.

My plan was to see what direction he was driving and just start walking that way—as long as it wasn't back into the ghost ghetto. I'd had enough of that for one night.

Hank burst from the kitchen, and at the hall closet, he took off one jean jacket only to put on another. He whisked right past me, through his screen door, and into the street. On his back pocket was a rectangular, threadbare outline. He reached back with two fingers and pulled out a pack of cigarettes.

After the visit, I had very little on the guy. I swung around him to get a closer look at the pack. They looked a bit like Marlboro Reds, but the writing on the package seemed odd. Not English. Maybe... Cyrillic?

Whoa! Was Hank some sort of Russian spy?

Um, would a real Russian spy be smoking from a pack of Russian cigarettes?

Der.

No.

When I thought about it more, I dropped it. In recent years, Minnesota had been jacking up the price of cigs. It raised revenue and got people to quit but also helped fatten a black market for cheap knockoff brands.

I kept up with Boyd, who kept glancing up the street. He seemed to be searching for something.

When I first died, I vaguely remember standing right in front of people and shouting, trying to get them to hear me. Now I get a kick out of standing face-to-face with people. Like nose-to-nose. It's pretty good to get intel on suspects. You can almost hear them thinking. Or, more correctly, you sometimes can hear them mumbling.

So many people talk to themselves when they think they're alone. Not always full words. Usually short bursts of word clusters. Like Popeye looking for his car keys.

As his eyes tracked in front of him then to each side, Hank said, "Motherfucker you, just... when, if ever anytime did you... prick had it coming."

Sometimes being able to hear someone's personal thoughts doesn't do you a single bit of good. Sometimes it offers a thread, a clue. But without the bigger picture, it can be hard to discern between those two instances.

Hank stuffed the Moscow Reds in his back pocket again and walked toward a row of cars. I made a quick wager with myself that he was in the shitty Chevy. He might have been in the shitty

Honda or shitty Subaru, but Hank seemed like one them proud 'Merican types. Not one to cozy up to his best girl in one of them rice burners.

Hank walked past the cars and continued up the street.

Seems Hank's car was, in fact, a Nike.

Or, more likely, Starter. Probably one of those "jogger" shoes with the useless mesh that ends up choking defenseless dolphins and baby seals. He probably flicked used, still-burning cigarettes at nearby baskets of puppies, too.

Okay, okay. For whatever reason, I just didn't like the guy. But in truth, I didn't like most people, so I didn't exactly feel like this was some sort of discrimination against dudes like Hank that, you know, likely cut their own hair. With rusted garden trowels. While drunk.

Most importantly, Hank was walking and not walking into the ghosty no-go zone.

At my low energy, I could shuffle along with him and, a benefit, I'd gain a bit of juice along the way. I'd feel better after a few minutes of it.

We passed out of the darker residential area to a line of rundown and shut-down stores along a strip mall. Trash was strewn across the street from an overturned drum. Either some homeless guy looking for aluminum cans or kids look for cheap thrills.

Either way, it's the world we get used to.

Hank stepped over the garbage without even looking then yanked the phone back out of his pocket.

"Yeah?"

Time for a little intel.

"No, baby, I... wait, later, right? If—"

Jesus Christ, this guy couldn't hold a conversation with himself or anyone else!

"I'll try, so—If, you know, it depends..."

Suddenly, I had an idea and burst forward, trying to see if there was a name on the phone's display. Of course, to do that, it's a game of inches. You have to get your field of vision right between the phone and their ear. Which means you've got to get your eyes into about a finger-width-sized gap.

And, of course, you've got to be a spook to do that. Because you have to pass through the guy's head or hand.

Which sounds cool, but the thing is, when you pass through buildings, trees, people, anything, you see everything along the way.

I matched Hank's pace and then put my face through the back of his head. Fucking gross. Hair, then skin flakes, then bone, then blood, and other fluids and juices. It's inside the skull, no light, so should be dark, right? Nope.

"So nasty, gross!" I yelled, not worried that he'd hear me.

Then I saw two floating dots on white Jell-O. And for a second I was looking out through his eyes. Walking for a moment like that, I felt silly.

"I'm a-wearing me some Hank glasses," I said.

"Whattya doing, Paint?"

The thugs were back!

I bent down on one knee and spun around, flinging my arms out to ward off any attack. I was terrified of that for good reason.

I got my ass kicked one time in the InBetween after I'd stumbled onto a tub filled to the top with water. Bubbles even. I had to get in. Water isn't exactly watery to spooks, but it has some strange relationship with our world. You can just barely feel it, and when you're dead, it can be nice to have a small taste of that. Relaxing.

Unfortunately, after a minute or two of me just chilling there, a woman came into the bathroom, stripped down, and got in too. Respectfully, I had closed my eyes, because I'd made a promise to myself not to intrude on the privacy of livies without cause. So I never saw the naked woman. And I never saw her dead husband, who'd come in seconds later. He was all about seeing the naked woman but didn't like the idea of her lying in the tub all cozy-like with me.

I almost didn't recover. Again, that beating had been while I was in water—which can be like a sort of very weak amplifier for spooks—so that likely was a factor in how I'd been drained of nearly all my energy.

It took me weeks to regain my strength. I'm not sure what happens to a spook with no energy. I'd asked the Professor, but she'd not enlightened me on that one. In the end, I stopped asking questions. Didn't really want to know. I just avoided it at all costs.

"Painter!" the voice called out, and I realized I'd squeezed my eyes shut, arms out in my laughable fighting stance. Less of a fighting stance, however, more just being indecisive about which way I should run.

"Up here, man."

Hank kept walking but was moving slowly. I could catch up easily enough, so I took a moment and looked up.

Gary was on a light pole. Doing pull-ups. Three stories up.

I let out the breath, or at least made the sound of letting out a breath, because I didn't really breathe anymore. Just leftover bullshit from being alive.

"Hey, man," I said. "How's it hanging?"

Gary let go and drifted down to street level in front of me. He'd shed the Ultimate Terror of the InBetween look he'd used with Allister the tax accountant. He now had changed into something that looked like a Power Ranger. That is, if that Power Ranger had been drawn by a felt-tip pen held between two trembling arms of a meth-addled wolf spider.

"You look… good."

My friend shrugged. I think.

"Just trying to get this one into shape," he said. He quivered for a moment all over then settled into a slightly different configuration. "What are you doing out this way?"

"I'm on a case." Even though I'd been on the job for a while, I still liked the way that sounded.

"You need a hand?"

I laughed. "You got any right now?"

He stood in front of me, and the head blobby-squiggle looked down at its body blobby-squiggle. "Five of them. I think."

"You're getting there. But nah, I'm just tailing a guy," I said, sharing some insights of my craft, which Gary always thought was pretty cool. "That's easy-peasy when you're dead. I can walk right out in the street and dance in front of a suspect, and they're never the wiser. So you don't have to worry about losing them."

Gary pointed a squiggle hand. "Is that your guy getting on a bus?"

"Ah. Yep, that's the guy."

"He's leaving."

"Getting on a bus," I said and exhaled. If I'd had real pockets, I would have stuffed my hands into them. Always sort of a reassuring feeling. Almost like hugging yourself, but it doesn't make others around you uncomfortable.

"You gonna go after him?"

"Can't. I'm tapped outta juice, man," I said and thumbed my chest. "I'm on the reserve tank."

Gary lifted his arms and appeared to clasp his hands together. "Take a bit outta me if you need."

"Nah, man, I appreciate it—"

"I'm good. I got plenty."

I knew this about Gary. Another quirk. "And how is that again?"

Gary dropped his arms. "I dunno. Just always do."

"Does that have anything to do with how you can do..." I waved toward his shimmering form. "... that?"

After a few seconds, Gary turned back into his InBetween hellbeast. I noticed he'd made an upgrade. He said, "No, I think it has something to do with being crazy."

"Crazy? As in crazy-crazy-type crazy?"

"Yeah, but at least for me, that was a brain abnormality," he said and folded his claws into both palms, making fists. "I don't got no brain anymore, man. I'm dead!" He laughed as he knocked on the sides of his head with both fists.

The image triggered something in my memory. I nodded down the street and said, "Hey, you have any idea why a couple of goons down in the Blind might be looking for me? Heard them call my name."

Gary's eyes got wide. The hellbeast looked over its shoulder. "You got some of those freaks in the Ghost Mob after you?"

I shrugged. In truth, I had no idea who they were. But we'd both heard stories of what the Mob did to other spooks

"Well, Paint, whatever's going on, you steer clear," he said, wiping some spittle and blood from his fangs with a hand as big as my skull then said, "Those dudes are scary."

"Right," I said and pointed to the new addition. "What's the second head?"

"Oh, I was getting bored of the old version. You like it?"

"Yeah, nice." He turned the new one toward me. The "face" was just a collection of dark, insectile eyes set with a mouth of sharp teeth. "Hope you got a good vision plan."

"Right?" He laughed. "I'm thinking about maybe adding one more. Something haunting."

"Yeah, because you're not haunting. Not one bit." I laughed. "You might have the best life here in the afterlife. You can do it all, man."

"Yeah?" The new head smiled, and a little bit of pee came out of me. "I'd trade all of it for my old Guns N' Roses album, though. All my life, that's all I listened to. Musta listened to Appetite ten thousand times. Maybe twenty."

"Might explain why you went nuts."

We looked up the street. In the distance, Hank's bus took a corner and was gone.

"You sure you don't want to belt me a few times? It won't hurt me," he said with almost a pained expression. "That's a faster refuel than spirit fingers or whatever you were doing when you were walking behind that guy."

"I'm good, man."

"Okay," Gary said as a car rolled down the street, low to the ground, its stereo blasting something with ball-busting bass. My friend smiled, drew his arms in, then threw them open again and roared so loudly it actually hurt my ears.

With all that energy output, for just a split second, a half blink, he was visible in the real world.

Even with the tinted windows rolled up, I could hear the guy inside let out a scream then gun the engine, smoking the tires as he flew down the block and disappeared in the darkness.

"See, I got plenty of extra. Never totally full but never totally empty either. I just pull it from around me, I guess."

"I see that."

"About a half hour ago, I scared this Toyota hatchback so bad, they knocked a garbage can halfway across the street!"

"Okay," I said and loosened my arms a little, raising my fists. "Maybe just a couple…"

Chapter Ten

The walk back changed my life—well, death—forever.

Until I knew who the spooks were who had jumped me—and more importantly, why the hell they were looking for me—I was going to be smart about how I got around.

And by smart, I mean I was going to be a little bitch about it and go the long, long way around any areas with gaggles of spooky spooks.

For us, the "bad" part of town isn't a simple, centralized geographical area, like this street to that street. When ghosts band together, trading stolen energy back and forth, this creates what we call a Blind Spot. It's a cluster. From high above, it might look like a blood stain on cloth. But it can also manifest into a fat stream with fuzzy boundaries. A river of dread that can go for miles and miles.

The Midwest Blind Spot cuts right through my home town. Minneapolis-St. Paul.

I did everything to avoid it. Or if it couldn't be avoided, I tried to ride using a vehicle as cover instead of walking or skating. It costs some valuable energy, but usually, you can slip right past any spooks looking to roll someone.

That was why I'd thought I'd be safe in the car with Mags. Still, I don't know how, but they saw me.

As I skated down the middle of the street, passing through the occasional car or motorcycle, I made sweeping curves to gin up some more energy. I took Excelsior Boulevard for a few blocks then hooked left.

My local Blind Spot is a little like a time zone. That is, it's jagged and uneven, and those who live near the line of delineation can't really tell where one area stops and the other begins.

Listen, that doesn't mean all the danger is confined to these areas. Not at all. Bad ghosts, like bad people, can be anywhere. But many do seem to be drawn to the Blind, and if a spook with a darker nature hangs around long enough in the InBetween, they eventually end up there.

There are places where Blind Spots do thin out, bodies of water have something to do with it, another weird aspect of H20. My early days here are fuzzy, but it's entirely possible this is why I made my home base in Minnesota, the Land of 10,000 Lakes.

Over time, I've memorized where some of the thin bits are in my neck of the woods.

But even just crossing a few streets in the Blind without somebody watching your back is asking for trouble. So I was going around, and since there was some sort of bull's-eye on me, I wasn't taking any chances.

The long way.

I began to build up speed, using a bit of the energy I'd swiped off Gary, so that I could skate up around the Great Lakes then come down the other side of them.

Skating is a bit like it sounds.

As a ghost, you don't really move based on the movements of your feet. It's your perception of that movement.

I played hockey as a kid, day and night, but in Minnesota, that's not unusual. Despite that, I'm the only one I've ever seen skate in the InBetween. There must be others. Maybe they whiz by me so fast I never see them. Because you can really, really haul ass.

Once you build up speed, it takes almost no effort to keep it going. A bit like space flight, I suppose—once you're moving, there ain't much to slow you down. Gravity gave up on you the moment you stopped breathing.

My plan was to pick up speed and hit the southern tip of Lake Michigan, which always looked to me like some teenage boy getting "stinky pinky." So I planned on skating to the base of the pinky, all the way up to the top, then crossing over Lake Superior, rocketing across the US–Canadian border, then coming back down to Minneapolis's west side.

Not even halfway there, I smashed into some fat, idiot spook dressed as a mailman and peeking into some woman's house, just after midnight.

In truth, running into another spook benefits me. If I'm the one doing the slamming, I'll pull a bit of juice from them. But it goes against my Short List of Rules to Live and Die By. Bashing some innocent ghost breaks a biggie:

Rule #1: Don't want no douchey, don' be no douchey.

You have to say it with a bit of a Jamaican irie irie mon accent to get the proper effect. Not sure why, probably has to do with Bob Marley or his buddy Pete, but there it is. I can imagine some reggae song must have wiggled that idea into my brain.

No douchey, no cry.

No… dou-chey, no cry.

I don't know. The world isn't a fair place, so I'm not naïve enough to think that being a swell fella will keep me out of trouble. It doesn't. Good people get dealt a bad hand all the time.

But if karma's a thing, then there's no use in stacking the deck against yourself. The world's tough enough as it is. Even the afterworld.

Crossing through Wisconsin, I could've kept skating on the interstate, but it goes through some towns that are more populated, so I opted instead to cut across a series of lakes. It's quicker, and there's that bit of a drip charge across water. They're also kinda pretty, especially at night.

However, you gotta cross a half dozen streets between Lake Mendota and Lake Monona in what my sixth-grade teacher learned me was an isthmus. It's a strip of land over water between two larger land masses.

A bit like when you first kissed a girl as a kid, you leaned back a few inches and, blechy, there was a line of spit between the two of you. That's kind of like an isthmus.

Now that I think about it, I believe that's how Mrs. Drake may have explained it to me. Realizing that trying to recall those exact circumstances more clearly was an emotional Pandora's box, I buried it back down to ignore it so it might continue to do untold psychological damage.

Back to smacking the hell out of the fat guy.

When I'm crossing near populated areas, I stick next to the curb, away from the middle of the street, in case some spook is haunting some moving vehicle. You're pretty safe at the street side of the curb.

Unless you've got a dead mailman named Bernard Grimsby who's parked himself next to a stone letterbox and is peering into the windows of some woman's house.

I'd been going at a good clip, so when I smacked into him, I tumbled a half dozen houses down the street, end over end. When I'd got back to check on the guy, I saw he was crying.

Or trying to. Spooks don't have tear ducts, but you can get a bit splotchy in the face if you've been wailing for a little while.

Grimsby was curled up on the ground, knees to his chest, sliding ever so slightly, drifting, and spinning in slow, small circles.

"You all right, man?"

"No," he said, not yet looking at me. "I'm not supposed to be here."

Looking toward the house, I saw a woman in a bra and blue jeans close the drapes. "Yeah, you mean peeking into people's houses? Probably not the best use of your time."

"No, no," he said, finally looking at me. His face: very splotchy. Ol' boy had been bawling his dry eyes out for hours. Maybe longer. "Here! I was sitting in my mail truck dri—uh, sifting through mail, and next minute, wham, I'm sort of tumbling through the street, not feeling a thing."

"Yeah, you're dead, dude."

"I get that! Where is this?" he said then rolled over to face me. "Is this Hell?"

I shook my head and reached over to help him up. "Not yet."

Bernie slumped back to the ground.

Eventually, he introduced himself and said he'd pretty much been hiding in the bushes the past few days. Never sleeping, never getting hungry, and avoiding everybody. He didn't know what to do.

"Painter Mann," I said, extending my hand. "My caseload is quite full, but I expect we can fit you in."

He stared at my pulsing hand. My entire body was probably undulating with light since smacking into him. For the moment, I kept to myself that the fact my energy was nearly tipping past the FULL line had a little to do with why he was now on a quarter tank.

No use in confusing the guy.

Putting my hand back at my side, I said, "I'm the world's only dead private investigator."

"You got a job? In the afterlife?"

"Self-employed."

"Do—do you like it?"

"Ah, the hours are good, but my boss is a dick."

Nuthin'. Not even a smile from the guy. Maybe I hit him harder than I thought.

I needed to get back on the road, but I took a few moments to get Bernie up to speed. I ended with the reason why he'd gotten snared in the InBetween.

His mouth hung open for a moment. He repeated, "Murdered?"

"Yes, that's usually what does it," I said then sat down next to him. "But the caveat is if your killer is caught—or at least revealed—then you can move on. It sets the balance right or something."

He stared straight ahead as a car rolled down the street. For a moment, he just watched as the lights grew bigger and bigger. I slid myself toward the curb as it roared past, running right through Bernard Grimsby.

"Somebody murdered me."

I moved back.

He then slowly turned and looked over his shoulder at the car that had driven through him. "You can see everything. Flashes of fluid, pistons, the driver's kneecap."

"Yeah."

"At least, I hope it was the guy's kneecap."

"Yeah, that's why I sort of avoid ghosting through stuff," I said and helped him back up. "It can be unsettling."

He walked toward a house, his feet not exactly going in the direction he was heading. He looked down, saw this, and once again began to sob.

"It's all so confusing," he said. "You can help me?"

"I'll try."

Bernard led me a few blocks away from where I'd hit him. Even a few days on, he was still really unsteady on his feet. Think Bambi on the ice. While tripping balls.

I had him gently grab my arm while I skated, and he directed me which way to go. Funny thing, I had faint memories of doing the exact thing on ice, many years earlier, with my kid sister. She couldn't skate, so I'd wrap my scarf across my chest and under my armpits so she could pretend she was in a sleigh being pulled by a pony.

For an instant, Bernie even looked like he was enjoying the ride.

When things get overwhelming, sometimes we just need someone to take the wheel. Even just for a little while.

"Here," he said, and we slowed near a corner. The curb was high, with squared-off edges. Above us, light spilled down from a street lamp, and the two of us shimmered a little, if only to each other.

I surveyed the scene. I couldn't stay long, but Madison wasn't too far out of my way. I could come back in a few days. "Your mail truck was here? On the corner?"

He nodded slowly, and his smile drifted away. On the other side of the curb, a beautiful, lush expanse of lawn rolled up toward a line of shrubs. From the street, you could only see a hint of the home's eaves, the roof.

I walked around to where I imagined he'd been sitting in his truck. With the windows at the closest house hidden, there were likely no witnesses to what had happened.

"What were you doing at this point? Where you leaning over to the other seat or—?"

"I was drinking," he said, not meeting my eyes. "Sipping a beer and watching a couple of people walk up the street."

"Hey, man, no judgments from me. That's gotta be a tough gig."

"Yeah. But I sort of loved it."

I bent down into a bit of a crouched position, but he came over and straightened me out. He said, "The seat was raised up on this carriage of springs. You're sitting a lot, so it helps the back." He then looked at me with a blank expression. "And I could see in the windows, you know, to see if people were, you know, home."

"Uh huh."

"No judgment, right?"

Standing there, I looked to my left and right as Bernie described how he'd been sipping his beer, then the next moment, a flash in front of his face, he sees this hand and something shiny sticking out of his nose.

"Wait, no," he said, closing his eyes. "Not shiny. It was dark."

"Like dirty or painted—"

"No, not… it was metal, so it was, like, rusted."

I put my finger to my scalp and so wished I could give it a good scratch. I said, "Rust ain't shiny, man. Are you sure th—"

"Hold on, his hand was shiny," Bernie said. "Really shiny."

I thought about it for a moment. "The guy who killed you was wearing rings?"

The dead mailman nodded, excited. "Yes, yes."

"Could you identify any of them?"

He squinched his eyes closed and grunted a little. "No, but I wouldn't know a class ring from a wedding ring or skull-and-bones ring or any of that. Still, I only saw it for a second," he said, opening his eyes. "But the guy had a lot of rings on. Like Liberace."

I put my hands on my hips. "You think you were killed by a dead, gay Las Vegas pianist?"

Grimsby frowned. "You know he was from Wisconsin, right?"

"You weren't killed by Liberace," I said and then had a thought. I moved toward the line of bushes on the nearby property.

"I know. Just saying the guy had a lotta rings on."

There was a steep slope, but it could have been a hiding place. I called back to him, as he stood in the street, glowing under the light, "You said two people were coming up the street."

"Pushing a stroller."

"Right," I said and glided across the line of shrubs. "Wouldn't they have seen someone walking down the street with all his sparkly rings?"

"They rounded the corner about a minute before…" He stopped and let out a sob. Increasingly, his death was becoming a reality. It's not easy to accept all your hopes and plans are over. Life always feels like there's just a little more time, and realizing that ain't true anymore takes a little while to sink in.

I moved down the row of bushes, which was continuous all the way down the property, up to a driveway. At the blacktop, I looked back.

"That's a long, long way to get to you," I said, and he turned toward me. "Especially in the middle of the day when you never know who might come down the street."

I moved back down the line of shrubs, this time more slowly.

They were perfectly manicured, squared off. You could have put a dinner plate on top of them, and it would have balanced perfectly.

Except for a small patch. It looked different.

"Maybe," I said, slowing, "he jumped the bushes." I eyeballed part of the hedge, wishing the streetlight were a bit brighter.

Bernie called up, spinning slowly in place, "Those hedges are kinda high. It would be a bit of a jump."

My eyes trained on an area about two feet wide. "You think you would have heard a thump or something if the guy jumped."

He was quiet for a moment, then said, "No, Cubbies were playing on the east coast, so I had the ball game on."

Then I saw it. And, in fact, it was only because the streetlight hadn't been brighter that I did.

"Holy shit, man," I said and moved back a little from the line of bushes. "Oh Jesus, I don't even know what to do with…" My voice trailed off.

"What is it?"

I jumped and yelped, not realizing that Bernie had slid up. His phlegmy voice terrified the bejesus out of me, just for an instant. "Whoa!"

"What?" he shouted back and began to slide quickly down the hill, his arms flailing in all directions. I grabbed his wrist and held him steady.

"Don't sneak up on a guy!" I said then pulled him toward the part of the bush that had been damaged. "You see that?"

"No."

"Look closer, man."

He moved in and pointed out the area I'd seen, too. About a dozen tiny leaves of the shrub had been sheared off.

"So the guy hid back here and jumped over," Bernie said softly. He shuddered. "He'd been waiting for me."

"Probably," I said.

"So it was someone… I knew?"

I shook my head. "Not necessarily. If the guy wanted something you had or was ripping off your mail truck for, I dunno, Social Security checks—"

"What? No, they stopped mailing those out way back in 2013. It's all electronic now."

"Okay, but if he wanted something in your truck, he could have followed you for a day or two to get your pattern down. Then picked where he wanted to, you know, do it."

Bernie went to straighten up, but I held him steady.

"Look closer," I said, my voice just above a whisper. "Do you see anything else?"

"Just the broken bits—"

"Come on, Bernie, this is important," I said, my hand actually shaking a little. "Look and tell me if—"

"Wait," he said then turned his head from side to side slowly. "Yeah, I think. It's hard to really—"

"Just tell me."

"It looks like…" The mailman traced his finger back and forth as he tried to find the words to describe what he was seeing. "It's… the tiny leaves here, they… they're like, barely, but they're a slightly different color."

He saw it. Same as I did.

"No, man," I said and put my hands up to my eyes, then looked again. "They're not a different color. It's a different luminescence."

"Uh, is that… isn't that kinda the same thing?"

"No, no," I said and looked up and down the hedge to see if I saw any other trace of it. "You know, as a kid, you ever catch lightning bugs in a jar or in your hand?"

"Sure, my parents took me out to a camp every summer. Dumped me there for two months," he said with a heaviness that told me somebody coulda used some serious couch time back in his livin' days. "Some of the kids would go out at night and catch 'em."

"You ever smash one by mistake?"

"Yeah, sure," he said. "It was kinda gross, right? That glow-in-the-dark goo would be on your hand, then you'd wipe it on your jeans, and it would smear across your pant leg."

Slowly, I nodded and looked at him. "Right. Just like that."

He swallowed hard then said, "Oh my god, you think a big lightning bug dressed as a man killed me? As payback for all them bugs I squashed wh—"

"No, Bernie."

"Whoa! Those weren't shiny rings, then, those were hundreds of tiny lightning bugs, thousands, that came to get their revenge—"

"NO, man!" I said, and seriously considered slapping the guy, but I'd hit him pretty hard once already. "You weren't killed by a swarm of vengeful, undead lightning bugs dressed as a dude."

"Then what?"

I told him the truth. "I don't exactly know yet." Mostly the truth.

"So how do you go about investigating my murder?"

I glanced up toward the southeast. It was time for me to get going. I had unfinished business back in Minneapolis. I said, "I got to get back home, but I'll swing on by within the week."

"A week!"

"Or sooner," I said. "I've got some ideas. Let me work this out."

Bernie told me where he'd been lurking, haunting, the past few days, and I promised to get back as soon as possible. I headed out a bit slow at first, but thanks to Bernie, I had picked up a bunch of energy. Soon I reached Lake Monona, a quick hop over land to Lake Waubesa, then on toward Chicago. From there, I'd head north up Lake Michigan, then cut across.

It was only when I'd gotten to Interstate 90 that I'd let myself reflect on what I'd seen.

That faint luminescence on the bush made no sense, but he'd seen it like I had. It was leftover energy.

Just like how those thug spooks tracked me in the alley, using juice leaves a sort of residue. It usually fades after a few minutes or hours. But if we were looking at where the mailman's killer had hopped the bushes, that was days ago! To leave that much behind? That would have had to come from a spook who was bursting, gushing with energy as if it was coming outta their pores.

The problem, of course, is that spooks can't kill the living. Nor can we wear shiny rings like Liberace.

Whatever this was, it was something new.

Chapter Eleven

The tug was back. Already.

Oh, come on!

It had been a couple days since killing the mailman, and one more since then, so it didn't feel like too many. The time between boosts was growing shorter and shorter.

The congressman would have to be dealt with sooner than later. But the man was always surrounded by other people! She just had to be patient.

A hand went down to loosen another button on the man's shirt. But this was already the third down, and it wasn't calming the awful swelling in the throat. Like taking a bite of steak that was too big and just didn't want to go down.

Breathing was getting labored, but it had nothing to do with breath.

This was just the fucking tug. Again.

Chandra could go another day without satiating that pull. It was always there in some way just outside the field of vision. But if you get desperate, you make bad calls.

A bad call. That was how this problem had gotten so much worse in the first place.

You wait, and the pull turns into an ache then eventually into something that feels like a charley horse in the mind. Judgment gets clouded, muddled. Then, a bad call.

It seemed like ages now since this man had become the new ride. The emergency ride. A lot of pain in the beginning. Part of that was the adjustment, of course. And it would have been all so much easier if things had gone to the original plan.

All of that screwed up by a drunk with a gun?

Didn't matter. If there'd been proper planning, that wouldn't have happened. She'd always been a meticulous planner. But she'd failed, and that led to desperation and a bad call.

I need to focus on now, right now. She'll be heading to the elevator soon. Time to go up top.

After the button was pushed, the lit numbered floors above the elevator indicated the car was moving downward.

It had taken just two days to get the young reporter's routine down. In that time, there'd also been the kid who was working some bottom-rung IT job. Working late, tired all the time, some of it from home, where he'd lived alone.

The boy had been an easy target but took a surprisingly long time to die. It was probably better for the boost; who knew. Jan Jorgensen's hand reached into a pocket and fiddled with the boy's glasses. He was in the machine now, feeding her.

The elevator doors, all dented and scratched, rumbled as the car approached. The scratching looked like some idiot gang banger had run out of spray paint and resorted to tagging the door with car keys or a busted metal pipe.

Stupid.

The elevator announced its arrival with a bell that had seen better days. It didn't sound so much like a bell but some tiny, curved iron hammer striking a bent-up tin can. Not aluminum, but tin like back in the seventies.

The doors parted, and the light inside was unnaturally bright. It probably gave those who used it, especially at this time of night, the illusion of safety. There was an emergency phone in the car as well, but its wires had been carefully snipped twenty-four hours earlier.

Dark glass that encased a cheap security camera in the upper corner had been covered up an hour earlier with even darker electrical tape.

Proper planning. No more bad calls.

The killer pulled a cell phone from a back pocket and checked the display. Just before eleven-thirty.

The pretty journalism grad—who'd just made reporter after moving through the Chicago newsroom from researcher to booker to digital copy editor—would right about now be wrapping up her workout. Heavy on the aerobics. Treadmill, bike, boxing.

The woman inside the man rode the car to the very top floor, the nineteenth, and waited.

Like clockwork, Brenda Matthews had hit the twenty-four-hour gym as she did every night. She was planning for her future, a TV gig. For now, she was happy with having scored a reporting position at the paper a few months earlier. She wanted Crime or Politics, something with meat. But for now, it was Lifestyle.

A breast-cancer five-k race.

An old couple, she in her nineties, he in his eighties ("Robbing the cradle, huh?") getting married at the retirement home.

One story about a coffee shop that let customers play with cats.

They never said it directly to female journos any more, too dangerous, but looks still mattered. It wasn't fair. But this was the field she'd chosen, and she had known what she was getting into.

She'd always carried a few extra pounds, and despite how unfair it was, she was determined to knock them off. Sure, it was playing by their rules, but those were the rules.

"For now," she said, smiling, and pushed the button for the elevator.

The killer had caught sight of her days earlier. Watching from the building across the street, and once again tonight, the reporter had been on the elliptical machine, the last exercise of the night.

Earplugs in, blond hair bopping along to whatever the latest ex-Nickelodeon tweenage, popped-cherry singing star was putting out.

When she headed for the dressing room, it was go time. Quick run four flights down, cross the street, dead this time of night, then into the target building.

Now the killer waited in the elevator cab. Top floor.

The doors hadn't parted at the top—this floor required a passcode. Didn't matter. No one was getting off.

Then the car began to move, heading down.

The killer pressed a button on the panel, B2, and just waited until the doors opened on the twelfth floor. Sure, the call could have come from another level. Maybe an employee was getting off work instead, but he'd planned for that. Make excuses and take the ride back to the top again and wait

16.

15.

She'd no doubt be counting on the security guard's protection. In truth, not much of a guard and light on security capabilities, it seemed. Minimum-wage gig. No permit to carry. Spent most of the night watching YouTube videos on his phone.

Once the young reporter got off the elevator on the bottom floor, lower parking garage, the guard would be right around the corner, about twenty feet away, at a small station that looked more like he should have been parking cars.

Floor B1. There she would be safe.

She would never make it that far.

13.

12.

Ding! The metal rod hit the pop-top seventies Sprite can, and the doors opened.

The killer had headphones on—they were attached to nothing, the lead just tucked down into his jacket—and looked engrossed in a paperback novel.

The reporter waved goodbye to the person at the desk and only gave a half glance at the tall, thin man as she got onto the elevator. Her eyes fell to the chains around his neck, the many rings on his fingers—some holding two or three!—but she was too polite to say anything.

"Working late?"

A forced smile. Barely a look up from his book.

The doors closed, and she dug into her bag, reaching for the elevator panel. Her finger hovered over B1 for a moment before pushing it. The button for the floor just above was glowing. Recently, that level had been closed off.

The killer sighed theatrically, eyes still glued to the paperback. "Must've been some snot-nosed kids riding the elevator again. It stopped at five different floors before it got to yours."

The reporter smiled, hit her floor, and leaned up against the wall. A good workout. She would sleep really well. A musky bouquet wafted up to her nose.

After a bath.

With a soft groan, the tall man put his hand behind his back, making circular movements as if rubbing a tight knot.

One floor away from the security guard, the pitiful sound of metal striking metal, Ding!, and the doors opened to a level that had been shuttered for repairs after vandals had come in nights earlier and taken the fire ax to most of the overhead light fixtures.

Dark, exposed conduit and wires hanging from the ceiling.

"Creepy," was the last thing she ever said.

Chapter Twelve

It had been a level of despair the Butterfly never thought possible.

Beyond sorrow, beyond anguish, beyond misery. The one saving grace—a term that bent her lips into a bitter smile—was that the pain was so terrible, so complete, that she felt almost detached from her body. Observing from the outside, looking in.

But she didn't have a body, so what was left now wandering the dark streets of the city?

"This must be Hell," she said, then flinched when a set of dreary eyes looked up from a heap of discarded clothes next to the doorway of a closed-up shop. She kept walking, and the milk-yellow eyes slowly faded out of sight again.

I'm dead.

Since leaving the old apartment, she'd become more and more comfortable with the phrase. It was beginning to feel more hers.

After wandering the city the first time, she had found the smallest bit of solace back home—the dimmest of stars in a dark, swallowing expanse of sky. But it wasn't her home anymore. Now it was just his home. And in some way, she was still there. Her fiancé was still living with the memory of her, the digital frame a constant reminder of what he'd lost.

Over and over, the CCTV footage from that night outside their apartment played in her head. Hunched over, she ambled through the darkness, gripping her stomach, wincing. Then she had a realization.

Even before the second trial had begun (that little boy! Christ, Christ, Christ, the look of horror on the faces of his family in the courtroom!), she'd "paid her debt to society" with her life. But she had an outstanding debt.

Would he still be on that road? What kind of parents let their kids sneak out at night? For what? Chips and a drink at three in the morning. Where does a seven-year-old even get money?

Would the dead boy be at his home even now, pleading to his parents, silently screaming, distraught that they would not answer? Horrified that they were ignoring their beautiful boy. Didn't they know he was there?

Her attorney had argued that the Audi's dent could have been the result of hitting an animal. A dead dog had been found on the side of the road, and despite that discovery being some four blocks in the other direction, there had been a chance, it could be—

No, no! I don't get that!

She didn't deserve the false hope. No one had believed the possibility anyhow. No one except for one poor, gullible sap in the first trial who wouldn't budge. Hung jury.

Her own attorney, who'd been brilliant, worked every angle, every possibility, and had obsessed about the prospect of a videotape, just outside the convenience store. There'd been five cameras. Two on the forecourt to cover the pumps, two inside making sure no one pocketed the Little Debbies, then one to keep an eye on the cashiers in case they were looking to make an unauthorized withdrawal.

One of the forecourt cams was at a vantage point to catch the moment of impact. And for an excruciating twelve hours, they waited for the footage. At first, she had held onto hope that she'd be exonerated.

But just an hour before it was supposed to be delivered, she also made peace with the other possibility. One that would show she'd indeed mowed down the little boy. Did she swerve? Had she kept driving? Did she realize she'd hit someone's child?

When the video clip arrived, she couldn't remember sitting down.

"Maybe it's good news," her attorney Bronwyn had said, shrugging. "I mean, for the case. That one camera was just static. Couldn't see the street where, you know, it happened."

The next day, the stories came out of how one of the employees had been stealing from the store, late-night runs from the storage room to a friend's car, and that the camera likely had been deliberately turned off to avoid detection.

The digital age's Irrefutable Truth, the god's-eye-view black-and-white CCTV video, would not play a part in her trial.

Didn't matter. None of it mattered. No jury necessary this time; her sentence had been handed down by a judge who already knew what happened.

She looked up, standing in the dark city street, and her head, ethereal and without substance, still felt heavy, leaden. In front of her was a home. She recognized it but couldn't yet place it.

The boy's home. Her sentence would be to comfort this child. Apologize. Soothe. Anything she could do to help him. Nothing would make up for what she'd done, but that didn't mean she was in any way free of that debt.

Walking up the steps of the two-story house, her breath clutched in her throat—there was a light on inside. Someone was home.

The Butterfly reached for the door's knob, but her hand went straight through. Of course. Stupid. She wrapped her arms around herself, then lowered her head and went in to begin her sentence.

A beautiful wrap-around staircase led to an upper floor. Afghan carpet under her feet. There was a soft light on a small table near the door. A wicker container held a set of car keys. Mercedes.

She didn't yet see the boy.

Her feet were still, but she continued to move forward into the next room. Light spilled from that one into the foyer, illuminating her path. But when she crossed the threshold, she didn't see a grieving mom and dad. Or a ghostly child hovering nearby.

A woman, sitting back in a plush leather office chair, the toes of her right foot slowly swaying her from side to side. Nearby, a large-screen television was rolling through one of the 24-hour news channels, muted.

When she came around to see the woman's face, it took her a moment to recognize her. When she did, it was bittersweet.

"Hi, Bronwyn," she said and momentarily felt the hint of warmth. "You look good. Where's Alexand—"

On a stack of blankets, she saw a cat, a mutt of a thing, lift its head.

"There you are."

Then the cat's head flicked toward her, staring. Its body tensed. Either ready to pounce or run away. Small tics, flicker movements, but its large eyes only grew larger, locked onto the ghostly presence in the room.

The Butterfly shifted a few feet, and the cat's eyes tracked her as she moved.

"Can you—?"

The cat groaned, low in its throat. Then a bit louder.

"Alexander, cut it out," Bronwyn said, words slurring from either wine or sleepiness or both. Admonished, the cat blinked, licked its lips, and calmed. Still, it kept one eye on their visitor.

The bottle on the computer desk looked to have only been drained of a single glass. However, on the floor, there was another. That one was empty.

If the Butterfly had any tears, she might have shed them for her friend. She said, "I'm sorry. I'm so sorry. You were so great, so brave."

Whatever Bronwyn had been reading drew a small smile from her.

"I think in the end, you were just about my only friend left. That happens with child murderers, I hear. We don't get invited to parties much." This was the gallows humor–type banter that she and Bron—a British woman, Welsh?—had always fallen into with ease. She'd been grateful for it. It helped loosen the ropes around her head and heart.

She looked at the pictures on the attorney's wall. Families. Kids. These were images of other families. Other people's kids. A workaholic, the woman of the house hadn't taken time for her own. Not yet.

"You need to find yourself a guy," the ghost said. "A rich momma's boy who loves to bake and work out who can help you make babies. You'd be a good mom."

A picture drawn in a frame was inscribed with "to Auntie Bron."

"Sorry we never did get to go to Disney World," she said and was struck at the sound of her own voice, the depth of sadness it betrayed. "But still, that would have been weird, right? Two grown women showing up at the park by themselves."

Bronwyn turned to her computer, one hand still on the file in front of her.

"Can you rent kids? They should have that service. Then you don't look so weird." She ran her fingers down the portrait of a tall man. Bronwyn's brother? "Or Fiji or Cozumel or New Zealand would have all been good too. That post-trial trip, yeah?" She turned toward the woman at the computer. "But that's…"

Bronwyn tapped away absentmindedly, taking another large swig of the dark liquid in her glass. The flicker on the screen tickled the corner of the Butterfly's eye. Bright colors, a castle with fireworks, a smiling cartoon mouse.

She turned toward her friend and slid up next to her. "Disney World? How weird is that…"

The attorney lazily clicked around the website, every few seconds squeezing the mouse with her right hand while nursing the wine with her left.

The dead woman bent down so she was eye-level with her friend. A thin, pretty face that was aging too quickly. Her heart hurt to think this was how Bron spent her nights. Wishing. Wanting.

"You were so great," the ghost said softly, stroking the woman's arm as she typed one-handed, poking sluggish fingers at the keyboard, click of the mouse. "I've never seen such a fighter like you."

Bronwyn smiled.

Click, click. Sip.

"You were my hero! Door knocking every business and residence and lemonade stand for a quarter mile to find some other video. My million-dollar attorney, rolling up her sleeves and digging with her manicured nails!"

Click, tap, tap. Click.

Then the look on her friend's face transformed. Not quickly. More of a shift, like a stack of magazines slowly sliding off a table and then tumbling to the floor.

Tap, tap. Click. Sip. Slide, click.

"What's wr—?"

The Butterfly turned toward the screen. Bronwyn was no longer looking at fairyland castles or character parades or sunburned tourists posing with actors in costumes."

The mouse pointer hovered over a small rectangle. When the dead woman looked down to her friend's hand, she saw the right index finger hovering over the mouse. Hanging in the air, trembling slightly. The look on her face was intense, and her eyes were heavy, watery.

"What's wrong, Bron?"

Click.

The movie began to play full screen. There was no sound, just the images of the world slipping by a cityscape. Traffic. A succession of taillights ahead of her, to the left, to the right.

"This is what you watch? Your dash-cam footage? I should have left you a list of movies. You like mo—"

Bronwyn manipulated the mouse, and the images began to flutter by more quickly. Interstate driving, taillights strobing all around the dash cam like a disco. Then the car was off the interstate, whipping past a corner store, silently slamming on the brakes at a set of red lights.

Of course, it hadn't slammed on the brakes, but at the accelerated pace, the car seemed to be racing through the streets, eager to get somewhere, somewhere important. Somewhere significant.

Another turn, then another.

The dead woman had to face away, the jerky video beginning to turn her stomach, which only reminded her that she no longer had one. When she turned back, Bron had begun to slowly rewind the video.

No, not rewind. The car was in reverse, backing into a driveway. Then a slight shimmer and a moment later the quick visual jarring of the car door likely being slammed.

"Did someone hit you on the way home, and you're looking for a plate or something? What are you..?"

No, this couldn't have been recent. When the ghost looked closer, there was a hint of snow on the ground. Frost. This would have to be late autumn. Earlier December.

Huh. That was right around the same time…

Again, Bron fingered the mouse. Despite being a bottle and a half deep into her wine, she still worked it with precision and purpose.

Wait. Hold on, wait…

These weren't images from Bronwyn's car. The dash-cam footage did not show this neighborhood but one the Butterfly was very familiar with.

Her friend advanced the footage quickly again, shuttling through until the daylight turned pale, the dusk turned to dark. The driver hadn't turned the dash camera off.

Oh Christ, oh Christ, oh Christ…

There was a quick flicker, then a burst of white as the floodlights of the Speedway service station across the street came alive unevenly, then locked in.

This was where it had happened. This was the tape they'd been looking for. Bron had found the evidence.

Why hadn't she told anyone?

Chapter Thirteen

The living don't realize how easy they've got it.

These days, you can't get lost any more, what with GPS telling you where to go. And even if that didn't work, your map software is likely on your phone. You can just call someone and tell them you got your dumb ass lost.

Hell, you might even come up on that person's phone as My Dumb Ass Friend Who Calls Me When He's Lost (mobile).

The dead don't have the luxury.

It's not like you've got a compass to tell you you're going north. You can see on the big rest stop map that you've got to take County Road 34 to 63, which'll take you to Interstate 70, then onto 35, but you'd be surprised how fast all them numbers jumble up in your head because you can't carry a notebook and a pen to write shit down.

Now, there is a bit of a fallback you can half rely on if you get lost: if you just keep going, eventually, you'll find yourself back home. We are the energy beings of the ether, so we are drawn back to the familiar.

It's almost like a faint scent that you can't name. Something vaguely familiar; you just can't put your finger on it.

I'd hit Chicago, which is goddamn chockfull of spooks, but thankfully most had been around long enough to know to keep out of each other's way. If there was any sort of spook Blind Spot in Chicago, I'd never stumbled into it.

I never thought Minneapolis would be more dangerous than Chicago. Never sounded terribly dangerous. The city's name always sounded a bit like what you might name a lapdog that pisses itself when the doorbell rings.

I skated 90 heading into Chicago, and my eyes fell closed. My arms spread wide as I flew past car after truck after motorcycle. I cracked my eyes open just slightly and caught sight of the big city's lights. I've got a little bit of a romantic in me, sure, but I'm not quite sure why a light-dappled city skyline does it for me.

Using the sounds of the vehicles around me as a guide, I let my eyes fall closed again and cast my arms even wider as I picked up speed, trusting that faint pull home would guide me where I needed to go.

Soon, I would bank north and head up the Great Lake, where I could go almost as fast as I wanted, then make the turn west and be back home in no time.

Taking a deep breath—or really, more like what I remembered a deep breath felt like—I was almost in a Zen-like trance, pleasantly in tune with the ghost world that blanketed the real one.

I should have known better.

I'd crossed somewhere near Lincoln Park when I hit something or, of course, someone on one of the overpasses.

The burst of ripped-off energy coursed through me as I rolled end over end over end, finally using a bit of the new juice to slow myself down, coming to a stop near the bank of the North Branch Chicago River.

Standing back up, I looked toward the city, so close to where I was going to make my turn north. But I knew I'd just smashed the hell out of someone—twice in one night. But as Rule #1 says, Don' want no douchey, don' be no douchey, so I headed back to see what I could do to help. Again.

I found her spinning in a small circle on the overpass, a big bush of blond hair trailing behind her feet as she went around and around.

"You okay?"

She tensed, not saying a word.

I tried again. "Sorry, I mean, I didn't see you. Why were you hanging out there anyhow? Major roadway arteries ain't good places to chill—" She was now up on all fours, sliding, then trying to crawl, but, of course, having no effect on the direction she was moving. "—but they're not terribly good when you're alive either."

She still wouldn't look toward me.

I added, "Which, maybe, is what got you here?"

Finally, her face lifted to show her mascara had run. That is, it had been running just before she died, so that's how she now looked in the InBetween.

She arched her back and tried to stand but didn't have the energy. She said, "Motherfucker!"

I nodded. "Yep, I got that coming. You feel weak right now because—"

"I know why!" she shouted, getting to her feet, all wobbly. "That's why I left the goddamn city. Hell, I thought it was bad guys taking swipes at me before. Now, it can damn near kill you."

"Well, uh, it won't kill you, of course, because—"

"I know that, motherfucker," she said, and I moved closer to stop her from sliding. She gave me a look that told me she still had enough energy to do me some real damage. I put both hands out like you might do with an approaching tiger, pushing them down repeatedly to indicate that I wasn't going to hurt her.

I reached for her and slowed her slide.

The pretty, makeup-stained spook, new to the InBetween, trapped in what must be such a strange and frightening world, hauled back and clocked me across the face.

It's a little embarrassing, but I went down hard. Really hard.

Thankfully, I'd taken a big swig of her juice moments before (not to mention the mailman I'd T-boned earlier), so I had energy to spare.

Back to my feet, I nodded, and my jaw actually felt like it ached. "I deserved that," I said. "I mean, I wasn't trying to hit you, you know, with you floating around the interstate like that, but yeah, it's probably good you got a bit of your juice back."

"What?" she said and turned her pretty face toward me. "My what?"

Ignoring the question because I didn't feel in the teaching mood, I asked her, "How long have you been here?"

"Man," she said and raised her arms. "I don't even know where here is."

"Well, you're dead," I said and waited for her to panic again. "You know, FYI."

"I got that part," she said. "But what is… all this?"

"When did you, you know, get killed?"

She looked over at a jogger's armband and tapped it a couple times. "I dunno. My phone hasn't worked since being wherever this is."

"Not sure if it has a real name," I said. "But everybody just calls it the InBetween."

"Right," she said. "As in… in between life and…?"

Smiling, I shrugged. "Dunno," I said. "We'll find out when we move on."

One of my weaknesses is people in need, I think. Especially when they're kinda cute, that helps. So I gave her my InBetween Introductory Speech (Abridged), including how she could also move on to the Next place.

When I'd introduced myself with my very unique job title, I suppose some part of me was bragging, trying to impress her a little with my vocational ingenuity.

She said, "That's ridiculous."

"No, it's not. I help people."

Shaking her head, she slid, stumbled, skittered farther from the roadway toward a bus-stop bench. She nearly sat down but then caught herself.

"Damn," she said. "I already miss just, you know, sitting down."

"You'll get used to it."

"I don't want to get used to it," she yelled, her damp curls swishing around her neckline. "You said you could help me get out of here."

"What? No, I didn't," I said, doing a quick review of the conversation up to that point. "I never said that. Did I?"

"You said you help people. And I don't suppose there's any way to go back and pick up where I left off."

"No." She'd been just in her twenties. Way too young.

"Fuck, and I was on the verge of really breaking through," she said, closing her eyes. With the rivers of mascara streaming down her face, it looked like she was permanently crying. "Within a year, I'd have picked up a real beat. A real reporter."

"You were on TV?"

"No, shithead! Real reporting!" she said and then scowled. "Sorry. I'm sorry. I've been in a pretty bad mood the last four hours or so."

"Huh. You've been here only for a few hours?"

She sniffed. "Yeah, I think so. There about."

I looked toward the city and envisioned its reflection in the water. Had to get back to Mags. And after what I'd seen with Bernie the mailman, my long-overdue catch up with the Professor was now, uh, longer overdue.

But if the young reporter had just been murdered, I had a shot at an easy case.

Four hours? There might still be an energy residue. One that, if you know what you're doing, you can sometimes follow.

"I don't have much time," I said.

"Far as I understand it, you got all the time in the world, dead P.I. guy."

"No, I mean people are waiting for me back home."

"Oh." Her face slightly darkened. She was thinking about her own family or a husband or a dog or friends. The people she'd left behind.

"Um, listen," I said softly. "You're probably thinking about going and seeing your folks or friends or something." She looked up at me with wide eyes. "It's not a great idea. It just really bums you out, and they will never know you're there."

"How do you know what I'm thinking? Is that a thing here?" Her eyes grew to nearly the size of vinyl albums. "Can everybody ready everybody else's thoughts? Oh Jesus, all that stuff about my cousin, second cousin, it was a long, lon—"

"NO, no!" I said, raising my hands. "We can't read minds, but I've been here a while." Using up a bit of juice, I sat down on the bench. "I know my way around a bit."

She looked at me, walked over to the bench to sit down by my side, then slipped right through and fell on the ground, feet up in the air.

"As I said, It takes a little getting used to."

I stood up and helped her up again.

"Okay, we're going to do a quick start on this thing," I said flatly, all professional. "Did you see the face of the person who killed you?"

It took a moment. Then, "Yes. He'd been on the elevator."

"So if you saw him right now, you'd recognize him."

She nodded. "Just over six foot, short-cropped blond hair. He was in pretty good shape." She pursed her lips. "He might have been gay?"

"Really," I said. "How do you know that?"

"Because he had a cock sticking out of his mouth."

Even though I was long dead and body free, I may have blushed. "I… uh… wha—"

"No, no," she said and laughed. "I'm kidding. He just had, I dunno, a slight feminine quality about him. The way he moved, the rhythm of how he spoke. Dude was probably gay."

"Not sure if that helps."

"Probably helps other dudes a whole lot," she said. It seemed the joking was keeping her from falling apart.

I walked in a circle, bouncing my fist slightly off my forehead. My big thinkin' pose. "Knowing his face is a big help. That way you can recognize him, and if we can get a name, you're fwoop! home free."

She looked at me a little confused, and I explained her ticket out via a short online entry.

"Huh," she said. "That's a bit like in the movies, then."

"Even a broken clock is right twice a day."

"What? No, it's not. The display is dead. Doesn't say anything. Just a big hunk of wrong-clock is what you got."

"Uh huh," I said. "How'd he do it... uh... damn, I don't even know your name."

"Brenda Matthews."

"That's a very reporter name, Brenda Matthews," I said, trying to keep the mood light, but it had the opposite effect, reminding the young woman she'd lost the most precious things of all. Life. And time. And love.

Yeah, I kinda suck at cheering people up.

"Coming down the elevator, the doors opened up onto a dark floor, and the asshole shoved me onto it," she said and combed her fingers through her thick hair. "It was dark except for the emergency lights above the exit doors."

"Did you see how—?"

"Yeah, it was like a screwdriver or something. Right to the skull," she said, then added a bit more quietly, "Right to my skull."

Hand weapons were easier to hide—knives, files, iron pipes— but that kind of close-up kill is often personal. Maybe someone who had a grudge. A jealous coworker? Someone she'd written about in a column?

"Do you have any enemies?" I said, but the words left a bad taste in my mouth. Sounded like an eighties TV detective. "Or, better, do you know anyone who had a beef with you at all? Something a bit recent."

She tugged at her shirt, trying to adjust it. She'd eventually find out that here, that just wasn't a thing anymore.

"Well, I am a journalist," she said. "So my bosses don't like me, the public doesn't trust me, elected officials hate me, and everyone who runs a company, coffee shop, or nail salon wants me fired." She smiled at that thought, then added, "My momma loves me, though."

"Cool," I said. "We'll cross one name off the list, then."

I asked her to give me anything else she could remember about what had happened four hours earlier.

"That's pretty much it," she said. "I remember lying there, more scared than I'd ever been. For a moment, I held out, thinking I'd get outta there. Soon after that..." Her lip quivered for a moment. She wiped her mouth and said, "You know, I remember which exact breath was my last one. Is that fucked up? It was shallow and thin, didn't get much air. If I'd known it would be my last taste of life, I'd have filled both lungs until they burst. And just held on."

I looked down at my feet. "I'm sorry."

"This guy, he got off on it like nothing I've seen before. Just stood over me, as if he were breathing me in, flexing his arms. Just ecstasy, right? I think he actually sparkled."

Bells went off in my head, but I kept my gaze down, listening.

"Then, final insult, the prick took off the St. Christopher's cross my mother gave me. And two of my rings," she said, eyes staring off somewhere far away. "Actually, I remember that now. That guy had rings on every finger. More than one."

"Right," I said, trying to get my head around it. "Right. Like Liberace."

"Who?"

"Did you know he was a Wisconsin boy?"

"My killer?"

"No, Liberace," I said and earned another blank stare.

For the first time in my dead P.I. career, I was on the trail of a serial killer. And if I moved quickly, I had a solid chance of finding him.

"If you wear that cross, those rings every day, you've still got a connection to them. At least for a while. That's something you can feel, something we can follow. And it could lead us right to this guy."

"Yes!" Brenda shouted, and it was the first time I saw her really smile. "And I can get justice for my death!"

"Or—" I said and grabbed her hand, pulling her along and picking up speed toward the city, "—at the very least, a succinct Wikipedia entry."

Chapter Fourteen

I felt a little like someone who was trying to put off some upcoming dreadful event. Which—and I'm pretty honest with myself now that I'm dead and all—wasn't the case at all.

For one, I wanted to get back with Harry and Mags to work on little Katie's case. Also, I missed them, which wasn't great. I'd had plenty of others work for me in the past. Retirement villages and nursing homes were the best places to recruit. All of my Temps are dying—that's how it works. So getting too close only means a broken heart.

Then again, getting close is really the only nice thing left for anyone in the InBetween.

I'd already told Harry that his wife Mags was my favorite Temp in a long while. She reminds me a little of what my wife would have been like if she'd gotten to that age. At least, I think she reminds me of my wife. Honestly, I can't even remember what she looks like anymore.

I'd promised their granddaughter, their living granddaughter (and I still hadn't figured that out either), that we'd look into the death of her stepfather Boyd. Someone had emptied a gun into his chest, so he should be hanging around the InBetween. Unless the Ghost Mob snatched him. There are rumors that's been happening more and more recently.

If he is wandering around, he might be Uptown. A lot of spooks hang out there. Probably all the theater. That's not a joke. Being dead and awake 24/7, a good midnight show can help pass the time.

But with all the recent weirdness, like I said a chat with the Professor was overdue. I've learned most of what I know about the InBetween from her. Despite that, she's a tightwad. She won't give you a nice bullet list of top secrets. But if you ask enough of the right questions, you'll come away knowing more than you did before.

Like any pseudo-prophet, you can't be too exact about things. Easiest way to put yourself out of a gig.

Following Brenda the ex-reporter's nose, we were led to Clark Street, just off Chinatown. We'd been barhopping for about two hours. If I'd had palms, I think they would have been sweating. Sure, we needed to find the guy, but I dunno, something about hunting down a serial killer was making me skittish.

Maybe it was my run-in with the spooks back in the Cities. Or perhaps it was the very faint luminescence I saw every now and then as we followed Brenda's lead through the city.

The same sort of stain the mailman and I had seen on the bushes.

"I know that guy," the reporter said, pointing a red-tipped nail toward a pack of young wolves who'd parked themselves in the corner of a loud bar called The Grind.

He was a scrawny dude with long arms and a haircut that would make you wonder why his barber didn't like him. His pants stopped at the mid-calf to show off horrific Dr. Seuss–style striped socks.

"That's the guy who killed you?"

"No, we went out a few times," she said, and I gave her a look. "Don't gimme that. I was a few years younger, and I was going through some self-esteem issues."

"Before or after dating that guy?"

I spun my back toward the bar and used a capful of juice to prop my elbows up on the rail, scanning the crowd.

"You have to show me how to do that," she said with a twist of her lips.

"Kid, you ain't gonna be around long enough to need to know."

"Don't call me kid."

"Why not?" I said, scanning the crowd. "I think it's a detective thing. Like Humphrey Bogart's Sam Spade." Every guy there, in some way, looked suspect. "Don't take it personal, doll."

"Ugh, maybe I should do this by myself," Brenda said. "I'm a reporter, after all. I can solve my own case."

"Maybe, but you need me to help you clear this place."

"Fine."

"Okay, you said you're drawn to this area."

"I definitely felt something."

"Yeah, but is that an 'I wanna drink' something or 'I think my killer's eating tapas over there' something?"

She closed her mascara-stained eyes, moving her head slowly, like a sat dish looking to lock onto a signal.

"I think," she said, slowly. "I think we're closer than we were before. When we first came, but–"

"Can I get you anything, Jimmy?"

Jumpy, I pushed off the bar as if someone had put a live wire to the brass rail. Brenda smiled sweetly and shook her head.

"That'd be great," I said, pretending to reach for a half-finished silver bowl on the bar. "Walnuts always make me thirsty."

Our bartender smiled, and his big, bushy mustache twitched.

The next moment, another bartender walked right through him, grabbed two Buds out of a cooler beneath the bar, then headed off.

Our barman, who looked like a fixture from a century ago, smiled again. "Fine, sir, what'll you have?"

"Oh man," I said and reached out to stop Brenda, jaw hanging open, from sliding away. "It's been a long time since I had a Kingfisher. Nice full-bodied lager."

The bald bartender reached down as if to adjust his apron, then raised one hand to the top of his head, rubbing slightly.

"Sir, I do believe I had one of those during one of my tours in the African campaign," he said, the famous memory of a bartender still good some, what?, hundred years later? "Indian brew, I believe."

"You too?" Brenda said. "Do all men have fake jobs in the afterlife?"

Ignoring the slight, I gave the bartender a broad smile. "Yes, from the subcontinent, I believe. That's the one."

"Ah, Jimmy, I can nearly taste it now," the guy said, smoothing down his handlebar mustache with his fingertips. "And the young lass I was with when I had it." He grinned, eyes twinkling.

I laughed. The guy was a charmer, natural bartender. "I bet, but my name's not Jimmy."

"He calls everybody Jimmy," said a skinny wreck of a man, one side of his face blackened with either dirt or dried blood. "And we don't allow no froufrou drinks in here, so your girl better not be thinking piña coladas or nothing."

"I'm not his girl!"

"Don't mind him, you two," the bartender said. "He's been a cranky old bastard since we got held up in '57. Sawed-off shotgun took off half his pretty face. That'll put anyone in a foul mood."

I was glad that all I saw was dirt. I'd seen guys who'd taken one to the head and, wuff!, some of those guys you don't want around during dinner. Even if you could eat in the InBetween, you wouldn't want Gooey Gus with his face full o' pus hanging around.

Sure, we're all dead, but that doesn't mean I still can't pick my own friends. Me? The less oozy the better. Weird part is that if he had taken a shot to the face way back then, he should have reverted to "normal" by now. Whatever his memory was of himself. He hadn't. I guess some folks can really hold a grudge.

The barman introduced himself as Handsome Dan, which was weird because he didn't look like, at least to me, a Dan. I told them our names.

Brenda finally found her voice again. "Handsome Dan, why do I get the impression you've been here a while?"

He nodded and gave her a wink. "My dear, I helped open the place."

When we'd come in, I'd seen the plaque screwed to a large rock outside. It'd read, Oldest pub on the South Side. est. 1917.

"Great," she said. "I'd love a shot and a beer."

Handsome Dan's eyes flickered. "Um, we're temporarily out of stock at the moment. Of everything." The living bartender then reached through Dan's chest, pulled on a tap, and poured a frothy Samuel Adams into a thick glass with a handle. The dead barman looked down and scowled. "Uff, what kind of flavor is pumpkin for a goddamn beer?"

The live bartender spun away from us, with the seasonal brew leaving a trail of foam on the bar behind him. We all momentarily stared at the bubbles as they popped, disappearing one by one.

I said, "What kinda bar is outta everything?"

Sawed-off looked at us, laughed, and took a drag of his cigarette. None of the smoke pulled into his lungs, the cig just burned brighter, stuck there between two fingers. He'd been smoking it when killed.

To carry that around for more than half a century? That had to be a bit of torture.

Handsome Dan was undeterred. He clapped his large, meaty hands and, I swear, a couple people nearby jumped slightly. Then they gave each other furtive glances and laughed nervously.

He said, "What we do offer is a place to rest your heels and engage in a little friendly conversation."

"That'll do," I said. First, a little flattery. "You guys, bartenders, you hear everything, see everything, don't you?"

"We know something about everything. From travelers such as yourself, those who pass through," he said, then laid his elbows on the bar. Where his skin met the wood, I saw just the slightest hint of a glow. Like a warm hand touching cool glass.

This guy was using the minimal amount of juice possible to keep himself propped up. Skilled. Very skilled.

And no, I hadn't missed the subtle hint. Travelers should "pass through." We were on a countdown clock.

Dan opened the door by saying, "Whatcha after?"

"You ever hear about a spook that wasn't, you know, just a spook?"

The mustache twisted. "Lad, I'm not following."

Suddenly, I was feeling stupid. Like one of those guys who won't shut up about 9/11 conspiracy theories at a party where the person who drove you isn't ready to leave.

I came at it another way.

"You've been here a while," I said. "Anybody come in here who looks a bit different than anybody else?"

"There are just the two types who come in here, Billy. The 'is' and the 'was,'" he said, then fell into a comfortable patter. "Oh, sure, we see the tall, short, fat, skinny, ugly, black, brown, and white. All sorts. But if you're getting down to brass tacks, son, there is just the 'is' and the 'was.'"

"Gotcha," I said, reaching out for the last of the bubbles on the bar. My fingers slipped through, and I wished for just a moment I could feel that again. "But you ever met anyone who was, you know—" I stared at him for a moment, then said, "—both."

Sawed-off leaped up from his seat. "I've heard enough of this, man. I'm outta here."

"You haven't stepped foot outta this bar since 1963," Handsome Dan said. "And that was just to peep up the skirt of a young lady who'd just walked out, Billy!"

The man with half a face waved him off and sat back down, but his shoulders hadn't relaxed. "It's Lonnie, which I told ya a thousand times! And, you know who that was, that girl?"

"I don't want to get caught up in your depraved stories," Dan said. "Keep it to yourself."

Brenda stepped up to my side, and for a brief moment, I saw her try to tighten the drawstring on her sweats.

She asked, "Have you seen anyone that was both alive and dead before?"

"Can't be that," the barman said, leaning back and crossing his arms. "It's like being pregnant and barren. Can't be both."

"The problem with analogies," I said to the dead bartender, "is they're a satisfying but false answer masquerading as a logical conclusion." Glancing toward Sawed-off, or Lonnie as his mother had apparently named him, I saw Handsome Dan shift his weight again.

The barman stood there like a drugstore Indian, not moving a muscle. "What do you think you're trying to say, son?"

"I've seen… there seems to be a guy who's both," I said. "Both 'is' and 'was.'"

Handsome Dan didn't break my gaze for a few moments, then slowly looked outside toward the lake, where Illinois gave way to Indiana. After a minute, as if he'd come and gone somewhere if only in his mind, he looked back.

"That kind of guy, Billy? That would be a dangerous, dangerous fella."

"I think you're right."

"If, and I'm saying if here… if that kind of guy were, as you explain it, possible."

Taking a step back, I put my hands gently on the reporter's shoulders. "I think this 'is-was' guy killed Brenda here," I said. "And there's a good chance he also offed a postman I met in Madison."

"A postman?" Lonnie whistled. "Dangerous sort, those. A lot of pent-up rage. I think it's all the circulars they hafta carry."

The barman put his elbows back on the lacquered wood. This time, I saw a bigger splash of energy than before. As if his concentration had been shaken.

He said, "That sort of man, in both places, would be a threat to anyone living or dead. If it's at all possible, of course."

"Of course."

"You get what I mean?"

"Naw, Dan," I said and leaned down to the bar, my elbows nearly touching his. "You ain't afraid of some spook, are ya?"

"No," he said and looked down then back up to me. He grinned. "But I gotta keep an eye out for patrons like Billy here—"

"Lonnie, for chrissakes!"

"—A guy like that could be bad for business."

Brenda leaned forward, tried to put her elbows on the bar, and fell to the floor with an "ooof." None of us said a word, perfect gentlemen, until she regained her footing.

She stood in the middle of the bar facing the two of us, the thick wood coming up just under her ribs.

"Seems like a guy like that might stir up more business for you, Handsome Dan. Hell, I wouldn't be in the InBetween without him. There could be dozens more in here if a guy like that really puts his mind to it."

Despite how loud it was in the bar, all the voices around us laughing, arguing, yelling for drinks, sound in the space between us dampened into an unsettling quiet. Dan leaned back on his heels, looked up to the ceiling for a moment, then disappeared under the bar. When he came back, he was holding a cracked baseball bat.

Which, of course, is basically impossible.

I glanced quickly at the bar patrons, who seemed too busy to even notice the floating baseball bat behind the bar.

Lonnie looked over and nearly fell off his chair. Even having steadied his landing, he still stumbled back and took a couple hasty steps, on all fours, away from the bar.

In the bartender's hands, the bat, one part of its end sheered clean off, gave off the faintest glow. Spinning it around, he held its grubby, taped handle to me and nodded.

This seemed important, so I poured a ton of juice into my hands and grabbed it. Unbelievably, it actually felt cold in my dead, ghostly fingers. I felt it! Turning the bat around, I tried to read the words on the side, but they'd been scored away long ago. Burnt.

My imagination running rampant, I thought the bat was actually humming, just slightly, in my hands.

"Drop it."

"What?"

Dan repeated, "Drop the bat."

Shrugging, I flicked off the flow of energy to my fingers so the bat could pass through them.

But it didn't.

Without a single drop of juice, I held the bat, lifted it up and gently swished it through the air. One of the short red straws in a nearby drink flipped out and fell to the floor. A woman with a frizz job gave it a lazy glance and kept on talking.

Then she saw the bat, and her drunken expression wavered. That was when Dan nabbed it out of my hands and tucked it back under the bar.

"No use in causing a fuss with the livies, now."

Brenda noticed something I hadn't. "It's broken."

Handsome Dan laughed darkly. "Yeah, split down the side, sweetheart." His small smile didn't last. "In '74, this guy comes in here. Spook, big mean-looking bastard with the wildest eyes you ever seen. I swear, not making this up, but the guy didn't even have any pupils."

"Dan—"

"Nope," he said, putting one hand to his heart, another held up like he was being sworn in by a judge. "White as boiled eggs, they were. He comes in and, without a word, starts swinging this bat around, knocking the lights out of all my regulars at the rail," Dan said, and his voice quivered. "We useda have a bunch of spooks hanging out in here, passing the days, laughing. Talking shite. You couldn't even hear the livies over the ruckus they was making."

"And this guy—"

"Don't rush me!"

"Sorry, man."

His features softened, and he nodded at me with a half smile.

"So he's just swinging this freakish bat—something no way he should be able to do, right?—and he beats four of my patrons until they're so drained they can't even move. Right in the middle of the bar, all these goddamn kids in here, the living, laughing away and having a good ol' time, and a couple of my boys are being beaten senseless. Eventually, his swinging hit some livie, who spun around and saw another guy, and they throw down. Huge ruckus then, the live and the dead. And there was nothing any of us could do about it."

Brenda and I waited, just listening. Lonnie got back up and slowly sat at the bar again, really, really interested in his dirty, cupped hands held a few inches from his face.

"He actually cracks it over the head of a good man, a livie, who'd been in here for years, from the very beginning when he was a wee lad… worked at the plastics factory. He hadn't been a spook up until that very night. He was… Christ, his name was…"

"Bill Mitchell," Lonnie said as gently as I'd heard him speak all night. "That was Billy Mitchell, Dan. You remember. His name was Billy."

The barman slowly nodded and swallowed hard.

"Then, um, the big bastard, he looks at the busted bat and tosses it to the floor." Dan's voice was nearly a whisper. We moved in closer to hear him. "And then he grabs all four men, and these spooks, they're frozen solid, not a lick of energy left in 'em. Then he just drags them away."

"Last we seen of him," Lonnie said, digging a nail into a dirty crevice in his hand, the ember of his cigarette passing in and out of his cheek. "Good riddance."

"That bat ain't exactly 'was,' but there it is," Handsome Dan said. "It shouldn't exist, shouldn't be here."

"But there it is," I said.

"Right. And if this 'is-was' man you're looking for is out there, it sounds like you folks are connected to him. I don't want no part of it." Dan reached down and casually propped the bat on the floor behind his back. The cracked tip by his feet was all I could see. "So if you don't mind, I'd appreciate it if you got the hell out of my bar."

Chapter Fifteen

As instructed, we got the hell out.

However, me and the reporter weren't exactly as one in that decision.

"Let me—" she said, struggling against my grip as I led her down a path that skirted the edge of the pub. "I wasn't done asking him questions!"

A rather bouncy group of young people bubbled up in front of us then through us, which briefly drained a little anger out of her.

"Ugh," she said. "I think that one dude might have head lice."

"Could just be dandruff. It goes by so fast sometimes."

"Whatever!" She twisted her arm back and forth until I let go. Another pack of people, apparently having preloaded at home or in the parking lot (or more likely both), were coming towards us like a hip, H&M amoeba.

We walked to a quiet corner of the lot next to The Grind.

"That bartender knows more than he's saying."

"Most bartenders try to give that impression," I said. "It's part of their charm. Their mystique."

"No, no," she said and stuck her head through the dark window of the bar briefly then came back out. "He knew something about just the type of guy we're looking for. Some superspook. And you said you think that kinda guy might have killed me!"

"Did you hear him?" I said. "When'd he see the guy with the bat? The seventies? Hell, girl, that was thirty years before you were born."

"Not quite."

"Close to it," I said and waved her toward the alley behind the pub. Two guys crouched near the dumpster, apparently waiting for the next wave of puke to hit them so they could go back in and party some more. We gave them a wide berth.

"Why'd you leave, then?" she said, trying to grab my shoulder to spin me around as we walked. "You some kinda pussy?"

Sensing her fingertips, I was always a quick twist of my body out of her reach.

"Listen, the big guy with the big mustache had a big bat. Normally, we don't care about things like bats, unless, of course, they turn into vampires."

She stopped walking.

"Wait, what? You never said any—"

Glancing over my shoulder, I said, "Nah, what are you, nuts? There are no vampires. Or werewolves. Or zombies."

"But ghosts, that makes total sense."

I shrugged. "Obviously. Part of the natural order of things."

Ultimately, she had a sweet nature, so she couldn't maintain her rage with me long. She came up beside me, a bit moonwalky as she moved along, but she was getting the hang of it more and more.

I hadn't said anything about it yet, but out of the corner of my eye, I caught the tiniest flicker of light. We were being followed.

"So do you still feel the guy?" I asked. "When you close your eyes, can you still feel him in this area?"

Once she'd shut her eyes, I gently put my hand on her arm to keep her moving, taking the chance to cast a quick glance behind us. There it was again. I moved us along toward the bar at the end of the alleyway.

"So? Can you?"

"Yeah," Brenda said and rubbed a spot between her eyebrows. "He's close." She opened her eyes. "Paint, I don't want to lose the guy if he's my way out." Her face turned a bit stiff again. "And I deserve the justice." Then she was soft again. "It'll be like my last story ever."

"We'll find him."

"How can you be sure?"

I stopped and turned her toward me, so we were face-to-face. Her eyes widened, and then she started to look back where we'd come from. I said, "No, no. Keep looking at me."

She began to tremble. Her voice was thin. "Wha—why are we stopping?"

"Just wait."

"W-w-wait f-for what?" she said. "Jesus, Painter, what's—?"

"Just give it a sec."

In the next moment, a dark light came up to us from the side, not wavering. It sped up slightly then slowed again but stayed on target.

Brenda went to turn, and I said, "Don't—"

At that moment, the tiny orange light passed right through her pretty face, into her brain, and out the other side. She shuttered briefly, squinted, then turned to see where it had gone.

Clopping down the street, cigarette forever in hand, Lonnie waved the ember in the direction he was walking.

He said, "I know a quiet place where we can talk. And I might know something about the guy who kilt ya, young lady."

We were led by the old ghost into the next alley and then two streets over. Most of the shops were closed except liquor stores and mini-markets.

Lonnie pointed, saying, "That there used to be a corner diner. Served fifteen-cent phosphates. Cherry was my favorite. My wife Diana, she loved lime. Couldn't never stand lime."

"That's a nice memory," Brenda said wistfully.

"Shortly after we married, Diana couldn't much stand me," he said. "After that, lime didn't taste so bad no more."

We followed him through the brick wall of a warehouse space that looked like someone had taken the effort to whitewash it. Just before we passed through it, I couldn't help but think it looked like decaying bone.

The first room was choked with dust, large sheets over hulking furniture.

"I spent the first few weeks hanging around my Diana—you know how it is," he said and threw a quick glance over his shoulder at me before moving deeper into the building. "Thinking if I shouted loud enough, if I loved hard enough, she'd eventually know I was there."

I nodded.

"But after less than a month, I had to leave."

Ever the reporter, Brenda asked, "Why?"

"It was a waste of time. And you learn that people ain't their best when they think they're alone."

"What's that mean?"

Lonnie was quiet for a moment and waved us past a line of offices, some with broken furniture scattered across the floor.

"I dunno," Lonnie said and stopped at the edge of a wall leading into a wide space. The air grew a little heavier, and I caught the slight odor of metal and oil. "Just disappointing is all, mainly. Think about when you been alone, maybe talking to yourself, what have you. Not at your best, probably."

"No, I suppose not."

"That and she started sleeping with my brother," Lonnie said and slipped through the wall. We followed him into a large space with the hollowed-out shells of cars from the thirties and forties. "And my sister, actually."

"Wow," I said, nodding. "So where does this wife of yours live?" Brenda gave me a scowl.

"She don't anymore," Lonnie said with an expression that looked like he'd just swallowed a bug. "She died about seventeen years after I did. Didn't make no stop in the InBetween," he said and looked up to the windows, high on the wall above us, lining the bottom of the ceiling. "She passed right through. Might be waiting for me there right now."

"Or your brother," I said.

"Or your sister," Brenda said.

"You wanna hear what I got to tell ya or not?" the bent figure of a man said as he walked toward the shell of a prewar Buick. The engine was long gone, while the compartment that had once held it—at one time nearly half the length of the car—was smashed to the windshield.

He waved Brenda toward the car. "Come on, young lady. You, now, fella," he said, waving me toward a wall to my left.

"Painter. I prefer Painter over fella if you don't mind."

"Don't know why. That's a stupid name," he said. "You look like you're carrying some extra juice about you." He looked at Brenda closely. "In fact, kinda looks like you mighta knocked it off her, but whatever you spooks are into is fine by me."

"There was no knocking, man. I didn't knock. We haven't knocked or—"

"Ain't got no time for all that conjugatin', Painter. There's an electrical panel on the wall. Flip the double-breaker marked E-14 and -15."

True, I had a bit of extra juice, but the thing was to hold onto it when you could, not blow it. Just in case, you know, you get jumped by thugs in a shit part of town. Still, it seemed he was about to tell us something important. Fair enough trade.

Holding my first two fingers above the breaker box, I willed a bit of energy to their tips and gave it a push. It took four or five goes, but they eventually tripped to their ON position.

Behind me, I heard the thump and hum of a speaker charging up. When I turned around, a beautiful sight: an old Wurlitzer jukebox. It looked a little like some fifties notion of a high-powered computer of the future.

The bottom half was beveled on both sides, flushed with an emerald-green light, orange on its corners. Above that, tiny yellowed strips of paper all lined up in rows and columns that told of the selections inside, held in a carousel of forty-fives just above them.

Elvis Presley, Buddy Holly, Paul Anka, and the Everly Brothers all looked like skinny black teeth underneath the wide dome of glass that held the records' carousel.

It came from a better time when rock stars ruled the world.

"This place here has been sealed up for decades. Nobody comes in here no more. It's paid out for a while longer though, so… I enjoy it while I can."

I looked around and walked toward them. "There's gotta be a dozen old roadsters in here. Surely they've got to be worth some money."

"Maybe, maybe not," he said. "Most of them were bought smashed up, and what's left of them is a lotta rust and bad memories."

My eyes had been trained on the jukebox, but when I finally looked at Lonnie and Brenda, I noticed they were sitting in the front seat of the old Buick.

Sitting in the seat.

Lonnie grinned from ear to ear when he saw the look on my face. Then he laughed out loud and pounded his fist for a moment, as some men do. His hand passed through the dash several times.

"Ain't it grand?" He laughed again. "This here old '37 was a beaut in her day, whoo-hoo! That's until some teenager took it out on a joy ride with his girl and went over the side of a bridge." He looked at Brenda in the seat next to him, who was loving that she was sitting down. "Down they went." He held his hand flat, then arched it downward with a ptchoooo sound escaping from his lips. "Then, whammo-splat."

I finally said, "How are you sitting in there? Why aren't you—"

"Falling through? Nah, those two kids when they passed—and they passed violently—they left a remnant here on the seat. Leftover energy, a stain been here for more than fifty years now."

"I had no idea."

"Painter, there's a lot most of us don't know about this place," he said, the light from his unsmokable cigarette bopping up and down between his fingers. "Sometimes I wonder if this is the InBetween at all. Maybe this is Hell, and we just don't know it."

Brenda made a small noise then closed her eyes for a moment.

Lonnie shrugged and took an empty drag of his cigarette. He said to me, "G-7 if you will, sir."

"Why don't you get up and—?" I started to ask but then stopped, spun on a heel, walked to the jukebox, and expended yet more energy, lowering my stash more, to push the G (six tries!) and then the 7 (not bad, just two).

The carousel began to move with a snap then settled into a grinding trip, clockwise. Tick-tick-tick-tick-chunk!

The selected record, the mystery G-7, was then lifted by a white wand up into the playing compartment, settled into place, cha-chuk!, and then it began to spin.

It fired up as I returned to stand next to the busted-up Buick.

"Nice," I said. "Bobby Darin." Lonnie gave me a half look then nodded. "You know, I'm all for nostalgia and shit," I said. "But "Mack the Knife" is a dark, dark tune, man."

"Especially for 1959."

"Serial killer is dark for any age, man." The tune was a strange choice given the guy me and Brenda were tracking. Lonnie knew something.

He looked at me over his forever cigarette, like he was peering through its smoke. "It's not really about a serial killer."

"No," I said and sat on the floor. "It's about the haves and the have-nots. The rich and the poor."

The old ghost looked at me, but this time the smoke I'd perceived had cleared. With his cig, he threw me a small wave, a nod that told me I'd scored one tiny point in his books.

Brenda said, "You were going to tell us about the guy who killed me. Are you saying this guy's been around more than fifty years or something?"

"No," Lonnie said. "That spook, all those years back, I never saw 'em again. But man, I waited. I was sure he'd come back and pick off another handful of us like he was shopping."

Brenda shifted, pressing her back into the seat, stretching. "But he didn't."

He shook his head. "But far as I understand it, those guys he went and drug off? He had those boys in a place, tucked away, where he could drain the little bit of energy they'd recoup, like harvesting it, which meant they could never leave. They could never get away."

I'd heard of this before but at the time thought it was, well, a ghost story for ghosts.

"I don't think they were the first. When he come in the bar, that creep had buckets and buckets of juice just oozing off him." Lonnie said. "Left a trail like a wet dog. Or a lion after a fresh kill."

Brenda chimed in again. "What was all that stolen energy for?"

"Who knows? It's currency in the InBetween, the only wealth there is," Lonnie said. "Or maybe he had bigger plans. How would I know?"

I was getting tired of the old guy's dodge. He could be bullshitting or stalling.

"So what does that have to do with the one who killed Brenda?"

Lonnie looked toward her and, for a brief moment, a softness passed over his dark eyes. He reached out but then thought better of it and pulled his hand back.

"I been hearing about some new creep or creeps trolling around these parts," he said. "Using spooks like diesel for your car. They might have a place nearby. Maybe."

"Where?"

The song ended, and it got quiet for a moment. We just listened to the Wurlitzer's clack and rattle as it lifted the record from the playing surface and returned it to its home.

Lonnie was the first to speak. "We're done," he said. "I need a drink."

As the old man began to lean out of the car, looking to head back to the sanctity of Handsome Dan's pub, Brenda reached out and stopped him cold with a clutching hand.

"Wait, he's close. Really close."

Lonnie put his hand over hers, not quite touching. "On the other side of that wall, there's a Chinese food restaurant. If anybody's nearby, they're there."

Brenda looked at me and nodded quickly.

After Lonnie lumbered out of the car, she came out swiftly behind him. She looked at me and then motioned to the wall.

"Thanks, man," I said. "I appreciate you helping us out."

"Ah," Lonnie said. "Just wanted to hear that ol' song. Do me a favor and pull the breaker. There's still power to this old shed because it don't raise much of a bill. I'd like to keep it that way."

I was about to protest, but Brenda slid past me in one quick motion, got to the panel, and it took a couple of swipes, but she clicked it off.

She turned to me then swayed a little bit. "Whoa, I feel... swizzy." Steadying herself with a hand on my shoulder, she met my eyes. They were the tiniest bit crossed.

"Swizzy?" I asked and raised an eyebrow.

Brenda then lifted a hand as if to place it on my other shoulder but instead swung at my arm and clipped it with a crackle I felt all the way down my spine.

I said, "I feel swizzy."

She pulled in a deep, satisfying breath and said, "Come on, you owed me for running me down on the road."

"You were in the middle of the road!"

"Total technicality," she said and let go of my shoulders. Her eyes went hard. "Let's go. I feel like Chinese."

Chapter Sixteen

"Jesus!" she said for at least the fourth time. "Jesus, Jesus!" Fifth, sixth.

We had been standing outside, hesitant to go in right away.

"Jesus." Seventh. Maybe eighth.

The restaurant was part eatery and part hipster bar. It looked like there were no spooks inside, which was strange. But a ton of livies were coming in and out, and Brenda was just sort of enduring it as if she should be used to it by now.

"That dude doesn't floss very well," she said.

Tired of waiting, I pushed in. Moving to the far side, the wall that was closest to the car graveyard, I kept looking back at her as her eyes scanned the crowd.

A burst of raucous laughter came from a rather large group in the back corner, mostly men in dark suits and power ties, a couple women, all wearing gray skirts and yucking it up just as hard as the guys.

Brenda pinched my arm and spun toward the windows.

"Shit, that hurt," I said and looked down. She was cupping one hand over a finger, which was pointing toward the bar.

She whispered. "There." Throwing a quick glance over her shoulder, she turned away and quickly squeezed her eyes shut. "That's him. The guy at the bar. He's the Ringman."

"Which guy?"

Her eyes still closed, she said, "Purple shirt, trimmed goatee, fake glasses, light-blond close-cropped hair."

The man was at the bar waving his credit card in the air, trying to get the attention of a swamped bartender. At least four others were doing the same thing, waving their plastic above their heads.

It looked like an auction-house crowd sped up. Or a nest of baby birds demanding food.

But this guy stood out with all the jewelry on his fingers and bracelets on his wrists that twinkled in the bar light.

"Jesus," I said, despite myself. "How did you—how can you tell he's wearing fake glasses?"

She slowly opened her eyes and started watching the bar in the reflection of the windows.

"They don't fit right on his head. They're just for show," she said, eyes fixed ahead, scanning. "I had a pair just like them."

"Why would you have those?"

"In case I had to anchor breaking news on the paper's webcast," she said, swatting at my line of questioning like a buzzing fly. "Breaking news glasses. Every anchor has them."

"Why?"

"Can you focus, Painter?" She glared at me, and I nodded. I realized there was a tickle in the back of my brain, and for the life of me, I didn't want to scratch it. But if we were going to get to the bottom of the reporter's case, I needed to be a pro.

I said, "Do you think that's your doer?"

"Doer?"

"It's a cop-slash-detective thing," I said and looked down my nose. "Totally legit."

She nodded slowly, but I didn't think she was validating my word choice.

"That's the guy," she said, looked at me, and then bit her lip. "I've got an excellent memory for faces, and you don't forget the face of the guy who killed you, so yeah. That's my doer."

"Okay."

"So how do we get that guy?"

"Get? We don't 'get.'"

Brenda turned back around to catch sight of her killer again, but a group of wobbly young women wearing plastic crowns now stood in the way. She took a couple of steps forward then stopped. I thought she'd lost her nerve for a moment, but then I saw she wasn't looking at him. She was locked on the glowing, giddy expression of the soon-to-be-bride's face.

Her lower lip trembled. Her shoulders fell, and she bent over slightly at the waist.

"I'm... I'm never gonna have that now," she said, and the mascara that traced down from her eyes seemed to turn a shade darker. "Never gonna be a bride. No kids. No one to love me forever."

She began to softly cry, but no real tears came.

"Hey, hey..." I said. "It's not all roses being married. You might have hooked up with a drunk. Or a guy who wore your heels when you were at work." She gave me a blank look, eyes unfocused. "You probably dodged a bullet."

The reporter looked back at the bride as the hen party lined up to order shots from the bar. Just to their left, the killer continued to wave his plastic money in the air, fingers sparking like camera flashes on the red carpet. For the time being, everyone was going to have to wait for the wedding party to get their drinks.

"She looks so happy," Brenda mumbled.

"Sure," I said. "That's only because she's sucking on a lollipop in the shape of a dildo." I saw a couple of long, candy-less plastic sticks in the hands of several bridesmaids. They'd apparently already finished their phallus candies.

"I..." she said and sniffed. "I never got to... never got to have a party, have my friends celebrate my last day as a single girl. No lollipop dildo," she said, trembling slightly. "I'll never have that."

We needed to deal with the killer, but some moments are too important. I'd been in the InBetween long enough to recognize one, so I stood in front of her and said, "Who knows what's after the InBetween? In the Next, if the bible's correct, there may be warehouses of candied dildoes for you. You can put as many as you want in your mouth, all at the same time!"

She gave me a funny grin, trying not to smile. "That's not in the bible."

"Pretty sure it was in mine."

"Might be why you're stuck here."

"Could be," I said, gave her a squeeze, and turned toward the bar. "I have an idea. Wait here."

She nodded.

I did my best to weave through the crowd and avoid any pass-throughs. I'd had my fill for a while and couldn't stomach too many more. However, they couldn't entirely be avoided. Between me and the Ringman were a dozen tables. As long as anyone didn't stand, I could just walk through them. A small smile crept to my lips.

People sitting there had no idea, as they guzzled their drinks and nibbled on tapas, that a ghost johnson was passing right through their heads.

A surge of laughter came from the executive corner, all the men and women in the gray and blue suits. I saw the killer's head turn just slightly toward them. Was he part of their group?

In the purple shirt, it didn't seem likely. Theirs was a strictly red-tie, dark-suit, and high-collared Eton Diamond crowd.

A squeal from the bar pulled my attention back. "Three..." the hen party all said in unison.

I was a stone's throw away and looked up at my target. The bartender had turned to the rail and was making his drink, arms moving like a Toyota factory robot. Fast, efficient.

"Two..."

Naturally, as I crossed the last table—I was close enough now to see individual hairs on the back of the guy's neck—that was when the group at the four-top decided to stand. They turned toward the young women and began clapping, cheering them on.

"Go, go, go!"

Seven girls had their arms out, bodies bent like they were ready to bob for apples as they held shot glasses in their mouths, no hands. One laughed, and her drink fell and exploded on the floor. No one cared.

I swerved around them, through them, passing through heads (Yuck, gray matter!), hands (Ick, sinew!), and chests (Hey, implants!) until I was beside the Ringman.

Squinting, I went up on my toes to try to read the name on the card he held above his head. I saw it! Finally, I had a name! But then I saw something else.

He was looking at me in the bar mirror's reflection.

As he spun around, I tried to dodge him, but the hand without the credit card was at my throat, and he looked me right in the face, scowling. Then his attention suddenly shifted.

"One!"

The girls, in unison with a crowd around them, were all shouting, screaming. Hair and crowns flew everywhere as they tilted their heads back, taking their milky shots, hands at their sides. Another glass bombed the restaurant's floor, shattering in a million directions.

In the panic and joy and chaos, I slipped into the crush of people, no longer worried about my eyes passing through shoulders, spleens, legs, arms, heads, just trying to get away.

He'd seen me.

The Ringman, a livie, had seen me. Christ, he'd grabbed me! And that was impossible.

And one other thing. I recognized him. Reporter Brenda Matthew was right.

You don't forget the face of the person who killed you.

Chapter Seventeen

"Can I help you, man?"

Chandra scanned the crowd, briefly looking away from the smug group of guys in the corner. They weren't going anywhere for a while. Then she couldn't help it. She glanced back.

All of them in crisp suits, the second outfit of the day, no doubt, after a late-afternoon stop at the 24-7 Total Fitness. You can always spot the lackeys, hangers-on, sycophants. And tonight something different. Some woman. She was new. Probably an assistant. An aide. She was sitting a bit close.

They were all hanging on his every word, like the congressman was telling tales of former conquests or sharing the secret to everlasting life.

Everlasting life!

That thought drew a laugh.

Yet another squeal from the group of drunk bitches who looked like a wedding party sponsored by a consignment store. Jan Jorgensen's head turned back toward where the spook had hightailed it out of there.

Gotcha!

At the front of the restaurant, Curious Casper was slipping through the front wall. Right behind him, another spook. Gym clothes, still-damp hair. Chandra stood to leave, but he'd never make it through the crowd, let alone the clutch of flannel and hair of the bachelorette party clinging around the bar.

She sat back down and looked up to the front again. The woman with Casper turned back, and Chandra thought she recognized her. It was hard to tell with the mascara lines running down her face.

"What can I get you, buddy?" the bartender yelled again. Jorgensen handed the card over with the promise of a G&T. Then his finger pushed the dead IT kid's glasses back up his nose as the woman inside went back to watching the politician and his crew of idiots.

* * *

"Wait, wait, wait!" Brenda shouted at me after we'd rocketed out of the sports bar and gone nearly six city blocks. I slowed and spun around, seeing the reporter coming at me, wobbly and out of control.

There was no sign of the killer behind her, and I exhaled a breath I'd never taken in then reached out to slow my client down. I glided along with her down the residential street with its long rows of greystones and brownstones.

We slowed, turning in small circles under the sodium streetlights, and from a distance might have looked like a couple finishing up a dance as the band plucked out the final strains of some forgotten waltz.

"So," I said and released her. "Gotta go."

"What?" She began to slide slowly toward the curb.

"Don't worry. I got what we needed."

"What does that mean?"

"Jan Jorgensen," I said. "His name is Jan Jorgensen."

"Okay, so what now?"

"Nothing now. I head back home and—"

"You can't head back! You're gonna just leave me here? You said you'd help me, Painter. I thought…"

I wasn't listening. All up, it would likely be a few hours before I could get to Shady Hills. I wondered if Mags was getting antsy without me around. That might freak her out a little, calling out and finding I wasn't not there. I'd had other assistants before, but Margaret would always be a favorite. She'd reminded me not to take shit from anyone.

Unless, of course, they were an ultra-terrifying livie-spook that posed more danger to you than all the Ghost Mob thugs put together. In those cases, you run like hell.

"Listen, all I have to do is get back to the home and have Harry post this."

"Post… what?"

"'Junior reporter Brenda Matthews was bashed to death by a man named Jan Jorgensen on the seventh floor of her gym building.' Or something to that effect. That actually sounds a bit cumbersome."

He face darkened. "You put junior reporter and I will kill you again."

"No junior, then. 'Fresh-faced, game-changing reporter Brenda Matthews.'" She gave me a nod. "Harry puts that into a Wiki or something and you clear. Case closed."

"That's it?"

I smiled. "That's it!"

She put her hands to her damp hair and spun in a slow circle then said, "Fuck that! I want that guy nailed. He killed me, Painter!"

"Brenda, that's… I'm sorry, but all that doesn't matter anymore. What does is you getting to the Next—"

"It matters to me," she said, the mascara streaks darkening as she passed out of the lamplight above her. The reporter slid up toward me. "I don't know about you, Painter, but I've got parents who are heartbroken. An older brother. And friends at the paper."

"That's all the past, though!"

"Not for them," she said. "Not for them. We need to do this right and get this Jorgensen busted. Have them raid his apartment or hidey-hole or whatever."

"No, no—"

"And, wait, you said he killed the mailman, right?"

"Maybe. I dunno. He could have."

"Painter, this guy's a serial killer, for chrissake! Who knows how many people he's killed."

Well, as of five minutes ago, I now know of at least one more.

"Brenda, that's not how this works," I said, but it came out more like pleading. Her eyes dropped to half mast, searching for something in my face. "I get my Temp to put in your death details and the mailman's and whoosh, you're off. Case closed."

Brenda reached out and grabbed my hand in hers.

"Think of all those other people. People you haven't even met just wandering around somewhere in the InBetween. Don't they get to move on, too?"

"No, listen—"

"This creep gets busted, properly busted, and all those people move on. You want to make cases, right? You'd be responsible for maybe dozens of lost souls finally getting to move on!"

"What if they're not all ready to move on?"

Like me.

"What are you afraid of?" She stared at me for a moment, then a strange look passed over her face. "Wait. You recognized him, didn't you?"

A car turned toward us, taking the corner a bit too fast. Its wide arc was then managed by a few jerky tugs of the wheel, and the driver more or less was headed in a straight line.

"I promised to help you along, and I'll do that," I said and motioned for her to step out of the street. "That dude's drunk, and if he runs down some guy biking home late from work and takes off, then I got another person to help."

She eyeballed me, trying to read my face. Shit, she really would have been a hell of a reporter. She said, "I thought you were a detective."

"Dead private investigator. I'm the best in the world."

"You're the only one in the world."

I nodded. "Which means I'm busy. I do what I can."

She slowly began to back away from me. "Okay. Okay, Painter."

"Come on, don't be like that."

"You're right," she said, spinning slowly as she passed in and out of the spotlight in the street. "You go do what you've got to do. Have your Temp log the mailman and me. But give me a day before you hit publish. I'm going to look into this Jan Jorgensen before I go anywhere."

"Why?"

"Because maybe you were a great P.I. in life and now you're just doing what you know here," she said, tugging at her sweat clothes to straighten them. "But I wasn't yet a great reporter. Good but not yet great. I never got that. So I got one last story to do. Mine."

I thought about it for a moment. "I can understand that."

"It's my story, and I'm gonna do it. It'll take you a while to get back, and you said you got that other case. The little girl."

"Katie. Her stepdad."

"Great. Spend a day or two on that so I can find out why this guy killed me."

"Like you said, he's a serial killer. They're nuts."

"If so, so be it. That'll be the story, then."

"But who'll know? Anything you find out, who'll know?"

Brenda took a couple of long strides away from me, heading deeper into the dark. She was getting the hang of moving around the InBetween.

"I will. I'll know the story," she said then slowed to a stop. "Hey, so why do you think this Jan Jorgensen was in the bar?"

"I dunno. Maybe he was thirsty."

"He killed me. He killed the mailman. He's killed dozens maybe," she said. "But we find him hanging out in a bar by himself?"

I thought about that for a moment, trying to recall what had happened just before the scariest thing I can ever remember. Then it clicked.

"He was watching a group of people. Or maybe it was just the guy in the center. Everybody seemed to be eyeballing that guy."

"Who?" Brenda put her hands on her hips.

I closed my eyes. "Nice-looking dude in a suit. Actually, uh, he looked familiar. Young guy. I'd seen him before. Arguing." I concentrated, trying to pull out the images, like A.K. had taught me. "He'd been on television. Not arguing. Podiums."

"Like a debate?"

"Yeah, maybe."

Chapter Eighteen

It took me less than two hours to get back to Minneapolis.

Once I got onto the lake circuit, up then across, I started moving much faster. In part, I think my frustration was fueling me.

The Ringman had grabbed me by the throat. I hadn't imagined that. At least, I didn't think I had. And he'd done that after he'd seen me. An improbable moment followed by an impossible one.

Did he know who I was? It sounded nuts, but maybe he was the one who'd sent those three spooks in the alleyway after me. Either way, I needed to ask around a bit to find out why they'd targeted me.

Maybe it was a former client I hadn't cleared. There'd been a handful of them.

On the bright side, I'd returned home with two more cases solved. Two I hadn't even planned on, so bonus there. I just needed Harry to start setting up the doc.

"Harry!" I said, sliding into his room. "Fire up your computer, man!"

Except he wasn't there. His laptop was. His clothes hanging in the closet. No problem. Maybe he was hanging with his wife. I headed to Mags's room.

Then it became clear. In her room, her bed was perfectly made, not a wrinkle. Hospital corners. On top of the bed were three boxes—two medium-sized, one small. In felt-tip Sharpie, someone had written Margaret Anderson with a local address underneath it.

But of course, she hadn't moved. She'd moved on. And I hadn't been there for her. I dropped to the floor, pulled my legs into my chest, and wished I could shed real tears.

Mags deserved real tears.

The funeral of Margaret Anderson was naturally a somber affair. Quiet, dutifully attended, and short. I'm not entirely sure who the service was for other than Harry. I told him I was there, but, surrounded by family, he could only acknowledge me with a nod. His eyes were red and raw.

Some said they could feel her presence, but Mags whoosh! was gone. She'd rocketed right through the InBetween to whatever was Next and wasn't around to hear all the nice things said about her. Despite the kind words, all those mourners at Grady Memorial, to me at least, seemed to be checking their watches, messing with phones, tapping feet... waiting for it to all be over.

What was the point?

I stood next to her casket as strangers shuffled by. She looked lovely, but you'd be dumbfounded how many people said, "You look good."

She's not here!

See the lady in the box? She's dead, can't hear you!

About a dozen relatives made a quick stop by the open casket, lowered their heads, and said the most unbelievably banal things. One woman, only a few years younger than Mags, reached out in a tender gesture, petting her softly on the lapel. She then slipped Mags' broach into her palm and dropped it into a jacket pocket.

The crazy woman stole from a dead person!

"I expect I'll see you soon enough, "I said, just inches away from her face. "No questions somebody like you's going to get a brick to the head one day."

For a moment, I considered following the broach stealer back to her seat then even back to her home. You know, nothing weird, but maybe, totally a small possibility, I'd just haunt the living fuck out of her for a day or two.

Maybe.

But a small voice made me turn back.

"I miss you, Granma," the little girl said. "You were my best friend."

Drifting back next to the dead body of my friend, I came face to face once again with the little girl who'd hired me to find her stepfather's killer. She had a soft face, eyes red and puffy, but was likely trying to be strong for some parent or uncle or aunt who said it was better not to cry.

Why not? That's why you have the damn funerals. The living have no idea how to handle death.

Suddenly, I felt like I was intruding, because this was time between Mags and her granddaughter. I had no business hanging out and listening in as if they were on an old-school party line.

As I began to pull away, I heard the girl say to Mags, "Are you here? Are you close by?"

My eyes actually began to ache from the tears that would never spill and, frankly, shouldn't be causing the slightest amount of pressure on my face, but they were. Obviously, it was all bottled up in my own stupid head.

"Painter?"

Ah. Okay. She hadn't been talking to Granma.

"Are you here?"

I looked around, a little bit self-conscious, then knelt next to the girl. For the life of me, I couldn't remember her name. What I would give for just one postmortem Post-it note.

I said, "Yeah, I'm here. Don't be afraid."

"I'm not."

"Your grandma loved you very much," I said. "I think I remember her saying you were one of her favorite people ever."

"She did?" The little girl's lower lip trembled.

"Yep. And I can see why." Then it finally came back to me. "You're pretty awesome, Katie."

She sniffed and rubbed her face with her hand. "I peed myself a little a few minutes ago because I wasn't allowed to leave."

"Totally fine," I said. "I did too, but you know, since I'm a ghost, nobody can see me. Ghost pee."

The girl smiled.

"Actually, I thought you could see me. Did I imagine that?"

"No, I can sometimes. Not all the time." Her smile faltered, and she said, "Have you been looking into who shot Boyd? My mother's very sad. Not doing too good."

"Yes, sweetheart," I said softly. I moved so I could see her big, brown eyes. "I'm working on it. It just takes time."

"Okay."

From behind the little girl, a voice called out, a few rows back. It was the thief. "Uh, Katie? Granma can't hear you, sweetie. If you're done, we can start the service."

Annoyed, I asked Katie to repeat aloud what I was about to tell her but say it was from the dearly departed. The girl turned, wiped the dampness from her eyes, and said, "She can hear me. She says I was her favorite. And she said to give the goddamn broach back you just stole."

After Mags' service, I was a bit numb. Something had changed. Death felt more real or important. Then I realized it.

This wasn't about the funeral. I'd seen the face of my killer, which meant I was in trouble.

You see, most of the spooks you'll see around my neighborhood, they're looking to whoosh! to Level Two (or Three or Four, or whatever the Buddhists/Hindus/Scientologists think the Next is).

But me, I'm different in that regard.

I know in my heart—or at least where my heart used to be—that I'm supposed to be helping people caught up in the InBetween. I get a tiny spill of joy from it, but for as much as some people tease me about the job, I'm the only one doing it.

I can't go.

But if Brenda's investigation discovers all of Jan Jorgensen's victims, her "final story" will list her, Bernie the mailman, who knows how many others, and me.

As I've said, my memory is shoddy. But I'd looked into the face of my killer.

And while I am duty bound to help all those other people, helping Brenda finish her final story means I will never help another lost soul again. I will clear with all the rest of them.

Solving this case would mean that it was over.

I don't want that. But there are times when you have to do what's right, not what you want.

Maybe this was one of those times.

However, if I discover this is in fact not one of those times, I'm gonna back away quickly and find some other cases to get really, really interested in. There's still plenty of work to do.

Slipping out of the reception hall, I headed back to Shady Hills to find Mags' room again. Outside, the sun was shining, so brilliant and yellow that if you could drink it, it would go down like fresh lemonade with a little too much sugar.

Which is the best kind, in my opinion.

Some of the residents had drifted into the courtyard, a cordoned-off atrium replete with benches, some gurgling fountains, and plenty of shade. Two nurses—one male, one female—were making rounds to the dozen or so oldsters who'd opted to enjoy the beautiful afternoon. These were my candidates.

Sure, I still had Mags' husband, but Harry needed some time to grieve.

I spotted Anton Abrams, who seemed like a bright guy for eighty-two while also making it pretty clear he'd not make eighty-three, and remembered how Mags thought the guy was potentially a Nazi. That was ludicrous, of course; the guy went to temple twice a week. But knowing Mags, she was warning me away from the guy because something about him rubbed her the wrong way.

Who knows?

Maybe she'd rubbed him the wrong way. It's an old folks' home, and Harry was a bit of an invalid. Stuff like that happens. And you may go, "oh, gross," but if you're lucky one day, you'll be that old. And bilateral rubbing might be pretty high up on the to-do list.

Me, I try not to judge.

I fail miserably very often, but I do try to map out a quick route through the moral high ground. However, admittedly, there are often unavoidable rest stops along the way.

For a moment, I considered testing the group as a whole. All I would have to do was say a few words, ask if anyone could hear me, and tell them not to be scared, all was well, but please give me some sort of sign they'd heard my voice.

A simple, easy plan. A simple, easy plan that had once killed ninety-two-year-old Thomas J. Bernard III, who was convinced his dead wife (the second, not the first) had returned to drag him to Hell.

In the end, not the best recruiting method.

Something told me, though, that Mags had picked out her successor. I just had to find out who that was.

A minute later, I was back in her room.

The boxes that had been on her bed were gone. I put my hand over where they'd been, wondering if I could still feel her. I couldn't.

The drapes were drawn and, for such a warm day, the room felt cold. Abandoned. Dead.

But Shady Hills was a business. Soon enough, there would be a new resident in the room, and the entire process would repeat itself.

"Where'd you put it, Mags?"

I drifted around the room, convinced she'd made some arrangements while I'd been otherwise occupied in Chicago. That thought pinched a place in my chest. Mags had died without me nearby.

"Painter? You there?"

I hoped she wasn't alone.

"Paint?"

I stared at the bed again. Thankfully, Harry would have been nearby. But time slowly steals a lot of things from us. One of those is our friends, the ones who die before us, as we are stolen from someone else.

She was my friend, and I hadn't been there in the end.

The clock was ticking, even in the InBetween, so I got back to it.

"Where would you have left a note?"

It wasn't as if she could leave a message for me in the bedside table drawer. For one, the facility's staff would have searched the room to make sure none of her possessions had been left behind. Also, after she'd departed, some of her family would have rummaged through the drawer for loose change.

That didn't leave too many places.

The room was basically a single hospital bed, the bedside table, and a four-drawer dresser on the far side of the room. There was a closet adjacent to the chest of drawers, but I didn't remember her ever using it.

Not that I hung around when she was dressing.

I did remember an orderly coming in to reset a circuit breaker in a panel inside the closet. There hadn't been many shirts or dresses hanging up in there. Just the one, in a dry cleaner's plastic bag. That was the dressed she'd picked out to be buried in.

I supposed that might seem morbid to some, picking out the outfit in which you'll rot. But this will be the last thing people ever seen you in. You wanna look cool, yeah? You wouldn't want to be caught dead in a pair of Hello Kitty jammies.

I thought for a moment that she might have tucked a note into that breaker box, which would be a good hiding place. But you gotta know Mags. That would be too boring. She'd leave me with a laugh, no question.

There were two paintings in the room. For whatever reason, both were sailboats, on opposite walls from each other. I wondered if that had been some metaphor about a transition from the world of the living to the Next. Or if one day there'd just been a Shitty Sailboat Painting Day Sale! at Costco.

Examining each of the prints, I didn't see any writing or any pencil scrawling that could serve as a note from Mags.

There was a single light fixture in the room, but any note tucked up there would be seen the first moment anyone turned on the wall switch. Or, worse, it could have started a fire. Old people are tinder dry and can go up like kindling.

"No," I said to myself.

There was a fumbling near the door, and I heard, "'No' what?"

A moment later, an old man shuffled into the room wearing a robe that could have doubled as a parka on an Arctic expedition. His mouth hung open slightly as he slid toward the bed; on his feet were slippers that looked as though he'd kicked at two advancing Persian cats and they'd just stuck there.

He stopped and looked to each corner with a big, friendly smile.

His dark skin was contrasted by the whitest hair I'd ever seen on another human being. His pleasant face was scored deep with laugh lines. The lenses of the prescription glasses that rested on his nose were so thick he could have looked up at night and read newspapers on the moon.

"Hello," I said. "I'm—"

"I know who you are, Painter. What the hell kinda name is Painter anyhow?" he asked. "Your daddy a wannabe artist or something?"

"I don't think so."

He looked in my general direction. Hmm. "You don't think so?"

"Not trying to be funny, sir. It's just… your past gets fuzzier as time goes by."

The old man sat down on the bed with a groan. He said, "Tell me about it."

"Well, each day, maybe not every day, it's like there's an hourglass in your head. Each grain of sand a memory. And…" The old guy looked up, huge eyes in those Coke-bottle lenses, just staring ahead with a funny smile. I said, "Ah, okay. That was rhetorical, huh?"

"Yep."

"Okay. Guess I'm a bit off my game after losing Mags."

"Now, don't go blaming how dumb you might be on the dead. If people dying around you made you stupid, by now I'd be wearing funny clothes and listening to dubstep."

"Sir, I wasn't—"

"Oh, settle down now. I'm only playing with you." He chuckled and slowly turned until he was lying on the bed, his head on the pillow. "Shoot, she got a much nicer bed than I have. Mine, I got two springs jamming me in the back on the right side. For two nights straight, I dreamed all night I was being held up."

"Listen," I said. "Do you know if Mags left a note for me anywhere? Or did she leave a message with you?"

"No message with me," he said. "As for a note, I thought you were some great detective or something? Boy can't even find a note in a dead woman's room."

"Private investigator. I'm the best dead one there is, sir."

"That's what Maggie told me, but I don't know if that accounts for much," he said, then was quiet for a moment. After a quick couple of snores, he was back. "What'd you say?"

"Nothing. I think you fell asleep."

"On purpose, Painter. Catnap. Like da Vinci. He was a big proponent of naps during the day," the old black man said. "And he invented the airplane."

"I don't think that's true."

He waved me off. "Doesn't matter. My name is—"

"Julius," I said. "Julius Wilner."

"Huh," Julius said, leaned up, and trained his bug eyes in my direction again. "Mags said she hadn't told you about me yet."

"She didn't."

He laid his head back down on the pillow and gave me a half nod, eyes still open.

I waited a moment, then said softly, "Julius?" but only got a couple of sharp snores in return.

As he lay there like that, I realized where she'd put a note. I went to the floor, flipped onto my back, and slid under the bed.

There it was.

Dear Painter,

So, if you're reading this, I'm dead.

Also, if you're reading this, you're lying on your back under my old bed. Makes me laugh a little because, to be honest, I didn't always make it to the bathroom in time.

Not sure why you didn't make it back so soon, but I hope you're okay. Actually, I have no idea if you can be dead and get worse off. I suppose there's always worse off.

Please, do what you can for Katie. I broke your rules a bit and told her a little bit about you. Not a lot because, frankly, I don't know that much. You weren't much of a sharer. Might want to work on that. Or not, doesn't matter to me anymore, I'm dead.

Deader than you, actually, when I think about it.

I certainly hope that doesn't mean gone. As in gone gone. I get the feeling that's what you're afraid of. That you hang out in your in-betweener world because at least it's some sort of echo of living. If that is the case, don't wait too long.

No risk, no reward.

I narrowed my successors down to a couple of choices. Coulda just picked the smartest one of the group but Harry was convinced he was former SS. Still, I knew you for a while. You need more than just smart.

I hope you like Julius. He's got a strange way, but you're a damn ghost. You two should be perfect for each other. Still, I don't have much faith in anyone who might take my place.

Big shoes to fill, you know.

Mags

It was nice to hear her voice one last time, if only in my head.

First things first: I needed to get Julius up to speed a little and then get him started on preparing to clear Bernie the dead mailman and Brenda the dead reporter. These would be the first victims on my list attributed to Jan Jorgensen. It seemed there would be many others.

I slid out from under the bed and stood next to the sleeping man. For just a moment, I watched him, jealous. The bliss of sleep. What I would give to just turn my head off for a few minutes.

Maybe Mags was right. Maybe it was time I thought about clearing myself.

I had the guy's name finally. And to be honest, I had a duty to all those who'd been killed by Jan Jorgensen and were now stuck in the InBetween. But this case was far too big to be ignored by the living world. The moment I published a tiny post about all those killed by the Ringman, even if Brenda hadn't written her final story, many others would. Soon, feverish investigations would follow and my name would appear on that victims' list. Without notice, I'd get cleared as well.

But not yet.

I wasn't done yet.

"Hey, Julius," I said and tapped on the man's heavy robe. My fingers passed right through him because I wasn't going to spill any juice to put some actual weight behind my finger taps. It just felt like some motion you should be making when you wake a guy up.

His eyes split open slowly.

I said, "You got a Wikipedia login yet?"

Chapter Nineteen

I felt better now that I was back on my original case but was already stumped. I'd spent half a day searching the office park where Katie's stepdad Boyd had been shot, but there was no sign of the guy.

Spooks don't necessarily hang around where they died. But I'd searched all over Katie's house in Brooklyn Park and nada. Just her mother holed up in the master bedroom in the middle of the day.

I'd have to get back to Hank's Casa de Nasty and push him a little more. But that very likely meant going back through the Blind again to get there. Those three Mob members would be looking for me. Not just looking for me like they'd forgotten a white sauce recipe I'd once told them about at a cul-de-sac barbecue. These guys had pulled me from a moving car.

So why were they hunting me?

That was one of the many questions I had for the Professor.

No one knew much about her, but it was believed she'd been in the InBetween longer than anyone else. Maybe hundreds of years. Or thousands. Perhaps tens of thousands. Maybe more.

That was probably bullshit, because even according to her, everyone stuck here eventually gets out in one of two ways.

The first: they clear after their killer is revealed by police, by some confession, or possibly by a hard-working dead private investigator with a small team of near-death retirees.

The second: bit by bit, you slowly drift away after a very long time.

I'd just seen that in Handsome Dan. Slightly wispier in body, more fractured in the mind. Confused. In the dead bartender, I'd seen my future self. My past—places, people, events—was a dream I couldn't quite remember. Every effort to recall it was like trying to catch a handful of smoke.

Rarely, you could wrestle some of it back if you concentrated really hard. But sometimes it was so foreign, hell, maybe you somehow grabbed the wrong thing. It didn't seem like yours. Strange and unsettling. After a while, I just stopped trying.

I wasn't sure where you might drift to in the nonclearing way. Maybe you went to the Next, you just took longer. Or perhaps somewhere else.

The Professor would never tell me. Or she just didn't know.

The Professor wasn't her real name of course. The Guru would have been more apropos. Not because she's wise, which she is, but because she actually hung out on top of a mountain. I'm not even kidding.

Stone Mountain, Georgia.

I'd been to the place many times, but I wasn't not sure if all of those were after I'd died. The site is a mash of a state park, concert grounds, low-fi bobo theme park, and stone monument.

Carved out of rock, behold: three kinda sketchy dudes on horseback.

Think Mount Rushmore but instead of big, well-sculpted faces, this was more like the Etch A Sketch version of that. Three guys in relief. Pretty sure one of them is Robert E. Lee. And I'm not entirely clear on the theme, because—no joke—one of the dudes looks like Dracula. Who knows, maybe it's hard evidence that ol' Vlad had slapped on a gray uniform and fought in the Confederate Army.

Of course, that's totally ridiculous. If they'd had Drac, they'd have totally won. No question.

I'd left the details I had about the mailman, the reporter, and their killer with my new-Temp Julius, and he'd started a Wiki. When I first started doing this, I'd hoped for a more appropriate "web shrine" for my clients. But my Temps are usually ancient. Web designers they ain't.

It had taken me more than an hour to get from Minneapolis to Georgia. I'd skated down my "interstate"—the Mississippi—to Memphis then hooked east, picking up Pickwick Lake on the Alabama border. And I was in a hurry, so I didn't make any stops. Not even Dollywood, which, make all the fun of me you want, I've got a real soft spot for.

As my girl might say, if you don't like it, you ain't never been there, so your opinion don't matter no how anyhow.

Actually, Ms. Parton is brilliant and articulate. That quote sounds far more like a character she'd play—with aplomb, mind you—but the sentiment doesn't change.

Dolly also has very lovely boobies. FYI.

Okay, got sidetracked there for a moment. Grieving Mags' death and all, so, you know, we've all got our processes and stuff. Ahem.

Looking up to Stone Mountain in the fading light, I sighed. You never knew what you'd get with a visit to the Professor. Never what you came for but sometimes more than you expected. I had too many questions and knew that, if the past were any guide, there wouldn't be a lot of answers coming my way. But maybe one or two might satisfy.

Groups of picnickers were filing away from the base of the giant stone dome, which, according to one of the many signs around the massive slab of gray rock, was eight hundred twenty-five feet at its highest point.

The Professor was on top.

She claimed she chose this as her home because the view was calming. That's true, of course. The Georgia countryside, especially when the fall colors chase away the green of summer, is breathtaking. For some, it's more breathtaking than others—those who don't have pollen, grass, or weed allergies before they get to Georgia will have them soon enough.

Luckily for me, that was just for the living.

"Hi, little lady," I said when I found her, sitting cross-legged on a steep slope on the west side of the giant stone outcropping.

Slowly, she spun toward me, as if sitting on a Roomba maneuvering around a tabby cat. She always theatrically met my far-too-casual greetings with an exaggerated frown. It never took long to turn to a smile.

"Painter. How are you?" She must have been a religious teacher when alive. Or a karate instructor. She wore what looked like a karategi: white jacket and pants, white tie at the waist. It was perfectly clean, except for a series of red slashes across the back. She'd never explained them, and something told me she didn't know they were there.

I said, "I'm good. Still here."

"You didn't happen to bring any beef jerky or anything, did you? Like, I dunno, an offering?"

I was increasingly convinced the guru thing was a cover. So you'd assume she was like some old Greek who made a bunch of other old Greeks mad enough to poke her with pointy things until she bled out.

"How would I even carry that around?" I said and sat down an arm's length away. "Can you eat beef jerky?"

"No," she said. "I just miss it a lot. I like the smell."

"They had beef jerky thousands of years ago?"

She smiled widely. "Ah, well, my group, my people, we never called it jerky. But yeah, you know, meat's been around for a long, long time."

"Right."

"I miss it," she said wistfully.

"Yep. You got a sec?"

She blinked a couple of times then put her palms on her knees. Then the nod. The Professor was open for business.

I told her about the attack.

"They said your name?"

"Yeah."

"Well, you certainly don't have anything any other spirit doesn't have," the Professor said.

"What?" I smiled. "Tenacity? Charming wit? A small selection of moderately inappropriate knock-knock jokes?"

She ignored me. "I suppose you have memories others don't. Maybe that's what they're after."

"I dunno," I said. "I wasn't under the impression they wanted me for Trivia Night."

"Oh, I miss Trivia Night!"

"You had Trivia Night way back then?"

She looked at me. "Some version of it. A bit more lethal than today. And far fewer pop-culture questions, thankfully. So in that regard, an even trade."

"I don't think those spooks want me for my mind."

"Why?"

"Because I don't know these guys. They don't know me," I said and thought for a moment. "They couldn't."

"Then do you think it's something you do?"

"My work?"

The Professor shrugged. She liked to lead you to your answer. Maybe it was all wise and Socrates-like, but it could have been a dodge, too. If the answer was wrong, aha!, then you just misunderstood her questions.

It's all about the rep. Even in the InBetween.

Ah. Maybe that was what she was getting at.

"You think whatever I'm doing, clearing spooks, is somehow messing with the Ghost Mob?"

Another shrug, then, "Painter, if that's the answer, it does lead to more questions."

"Right. Like how does my work somehow hurt them?"

"Or another version of that: what might they be doing that your job interferes with?"

"Interfere? Interfering with what?"

Another shrug. This woman was going to get a kink in her neck. Even if it was a ghost neck. She began to spin away from me as if

I'd put a quarter in and asked the carnival genie a question and now it was time for me to go.

"Maybe you can help me with this, then?" I said, rising a little to try to catch her eye. "How'd they even know I was in that car?"

"Is it a convertible?"

"Does that matter?"

Shrug. "Easier to see you with the top down. Also, a much more pleasant ride, in my experience."

I exhaled. She could be frustrating.

"Or," she added, "they might have something of yours."

"Like what? We're dead; we don't have anything."

"Well, you certainly don't have any beef jerky, I know that!"

"Come on," I said, pleading.

She sighed and watched the last few stragglers far below us leaving the park. For a moment, I stared up at Georgia's big sky and missed the stars. Someone in my brain noted that this was an odd thought, but she spoke, and the voice quickly flitted away.

"There's a connection, a link, between spirit and some things physical. A favorite possession. There's a thin tether that can last for years. Longer."

"Yeah," I said, my thoughts swirly. "I've seen that, sure. How does that work?"

"I'm not a physicist, I'm just some chick who sits on a mountain," she said. "There's a link, sometimes very tenuous, between living creatures and some objects. Part energy, part emotion. The more important it is, the stronger the link. Especially if they carry it all the time."

Wait.

I asked, "You mean like maybe a ring they'd been wearing when alive?"

A nod. "Especially if they'd worn it a long time," the Professor said, and her hand absentmindedly slipped into the folds of her clothing, the tips of her fingers disappearing. "Necklaces, that sort of thing. Even for things like fillings in your teeth, there's like this very thin wire, a link. It always fades over time. Except for when it doesn't."

My hand went to my throat, and I felt where my aunt's necklace used to lie against my upper chest. No mirrors in the InBetween, but my best guess, in the projection of myself, it was still there.

Was it still with my dead body? Or did someone else now have it?

I came out of my daze and saw the Professor spin away again, her eyes off in the distance. "Another quick one, please?"

She stopped again, arching an eyebrow at my tone. I said, "I came across something bizarre in Chicago."

"That's a phrase likely uttered dozens of times a day."

"No, this was different. This living guy. He saw me. He grabbed me, actually."

The mountain lady shook her head, resuming her slow spin, like a telescope tracking toward the Crab Nebula. "The living can't see us, can't touch us, because we don't have any form. Our spirit, call it what you like, is represented here by how we express our energy. Livies can't see you in their world." Then she paused. "Usually."

"Usually?"

"I don't like absolute statements. Goes against the whole guru thing I'm going for." She smiled, still half turned away from me.

"Right. But we can be heard, obviously. What's the difference?"

"Very few can hear us, and that's only those who will soon cross over," she said. "But of course that's not really sound they're hearing. They've been opened to a sort of empathy usually denied the living, sadly. Seeing? That's different. Energy manifesting into light, that sort of thing."

"Right." I thought about Gary and the car with the thumping bass. Then my thoughts were back to the bar in Chicago. "This livie knew I was there, no question. A real bad-news dude, too. And one other thing…" I thought back to when Brenda had been tracking the Ringman. The bushes near the mailman. "I think he left residue like we do."

"Residue? What is that?"

I gave her my lightning bug metaphor, which I was quite pleased with. The mailman was into it. Everybody totally gets that one. It's a classic and easy to understand! However, the Professor does have a very soft heart, and my analogy had the wrong effect entirely.

I pleaded with her, "Can you please stop crying? I'm sorry. It was just—"

"You killed them? They're so pretty! How could you? I thought you were good!"

"I was. I am! This was years ago. I was very young."

"Uh, it always starts when they're young. Lightning bug killers today, ax murderers tomorrow."

I waited a half minute then tried again. I said, "Let's put the analogy aside like it never happened. But there was like a faint glowing film there where he'd been."

Not meeting my eyes, she finally said, "Stain."

"Stain?"

She nodded. "When spirits interact with matter on the livie plane. It can leave a very thin stain. Goes away after a while. Usually."

"But this guy wasn't a spook. He was, you know, a guy. Living."

"Not possible but..." she said, her voice trailing off.

"I'm sure of it."

The Professor stood for the first time since I'd arrived, moving in a small circle, her feet perfectly still, tapping her fingers at her sides. She was muttering as if she was trying to remember the last number of a combination lock.

"Could a spirit have been following the livie for some reason so that they're on the same path? That would explain the stain."

I nodded. "Thought of that. But no, I never saw one. Just this guy."

"Well, I mean... sure, but—" She was quiet again. "But if—I mean—if it's something else, it could be very, very bad."

"Bad?"

"Very, very bad," the Professor said, and there was something on her face I'd never seen before.

Fear.

Chapter Twenty

Now, I'm not sure if I've given the wrong impression, but I don't want to make it seem as if the InBetween is crawling with spooks like the Sunday before Christmas at the mall.

Take my city, for example. Last year in Minneapolis-St. Paul, there were like forty-something murders. That's for three million people. New York, it's closer to three hundred killings, but there's like ten mil there.

Remember, too, most murders are solved. We hear about the big splashy ones they put on the news, but usually, it's someone in the house pulling the trigger (wife, husband, grandma) or a robbery gone wrong (Crips, Bloods) or some maniac who's flipped out and gone on a shooting spree (Republican, Democrat).

The number of unsolved murders is really quite low. In my city, many of us know each other or at least have heard of one another. That's why it was odd to see those three ghost goons looking for me in the Blind. I didn't know them from Adam. But they knew me.

To get to Hank's house, I could go way around and do my east-north-west track. But I wasn't in a hurry to head back to the Chicago area. Not yet. I could have gone south from Stone Mountain, but the Blind extends all the way to the Gulf Coast. And with fewer lakes and rivers, it's a lot slower.

It's faster to take the Mississippi and then cross through the Blind. Faster, not necessarily safer. Luckily, the Mississippi cuts right up through the Twin Cities.

You come up and head east around 94 and you end up in Dinkytown near the university. Lots of cool little bars and places to eat. At least there used to be. Mostly secondhand clothing stores in many of those spots now.

To the west was Eden Prairie, where Hank lived.

Between the two was a ribbon of the Blind. In these parts, it seems to center on the fairgrounds, which, if you've been to the Minnesota State Fair, won't come as much of a surprise.

Just north of the cities, there was a series of lakes I could have taken to get past that narrow, dark band faster. But if ghostly goons were looking for me, they were likely keeping an eye on the obvious paths. Maybe.

I hit surface streets, moving slowly because somehow that felt safer. In part, so I didn't smack into any more dearly departed reporters or mail carriers. Also, I'd been ripped from a car doing thirty miles an hour in town. Going fast through the streets again was a déjà vu I didn't dig. It made me feel vulnerable.

Still, I clung close to the edges, even when I caught the always-busy Snelling Avenue and headed north, crossing University Avenue, traveling deeper and deeper into the Blind.

In the "real" world, you can usually tell how bad an area is based on two basic measurements: how many liquor stores and how few trees.

As the former number goes up and the latter goes down, the slum factor of a livie neighborhood increases. There's probably a ratio somewhere in there that would make a nice little grad paper. Most likely belonging to someone who would never set foot there.

In the InBetween, there's no real way to tell "bad" areas. It just happens when the wrong sort just starts hanging out. Maybe they'd been murdered nearby. But as I've said, evil spooks will generally migrate to areas where other ones are. And if you realize you're in a dangerous area—this always comes a second or two later than you'd hope it would—you get the hell out and stay out.

Going in on purpose, like I was, even just passing through, was generally a really, really dumb idea. But I'd already blown too much time. Obviously, Brenda the reporter wasn't some shrinking violet, but she was my client. I've sworn to protect them the best I can. And she was a newbie tracking something very, very bad. I needed to clear Boyd and get back to Chicago.

To get to Hank's, I'd have to slide past the fairgrounds, then it was a straight shot. Still, I was on my guard as I whizzed by grungy corner stores, pawn shops, a closed-up drum shop with busted windows, and drugstores.

Outside a funeral home, I saw a procession of mourners, all dressed in black. A heavy woman was following a casket, hand outstretched toward its lid, as it was being carried out by six men, who, despite all being young and looking pretty strong were struggling under the weight of the dearly departed.

Who, it turned out, was just off Mom's elbow. He was wailing even harder than she was.

It was unfortunate for him—maybe he'd been shot in some North Minneapolis violence—that the family had gathered here and he'd followed. Guy didn't know it, but his troubles didn't end with a dirt nap. Right now, he was in a bad, bad part of the InBetween.

I slid past the guy at first but then spun back as the casket was being loaded into a hearse. The dead guy, a huge man with arms as big as hogs on spits, was kneeling on the ground, crying dry tears.

"Hey, man," I said, and he looked around as I came up. "Sorry about you being dead and all that, but you gotta get outta here."

That had startled him, and I took a couple steps back so I didn't get smacked with pork fingers. I needed all the juice I had. No reason to lose it on some hysterical guy flailing. Then I caught the side of the guy's face.

He blinked at me with his right eye, and a painful, sad smile rose on his lips. The left side of his face was open. Missing. If he hadn't died well, which he hadn't, at least he'd apparently gone quickly.

"Who are you?"

I started to tell him but then thought better of it. The Ghost Mob was looking for me. Handing out business cards to strangers in the Blind wasn't the best way to keep a low profile. I made a quiet promise to myself to find the guy later and help him along.

I went into Undercover Dead P.I. mode and gave him a false name. He was in his twenties, so I dropped a name from a generation before this guy had even been born. It'd be my own private joke. See, I'm smart.

I said, "I'm Tommy Kramer."

He stared at me for a minute. "You mean the old Vikings quarterback?"

"No, no," I said, raising my hands all unclever-like. "Not the same guy. Who's that? Never heard of him. Except for the name. Which is mine."

Me, as you can see, I'm smooth as silk under pressure.

"Okay." He put his face—at least what there was left of it—back in his hands.

Kneeling, I cast a glance left and right again. The hearse door closed through me, and he stood as if he was about to chase it down the street to his final resting place. At least the final resting place of his body. Who knew how long he might be here.

"Man, you have to clear out of this area," I said. "It's not safe. Head east of the river and hang there."

"Why, Tommy Kramer?"

"There are spooks out this way that like to sap the energy off people. They take a couple swipes at you, you go down in a heap. From there, I don't know what might happen. I've never hung around long enough to find out. There are rumors that they've been sending out hunting parties lately. Dunno why."

The big man looked around, blinking again, his eye darting around as if he was watching a wasp. "Those sound like bad folks."

"They are," I said. Then I put a reassuring hand softly on his shoulder. "You got somewhere you can go? Away from here?"

He nodded slowly. "Got a sister in Brooklyn Park. She works at the movie theater."

"Perfect! Go catch a couple movies, man. All of them," I said. "We can still enjoy that, can't we?"

"I suppose so."

"If you gotta stay, you know, be near Momma for a while, keep a low profile. I'll find you and we can see about getting you out of this place," I said, smiling. "That is if you're still here."

"Right," he said, his arms pumping a little as he walked in a tight circle. "Don't wanna end up like those dead folks over on Cosgrove. That don't look good for them, whatever they're doing there."

"What? What who are doing?"

"Dunno. Got spooks all lined up in rows. But they ain't moving or nuthin'. Hunched over like they're in a plane about to crash. And it's bright as all hellfire in there. Terrifying. Saw it once on a wander and never went back."

"Where?"

"I said on Cosgrove Street," he told me, his eye flickering around. "Couple of scary dudes circling them, too, like they're some sort of patrol." Then he faced me. Or, well, half faced me. Because, you know, the shot part. He added, "Some of those guys looked weird, to be honest. No shimmer."

"What are they doing? The ones all hunched over. Are they in pain or something?"

"They're doing nothing, man," he said, his voice getting dimmer as he slid away. "But in the middle of them was this crazy pillar of light. Not like from a spotlight or anything, you know? A real crazy glow about it. You know what I mean?"

I knew what he meant. What the Professor had called "stain."

But a pillar of it?

What the hell was it for?

I passed over Como Avenue, keeping a sharp eye out for spooks of any kind, but didn't see any.

Dusk was settling in, waking up the lights high above Snelling. The sodium-vapor lamps produced a burnt yellow as if each held a mini dawn of its own. It also cast a real spooky pall over the area.

Something it didn't need. I was already dealing with a serious case of the willies.

I hugged a tree line on the east side of the street, also known as MN-51, but nobody calls it that. It's just Snelling. One of those names that pop up all over the Cities, so it's probably some political family from way back.

Must seem a bit funny. Old man Snelling was probably feeling pretty proud of himself, whoever he was, crafting a political domain up from nothing, because back then, everybody had nothing for the most part. Then he was able to pass the baton along to his kids, right? Maybe a couple of loud-mouthed boys who had their heads firmly up their asses. But in the end, he was able to help get them a little station—enough to push off and up from.

Legacy.

But in the end, a century later, that legacy is just the name of the street where prostitutes sell handies for fifteen bucks near the Job Corps Center.

Skirting the edges of the Center, I came upon a familiar site, a behemoth sprouting from the soil. Some thought it looked like a tall mushroom, but I always felt it resembled a white plastic car lock, popped up.

Something was skittering around my mind, tickling there since chatting with the Professor. I couldn't grab it, though. It was like a raindrop on a tin roof during a storm, rolling around, changing shape. But at some point, it had to drop.

I cut left just south of the water tower and headed to the northern-most side of the fairgrounds.

The closer I got to the fairgrounds, the darker it got.

I grabbed Cooper Street, now walking off the path entirely, passing through brush, bushes, and trees. It wasn't good cover, but it was all I had.

Cosgrove was two streets up, from what I remembered, so I passed over Randall, a big fat road that helped fairground traffic get to the deep-fried cheese curds, then back out again, to make room for more of the curd hungry.

There were far few streetlights here, about fifty yards between them. This wasn't really a residential area, so there was less need for them. Not a lot of crime here because there was damn near nothing to steal. Just empty pavilions, one after another, for when the State Fair fires up or, off-season, where they bring car shows and soccer clinics.

Most of the grass was worn away, looking like the head of a man who dropped his vanity the moment he began dropping his hair. Patchy, scarred, crisscrossing lines in the dirt.

Here the streetlights weren't the towering War of the Worlds stanchions I'd seen back on Snelling. These were those quaint, Victorian-style lights you see in theme parks that help move paying customers from one till to another. Most were either off or had been knocked out, but I couldn't be sure if that was how the area usually looked or if this was a new development.

There was a strange glow to the area, and I glanced back over my shoulder, looking for a big, bright moon. It wasn't there.

But then, like the dead man at the funeral parlor had said, there was a bright line stretching from the ground and piercing the thin clouds above me.

I walked toward it, crossing the empty gravel lots where thousands of cars park each year. Right now, they were as barren as a moonscape. A moonscape with oil stains.

The slipstream to heaven looked like a giant had drawn a line with a cheap highlighter, the kind that runs out of color too quickly.

I was one street over from Cosgrove, having cut farther over than I needed to. When I looped back, I passed by an abandoned food cart, the sort big ol' Ford 350s pull around. It promised FOOT LONG HOT DOGS, with a couple of smiling bottles of ketchup and mustard. Someone had tried to break in by bashing a window, realized there wasn't anything to steal and no damn hot dogs, so they gave up and skedaddled.

The giant hot dog on the marquee made my stomach growl, despite not having a stomach to growl. All in my head. Despite not having a head.

It's really best not to dwell on such things.

I saw the unmanned gates of the state fairgrounds. Six lanes wide, each path capped with a Minnesota state flag. With no wind, the lifeless flags looked like some discarded blue wrapping that had gotten caught up around the pole. Beneath them, arching lane dividers held paneling to protect fairgoers from the sun or rain as they handed over their cash.

In the dark, the huge curved lane splitters looked more like the ribcage of some giant creature who'd fallen and just lain there to die. Everything now rotted away but the thick bones of its chest.

The buildings on either side of Cosgrove were long, large structures, many flushed damn near right up to the street. Few places to hide, so that meant a quick recon and getting the hell out.

As I approached, the thread of light grew brighter and thicker. My breath was turning ragged, and I was convinced I could hear my own heartbeat, some leftover memory of what being scared meant to the body I no longer had.

A large white building on my right side. Some old fifties-style script across it.

I cast my eyes to the left to catch hidden lookouts, any spooks floating around and keeping intruders out. The only figure I saw was a livie—but still barely that, it seemed—passed out on a bench next to the building.

At the sight of him, the heartbeat drumming in my ears grew louder, thun-thun-thun-thun.

He was lying down, wearing at least two coats pulled so high up on his body I couldn't really see a face. The snore was the only thing that told me he wasn't dead. Above him in script were the words Gass Station. The marquis even had one of those old-timey service-station pumps, with the large readouts and red rubber hose hanging off the side.

In season, this was one of many places people at the fair could "fuel up." Next to the old cartoon gas pump, it read, "Brats, Steak Sandwiches, Burgers." Probably one of those Minnesota-nice jokes. Like it's a gas station, right? If not now, give it a few hours.

Above the massive, warehouse-style building, that's where the thin ribbon of light was coming from.

"Hey, buddy," I whispered. Then I moved closer and repeated myself. One more time, I said, "Dude, wake up."

He looked like hell, but either he'd never be able to hear the dead—it doesn't happen for most livies—or he wasn't yet close to death. So no help from this guy.

I gave one last glance up and down the street. The drumbeat of my heart was getting louder every second I hung around.

"Okay, okay," I said to myself, which sometimes I find calming. Not this time. "Don't wanna see but gotta see."

The words Gass and Station loomed large above my head as I slid up and slowly pressed my face through the side of the wall. Dirt, insects, paint, mold, and then the darkness of masonry and the occasional shimmer of light. A moment later, my face came through the other side, and I hung there.

It was a wide, open eating area. A massive concrete floor with vendor booths lining most of the walls. The long rows of lights hanging from the ceiling were dead. The roof was thick and solid, but the occasional skylight dotted the ceiling. But the room itself was bright as a baseball stadium during the season opener.

The stream of light at the center looked only about as wide as a garden hose but was spilling out a brilliant white wash so harsh it made the lettering on the vendor booths impossible to read.

There was movement to my left.

And then to my right.

I stayed perfectly still as if I'd been some theater mask thrown up on the wall near the entrance. Right now, I wasn't the happy one.

Thun-thun-thun-thun.

Fighting the urge to pull away and run, I tried to convince myself that with the overpowering light, my spook face would get lost in the glare. The two guys I saw were, no question, Ghost Mob. And if I tried to bolt, they would see that, and they'd be on my ass.

One of the spooks slid past me, not even moving his feet, just making a wide circle around the white light in the center of the room. I recognized him. He was the one who'd come almost nose to nose with me without knowing it, when I'd hidden in that big livie's boob tube back in the slum.

My heart was pounding so hard, I was sure it was making the eyes dance in my head, but I kept still reminding myself that I didn't need to blink because I really didn't have eyes anymore. Still, they burned, but if I could just ignore another minute or so, I'd be okay.

Another spook was coming up from my left. There was something horrifically wrong with his head. Elongated! A moment later, I realized he was wearing a stovepipe hat. No bush mustache or monocle or any other old-timey accouterments. This guy wasn't some nineteenth-century relic but instead just a bit of a douche.

Stovepipe was closing in on one side as his partner slowly passed the other direction. Staring straight ahead, I tried not to twitch my nose or part my lips. Of course, had the guy just looked over at the wall with the fucking face on it, he'd have known something was up. But the pillar of light was bright, like the big dead guy said, washing everything out.

I fought every urge to pull away and realized my arms were pumping behind me, trying to drain the buzzing, deafening fear from my brain.

"You think we gotta go out? Maybe go on a hunt, just around the area?" the taller one said to the dude with the hat when they grew closer to each other.

"Not yet. Have faith, asshole."

Tallman pushed the other. "I got faith, but that stream is dimming. Calks made a deal to keep pumping out the juice, so maybe we should—"

"He doesn't need your help."

At that moment, the doors to my left burst open, and I let out a tiny yelp. Stovepipe swaggered toward the center of the room, while Tallman got a queer look on his face. He turned toward the wall as his eyebrows danced a very slow waltz. He'd heard something.

Then everything changed.

Three men came in the door. Not ghosts. These were livies.

This made no sense. Probably some poorly thought-out break-in. To the living, this was a vast, empty, and dark hall. The booths would be locked up tight, and like the hot dog stand on the street, there was nothing left to steal.

The three livies were followed by a fourth, who came in just enough to guard the door at the adjacent wall. From where I hung, I could see a bulge in his jacket. But he was no threat to me.

It was a totally different story for the Tallman, the swaggering Stovepipe, and now another spook. This latter was making a beeline for the brilliant beam of light.

Three of the livies began walking toward a corner of the room, methodically shaking rollaway blinds at each station. What were they looking for?

With the distraction, I knew this was my shot at clearing out of there, but something told me I had to wait it out. That and the coward in me couldn't get my legs to work; they were just frozen in place. But I'll go with the fact-finding nature of my decision to, for the moment, not run like a motherfucker.

The big bastard at the door glanced around the room then pulled out a cell phone. He punched a finger into it a few times, maybe checked his Facebook feed for all I knew, then tucked the phone back into his suit pocket.

A moment later, a fifth man strutted in. Another livie.

What the hell is going on?

Didn't matter how tough they were, if these guys knew this place was crawling with spooks, they'd run screaming like four-year-olds.

The fifth man was incredibly tall, even bigger than Tallman, so I'd jumped the gun on my naming convention, obviously. He also had a nicer suit than the livies. That and the way he walked, casually bent at the waist, head bobbing slightly, told me all I needed to know about the pecking order here.

At first, I thought the livies had just stumbled into the Ghost Mob's operation, whatever it was, with plans of thieving. That changed a moment later.

The tall man in the suit said, "I ain't 'fraid of no ghosts." Then he laughed. His words had a cadence to them I wasn't familiar with. Some kind of, well, foreign-type accent.

Given the number of spooks in the room, these livies must have been warned off with rumors of the place being haunted. Maybe that was why there was possibly some loot still here to pilfer. Don't go in that one, man. It's haunted.

Then I saw them, and my heart fell.

In the center of the room, thick arching veins of electricity crawled across the backs of at least fifty ghosts, each of them on their knees and bent slightly as if in prayer. There were whip-snaps of light and crackling, and I actually could smell something. Burnt, electrical.

The swaggering fireplug of a spook walked to the center of this unholy prayer circle as if he were a preacher prepared to change their evil ways. But he ignored the hunched-over people around him as if they were furniture. Or livestock.

Watching their bodies thrum in time together—a controlled, slow writhing—I realized something. The machine's tendrils of light moving along the rows of spooks wasn't using some force to trap them in place. The energy was flowing not into them but out.

These people, trapped and contorted, were powering the machine. They were its fuel.

As this realization hit me, there was a sudden burst of light in the middle of the room as Fireplug spook began to glow, his hand now gripping the stream, and his features almost indiscernible with so much juice flowing through him. It was more than I'd ever seen in any ghost. Ten times, maybe a hundred times more.

I never knew such a thing was possible in the InBetween. Crafting machines from our energy. Was this where the disappeared had gone, those who hadn't cleared? Was this why the Mob was hunting spooks? To put them here?

What can a spook so supercharged do? Or, more importantly, what was the Ghost Mob planning to do with all that juice?

Then the very tall foreign man headed toward Sparkplug, walking directly over to a ghost on a parallel plane of existence. The man held out a hand as if to shake and then laughed and dropped it to his side.

"'Bout time you come out from hiding," the livie said, walking past the ghost. No question though, he could see him!

The squat ghost held onto the stream of light as the livie spun on a heel and stood in front of him. He towered over Sparkplug. The two other spooks, this one's lieutenants, came up behind Tallman. They weren't supercharged, so he had no idea he had two spirits of the dead breathing down his neck.

"We have been waiting. You know better than to keep me waiting," Sparkplug said in a voice that made every cell in my body want to flee. Didn't sound like anyone dead or alive. Unsettling and unnatural. "I don't have long here." He looked up to the power in his hand. "My arrangement with the old man's kid. This will drain the power I promised. Just for a while, but it won't go unnoticed. And we need that secret, or all of this—"

"Yes! But…" The tall livie's voice boomed, and he raised his hands, long arms with massive palms, as if he was about to give a blessing. "That is your problem, induna. I am making all the arrangements on my end."

"It is the only problem!" Sparkplug's voice, filled with sudden rage, may have sounded louder to the livies, but on our plane, with all that power, for just an instant, it was like getting hit by a runaway truck filled with angry bees.

It was brief, but in that instant, it was too much noise, too much light, too much pain all at once.

I fell to a knee, buckling, but thankfully the other two Ghost Mobbers also felt it and were dealing with too much of their own pain to notice. One of them looked up to Sparkplug, yelling out in anguish and anger, "Don't do that again, Calkin. Fuck, man, that hurts!"

Sparkplug—the spook called Calkin—just put a handout, dismissing him with a half wave. Even still reeling, I noticed something very subtle about the exchange. The spook boss man never looked toward his whining underling. It occurred to me that he was hiding from the livie that he had his people there, other Ghost Mob members.

Schemes within schemes.

From my vantage point, lower to the floor, I got a slightly better look at those trapped by the power generator. Each was hunched over, curled forward into a sort of crash position, but instead of preparing for disaster, they were in a nightmare that had already happened. And was still happening. Pain. Suffering.

The flux of light ahead of me, I tried to get a lock on the faces of those crouched to the floor. They were hunched over, spaced out evenly, bent in agony, penitent worshipers forced to face but not look directly at their god.

And they were each rocking slightly in rhythm, uttering a very low, guttural, animal-like noise. The sound I'd heard earlier hadn't been my heartbeat. It was them.

Gnuh-gnuh-gnuh-gnuh…

Dozens of spooks frozen in spasms of agony that fueled some impossible machine; a conduit of juice powerful enough to make the dead temporarily real again.

It just wasn't possible.

Then something drew my attention to a group of crouched, throbbing ghosts near the center of the room, just off to the right. The tall man was laughing again, but I couldn't hear that now. My senses were being tugged at by an echo.

No, not an echo. But something familiar to me, something I recognized. A voice?

I pushed farther in, exposing my shoulders, my chest, my waist, and my attention was drawn to one ghost. In the light radiating from the spook named Calkin, I could now see the side of the face of one of the trapped, hunched, writhing victims who were feeding the energy collector.

It was the mailman.

"Oh shit, no!"

The heads of the two ghosts behind the tall man in the suit snapped toward me, their eyes blazing. When the Ghost Mob leader Calkin turned as well, the livie looked to see what had drawn his attention.

"What is it? Who is there, Calkin?"

The squat ghost ignored him and pulled his hand from the energy stream, disappearing from the land of the living. As he did, four more spooks burst through the opposite wall.

And all of them were headed my way.

I spun around to hightail it out of the Gass Station, but before slipping away, I'd heard Calkin call out, "It's Painter!"

I crossed back over Snelling again, down Midway Parkway, not taking the streets, skating as fast as I could through house after house, not caring at all that I was near blinded as I burst through plaster, brick, metal, furniture, dogs, people.

The fleeting, panicked images of grit, stone, and sinew punished my eyes as I prayed some stray spook wasn't splayed out on someone's floor binge-watching Dancing With the Stars or something, which would have sent me tumbling end over end and crashing into the floor. At that point, I'd be an easy target.

Still, I couldn't let that worry slow me down. I had to move as fast as I could or end up like the other tortured souls in the horrific machine.

Skating uses very little energy once I get going, leaving behind almost no stain. If I could get a half minute ahead of them, any trail I might be leaving should dissipate enough for me to lose them.

Every few blocks, I ran a tight circle around some livie's home, at random intervals making switchback turns. This wasn't an original move—the Professor had shared it with me in those early days. Survival 101.

It eats up getaway time, but if you just go in a straight line, you're easy to track. Ultimately though, whoever has the most energy can eventually outrun the other guy if it comes to that. And only minutes earlier, I had seen the Ghost Mob leader, Calkin, take in so much juice he was momentarily whole again. Solid again!

What the fuck was that about?

Sure, he wasn't connected anymore, and now he was chasing me with a few other goons. But juiced up like that, he'd officially be the most dangerous spook in the InBetween.

At least to me.

"Hey, hey!" I heard a yell somewhere behind me. "The bastard's gone down Midway!"

"Go, go, go!" another voice yelled back. They were too close.

Logically, I should have headed south or west to get back to the Mississippi and use that to skate the hell out of there as fast as possible. I'd hoped I'd sent them that way after burning a few precious seconds tattooing a basic buzz saw shape near a band shell just west of Cosgrove Street.

It wasn't a full-fledged countermeasure, just a couple of jags on a circle, but if I'd just headed out in a straight shot, I'd be caught, no question. A couple of their voices were getting dimmer, and I smiled when I realized I'd split them up; at least two of them rolled the dice and headed in the opposite direction. Still, there were others on my tail. If I could hold them off for a couple more blocks, I had a chance.

"Come on, Como Ave., where are you?"

Just as I reached the edge of the Blind, nearly out of their territory, a tingling began on my shoulder blades. You can sense when another spook is really close, reaching for you. I've even heard some livies can feel this occasionally, the sense of a presence.

Animals do, especially cats, for whatever reason. That would come into play if I could just—

"Gotcha, asshole!"

The spook with the stupid stovepipe hat had swiped at my back with an outstretched arm, knocking me off my feet. I fell slowly and, twisting backward, caught sight of him and the horrific gash across his throat, ear to ear. I then thrust a fist into his gut, so that the two of us began tumbling in unison as we rocketed down Midway Parkway. Just above me, blocking out the sky, his scowling face strobed in my vision as we passed through homes, shrubbery, cars, and people.

As we slid to a stop, I heard another voice somewhere behind him.

"Anders, you got him? Anders? Pin the asshole!"

It was Calkin. I couldn't see him yet, and I could tell he was spilling off energy, but the prick was still so juiced up it made his words sting. Once Anders and I had slowed to a near-stop, I got to my feet first and kicked him in his stupid hat.

The Ghost Mob member on the ground called back, his breath hitching after I'd tagged him. "Calks! He's here, come on, he's here!"

We were in the middle of a suburban two-car garage. A seventies Chevy Nova was in one stall, no wheels, held up on cement blocks. Its hood was propped open, and various bits of its innards were strewn across the floor.

A teenage kid was under the car, cranking away with a socket wrench.

In the adjoining stall, Anders was on all fours over a massive oil stain in the concrete. On my feet again, and now with a bit of juice I'd stolen back from the spook, I turned to bail, but then a fist— white hot at its edges—flew through the Nova and launched me through the wall.

The kid dropped his socket wrench.

I was on my back with Calkin gripping either side of me, squeezing my arms so tight, if they'd been real, he'd have easily shattered the bones on each side. He then pulled his knees up onto my chest and was riding me like a surfboard, hovering over me, both scowling and grinning madly at the same time.

He laughed as the family homes melted away from us and gave way to successive copses of short trees and platforms on risers, topped with rainbow umbrellas.

Wait. What?

Did I imagine that last part? What was he doing to me?

Slowly, we spun to a stop, him still riding on top of me, holding my arms tight. The strange umbrellas in my head gave, and there was concrete below us. Under the ragged breaths he was sucking in, despite not having lungs, there was the faint sound of trickling water.

"Painter Mann!" he said then actually howled. "This day couldn't get any better!"

"Get off me," I said through my clenched jaw. The memory of my heart was banging away in my chest.

"We've been looking for you," he said. "Now we can add you to our collection. And you won't cause us any more headaches."

I only raised my hands inches off the ground, but he then squeezed even harder, leaning forward to press his knees deeper into my chest.

"I got no…" I choked out. "I got no beef with you, man. Get off! Leave me—"

"No, no," he said. His voice had a queer trilling sound as he oozed juice from every pore. "You're ours now. All the pieces falling into place, falling into place."

The guy was actually singing as he perched on top of my chest. Little hopping motions, which were making my head spin. His buddy, Anders, slid up behind him, along with another spook with a big stupid grin on his face.

"That him?"

Calkin raised his hand as if to give the new guy a high five then spun back and smashed me across the face. My mind split and split again and felt as if it had fallen onto the damp concrete below us.

"Yes!"

Another sledgehammer to the face. I'd been smacked before, but this was altogether different. I could see the juice fading in the guy, spilling out—despite him stealing handfuls of mine with each swipe—but it was still giving him strength like I'd never seen before.

Anders with the stovepipe hat just watched with a horrible double grin, a smile above a slash, really enjoying my beating like it was some sort of ghost porn.

The Ghost Mob asshole named Calkin leaned toward me, inches from my face. He said, "I'm going to put you in our little pipeline, so your juice will feed the machine. I hear it's the most painful, most awful."

His teeth came close to my face.

He added, "And it never ends. That pain goes on and on and on, Pain-ter!"

Anders' face had been eclipsed by the crazy bastard's head, but I could see flashes of his legs and feet as they slowly slipped from my view.

"Calk? Let's go, man."

The vise grips on my arms released and reappeared on the front of my shirt, grabbing me where his knees had been. But instead of yanking me to my feet, he let me go, and I felt him stand.

Then I heard a new voice. A deep baritone. Calm.

"Why don't you just let the man up and be on your way?"

Calkin then lifted me with one arm and held me high above him. I could see the crown of his head with a hole in it the size of a fist. Bits of gore and skull caved inward.

"He's up," Calkin said to the voice. "Why don't you mind your own business, Sheriff?"

I got a fleeting glance of the man with the baritone voice. Not his face so much but his dress blues, shiny belt buckle, and badge. Off his belt hung a baton.

Unreal.

"Ah, see, you bust up in our park? That is my business," the cop said. "Drop the man and beat your feet."

Calkin shrugged and, in his grip, I bobbed like a doll.

The Ghost Mob leader said, "Drop?" and then let me go, and I thudded hard to the ground. My breath shot out of me as if I'd been kicked by a pissed-off horse.

I mumbled, "Please stop helping."

Above me, my eyes not quite working as a team yet, I saw Calkin reach down for me again, but impressively, the sheriff's voice alone stopped him.

"Leave the man be," the cop said. "You spin around on the spot and head into your territory now. This is ours."

The juiced-up spook wavered. The look on his face said he wanted me dead. It takes a lot of hate to want a dead man dead. For the life of me, I still didn't know why the Ghost Mob boss gave a shit about me. Our paths had never crossed. Or if they had, I hadn't been aware of it.

Despite the big cop's size, the mob boss was the far stronger of the two. But then he took a half step back. He shot a crooked, glowing finger toward the man in blue. For the first time, in his voice, I heard an accent.

"You will pay for this!"

And yeah, it was a foreigny accent. Strange that I hadn't noticed that before.

The big man laughed. "In stories, people say shit like that when they lose. But at least you got the score here right."

With that Calkin spun away, trailed by his lackeys, and he punched the air every few steps, leaving a stain trail behind him that looked like a faint, sideways ECG reading.

Getting to my feet, I couldn't work out how one fat, dead cop had gotten the three Mobsters to back down. Then I felt them. On the periphery. He was not alone.

Up on my feet, I saw now that I'd made it to the Como Zoo.

Originally, I'd been heading here not because of any thoughts of help, but I knew that the zoo was popular with some spooks because of its familiarity when they'd been alive. And, like I said, the cats.

Cats can see ghosts.

You see Fluffy shoot a look to a corner of the room, staring wild-eyed, and you don't know why? Someone is likely hanging out. Say howdy.

And it's not just domesticated kitties.

Big cats, too. And they're not so skittish about us, even putting their heads out to get petted. That sort of companionship, offered up from the world of the living, can bring spooks from all over. Some never leave.

I looked behind the cop. There must have been hundreds of them—men and women, adults and children. Brown, white, and black.

Como had been my target because I knew that I could cut through here and my trail would get lost in all the others that crisscrossed through the zoo. Stain camouflage. But I hadn't made it there. Not his intention, but it had been Calkin's Hulk-smash punch that saved my ass.

The cop extended a hand to me and smiled. "Bullies are all brave until they ain't, huh?"

I shook and nodded. "Thanks for that, Sheriff...?"

"Not Sheriff. Sergeant Peterson," he said, flashing his security badge. Across the top, it read ALERT WATCH. "He only calls me that the way some people might call you stud, but they don't mean stud."

"No one's ever called me stud. Not even ironically."

The Sergeant nodded. "Hmm. Yeah, I can see that."

"So you're a security guard? In the InBetween?"

He smiled with crooked teeth, but it was still a warm, beautiful grin, and said, "Hey, man, this is the afterlife, right? New ballfield, whole new game. You can be what you want if you put your mind to it."

Of course, as the world's only dead private investigator, I deduced he was absolutely, one hundred percent correct.

Chapter Twenty-One

There really isn't much to fear in the InBetween because you're already dead. Your survival instinct shrugged, put on a hat too big for itself, and left without a goodbye kiss.

Of course, that doesn't mean there aren't dangers here.

Not from food poisoning or drunk drivers or falling anvils. Just other spooks. Most will leave you alone because they're usually dealing with their particular circumstances ("What? I'm what?").

However, anecdotally, there's been a recent uptick in spook-on-spook attacks. I say anecdotally because there really ain't a newspaper or a website dedicated to the InBetween.

Well, that's not entirely true.

There are a couple of websites that speculate about it, propped up by apocryphal accounts of people claiming they died momentarily and came back with news from the other side. I had one of my Temps read through a bunch of them, and nearly all of them are unequivocally and entirely wrong. Good for a laugh.

Nearly all of them. A few though… At some point, I'd have to look into how they knew what they knew. Thankfully, those sites are laughed off like all the rest.

I'd always heard rumors about some Ghost Mob lair, where they'd leech energy off of victims. Like harvesting. Get a bit of juice, and if you can set up a drip feed, the victim never drums up enough energy to escape.

For the longest time, I thought it was all bullshit. Until this one guy I knew named Randy came back after a spell and claimed he'd gotten caught up in one of those lairs for a few weeks. He eventually snuck away. He said when you're in the ultra-low-e state, you have these terrible fever dreams, reliving the moments before you were killed over and over again.

Even ghosts have ghost stories.

But that was a story, a nightmare, the mailman was now stuck in. I felt responsible and knew it was on me to get him out.

"Show's over, y'all," Sergeant Peterson said, waving his big arms in giant scooping motions outward. "See what we can do together? Did good." One of his crew shuffled in the crowd, theatrically crossing his arms. "Even you, Cy."

"Cyrus!" This guy looked a bit more motley than the rest of the sergeant's crew. The tiny man wore a faded sweatshirt and grubby jeans. However, he sported elaborate headgear, held to his skull by what looked like one of those old leather football helmets. On top of that was some sort of crown that looked a bit like a steam-punk menorah, dented, scuffed, and a dingy yellow. "Cyrus the Great!"

"Not great, but yeah, you didn't do too bad." I could see a tiny smirk on the sergeant's face.

"All fear the King of Anshan! King of Medes! King of—"

"I think all fear your danger hat, Cy." Sergeant Peterson smiled and nodded. "You did good."

The man shuffled back and, to anyone who would listen, he kept muttering. "It's not a danger hat, you know. This isn't a hat. It's a crown. It was only designated…"

As Cyrus faded into the crowd, Sergeant Peterson cleared the rest. "Appreciate the show of unity, everyone. We're done here for the night. Thank you."

The small army of spooks slowly shuffled away. They looked a little disappointed, as if they'd been spoiling for a fight and didn't get one.

I said, "Those your people?"

He shrugged. "They're just folks who were looking for something familiar and ended up here. I recognize some from when the zoo used to be my paycheck. But the others, they're just spirits who were lost, alone. And, I guess, didn't want to be that no more."

"I get that." I took a half step to follow his Zoo Crew. I might be marginally braver than most, but I had no plans of getting snapped up by those thugs again. Peterson, though, wasn't quite done with me.

He nodded, winced. "Just need to check, right? My job is security 'round here, so I need to, you know, secure."

"Understandable, man."

"Great." He flashed a smile. "So I'm all good with the enemy-of-my-enemy-is-my-friend and all that, but I just need to be clear on something." Sergeant Peterson gave me what I could only imagine was his cop stare. Maybe one he'd practiced in the mirror for a while. Wasn't too bad. "So why were the Unsettlers looking for you?"

That made me laugh a bit. "Unsettlers?"

The big man smiled. "Yeah, that's what we call the folks who settled in the Blind. Heard some call 'em Ghost Mob, but that's too much credit, right? Too cool of a name. They're a troubling kinda folk, so sure, we call them Unsettlers."

"I like it."

"Yeah, it's not bad. You ain't one of them, I suppose."

"No," I said. "But what they're doing there troubles me. You know anything about it?"

"The bright, shiny cord of light that stretches up to the sky?" I nodded. "Nah, don't know anything about that. Anyone who does, I reckon, is a part of that whole mess. Either some Unsettler or one of the poor souls plugged into it."

"Well, then you do know a little about it."

The security guard fixed me with a glare. "I didn't say that. But I do know those who poke around and get into somebody else's business are setting themselves up for hurt."

More and more spooks slipped away from us, back behind the barriers. In the distance, I heard the halfhearted roar of some big cat deep in the zoo. Like a lion or tiger. Who knows, maybe a puma? Foreign accents and roars weren't part of my expertise.

"Are there some of your people trapped up in that?"

He looked away. After a long moment, he nodded once.

"And you have no idea what that's all about?" I said then pushed a bit, despite my instincts encouraging me otherwise. "Not much of a protector of the people, then."

He leaned toward me, big towering guy, his face bent into a hard frown. Then a moment later, he softened. As if he remembered to count away anger or something.

"I ain't Superman or nothing, but I did help save you, right? If folks around here are looking for a bit of security, I'll do what I can. But if they go sticking their noses into other people's business, not much I can do about that."

Standing, I shuffled around for a moment and slapped my hands across my jeans, like you might when clearing them of dirt. Bits of movement to get a trickle of energy back after I'd taken blows from the Mob thugs. The Sergeant knew I was also just buying a bit of time, thinking.

He hit me with a small smile and shook his head.

"You know," I said, "people I don't even know, more often than not, end up laughing at me."

"You must be a hell of a comedian, then."

"I'm not trying to be funny."

He shrugged. "Shit just comes naturally to you, then. You got a gift, Painter."

That caught me off guard. I stiffened for a moment. "Wait, I didn't tell you my name."

"Your rep precedes you, little brother."

"Oh?"

"You doin' good, I'll say that. Had a cousin a while back that was wandering around these here parts. He wouldn't stick around the safety of the zoo, so I worried about him. Not a cat person, you see. Before he cleared, he told me some crazy sonofabitch stepped in and was helping him move on." His face went a bit soft. "You remember a dude named Martin? Martin Stipple?"

A bit ashamed, I looked down. "I'm sorry… maybe, I think?" My memory wasn't my biggest asset anymore. In truth, it really never had been. But at least now I had an excuse.

"Don't matter," Peterson said. "That just tells me that you helped so many folks by now that you can't even remember all their names."

I nodded, tried to say something, then just nodded again.

"Listen, you ever need a moment to turn your head off and hang out with some big cats, man, this is the place. And I don't mean, you know, cats as in some hip vernacular for other cool dudes. I mean we got big-ass cats all over here. Lions, tigers, all that shit. You're always welcome." He laughed at the absurdity of the offer, but I was grateful for the kindness. "But I'm thinking you got business to attend to. Especially when those Unsettlers are gunning for you."

"Yeah, not the best scenario."

"But if they've got a bull's-eye on you, you must be doing something right."

Again, I was wracked by shame, because the investigator had no idea why he'd been targeted. Had I crossed paths with one of their members previously? Maybe I cleared a girlfriend or boyfriend of theirs? Maybe it wasn't something I'd done but might do?

"Go or stay," the sergeant said. "Doesn't matter either way to me. But I will say we don't have enough folks in the InBetween trying to make things better, so… if you got something you gotta do, I won't keep you."

He was right.

My investigation into Hank's role in the death of Katie's stepdad was going to have to wait a little longer. The mailman would have stayed put, off the radar until I'd come back. Someone had hunted down Bernard and plugged him into the power station.

Other than me, only one person would have known where the mailman was hiding out. The Ringman.

Time to get back on the road. My answers would be in Chicago.

I crossed back over the state of Wisconsin, heading east. I took a winding route, but there was a lot of water along the way if you knew where to pivot and turn. Quick trickle recharge. And the slightly longer trip would give me some time to piece together what was going on in my hometown.

Since day one of being in the InBetween, I'd known about the Blind. Gary had been the first to tell me about it, giving me a rough idea of the area I needed to avoid with a caveat that it was growing in size. Spreading out.

Far as I could tell, the Ghost Mob was a big part of that.

As I skated closer toward Chicago, taking the Mississippi south, passing Midwest college towns like Winona and then heading deeper into Iowa, I drank in the bliss of flying down the waterway as if it were a sheet of crisp, clean ice.

I could still remember playing hockey as a kid and that feeling of pumping your teenage legs as hard as they'd go—the schwit-schwit-schwit sound as you cut across the ice—then sitting back on your heels at your top speed, feeling the breeze whip through your helmet and jersey. The thrill of it, plus the bite of your sweat freezing against your skin, would send a shiver through your body.

Skating down the big river elicited an echo of that feeling—the sweat was long gone, but the joy of rocketing faster than any human could run, even faster than some cars could go, was intoxicating.

Power, strength, and freedom that started as an electric tingle at your calves and by the time it hit your head, it was a full-on buzz.

I doglegged it directly east before reaching Davenport, Iowa. From a town named Clinton, it'd be a straight shot to Chicago.

Really moving, the world a blur, I turned my head slightly to the north. A few miles up, I had run into the mailman. He'd been waiting, hiding, and passing the time by peeking in windows. Now he was plugged into whatever was back at the fairgrounds.

Then I remembered the Mob leader Calkin had said something about an arrangement. Concentrating with some tricks I learned from the Amazing Kreskin, I pulled the words I'd heard in the Gass Station back to me. Whatever the mob and the livies were doing, there was some side thing with "the old man's kid." An arrangement to trade the energy of the power station for… something.

I put that aside for a moment. The other terrifying part of my fairgrounds visit was the news that ghosts and livies were working together. Whatever they were planning, as the Professor had put it, it would be very, very bad.

For both worlds.

From County Road 30, I hit Interstate 88 and would take that almost all the way to the Windy City.

That was where Brenda Matthews had been looking into the Ringman who was, what? an assassin for the Mob? That didn't seem quite right. Maybe the reporter had some answers. All I had were more questions.

Once back in the city, I headed straight for The Grind to talk with the bipolar bartender. I hoped I was catching him in a good mood.

"Handsome Dan!" I said, easing through the doors. The livie pub was closed for the night, with just the cleaning staff left to clean up after hundreds of drunk hipsters. The bartender looked up with a big smile on his face. Once he caught sight of me, however, it dimmed quickly.

"Well, hello there," he said, crossing his arms across his chest. "If it isn't Jimmy."

This guy.

I started in. "I was hoping—"

"And I was hoping you'd spin back 'round and head to another bar, Jimmy." Dan took a half step back on the other side of the thick, mahogany rail. It seemed the spook bar was closed, too. At least to me.

There were still a couple of spook drunks milling about. Some woman wearing several different coats at the far end of the bar, next to the wall. Two more standing near the pool tables, arguing in low voices about whose turn it was to pay for the next game.

But the place wasn't packed full of spooks, not hardly.

I asked, "Where's Lonnie?"

This observation, not surprisingly, did not win me any brownie points with Handsome Dan. The bartender looked down to an area in front of him, adjusted his white apron, and looked as though he was wiping a spot off the bar.

I stepped closer. "Where's our man with the perma-cigarette? Where's Lonnie, Dan?

The bartender didn't look up at me, just slid sideways, further down the bar. Not letting him off that easy, I turned to follow, and he spun back and exploded in a chaos of sound and rage and light.

"Get out of my bar!"

The lights flickered all around the tavern like a Las Vegas slot machine paying out the jackpot. One of the cleaning crew yelped, dropped the mop with a loud clack! and ran out the door. At the end of the walkway, he turned down the street and was gone.

Another older cleaner who was wiping down the tables didn't even look up. He sighed and mumbled to himself, "Malditos fantasmas…" Without missing a beat, he kept up his work, slowly shaking his head.

But back to the rage-fueled century-old dead bartender.

I learned early on you need friends—or at least not enemies—in the InBetween (see: Rule #1). No man is an island. Especially a ghost island. Sure, I could have pushed it, but a couple things were certain.

First, I wasn't getting anything out of Handsome Dan. He was shut down to me.

Which led to my second thought: he was angry at me for something. We hadn't parted on super-friendly terms, but this level of rage seemed disproportionate. Then I realized it: he wasn't angry. The guy was scared. Freaked out. Terrified.

Nothing I could say, at least for now, would change that. So I left.

Wandering Chicago aimlessly would be dangerous. If there were a Blind around, I'd waltz in and never know it. But I needed to find Brenda, wherever she was. Even just to prove to myself that she hadn't gotten caught up in that mess at the fairgrounds. But mainly because I knew she'd have something. She was a reporter.

One option was to roam through the city and wait for that pull. She was now familiar to me, so eventually, it should lead me to Brenda. But there was another option.

I needed some local intel. With that in mind, I headed a couple of blocks down and over toward a row of warehouses on the west side. It took me a moment to find it. Looking up and down the alley, I waited a few moments to be sure no one saw me go in.

I passed through the small graveyard of old cars, some surrounded by dark liquid stains as if they'd died here on the spot and vital fluids had leaked from the broken bodies and dried. My energy levels weren't ideal, but I had to spend a little if I were going to find help in a city unknown to me. I flipped the breaker on the wall. The old jukebox lit up, expectant. Waiting.

I headed over and pressed G then 7.

Bobby Darin began singing me his dark tune, so I wobbled over to the car Lonnie and Brenda had been sitting in. Using up that much juice, as low as I was, I needed to sit down. The old car would, at least, give me that.

By the third go-round of "Mack the Knife," my gamble paid off. I felt him before I heard him but waited until he made himself known.

"You know, that ain't like the Bat Signal, Painter," the man with half a face said, looking at me through the cracked windshield of the car.

"Clearly," I said to Lonnie. "Because you ain't Batman. Two-Face, maybe."

"Aw shit," Lonnie said and waved his ever-lit cigarette around as if he was wafting away the smoke. "You talk to me like that, and you want my help? You got a lotta nerve."

I shrugged weakly. "Look at me, man. Getting you here wiped me out," I said. "Hell, all I got left is nerve."

He looked at me hard for a moment, and I could tell he was making some decision up in his head. Pushing Handsome Dan had gotten me nowhere. I waited until he made his own mind up.

He did. "What do you want?"

"What do you know about that guy you were telling me about? The one in the bar all those years ago. The one who'd dragged some of your friends out."

"I told you what I know, Painter. Which ain't much."

Lonnie was leaning on the old Buick, his arm atop the hood of the car. He looked toward the wall then back at me. I'd say he seemed nervous, but with a guy with half his face blown off by a shotgun, it's hard to tell.

The song was in its second refrain, and I had a feeling that once Bobby stopped singing, Question Time was over.

"Why aren't you over at The Grind anymore? Thought you never left."

He shrugged. "I left to help you and the reporter, didn't I?"

"Sure. That mean you didn't go back?"

Another shrug. "I went back," he said and pulled on the dead cigarette between his fingers. "Then I left."

"Why?"

He looked toward the jukebox, frowned, then gazed back down at his hands. His expression told me he was thinking something through. Weighing options.

"A couple of guys came into Handsome Dan's bar. They were looking for you."

"Me? What'd you tell them?"

"I didn't know where you were, but I knew you'd come back looking for the reporter."

"So what, then?" I said, slowly running my hands across the front seat of the car in small circles, trying to generate a bit more energy. "You left after they left?"

"No," he said. "Not exactly."

At that moment, two spooks slipped through the wall, coming toward me. Exhausted as I was, I tried to stand, but a third had come up behind me and put a fist into my lower back and another into my brain.

Flat on the seat of the old car, I couldn't see his face. Just a stupid stovepipe hat. Another fist, this time to my face.

I crumpled to the floor.

Lonnie looked down on me, flicked his dead cig, and said, "Sorry, Paint. I really am."

Chapter Twenty-Two

When you're dead, at least in the InBetween, you never sleep, and you never get tired. A sort of mental or emotional exhaustion is ever present, but you soon learn to relegate that to the parliamentary backbench. Still, it's in the shadows waving its arms and blowing raspberries.

Here, the only time I'd ever sailed upon what you might describe as the gulf between conscious and unconscious was the few times I'd been clobbered really hard by some other spook. Usually, it's just an accident. Someone slams into you. It happens.

A few times, other ghosts had taken swipes at me. Usually, they were spooks with something wrong with their heads. But really, we were all a bit off kilter because we'd been killed by someone. That can fuck you up in the head.

But for the first time since I'd died, I felt like I was in Hell. Not flames and hot pokers and forced to grab cotton balls with freshly cut fingernails... but it was sensory overload. Painful, no question, but also the world around me was whipping past in streams of color. Ribbons of reds, yellows, and deep blues and blacks, racing past my eyes, and I wasn't even sure if they were opened or closed.

Then I tried to open my eyes. The echo of resignation hit me, informing me I'd already tried that and failed.

There were images in this psychedelic wash, brief flashes of people's faces that I felt I should recognize but couldn't place.

Old, young, male, female. All of them in agony.

Every now and then, one would launch straight for me, I'd tense—or feel like I had—and then it would pass through. But it wasn't like a real face. No lingering images of skin, tissue, veins, or bones. Just a terrible rush of emotions that weren't mine—all of them at once. Then waiting, bracing for the next wave.

Massive, horrifying snakes were writhing just above me, their fangs locked deep into the flesh of my back, but instead of squirting their venom into me, they were sucking deep from my body, draining my breath, my will, my energy.

Then these serpents would lift off briefly, leaving a painfully cool ache in the dried-out cavities they'd left behind, raw nerve endings so overstimulated the air actually hurt.

Slowly, I felt some strength return to my hands and thighs, and I realized that I was hunched over and on all fours. As I felt the distant rumors of feeling return to my body, I sighed heavily. This I'd felt before. This was all I felt. My only memory now. Over and over again.

With the hints of strength returning to me, I willed my dropped head to turn to the left or right. It wouldn't budge, far too weak. So I rolled my eyes to one side, to my right it seemed, trying to see if I could catch sight of anything nearby.

The strain the muscles in my eyes hurt as if I was doing some sort of damage, but I had to see.

For only a moment, I caught the sight of an animal next to me.

No, not an animal.

It was another person, on all fours, prostrated as if fiercely praying to some insatiable god who'd granted us an audience.

The teeth of whatever had latched onto me returned, the mad rush of colors again filled my vision, and once again I lost sight of anything around me. It drained my strength, replacing it with pain, and I couldn't be sure if I was falling or floating. The harsh, shapeless images melted into faces, full of lines and contours, then each would slowly flatten and gray out as it was replaced by another.

The dark yellows, oranges, and reds that punished my mind slid toward the blues, and I saw faces again, pulling through me or over me, it wasn't clear. My insides were sucked out by some creature as if I were a tiny snack.

Then my mind drifted, drifted, drifted, and the world came back to me—this would be only brief clarity, I knew that now—and with my face to the floor, I saw the spill of brilliant white between my hands and knees.

And for the first time in as long as I could remember, I was terrified.

Death makes an unspoken promise to all creatures: I have taken everything so you shall fear nothing. But as it's our nature, humans had found a way to distort the purity of that contract.

Were the rest of my days going to be like this? Was I trapped? Had I always been?

The mind snakes struck again, biting deep into my shoulders, and I felt the muscles that knit my flanks together rip and split apart.

Above me, then, a new face.

This one was far more clear than others. I recognized it but couldn't recall who it belonged to. I squeezed my eyes shut, waiting for its impact. Wracked with pain, I couldn't wish for death, because of course, I was already dead.

The face said to me, "Painter, I'm getting you out of here."

And all went dark again.

Chapter Twenty-Three

My mind slowly drifted back to me, and I felt a hangover come on like I'd never had when alive. And trust me, collectively, I'd had years of them. But none felt like my brains had been stomped upon by a jealous elephant, forced through a rusty kitchen meat grinder, then eaten by a yippy lap dog and shat out the other end.

"How are you feeling?" the reporter asked, her mascara-stained faced hovering over me.

"I'm fine."

"You don't look fine," she said, scowling. "You look worse than dead."

"What—" I said and tried to sit up. Then, realizing that was a horrible idea, I inched back down. "What does worse than dead look like?"

She lifted my arm up and dropped it. Brenda was sitting next to me on the cement floor of what looked like a parking garage. Again, she raised my arm and released it. I looked down without moving my head and saw she was letting it fall onto her leg.

Fast learner.

I felt rivulets of energy seep back into my body, took a deep shuddering breath, then felt as though I'd actually exhaled for the first time in my life.

The emotions of the experience in the power station were still fresh, raw, in my mind. I could feel a swell in my throat. I felt like weeping and was glad there just wasn't the strength for that.

I said all I could at that moment. "Thank you."

"Not a problem," she said and stood, yanking me up to my feet. "You feeling a bit more… uh, normal?"

Nodding, I looked around at the parking garage and saw that we must have been a few levels underground. Seemed like a good place to lie low for a few minutes.

I said to her, "So you're still here."

"I noticed that."

"I thought maybe Julius might have inadvertently uploaded your details by now. You and the mailman."

She spread her arms out wide and actually gave me a small smile. "Still here."

"So, Bernard?" I said, choking on a sob. "I saw him trapped in that thing you pulled me out of."

"He's here?" she said, a little distressed.

"And how'd you do that, by the way?" I said. "How'd you know how to find me?"

Brenda turned in small circles, generating a bit of energy, recouping a small part of what she'd given to me.

She said, "It was a mistake, actually. I'd been tracking the Ringman, Jan Jorgensen, you know, like the way you said. The pull, right? And Lonnie and I must have crisscrossed paths, because next thing I know, I'm looking at him."

"Yeah." I nodded slowly, having had the same experience myself. "That used to drive me a bit nuts early on. But after a while, you do start picking up differences. Almost like a cologne or perfume. Everybody has a different, I dunno, scent. Takes a while to get down."

"Right. Well, I was going to break off but saw Lonnie talking with some spooks, and they didn't look like pals. Real aggressive, threatening. Then I heard your name. A few hours later, I'm dragging you out of that crazy monstrosity. What is that? It looked like you and the rest of them were being tortured or something."

"I don't really know yet."

Brenda looked at me and began nibbling on a fingernail. She said, "Followed Jorgensen for quite a while. Tailed him."

"You gunning for my job?"

She grinned at me. "Why would I want a demotion?"

"Harsh."

"Painter, I saw Jorgensen talking to those same guys who'd strong-armed Lonnie. He was talking to ghosts. "

"The living talking to the dead."

She nodded again. "Don't ask me."

Then I realized something that didn't make sense. "Wait, you followed Lonnie? He came all the way back here to St. Paul?"

"What? No," she said. "Here? Do you think you're back in Minnesota? You came to Chicago, Painter. Don't you remember?"

"Yeah, but…"

Feeling, uh, swizzy, I sat back down as another puzzle piece clicked into place. The power station at the fairgrounds wasn't one of a kind. There were two of them. And despite their efficacy as torture devices, those setups weren't about punishing spooks the Ghost Mob didn't like.

But what were they for?

I wondered how long it would take for them to notice the missing ghost in the machine. Or if they'd realize I was gone at all. Obviously, that attack, when I'd been with Mags in the car, would have ended with me in the fairgrounds power station.

Those spooks wanted me out of the picture, and so did their leader Calkin. It was time to be the threat to them they were making me out to be.

At that moment, feeling limp and fried, spinning slowly on the floor of a subterranean parking garage on 17th Street in West Chicago, I didn't feel much like anyone's arch-nemesis, a king slayer. More like a scaly, bloated fish in the king's putrid moat, blub blub blubbing, wading in circles waiting for his eminence to return and toss me a bread crust or a chicken bone—

"What are you doing?" Brenda asked, staring down at me doing slow circles on the concrete. "Why are you blubbing?"

"Uh, I didn't realize I was. It's a type of, you know, meditation. East Asia thing."

"Right. I don't think it is. But whatever floats your ghost boat."

I got back to my feet, wobbly, catching Brenda's face. Her mascara didn't look as dark as before. She was starting to settle in, her own perception peeking through. She was doing really well. Even joking, like the ghost boat thing. But I should have helped her clear by now. Who knows? Maybe she didn't want that anymore.

The reporter must have seen the look on my face. "What?"

"You're doing okay. Adjusting. More than adjusting, you're precariously close to knocking me off my 'best dead private detective' throne.

That made her smile. She looked away for a moment then back.

"Paint, you were right. This world here—" she said, looking around the crumbling concrete structure "—isn't home. It's like a photocopy of a photocopy of it."

I nodded and said, "Colors ain't quite right."

"Yeah, but more than that," she said. "It's just not right for me. But thanks to you, I've got something I didn't think possible."

"What's that?"

She smiled. "A second chance. I'm going to write one last story. The big one I never got to write. It's my story. And that of all of those whose lives were stolen by the Ringman."

Like me, I thought. For a brief moment, I considered telling her. When I caught her face, she was looking at me strangely. Quickly, I changed gears.

"That's a once-in-a-lifetime story, Brenda. And you save yourself at the same time. You save all those people," I said and felt my voice hitch. "That's brilliant. Maybe that's what this place is for after all. The InBetween, a second-chance store. I just haven't worked out my place yet."

The reporter leaned in and kissed me on the cheek. "But you have! If you hadn't bumped into me—sure could have been a better intro, but I'll give you a pass on that one—hell, I could have ended up in one of those glowy things. I would have. Like the mailman. Instead, here I am. You did that. You do that."

"We need to help Bernard. I said I'd take care of him."

"You can only do what you can do, Paint," she said, and we started moving toward the stairs. "I've got my big story, then for me, it's on to the next adventure. Now you know who killed you, you can go too."

She'd worked it out. All from a look on my face.

Smiling, I could only think about how the world had lost so much when she'd died. She would have been a great reporter. As we headed into the street, she confessed to me that she'd done what we all do in the InBetween.

After I'd left for the Cities, she'd pushed pause on her hunt for the truth and gone looking for her family. She spent some time in the basement of her parents' home, just outside of Chicago, in a city called Rockford. It made her feel safe, but she knew she couldn't spend her days hiding and lurking.

"In part because, you know, it's my folks," she said, rubbing her eyes. "It's kind of comforting to be around them, but it's still an intrusion, right?"

"Sure," I said. I knew exactly what she was talking about.

She seemed to sense that. "I mean, when we don't think anyone else is around, we're not really at our best, sometimes."

It always seems like an almost romantic, loving gesture to haunt the people we'd once cared about, but when folks are alone, there's a lot of nose-picking, farting, and far more personal bits that are private and should stay that way.

Nobody's a saint. Maybe your mother spies on the neighbors through the sheers or your father drinks a little before work. At work. Then on the drive home. Or that loving aunt you knew, maybe she likes Czech exercise sites where nobody grooms themselves terribly well, ugh, and then they slather all that pudding, with the licking—what's the point of working out, then?—all that stuff gets caught up into the hair and…

Just examples, mind you. Totally made up. Could be anything.

After her parents' house, she got back on the trail and made progress.

"It's not easy," she said.

I shrugged. "Tell me about it."

"There's really no way for me to find out about Jan Jorgensen, you know, google him or anything."

"Not directly, no. I have my Temps do some of that, but it's hit and miss."

Brenda told me how after she'd found the Ringman again, she pretended to sit down at tables and chat with people. A group of two or three suddenly became a group of three or four. If Jorgensen happened to look around, she was there smiling and laughing along with her "friends," who had no idea she was even there. Neither did he.

"Damn. That's smart. I need to take lessons from you."

"I was a reporter for a little while," she said, then her eyes cut to the door on the bottom floor of the parking garage. We stepped out into dawn's dull sunlight. "I would have been good, Painter."

"I know," I said and was quiet for a moment.

A woman pushed a stroller past us. Next to her, a man walked as he carried a toddler who wasn't yet ready to face the day, still zonked out. Brenda gripped her elbows with opposite hands as if she was cold or rocking a very smelly baby. This was some sort of habit or tic left over from when she'd been alive.

"So remember the young guy in the nice suit from the bar? The debate dude. Looks like Jorgensen is targeting a congressman," the reporter said. "Just like he'd gone after the mailman and me and who knows how many others."

"But why not pick someone less, you know, visible? The guy was surrounded by people and probably always is. There's gotta be much easier targets."

"Why's he killing at all?"

"Dunno, but those power stations have something to do with it."

Brenda raised her arms above her head and brought them down again. Her thinking process was more aerobic than most. "Congressman's name is Stephen Lee. You ever heard of the guy?"

"No," I said. "But I bet they know him at the state capitol building."

"If we can find anyone to talk to us."

"Chicago politics?" I said, smiling. "I'd be surprised if there's any room for the livies in the building."

Of course, Chicago isn't the capital of Illinois, so the capitol building ain't in the city limits. Still, a lot of legislators live in the Chicago area and make the daily hop by plane.

Brenda told me there was a canal system leading out of Chicago to the southwest, and we followed that until it merged with the Des Plaines River in Fairmount, then grabbed the Illinois River near a town called Millsdale.

"I lived just west of here," the reporter told me as she directed me along the Illinois waterways. "Little town called Channahon. Very heartland. Very Lee Greenwood, you know?"

"Sounds nice," I said, skating the river as she gripped the back of my sweatshirt, riding along.

"Hated it."

Near Browning, we crossed a beautiful group of lakes, whizzing past early-morning boaters, who, after grabbing the early bird's worm before it could wriggle away, slapped it on a hook and went after panfish. Crappies, sunfish, bluegill.

There were trout and smallmouth bass, Brenda told me, but it was more fun to catch the panfish.

"Limit's much higher for the little guys, so you can spend most of the day reeling them in if you catch a good spot."

From there, we banked east again, along the Sangamon River, then to a little tributary called Salt Creek. From there we grabbed Interstate 55, heading south into Springfield, the state capital. That was just thirty miles farther than the hundreds we'd taken up to that point, but over blacktop, it was nearly the longest part of our journey.

When we eventually got to the capitol building, it was just before opening time, but there were already plenty of bees buzzing around the hive. The building towered above the rest of the city nearby. Far less squat than its big brother in DC, it was still impressive. Unlike most capitol buildings I could remember, its dome was not gold colored.

It was silver.

"Zinc," the reporter said with a broad smile, bending the now-faint mascara marks trailing down her face. "Keeps it from going green or anything."

"Odd, though, huh?" The sun sparkled off the ribs holding up an impressive spire. "Silver. Like, not quite gold. Second place. So sad."

"Not sad for the maintenance men who don't have to climb up there and brush it clean every spring."

"And it takes away jobs from the working man, too?" I said and tsked. "Empty promises. Sigh." Yes, I actually said the word "sigh."

"Painter," Brenda said. "Don't be dumb."

"Why? I'm good at it."

We passed up the capitol steps as maintenance workers brushed leaves and branches from cement. There'd been a storm the night before.

Brenda had interned at a Springfield television station for a year and a half as a lifestyle reporter, but when one of the political editors had had a baby, she'd filled in.

"At first, it was shaping up to be the worst six months of my career."

"Why's that?"

"I thought politics would be dry, dull, and boring. But it's a soap opera. Sex, drugs, betrayal. The whole 'power corrupts' thing, I suppose. Sure, there are good people. And some just look like good people."

"I've seen that."

"You know, Lincoln said 'If you want to test a man's character, give him power'," she said. "Problem with that though is by the time you work out they shouldn't have power, they've already got it."

We slipped passed a pair of statues, two bronze maidens spending eternity holding up a single light fixture, and climbed the stairs to the second floor. At the top of the staircase was one of the largest paintings I'd ever seen.

Brenda told me the mural, forty feet tall, depicted a man named George Rogers Clark horse-trading with Native Americans. The reporter said the painting bubbled up as off-and-on controversial. Something to do with how the Indians were dressed made some folks angry. Probably Native American campaigners, not fashionistas.

We found a clerk's office and slipped inside.

It wasn't yet open to the public, but there were already half a dozen workers inside, busying themselves with morning rituals as they had likely done for years.

Another came around the corner, gliding across the floor more smoothly than the others.

"Hello?" Brenda said, but none looked up. She repeated her call, then the new woman glared at us. She held up a finger and shushed us.

I mumbled, "Whatever, dead lady clerk person," which earned me a second shushing.

Brenda turned toward me, eyes big, eyebrows raised. She said quietly, "You catch more flies with honey, Paint."

I said, "Who wants flies?" but then smiled wide and offered it to the dead lady clerk person. She ignored me.

On the counter was a sign that read "Ring for Service." With a big smile, she swiped down on the bell next to it and said, "Ding!"

The dead lady clerk person was making the motions as if she were filing, right next to another woman who was actually filing. The live clerk finished what she was doing, the drawer slammed closed, and the ghost moved on as if that was what she'd planned all along.

I wondered how long she'd been in there.

"Ding, ding!"

The room was large, made smaller by hulking file cabinets and boxes of paper. In the center of the room was a workstation with two printer/copiers and, unbelievably, a fax machine. Every desk had a computer with two or even three monitors.

"Ding!"

Dutifully ignoring Brenda, the ghost clerk turned toward a newly opened file cabinet, and that's when I saw that her neck had been sliced open and gore spilled down a ruffled top, pleats at the neckline stained black and draped in faded pink chiffon.

"Ding, ding, ding!"

Brenda's honey needed a bit of vinegar, so I pushed some juice into a fingertip, gave it just a bit of grain, and smacked the bell.

DING!

That got all the ladies' attention, several of them gasping and cursing, shocked by the bell that had dinged all by itself.

The ghost clerk fixed the two of us with a glare and glided toward us. I pointed at Brenda, spun on a heel, and slid over to an incredibly exciting set of photos on the back wall that showed old buildings or something.

There was a quick, fevered exchange of words between the two women, and I glided back when the voices came down near the floor level again.

"—don't have the first idea why I should," the dead file clerk lady ghost was saying. "You two coming in here creating a ruckus."

"I don't recall a ruckus, ma'am," I said and then pointed at Brenda. "Is this pretty young lady bothering you?"

Now I had two women glaring at me. Disapproval in stereo.

However, now that they were effectively on the same side for a moment, the dead lady ghost clerk worker capitulated. Slightly.

"We're terribly busy today, I'm sorry—"

Brenda stepped in. "We don't need anything serious. Just wondering if you could tell me about a lawmaker who used to work here."

"Oh?"

"He's now a DC boy but splits his time in Chicago."

"Right," she said and squinted in thought. "You mean the colored fella that made it all the way to the White House?"

Colored fella? How long had this woman been dead?

Brenda shook her head, looking as if she'd swallowed a bug.

Intrigued that our query involved a player inside the Beltway, she fixed us both with a conspiratorial look, her mouth a fine line, and then made the motion of lifting a hinged portion of the wood laminate counter. She looked over her shoulder and was waving us into the clerk's office inner sanctum.

I glided through, and once Brenda had followed, she theatrically reached over to "grab" the countertop, making a motion as if she were returning it to its rightful place. This earned a delighted smile from the ghost dead clerk lady person, Mrs. Ulesich. She spelled it, then pronounced it again, in three syllables.

"You-leh-sitch," she said, as if somehow we were writing it down somewhere.

We headed to the back, following her lead as we unnecessarily wove in a serpentine pattern around tables, around desks, around filing cabinets, and around livie clerks.

When we got to one of two offices on the back wall, she reached out as if she were grabbing the knob and "pushed" the door wide. We both stared at the closed door, muttered a thank you each, and headed into the small anteroom.

Inside, the oldest living human on the planet was stationed at a gray, dented metal desk sitting on the oldest stool ever invented. I was pretty sure that if we'd flipped over his wooden chair, with its threadbare and faded red cushion, it would have been signed by Benjamin Franklin.

The old man looked half asleep, arms crossed tight to his chest as he stared at the computer screen in front of him. The text had been made so large that only a couple dozen words could fit on the screen at any given time.

Glasses perched on the end of his nose had carved a dent in the skin above both nostrils. He stripped them off briefly, rubbed the bags above and below his eyes, then returned the spectacles to his face, a bit too high on the bridge of his nose, and they slid down, locking back into place near the tip, like tongue-and-groove flooring.

We collected behind the old guy at the computer, and she hovered her hands over the livie's shoulders. She whispered, "This is Albert. He's been in this office his whole life, but despite his age, he's a wiz on the 'Net."

Puh-leeze. The 'Net?

Then Mrs. Ulesich leaned down toward Albert and hummed sweetly. Brenda and I traded glances.

"Albert? Albert?" she cooed softly. The woman had to be in her eighties or nearly there. "Hey, big boy, you working today, are ya? There, yeah, that's my boy."

It was unequivocally the most disturbingly sexual moment I'd witnessed in a long time. And even worse, I was somehow a part of it.

Albert leaned forward, concentrated on a collection of words on the page, and made a notation in a leatherbound book on his desk.

He murmured, "Hmm… working."

"Yes, yes," the old clerk cooed. "You are a working man, aren't you?"

Brenda smacked her lips and gave me a sideways look.

The old man hummed slightly to himself, whispering, "Working, working. Working man."

"Mommy needs a favor, now, would you do me a big, fat favor? Hmm?" Mrs. Ulesich knelt down next to the old man, who looked oblivious to her octogenarian wiles. "Can the big working man do a needy girl a favor?" She made a motion of stroking his bony thigh through his brown polyester pants. Her fingers paused at the sharp peak in his slacks, where he'd ironed a perfect crease. Her fingers wandered up and down and across the ridge.

"Mommy wants to know about a naughty boy named Stephen." She fixed her big doe eyes on the man, a smile that was borderline obscene. "Stephen Lee. Congressman Stephen Lee, who's a dirty boy in Washington now. Stephen Lee is a naughty, dirty, boy. Like Albert is, dirty, naughty—"

Brenda faltered, appearing slightly dizzy, and I reached out to steady her. She looked toward me, about to speak, but I put a finger up to my lips. I may have put it there less to keep her quiet and more to prevent ghost barfing on her.

"Lee, hmm… Congressman… Congressman Stephen Lee." The old man, despite himself and not fully aware of the three dead people surrounding him, put the lawmaker's name into the search field and pulled up the Congressional Record.

Brenda and I read over his shoulder as Mrs. Ulesich continued to pass her hand through the old fella's pant leg. Every time she gave it the slightest stroke, he'd move down the page.

Congressman Stephen Lee had been a Republican representative of an area called the Western Springs district. He'd been elected four years earlier, and despite being one of the younger members of the Illinois state legislature and still in his twenties, he now was a representative at the federal level. He was the youngest of the eighteen members of Congress representing the state.

Despite being a member of the minority party, he had been described as a popular legislator, liked by reps on both sides of the aisle. Earned a law degree from Northwestern. Two years at Harvard but dropped out before completion when the previous representative in Western Springs, a Democrat, had announced her retirement.

Lee had run against a Democrat who'd been supported by big party dollars to retain the seat but, in the end, won over even bluest parts of the district. He made promises of fiscal prudence and smaller government yet also championed more liberal social policies that, in more conservative parts of the country, would have planted him in a seat firmly on the opposite side of the aisle.

Brenda and I read through the record, seeing nothing that appeared to stand out. He served as a minority member of the House's Conservation and Forestry subcommittee.

There was a small slide show of pictures showing the young congressman shaking hands with lawmakers from both parties. Even one with the president in front of the Congressional seal, which looked like the sort they all might get that first day in office.

Lee was a good-looking man. His surname and appearance led me to believe that his ancestry was likely Chinese. I'm sure that couldn't have hurt in a party known for a moderately less platonic relationship with big business, now that China had begun snapping up troubled companies—and some not so troubled—across the United States.

The cooing and stroking continued for about fifteen minutes until we got to the end of the record. Jorgensen wouldn't be targeting the high-profile politician just for his Harvard ring. We'd missed something in the bio. Or it just wasn't here.

Mrs. Ulesich spent another half minute praising Albert, thanking him, whispering to him in a tone that made both of us feel as if she'd forgotten we were there.

She gave us the nod, and we headed to the door. Despite both of us looking to clear out of there quickly, Brenda had the presence of mind to stop and mime that she'd opened the door. I followed her.

A moment later, the old lady clerk followed us. She exhaled a deep breath, and it appeared as though the spill of blood beneath her neck had turned a shade redder. She fanned her face slightly.

"Such a tiny little office," she said. "I don't know how the man stands it."

"Thank you for the help, Mrs. Ulesich," I said. "We appreciate what you, you know, did."

With a wan smile, she shrugged. "All part of the job."

I raised my eyebrows at Brenda, and we both headed to the counter, retracing our earlier path. Then, as the reporter reached out to "lift" the hinged piece, the old clerk called out.

"Wait a moment, I think I do remember the young man," Mrs. Ulesich called to us from in front of the door of Albert's office. The living clerks around us went about their business, one heading to the front of the room with a large, jangling set of keys.

"Anything you can think of would help," I said.

"I don't think it will. I'm sorry," she said, straightening out her dull, wool skirt with wide palms as if drying them. "But I remember the ladies talking about some young Congressman who'd lost a loved one. I only remember now because I recall he'd been a Chinaman. "

Yep.

"Okay," Brenda said, perking up. "Family member?"

"I can't recall." Mrs. Ulesich fanned the air. "They'd died in prison. Devastated the young man."

I asked "The young Chinaman?" and earned a punch in the arm from my friend.

"That's right. He nearly dropped out of his campaign but then championed more robust prisoners' rights or safety or something useless like that."

The first customers of the day began streaming through the door, bleary-eyed, each holding folders and stacks of papers clutched in tight fists or to their chests. Weary faces held stories of long, hard battles filled with both joy and loss, their eyes the only hint at which way the scales were now tilting.

After we passed through the counter, I turned back to wave goodbye, but she was again heading back to the far office—for more tawdry naughty talk, I guessed.

"Blechy," I said.

Then, as she disappeared, I caught the faded nameplate on the door and felt a little heat rise to my cheeks.

It read, Research, Albert Ulesich.

Chapter Twenty-Four

Heading back north, I picked up Interstate 72 west, then skated the Mississippi to get us to Minneapolis. Time to check back with Julius.

I'd been tempted to head back to the fairgrounds to try to help the mailman. With Brenda, we might have a better shot, and it didn't seem that those trapped in the power station had been guarded terribly well. Why would they be? Nobody was escaping that place under their own steam.

But first we needed to learn more about what was going on. Hopefully, the Ghost Mob had forgotten all about me, thinking I was out of the picture. For now, they wouldn't be hunting me. Why they had in the first place I still didn't know.

Back at the Shady Hills rest home, it was easy enough to find Julius. Each time I'd seen the guy back when I was working with Harry and Mags, he'd been in the canteen. Initially, it seemed like this had been a coincidence. But really, the guy was just always eating.

You can't constantly graze at the home; they have set eating times. But given the infirmity of their residents, those "set" times are open to a certain amount of personal interpretation.

We'd found Julius chatting up a young woman who looked like she might be a high schooler making an extra couple bucks to buy more posters for her bedroom wall. She turned out to be a doctor in residency, so what do I know?

I told Julius I was standing nearby, and he only betrayed the slightest of hesitations, catching himself before he turned to answer. At the door, he tried convincing one of the cafeteria ladies that he would return the plate, despite her insistence he transfer his half-eaten pecan pie onto a paper one that could be disposed of in the rooms.

"I don't like chasing after all y'all's dishes," she said, looking down suspiciously at the pie in the old man's arthritis-cragged hands. "You hide 'em too good for me. It's like going on an Easter egg hunt in your rooms, except insteada finding pastel-dyed hardboiled eggs and jelly beans, I come up with a gravy-caked saucer under the bed."

Jules gave her a perfect smile, brilliant rows of white teeth underlying a warm, dark face. "Don't like eating off paper. They used to give us paper plates after they first let us sit at the counters in all the white restaurants. That way they could throw them away when we were done. But I suppose—"

"No, no, I'm sorry. It's fine," the woman said and suddenly headed for something very pressing on the other side of the room. "Please, I'm sorry, take the plate. I'll come by later. It's my pleasure."

Shuffling down the hall, nibbling on his pie, he whispered with a smile, "I never was made to eat off a paper plate, mind you." He took a bigger bite then added, "But that was a thing back then."

Once we got back to the room, Julius was all business, which I appreciated. I didn't have much time to waste. Then I reflected on that thought, a bit embarrassed: neither did Julius, actually.

"I got those names you gave me, but I haven't published the entry," he said, swinging a laptop on a plastic tray around. The bottom of the tray was attached to an elbowed metal bar, which stemmed from the frame of his hospital bed. "Just like Margaret showed me. You want me to fire it off now?"

"No!"

Julius jumped. It was the first time he'd heard Brenda's voice.

He brought up the draft Wikipedia entries for both the reporter and the mailman, and I read through them. Two brief passages. One detailed that the reporter had been killed leaving her gym in a Chicago high-rise, the other that Bernard Grimsby had had a railroad spike jammed into his eye while on his mail route on the outskirts of Madison, Wisconsin. Both listed their killer: Jan Jorgensen.

One already had been flagged with a super-editor's notation asking for reference and clarification of fact. It would likely get yanked down soon after publishing, but it would be enough to clear them both.

"So is your pretty reporter friend here now, then?

"Aw, did he say I was pretty?"

The smile on Julius's face grew. I got the feeling he had been a bit of a ladies' man some years ago. "Ah, no, darlin', I can tell by the sound of your voice. You sound lovely."

"If you weren't dead, I probably would have asked you to take a nice carriage ride with me in the park or something."

I asked, "Is that some euphemism, Julius? The ol' 'carriage ride in the park'? Is that like 'watching the submarine races' or something?"

Julius said, "Nah, me, I'm a gentleman."

"You could have always taken her to a movie."

"The pictures is a terrible date unless you don't know how to talk to a pretty woman," he said, tapping at the keyboard with two index fingers. "I am not afflicted with that particular malady."

I had Julius do a quick google for the Ringman.

There were nearly seven hundred thousand entries for Jan Jorgensen. The top one was a professional badminton player from Denmark.

"Badminton," Julius said, the words crunching in his throat. He thumped a fat finger onto the screen as if he were casually smashing a tiny bug. "I never trusted no man who swishes around a dainty racket like that."

I said, "I think we're getting off track."

"You know what they call that little birdie they got?"

"Yes, I don't—"

"Shuttlecock," Julius said with an emphasis on the last syllable. "Man looks like he's swinging a tiny little fishing net trying to scoop him up some shuttlecock."

"And to think of all the time I wasted with a pushup bra and six-inch pumps," Brenda said casually, then pivoted back. "Maybe he's not any of these guys. Maybe he's just, you know, some dude who flipped out. On a killing spree. I suppose that happens."

"Except he saw me," I said, shaking my head. "He can't. Livies can't see us."

Julius looked up. "I can see you."

"Then why are you looking in the wrong direction?"

He paused. Then, enunciating each word, he said, "I am contemplating my own mortality."

"There have been stories for years of people seeing ghosts," Brenda said. "Maybe some can."

I thought of little Katie, but in all this time, she'd been the only one. "Doubt it. And he'd grabbed me, remember. That's not possible. Livies and spooks don't share a physical plane. That's one of the first things the Professor told me."

"The who?"

I waved my hand in front of my face, trying to focus. "It... she, she's this person up on a mountain. Knows more about this InBetween than anybody."

"On a mountain? I'd like to meet her."

"You know, that may not be a bad idea," I said. "Last time I saw her, she was going to go look into something. She should be back by now." I shook my head. "Nah, not yet. I've got some business here. I promised I'd look into someone's case, and I haven't really held up my end of the deal."

Julius spun and looked into the space between us. "Margaret said you were investigating the death of her son-in-law, Boyd. For little Katie."

"That's the one. I'm looking into Hank, the girl's biological father. He was the first husband."

"You think he had something to do with it?"

"Apparently, he was no fan of Daddy Number Two," I said. "Blamed the guy for the breakup of their marriage."

Julius dropped his voice low. "You know that boy died from drugs? Overdose, they said."

"What? Boyd?" I said. "I thought he'd been shot during a robbery. Like the thieves caught him at home or something."

"Nah. He got shot, all right, but that wasn't what killed him," Julius said and pointed to the computer. "I read about it in the paper because Mags didn't like to talk about it. He OD'd. Then he was shot afterward. By Hank."

"What?"

"That doesn't make any sense," Brenda said. "Who shoots someone already dead?"

Julius pulled at his bottom lip with his fingers. "Somebody who was really, really angry at a fella, I guess. It also didn't help that same somebody was really, really drunk, too."

"But Hank was cleared of the crime, right?"

Jules nodded and tapped away on his keyboard again then pointed at the image of a medical examiner's illustration marked with six Xs. It seemed someone had posted some of the evidence files on a crime website.

"See the holes Hank put into Boyd there? They didn't even bleed 'causin' the heart wasn't pumpin' anymore. No blood, no crime."

I looked at the screen. "Who shoots a dead guy?"

Katie's father had been accused, jailed, and eventually cleared of her stepdad's death. According to what Julius pulled up on his laptop, the police didn't have anyone else on their radar, so without any other target, Hank took the full brunt of all that anger and grief.

Julius agreed to meet us at his home so he could do the questioning. I wasn't up for riding in a car again, not just because I had gotten attacked the time before, but my energy levels were just barely normalizing. I would have to hold onto the car and Brenda, who didn't yet have the skill to interact with the livie world. Not worth it.

Brenda and I slipped through the dark streets of the Blind in broad daylight. This would work in our favor, since it would be harder for us to be spotted by errant spooks.

Once we hit Snelling, we did a broad sweep that took us within a few blocks of the Fairgrounds. I had it in my head that we might try to sneak into the Gass Station and yank Bernie the mailman out of the power plant, but when we got close enough, it was evident that the Ghost Mob had posted sentries on the streets leading to the area.

Those guarding the perimeter streets often parked themselves in the alcoves of buildings or darkened recesses of homes. This only made them easier to see. In the end, I realized that may have been the point. Better to warn someone off a fight than risk a battle you might lose.

We'd arrived at Hank's rundown one-bedroom home and saw a Saturn coupe, faded silver with bald tires. Obviously, it had been years since a new Saturn had rolled off the line, and this one looked like it had been sold—and resold—in the years before that happened.

I had always been a fan of the cars because they looked a bit like what I'd imagine a slick, small spaceship might. That is, if a slick, small spaceship also had been equipped with a suicide door.

Brenda and I circled the car briefly. Not seeing anything of note inside but a collection of empty fast food wrappers in the back seat, we quickly headed up the stairs and ducked inside. That, it turned out, was a horrible mistake.

Not because it posed any danger to us. That is, no physical danger.

Hank and, I could only assume, his girlfriend were engaged in marital relations on the couch. Well, not marital relations. For one, as far as I knew, they weren't married. For two, uh, as far as I remembered, women didn't let you put it where he was putting it after you got married.

We quickly stepped back outside.

Brenda squinted and pressed both palms to her ears. "I can never unsee that." She sat cross-legged on the sidewalk. "Those two could lay off the beer and Cheetos a little. Maybe do a few sit-ups."

"Ha, what a snob!"

"No, I'm not," the reporter protested, then added, "I just—what the fuck is that?!?"

My head was deep in the Saturn's glove compartment, but it was too dark inside to get a good look at anything. I'd been considering opening it up to hopefully catch a glimpse of some ownership papers.

Brenda's outburst had me upright quickly, legs in a fighting stance, arms up, ready to cover my head if I saw anything scary.

I did. Then I said, "Hi, Gary."

"Hiya, Painter," the massive, hulking spook monster said as he trotted merrily down the street. Today, he was a purple bulk with a half dozen eyes. Naturally, he had included obligatory claws, spikes, and horns. However, a daisy poked out of the top of his head.

Gary eyeballed me. Which, given the number of eyes he had, was a little unnerving.

I said, "I like the flower."

"Yeah? Does that make it freakier?"

"Not really, but it's retro," I said. "Like a Bugs Bunny monster or something."

Gary smiled, his teeth flashing, and he snapped the fingers on two or three of his hands. He said, "Right! That's it. I was wondering where I'd seen it before." He then got a glimpse of the reporter, who'd now backed up to the front door of Hank's place.

Despite the horrific, ghoulish creature in front of her, she still didn't want to go back inside where the unnatural acts were likely ongoing.

From Gary's largest mouth, he rolled out a tongue, licked the hand of an arm roped with muscles, then pulled his fingers across his head as if to straighten out his hair, which, as noted, was just a flower.

Three petals tumbled to the ground.

"Ain't you gonna introduce me to your hot sister?"

"She's not my sister."

"Your hot aunt!"

That got her back in the game. "Hey, how old do you think I am, asshole?"

Gary the Monster's face caved, and his eyes (all of them) stared at the pavement. He's a sensitive type of guy for an utterly terrifying vision. He gave us a half wave and spun around in the other direction, loping away and dragging a tail I hadn't seen previously.

"Hey, Gar', the tail's a nice touch."

He looked back at me, and I caught the tiniest hint of a smile. At least I think I did. He said, "Thanks, man," and crept away.

Brenda watched, both horrified and a bit crestfallen.

"I didn't mean to hurt his feelings."

"Don't worry about it," I said. "I like Gary a lot, but in truth, he's a bit of a sulker. Big softie."

"He doesn't look like a softie," she said. "He looks like a double-burrito-and-cheap-tequila nightmare. Which, I suppose, around here may be a good thing. How does he pull that off?"

A hybrid car glided to the curb next to us, and Julius craned his neck as if he was looking for, you know, ghosts or something. He tapped away on his smartphone for a moment before getting out.

Answering Brenda's question, I said, "Dunno, really. Gary doesn't even get it entirely. It probably has something to do with being crazy when he was alive. People in his head."

"Jesus, really? You mean like voices and all that?"

I nodded, watching the old black man emerge from his Uber as I told Brenda what little I knew about Gary. Julius was moving slowly, but there was a spring to his fallen arches. I'd seen it before, and it made me just a shade proud. People are far too quick to dismiss older folks, to relegate them to some corner of the family so the younger people can reign.

Seventy, eighty years of life experiences? No, what's that know-it-all, twenty-something's plan? Let's go with that instead.

So when, literally in the last days of their lives, I give them a bit of a purpose, something that's important, at least to those directly involved, it reenergizes some of my Temps. Might even push them to hold on a few more days.

Which, actually, is good for me. It's very time consuming to break new ones in.

"Painter? You here?" he whispered once the car pulled away.

"Yessir, Julius. Me and Brenda are hanging out by the steps," I said, choosing not to inform the old guy why we weren't actually inside. "We thought we'd wait until you came 'round."

He tipped his hat and flashed those perfect Chiclet teeth. As he climbed the steps, I could see Brenda's expression change, fearing for the man's mental health, but before she could say anything, a heavy-set blond woman with dark roots and gray teeth burst down the stairs, unlit cigarette bouncing between her lips. The door banged against the side of the house, and Julius began to fall backward, but I slipped behind him and willed some juice into my hands, catching him momentarily. But I quickly started to waver, my energy draining.

"Oh, my gawd!" the woman yelped, seeing the old man falling back, away from the steps.

"Grab the rail, Julius!" I said. I felt him begin to slip from my grip, but there was suddenly another pair of hands as Brenda pressed hard, pushing whatever grain she could into creating a firm cushion behind the old man.

My Temp got his head back, reached out for the rail, and held on. To her credit, the woman in the Molly Hatchett T-shirt reached out to help him steady.

"Thank you," Julius finally said, trying to catch his breath, less from the exertion and more likely from the scare. "Thank all of you."

This, not surprisingly, earned him a pair of twisted lips from the girl, who lit her cigarette and flung a wordless goodbye all in one move.

Hank, still in boxer shorts and toting a long neck beer bottle, now stood at the top of the stairs and called out to the woman, already nearly a half block down the street. "Come on, Beth," he called out, drawing out her name as if it had more than a half dozen syllables. "That never bothered you before!"

Not even turning around, she flipped him the bird and tugged on the broad belt of her fashionably ripped ("fashionable" if this had been the eighties) jeans.

He looked to the curb in front of his home. "Hey! You forgot your car!"

She stopped, her fists at her sides, smoke wafting from one hand, the trail of the ember doing circles as she fumed, then slowly turned back, stepped into the street, and headed toward her car.

"Looks like you made your girl fearsome mad," Julius said, straightening out his thick gray coat. In the handful of times I'd seen him, it appeared that the man never wore less than three or four layers of clothes. "You want to go apologize?" Hank looked toward Julius, noticing him for the first time. "I don't mind waiting. I'm old. I do a lot of waiting."

Hank blinked slowly, a bit wobbly on his feet. Obviously, the bottle in his hand wasn't the first he'd opened that day.

"Who the hell are you?"

"I'm a friend of the family," Julius said and introduced himself. "I was told you wouldn't mind if I stopped by."

"What? What family? Who said you could come by?"

"Son, you know you're just in your shorts out here, don't ya?" Julius said, smiling widely. "Let's get you inside, and we'll jaw, you and me, for a little bit. My legs are killin' me."

Hank's beer-soaked brain couldn't process a clever response—or any response. Julius has already sauntered past him and was heading inside. Brenda and I were both a little weakened after the episode on the stairs but pulled ourselves up and inside as Hank slammed the door behind him.

My head, despite it not carrying even an ounce of weight, lolled low, my chin to my chest, as I tried to deal with even less energy than I'd started with that day. I nearly fell to the floor when Brenda yelled out, "Not the couch!"

Julius spun around slowly. "Why not the couch?"

Taking a deep breath, I wheezed out, "Chair, man. Just go with the chair."

Hank said, "Are you senile or something?" He turned into the kitchen. The clank of an empty beer bottle landing on a pile of others split the air. A moment later, he came back with two more and, surprisingly, handed one to Julius.

Despite his shortcomings, the guy must have had a good momma. So maybe not entirely a shitty guy. The younger man sat on the couch, got a queer look on his face for a moment, then slid to the far end of the piece of furniture.

Julius looked at the beer and smiled more widely. "Been a little while. Thank you kindly." He then set the beer down next to his chair and leaned forward.

Hank's eyes danced a little in his head, and then he said. "I don't even know why I let you in. I don't know you." He then looked upward, as if he was checking some files in his brain. "Do I?"

Julius regarded the man for a moment and said, "I mighta met you at Margaret's funeral. There were a lot of people there. She was a much-loved woman."

Hank suddenly got intensely interested in the paper label of his beer bottle. "I, uh, missed that. She was, you know, real great to me." His eyes watered slightly. "A lot of the other family, they saw me as some kinda piranha."

"You mean pariah, I think. The other one is a freaky fish with teeth."

"Whatever it is, they hate me," he said and took a swig of brew. "So I guess I figured people wanted me to stay away."

"Margaret liked you," Julius said with a grin. "I think she would have liked you to be there."

Hank shrugged, lifted the bottle to his lips again, then wiped his eye with two hairy fingers on his beer-holding hand. He shivered slightly for a moment, then asked, "Is that why you're here? 'Cause I didn't show up?"

"No, no, nothing like that. Funerals are more for the living than the dead. If you didn't show, Maggie will know you didn't mean no offense."

Hank shrugged, his mouth hanging slightly open now.

I quickly ran through what we needed to know, and Julius bobbed his head for a moment, listening. He then processed it and looked at the other man with kind eyes.

"Margaret did like you," Julius began. "You were one of her favorites."

"Favorite what?"

Julius blinked. "People."

"Oh."

"What did you think I was talking about?"

"I don't know. Maybe she knew a lot of guys named Hank," he said and took a slug of his beer. "And I was, you know, a favorite Hank."

"Uh huh," the old man said. "You know, there was an old ballplayer named Favorite Hank. Favorite Hank Anderson."

"Really?"

"No."

"Then why would you say that?"

"I don't know. I've lost my bearings in this conversation entirely," Julius said, then before Hank could protest, he added, "So Margaret told me as she lay dying—"

"Jesus, Julius," I said.

"—she said, 'Julius. Now you go see my son-in-law and—'"

"Ex-son-in-law," Hank said, his words fuzzy at their edges.

The old man shrugged. "She didn't see it that way. Anyways, she wanted you to clear your conscience, boy. She said you needed to get some stuff off your chest."

"About what?"

"That night," Julius said, his hands spread wide. "The night it all went wrong for you. The night you shot Boyd."

Hank leaned forward, shaking slightly. At first, he looked as if he was sobbing. Then I heard his low, scratchy laugh. It was phlegmy, unpleasant.

"Man," he said. "My life 'all went wrong' a long, long time ago. That night was just icing on the cake."

Julius sat back in the chair and softened his approach. Reaching down, he grabbed the beer Hank had given him and tipped it to his lips. "Margaret had a lot of faith in you. More than you got in yourself. I can see that."

"What do you know?" Hank said through gritted teeth.

"I only know what she told me. That she loved you, and it hurt her heart to see you hurting yourself."

"Sh-she…" Hank stammered. "She said she loved me? Even after, you know, the divorce and all that. And me, you know, shooting Boyd and all?"

Julius nodded slowly and pointed the opened bottle toward Hank. "She said you gotta just get right. You hafta clear the air."

Eyes wide now, as if he were about to hear some secret to happiness that had eluded him, Hank whispered, "About what?"

"About that night. About the night you shot that man."

Hank stood, arms hanging heavily off his shoulders, and he walked around to the back of the couch and leaned forward on his elbows. "I already have. I talked to the police. Told them everything."

"Not everything."

That stopped the younger man briefly, then he waved his hand lazily in the air.

"Yeah, I did. I mean, that was going to be my last night of freedom. I'd already planned it. Got lit on Wild Turkey and headed to the man's office. He had a shitty two-room space at a strip mall about two miles' walk from here."

"I hear ya."

"Had a .38 I got from a buddy of mine a little while back," he said and covered his eyes for a moment. "Never told Larry, but I wasn't planning on using it on anyone but you know, myself."

Julius nodded slowly, not interrupting the man's flow. Just listening, nodding.

"But then the night I was gonna do it, right, pressed it right to my head," he said, shoving a dirty finger to his temple. "Then I thought… 'this ain't right. I got a better use for all this lead.' So I grabbed my jacket and headed out the door."

Hank sighed then stretched out on the couch in the spot he'd previously avoided.

"I had the whiskey in this old Army-Navy surplus store canteen I got. Gun tucked into my belt, under my coat, right? I felt like some soldier heading off to battle. Like an idiot, tugging away on that whiskey, getting braver and braver as I went."

Hank went to take another sip of beer, but the bottle was empty. His eyes were damp.

"That man took my wife. My daughter," Hank said, sobbing but with angry eyes. "He took my life. So I was gonna take his."

"But Margaret told me it didn't go down like that," Julius prodded. "You showed up, and the fool had already died. Overdose or something."

Hank nodded, smiling through tears, "Son-of-a-bitch beat me to it. I came in and yelled at him, gun leveled at him. He didn't even move. I walked over, jammed the pistol into his neck, and he just lay there face down on the desk. Dead. Spit and shit dripping all outta his mouth and nose."

"And yet you shot him," Julius said. "You shot a dead man."

Hank shrugged and looked around the room. "I was angry. Then I passed out on his shitty little love seat. First thing I remember was the cops handcuffing me, reading me my rights."

"But you didn't kill him."

"Sure, they realized that, and eventually, they let me go. They didn't want to, no way," Hank said and let out a bitter laugh. "They did everything they could. Tried to say that I'd forced him to take the drugs and shit like that, but it didn't stick because it wasn't true. And didn't make sense, because if I tried to get him to OD, why the fuck would I shoot the bastard, then?"

That was my question. It still didn't make sense. I asked Julius to push him on the point.

"So," Julius said after a few moments, "why did you then?"

Hank looked back at him as if he'd just about forgotten the old man was there. "What?"

"Why did you shoot a man who was already dead?"

"I told you! He took everything from—"

Julius put a hand up. "I know you said that, and that's probably in some way true. At least from your perspective. However, if I may, my guess is that you helped drive your family away." This time, Julius's eyes watered slightly. "Trust me, little brother. I know all about that. Some men are stupid like that. We get a good woman and don't feel we deserve her or something is all fouled up in our head. And we do what we can to push the best thing in our lives away."

Hank looked at the man, opened and closed his mouth a few times, but no sound came out. After a few seconds, he merely nodded, wiped his face with a sleeve.

"But that doesn't make us shoot a man who is already dead," Julius said, leaning forward. "Now, I told you, your mother-in-law, she loved you, and she wanted you to get this right. Clear the air and move on, son."

"I… I mean…"

"And all that means is you get it out. Just clear the air and, clean slate, get back onto getting your life together."

Hank started to stand, then sank back down onto the couch.

Brenda looked to me and nodded, excitedly. She urged Julius to press him a little, but the old man gave the slightest shake of his head. He waited. Hank looked at Julius with such a queer expression that my breath caught in my throat. Then he drew his arm across his mouth for a moment, slowly shaking his head.

"Hank," Julius said softly, "there's just you and me here, and I'll be dead in a few days, maybe a week or so. But when I go, I wanna be able to go see ol' Maggie and tell her that you and me, we got her boy right."

Slowly, Hank nodded, and the words began falling from his mouth despite themselves.

"Never told the cops, because…"

"I'm not telling the cops anything," Julius said. "We ain't never been friends, no use in starting now."

"Well, I was mad at the guy, you know? He had everything I wanted, everything I worked for. It's like you're going through the grocery store, and you head to the back corner and grab the milk.

Then you make your way, slowly, to the front of the store. Bread, spaghetti, canned fruit, salami. And as you're standing there at the checkout and you go, 'oh shit, I forgot the beer,'" Hank said and snorted. "Then you come back, and some asshole's grabbed your cart, all the stuff that matters to you, and he's already in the parking lot."

I could see Julius pressing his palms into the fabric of the seat. Here was this guy equating his family, all that he held dear in life, to a trip to the supermarket deli counter. But still, it was hard not to see his point.

"Sure, maybe I shouldn'ta gone back for the beer…"

"Right," Julius offered.

"I coulda taken the, you know, cart back with me to the coolers."

"Got it."

"And there's a chance I may have stopped for some Cheezits on the way back to the—"

"Can we get outta the damn grocery store?" Julius said, finally breaking.

Hank sat motionless, his mouth hanging open for a moment, eyes wide. Then he slowly reanimated, like one of those old record players after someone had mistakenly tripped on the cord, then the plug getting inserted into the wall again.

"Right, well, it…" Hank said, looking at his hands as he twisted his fingers. "So I don't even knock on the door to the guy's office, bust right in. For whatever reason, I leave my half-drunk canteen outside the door. Maybe I'm afraid, I might spill it."

"In your mindset, understandable."

Hank said, his eyes staring out into middle distance again, "He's got the radio on, real low, which is annoying 'cause you can't hear the song. It's more like… it sounds more like this voice with no body, whispering. Can't make it out, it's just whispering."

Julius lifted the bottle from the chair next to him, patiently waiting, and tipped it to his lips again. I noticed for the first time that the level of beer had not changed from when it was handed to him.

"And…" the old man said, and waited for a moment. "You shot him."

Hank nodded. "A couple times in the chest."

Wait.

"Then I emptied the pistol in him."

I looked at Brenda, but she was staring at Hank, the mascara lines streaking her face looking darker than before.

To Julius, I said, "How'd he shoot the guy in the chest if he was leaned forward, face down on the desk?"

Julius looked around the room as if searching for the source of my voice. Then he seemed to remember something. He relayed the question to Hank. Then the younger man did the strangest thing. A small smile stretched his lips. Not malevolent, not menacing. Just a smile. One you might have if you'd just caught an old, sad song on the radio you hadn't heard in years.

"You know," he said. "The cops asked that, but I brushed them off, and they didn't care too much. After the undertaker guy, or whatever, said that the shots came after he was dead, I guess they all thought… what was the point?"

Julius saw it. "You're saying he wasn't dead? The man was still alive?"

"Not according to the cops. They split the guy open and said, hands down, the guy was dead when I shot him."

"But you think he maybe was still breathing or something?"

Hank again shook his head, the smile fading by a degree. "Not breathing, man. Walking. The prick who stole my family was walking right at me. He was supposed to be dead—hell, he even looked cold to me, and he had this look in his eyes."

"What do you mean 'look'?"

"I'd met Boyd a couple times," Hank said. "He'd handled our taxes for a few years before. I could always tell he had something… you know, the way he would look at Ally. Something there."

"Okay."

"But it was, you know, his eyes were always gentle or something, right? Christ, the guy was an accountant. Not like he was a taxman by day and evildoer by night. Hands soft, body soft, eyes soft," Hank said and went into the kitchen for another beer.

The empty went clank on top of the others.

Fresh bottle in his hand, he leaned against the door jamb that led from the living room to the kitchen.

"I don't care what the cops say. That guy wasn't dead. I didn't shoot no dead guy," Hank said, taking a slug of beer. "Hell, I may not have even shot him in the first place, probably would have chickened out. Gone back to my Wild Turkey at the door. But then he was just coming at me, you know?"

"The dead guy?"

"He wasn't dead, man. And those eyes, those soft eyes, they weren't soft no more. Hard as a fucking knife's edge." Hank said. "I'll admit it to you and, you... you can tell Mags. I shot that guy because he scared the shit out of me."

Julius was incredulous. "The accountant?"

Another swig. "I don't know who was coming at me, the guy that the cops say was dead and all. It may have been him, but those eyes? Whatever was behind those eyes, that wasn't the accountant."

Chapter Twenty-Five

The Butterfly watched as Bronwyn clicked and the video played. Each second ticked away like midnight drops of water from a busted tap, snapping against the thin, cold metal of a pristine kitchen sink.

Her eyes moved from the center of the screen, and for the first time, she noticed the time stamp on the images.

Nov. 27 01:13:47… 48… 49… drip, drip, drip.

Whereas the Butterfly had habitually been breathing since leaving the light, her ghostly chest lightly rising and falling, she now stopped. That was the last time she'd ever taken a "breath," alive or dead.

She began to tremble, her eyes inadvertently watering as she refused to blink, because she knew it was coming—

But that's impossible, you told me you never found a tape! No one knew you had this! Why didn't you tell anyone you had this?

—then, on the screen, a tiny spot about three inches from the Energy Star logo affixed to the upper right of the computer monitor, there was the metal wink of a door opening and closing. A figure walked out, and in the dark, it looked as if it was taking tiny hops in place but not growing larger. It seemed to be standing in one spot, but no, it was moving lower and lower on the screen then slipping out of the pool of lights from the gas station. It was then hidden in the abyss of black that engulfed the middle portion of the screen.

Oh my God oh my God oh sweet Jesus

The ghost was frozen, her head wrenched, locked as if held stiff by an EMT's neck brace, but her eyes traced away from the screen, just for a moment, to see Bron's finger again hovering above the mouse, the woman's eyes fixed to the street scene playing out before her.

No. No, no.

In the middle of the screen hung the slight tease of the moment. The blacks swirled ever so slightly in eddies of dark blue, purple, like an ill thought forming in an evil mind.

On the far left edge, the street frayed with a pulse of white, the hint of light approaching.

The boy was clearer now but still so dark that he looked like some image on a black-and-white film. On his arm swung a plastic bag, its sinewy handles straining against the weight of a bottle of soda. The ghost knew that inside, there was also a ten-ounce foil packet of barbeque chips. He had never gotten to taste either.

She began to moan.

No! No, no. No no NO NO NO NO NO!

Then scream. Over and over.

"NO NO NO NO NO NOOOOOOO!"

Click.

The image stopped. Frozen in time.

The seven-year-old Mason, head still down, was looking at his phone. She could just barely see the thin cord of his headphones. Despite the burst of light, very bright now, he hadn't looked up yet. The image was frozen at this point, and it wasn't clear if he had ever seen it.

Her eyes slid toward the harsh light on the left side of the dash cam footage. There it was. The hint, just the edge of chrome and a starburst so bright that it almost distorted the image.

Taken as a whole, the approaching menace seemed to have purpose, intent. The boy, its prey, was locked into its sites.

The dead woman stared, one part of her remembering that she'd made a promise to endure the pain and torture of this world as a debt, never fully to be repaid, so she should be forced to watch it. Forced to see this. See what she'd done.

But Bronwyn simply stared at the screen, almost disinterested now, as if she'd seen this dozens of times before. She took a casual, tired sip from her glass.

"Why did you keep this? Why didn't you tell anyone you had this?"

Bronwyn pulled a bit of something from her lip, and something passed over her face. The Butterfly moved closer to her friend, looked closely at her face, looking for some clue, some answer.

You kept this hidden. You found it. You never told me you found this, what we were looking for! Why didn't you tell me? The spirit looked back to the screen. Why didn't you tell... anyone?

The window clicked closed.

Her shoulders fell, and she said, "No. Play it. I need to see." Then something rippled through her. "Bron, play it! I have to see just... once and for all. I need to stop holding onto this shred of doubt. Wait. Have you shown this to Stephen? No, it would crush him. Poor Stephen. My poor Stephen. Play it. I need this. Play it, Bron!"

But she didn't. Instead, the pointer slowly skittered across the screen, and she clicked over to another image, a thumbnail, next to the blue-black rectangle.

Despite the horror promised by the video of November 27, this new one—she never saw it coming—would deliver an anguish she'd never known. She'd actually begun to brace herself for the carnage that would spill from the blue-black rectangle, the crush of bone, the burst of blood, a small body smashed and broken. Maybe a brief, silent scream.

But this new video clip was something altogether different.

At first, it was a canvas of soft white that rippled lazily like a pond in late summer, warm amber light flickering from a nearby fire. The perspective jerked, camera angle adjusted, and the white of the blouse gave up half of the screen to the interior of a home.

Soft woods, dark, inviting leathers.

The Butterfly instantly recognized the painting on a far wall in the dimmed light. It was nighttime, but she could still clearly make it out as the person in the soft white blouse manipulated some workings on the camera, the iris going too full momentarily, the warmth on the screen briefly revealing a harsh white light, too bright, then settling back again.

She didn't know who'd painted the piece of art. But she knew it.

She looked up across the room and stared at it. The painting was in this house. The images on the screen were from this very room.

The woman in the blouse stepped back, her face in slight shadow, her eyes focused just off to the right, maybe checking a small monitor? She then leaned in. The image jumped momentarily, her hands opened a drawer off camera, and then she turned away.

The dead woman let out a dry whisper. "What is this?"

Her friend's right hand manipulated the mouse, advancing the video, and the woman on the screen danced and dipped unnaturally around the room, then disappeared toward the door. Bronwyn slowed the footage now, playing it out in real time.

Something told the ghost she shouldn't see this. It was probably something private. This was a video of her friend, one of the few she'd had left in the world. This was too invasive. Briefly, a small wave of humiliation rolling through her ephemeral body, her eyes drifted away from the image to elsewhere on the screen.

For the first time, she noticed the name of the folder the video was in. It didn't register right away. Didn't make sense. The others in the structural tree on the left of the screen had standard titles—Documents, Downloads, Case Notes, Court Motions, Investigations. But this folder had been buried within a folder within a folder within a folder.

The one she was in now was called In Case He Gets Squirrelly. What is this?

When she looked back to the image itself, the woman on the screen was leading a man wearing a long, thick coat into the room.

He was holding something under his arm. The Butterfly moved in closer.

In the clip, Bronwyn was talking, her hands moving as fast as her lips, which brought a tiny smile to the dead woman. She remembered this. One of the attorney's hands went to her mouth, then reached out and brushed the sleeve of the man in the video.

A brief discussion. The guy shifting his weight, making some moves toward the door. The object held in the crook of his right arm looked heavy but was impossible to see in the low light. Bron had motioned to the table. A hesitation, then slowly the man removed his scarf, handing it to Bronwyn. He put the object on the dining room table and removed his coat.

Her smile faltered, traded for a flat line. It was Stephen.

Bron had taken the coat and scarf from the room as he sat in a chair. He looked small. His head seemed too heavy for his body, weighing down his neck, arching the top of his spine away from the chair back. Sitting in the dim light, his hands then went to his face, covered his eyes, and his shoulders began to quake.

He was crying.

Sobbing.

He looked up. His left hand on his mouth, his right reached to the object on the table. Hard to see. The ghost moved closer to the screen. It was like one of those ice buckets from the nicer hotels. Brushed steel, tapered cylinder, smaller at its base going wider toward the top, then tapering at the top.

A vase.

No. No, of course. She and Stephen had discussed it once or twice. Philosophical discussions that assumed they'd shared a life together, conversations that took for granted decades of joy and sadness and love and fulfillment. Children. But she had told him at the end, the very end, she didn't want to rot.

On the table, the thick metal object Stephen was caressing was an urn. Hers. The Butterfly was looking at all that remained in the world of her. In a tiny container not much bigger than a coffee maker.

She squeezed her eyes shut for a moment, tight, tight. But wait; she had to see more. And when she opened them again, Bronwyn was returning with a bottle under her arm. She sat across from Stephen and arranged the two glasses on the table.

Drinks poured, they held them aloft while Stephen spoke, his hand resting softly on what was left of the dead woman's body. All that was left.

They drank their drinks, Bron in one quick motion. Stephen, never much of a drinker, finished his in three pulls. Then a fourth. The spirit grinned sadly. In the clip, his chair edged and turned away from the table slightly.

But then Bronwyn leaned over the table in a sharp, almost aggressive motion, her hand resting on his. He looked toward the door, but then she'd poured two more drinks, her turn, and he nodded and turned back.

What were they saying? The Butterfly, embarrassed, wanted to hear what they were saying. They were talking about her. Was it horrible that she wanted to listen to it? Was it awful that she wanted to listen to some kind words said about her? After the horrible, horrible descriptions of her she'd heard repeatedly in the trial—which would have all been repeated in the second trial, she'd known that—these vile words that she would never forget, the dead woman selfishly wanted something nice for her morbid collection, too. Some "light in the shade," as a friend had once put it.

But they were still silent. Now her former defense attorney was speaking, their glasses raised, her left arm waving theatrically through the air in a gesture toward the urn. She couldn't hear them, but she actually let out a small laugh.

What she would give to hear them! Just something lovely to hear, that memory to cherish as others, good and bad, had already begun to flitter away from her mind.

She would have to settle for the intentions. Beautiful things, impassioned words, had been said after she'd died. Words about her. Words of admiration, of love, of friendship. That would be enough. That filled something in her, not entirely, but it was like some extreme hunger had been satiated by a few bites of something beautiful.

That wasn't why she'd come here. She was being selfish and needed to get to her duty, her penance. It was time to see if the dead boy was still wandering his parents' home. Alone. Distraught.

But as the dead woman began to slide away, the defense attorney again moving the mouse with one hand, and it was only now that the Butterfly noticed the other hand. She was stunned, dumbfounded, unsure at first at what she was looking at.

Well, she knew what she was looking at, but it didn't register. It was… out of place. Like some intruder.

Bronwyn manipulated the video with the fingers of her right hand, while the left had settled beneath her silken slip. The ghost flinched and shrank back, horrified.

The office chair was now tipped back slightly, one of the woman's bare feet resting on a filing cabinet under the table, toes curled slightly. The sheer fabric had risen up on this leg, crumpling slightly at her hip. Beneath that, her left hand made slow, rhythmic movements. The same sort that she'd employed when she'd consoled Stephen, soothing him, stroking his arm.

"What… what are you—uh—what… I don't underst—"

Bronwyn let out a soft, low moan, her eyes greedily taking in the blue glow of the screen. The look on her face was sharp, hard, and hungry.

The spirit looked back to the clip, which had been advanced, and her heart leaped to her throat.

Her friend had risen in the video and now stood behind Stephen, rubbing his neck and shoulders, both glasses refilled. He'd reached up once or twice weakly, in jerky yet languid motions, and she knew from the way his head was lolling around his shoulders that he was drunk. He wasn't really used to alcohol; she'd seen him drunk on a half dozen occasions. He was a silly drunk. Playful.

Horny.

Wait. Wait.

The ghost looked at her friend, whose eyes were hooded, her breathing deeper now, throatier.

Jesus, I'd told you that about him. That alcohol did that to my... You'd come for a visit to the prison, just girl talk. What was I doing? I trusted you. But I told you that.

She looked back to the screen. Bronwyn reached to loosen Stephen's top button, to get better access to his neck. Naturally, shirt's in the way; this will be better.

I told you that.

Stephen's hand made one last attempt at changing the flow of events, but full of grief, loss, and now single-malt whiskey, the pleasure of touch was a tide now too difficult to fight. The Butterfly could only watch as her former attorney, her former friend, bent down and put her lips to her fiancé's neck... whispers, the flick of a tongue.

Shock had turned to horror to disbelief, but now it was something new. Something strong. Rage was building, filling her, pouring into her the longer the video played.

Sadness too. Deep, bone-deep sadness. How could you do that? I get—but how could you do that? Christ, I'm right—

Stephen had motioned to the object on the table and, one caressing hand resting on his shoulder, like a toddler playing tag holding onto the not it tree, she grabbed the urn in one arm and quickly walked from the table. Bronwyn walked toward the camera and placed it on the cabinet, the same one that had held the camera.

She spun back around, a third of the screen now blocked by the metallic container that held the remains of the Butterfly, a steel vessel in which she would spend eternity.

When the attorney returned to the table, her hips swaying in long, determined strides, all bets were off. The ghost could actually smell her musk and then realized that wasn't something she'd conjured up in her imagination watching the scene. Bronwyn pushed the dining room table forward, pulled her gray business skirt up as a one leg crossed over Stephen's knees, her ankle wrapping around the leg of the chair as she pulled herself down upon him, straddling his waist, her damp mouth taking his.

The woman at first gripped the back of the chair, the other ankle now entwining the other chair leg, and she braced herself so she could rock her pelvis forward, grinding into the crotch of the seated man.

Bronwyn let out a gasp. Horrified, the dead woman turned to see the woman's hand moving faster now, needy, her face glowing in the blue glow of the screen, head tilting back, lips parted with a thin line of saliva arching from top to bottom, each panting breath making it shudder. Eye open, staring hard at the image at the screen, unblinking.

What did you do? What did you do?

Back on the screen, the two bodies were writhing in the chair. The woman how had the man's head wrapped in her arms, her breasts pressed against his chest, the shirt now open, buttons on the floor, the woman's hips bucking up and down, up and down, as if she were in a saddle, up and down, clench, up and down. Stephen now had his hands on her back, then one slid down the skirt and worked its way underneath to the grinding woman's buttocks. Beneath the dress, she wore nothing. No panties.

She'd planned this.

When did—?

Almost frantic, the woman leaning back in the chair convulsed as a sexual shockwave rippled through her. She began moving the hand with the mouse practically as fast as the other hand.

On the screen, the two people twisted and grinded at dizzying speed, then play-speed again, and Bronwyn was on her back, Stephen's hairline just above the woman's toned thigh, sheer stockings twisted, her arms stretched above her head like a black cat's, her right calf pressed against the back of his head, pulling him deeper and deeper.

At that moment, the ecstasy on the dark-haired woman's face bordered on obscene. It made the dead woman sick. Then the attorney turned her head ever so slowly toward the camera and smiled. Her eyes, partially hidden by the urn pushed up next to the camera, showed unmistakably that she was smiling.

The ghost knew she wasn't looking at the camera. Sure, she'd set it up and had planned this, she'd planned all of this. Maybe for months. Longer. No, she wasn't smiling at the camera.

She was smiling at her.

She was smiling at the urn.

The Butterfly knew precisely what the slut was thinking. "I've won. He's mine now. I beat you."

This was the moment something broke in her.

A barrier that had been in place. One she had built. Not alone but as a child. Through teen years, her mother had helped. A good woman who'd shown her the right path. Shown her the good in the world. The better.

Stop being such a fucking sniveling little cunt!

The voice in her head surprised her. But not a total surprise, maybe. Those words, of course, were not her own.

She'd been cunning and brilliant and aggressive and excelled at everything she did. It was just the way she was built. As she'd risen through the ranks at various employers, she'd been labeled cold. Or heartless. Or even "She-bitch" (a title she wore with pride).

That same passion, the same ability for total focus, the same bit of damage had also lived in her father.

You were always weak. Too much of your mother in you.

That was always a favorite admonition from her father. Condemning her in her weakest moments. A two-for-one, the statement also belittled her mother. It was also his attempt to dent the barrier the two women had constructed, the one that let slip through the passion for greatness but held back the darkness.

The darkness that had turned her father into something more than human but with little humanity.

In her youth, she'd seen less and less of him. Her mother had made sure of that through the courts and, when they'd failed, through picking up and moving to a new address. Sometimes at a moment's notice.

But he'd find her. There were bigger swaths of time between encounters, but he'd find her and try to get her to go with him on some grand, terrifying adventure. She'd never told her mother— she never would have done that to her—but it had been tempting. Despite what he'd done, the horrors he'd been accused of, it had been tempting. Had that been because she'd missed her father? Or maybe just someone in the role of dad?

No. She'd always known she had an appetite for that darker world. Very slight. Just an interest. But it did call. She'd always resisted. With her mother's help, she'd always resisted.

This was it.

This was the moment something broke in her.

She let the rage flow through her, empower her, and suddenly felt something she hadn't felt since she'd left the light. Something she hadn't entirely felt years earlier. Maybe ever. She felt strong, she felt confident but mostly—She. Felt. Free.

Took you long enough, goddamn pussy kid.

There was another gasp then a moan from the woman alone in the dark, but the spirit barely heard it. She now had a path. New plan.

She recalled that one night in her cell, as she lay listening to her fat cellmate snore and smack her lips. Her father had come, he'd found her, like he would in those years before. But of course, this time her father had long since passed. Died years ago. Violently, of course. He'd deserved it, of course.

Back then she'd been terrified and had put it off to a nightmare. Spicy food in the canteen. She'd nearly screamed when his grisly form, blade handle still protruding from an eye, slipped through the concrete wall of her cell.

But even then, the anger had been growing. The rage? Not yet. But the anger. And that, in the end, might have been what led her father to her cell that night.

"Death ain't the end, Butterfly," he'd said and laughed. "Or maybe it is for some folks but not for me. Maybe not for you." She had screamed at him to leave, and he'd only laughed more. "Right. I can see it now. I can see it in you. There's a crack in the door that your mother clamped shut. But there's a crack." She'd closed her eyes and begged him to leave. He did but promised to return the next day. And that he would have a surprise.

He had returned. But not in any form she'd expected.

She'd been informed she had a visitor. She didn't recognize the name, but remembering what her had father said, curiosity got the best of her. She'd sat down to talk to the young man, just in his twenties. Beautiful with dark circles under his eyes. But inside wasn't some young man. When he began to speak, it was her father. She was doubtful at first, but it didn't take him long to convince her.

As impossible as it was, this was her father. She knew it.

"You ain't the only genius," the young man said, searching his pockets, tapping his shirt as if looking for a smoke, then giving up as if realizing something. "I worked it out. The folks, uh, in the next world where I live. There'd been just rumors about it. Stories. But I worked it out. Your old man worked it out."

"What? What do you think you worked out?"

"I don't think, Butterfly. Girl, I'm dead. Yet here I sit," he said and smiled just like her father had. Terrifying. Too much pleasure in it. "Dying, ending up in the InBetween? There's a way back. I found a way back. I know the secret. I'm the only one that knows it now. And I'm going to tell you."

That was when this impossible creature told her about something called a "cab ride."

Now, watching the pitiful woman strumming away in the dark, alone in her big home, fucking her own hand because no one else would, she recalled what her father had told her. She remembered the secret.

Rage coursed through her like gasoline in her veins. And it felt so fucking good. Better than she'd ever felt. Ever.

Even better, now she had a plan. First, she had to see the rest of the tape, put that last bit of hope in her mind out of its misery. The rest of her mind was already swirling with inky black, and this last tiny oasis of light would soon be gone. She just needed to see the next moment of footage from the dash cam.

Then she was going to find a way back to Stephen. Her Stephen.

Then she would kill Bronwyn. She was a liar. Manipulative. She'd literally moved the Butterfly aside so that she might fuck her fiancé. With her body, what was left of it, still in the room.

She was transformed. The Butterfly was moved aside as she had been in the video, replaced by what she knew she'd always been. She was Chandra again, but not the one her mother had wanted. Not the one her mother had raised.

This was the real Chandra. Her daddy's daughter.

She headed for the door then threw a few words over her shoulder, a warning that wouldn't be heard.

"See ya."

Chapter Twenty-Six

Once outside again, I asked Julius to walk down to the bus stop, where he could sit down and we could all get our heads around what we'd just heard. The early-afternoon sun was reflecting off the storefronts of a strip mall. "For lease" signs stood in every window.

The bus stop was sheltered, and all the plexiglass was either marked with some gang tag or scratched so thoroughly it had become opaque. I began to wonder if the bus stop was used for more than catching the bus.

"I think meeting Hank that first time set a path for me," I said, thinking it through. "Brenda, you and me, we're just energy now. When we interact, it creates a shot of magnetism. That's how Lonnie's presence drew you off when you were following the Ringman. It was familiar. You had come close to Lonnie, and there's a link."

The reporter nodded. "Sure. I found you pretty easily in that power station because I sort of felt you."

"Right," I said. "Whatever was in Boyd, Hank had come close to it. After my first run-in with Hank, then I smack into the mailman, then you. It was... there was a draw. The familiar."

Julius was listening to us talk, his brow growing more wrinkled by the minute.

"I don't really get it," Brenda said.

It was starting to click now. "Remember how Lonnie had described the thug who'd come into the bar that night, all those years ago?"

Julius squinted against the sun. "Who's Lonnie?"

"Guy we met in Chicago. A ghost, that is."

Brenda said, "Yeah. The guy with the bat. You think that guy is the Ringman?"

I shook my head. "No. But the interaction between the living world and ours—the dead guy in the bar with the livie bat. The live Jorgensen with me. It's just not possible unless you're in both worlds. That's how Jorgensen could grab me by the throat in Chicago. He's both. One body, two people: one livie, one spook."

Julius shook his head, the conversation unnerving him. "Wait a minute, hold on. How does that happen? Is that a thing?"

"I've heard of it. But I never knew it was real," I said, looking south.

Brenda inched toward me. "Okay, what do you know about it?"

"Not much," I said. "But I know someone who does."

I needed to talk to the Professor, but the delay in getting Brenda back to her hometown was making her angry.

"The answers are in Chicago," she said. "And that crazy fuck is going to kill another person, and that'll be on you."

"No, it won't. I'm not taking responsibility for Sir Kills-a-lot," I said, leading her back toward the Mississippi. "I have the courage to change only the things I can and the serenity to accept that I ain't responsible for a guy who kills people with sharp object to the face."

"Nice. You should make T-shirts."

Impressively, Brenda was able to maintain her anger for most of the hour it took to get down the big river and then across to the giant pile of rock. When we'd hit the thick foliage of Georgia, she began to soften.

As we approached Stone Mountain, I slowed on the way up and pointed out the three stone men on horseback.

"I don't think he looks like a vampire."

"No?" I said, looking closely at one of the men on horseback. "Maybe he's at that awkward in-between stage, you know, where he's been taking the vampire-change-over medicine but still wearing some of the old human clothes, top hat, but underneath that he's wearing a frilly little vampire undergarment."

Brenda gave me a long stare. "You ain't right."

We glided up to the top of the rock and began looking around for my guru friend, as I had done many times in the past. She's always there, sometimes watching picnickers, often stargazing (or navelgazing).

After we'd circumnavigated it a second time, I headed up to the very center of the stone outcropping to scan it as a whole. Then I realized the truth.

"She's not here."

Chapter Twenty-Seven

As I'd promised, we headed back to Chicago, making good time up the river and planning to keep on the water, rocketing over through the Great Lakes and down into the city. The best part of that, in addition to possibly shaving a little time off our travel, was that going over the water was going to help replenish some energy.

We'd been pretty quiet the entire time, but swooping down Lake Michigan, Brenda piped up. "It seems the Ringman Jorgensen and the Ghost Mob are working together. Maybe it's like a marmite-and-Bass scenario."

I sighed. "Yes, I had the exact same thought. Totally a martinite and boss scenario." I didn't even have to see her to know she was rolling her eyes.

"What I mean by that is they may be working together for different results. Marmite is this century-old spread that British people put on toast. It came from all the crap left over from making beer at the Bass brewing factory. So they both benefit—the spread people get their ingredients and Bass has someone cleaning up their slop—but two different endgames."

"Maybe." I thought through what she'd said. "Why didn't you just say the last bit. Working together but having two different goals. Instead of all that stuff about beer and jam."

"It's not jam. It's spread. Like a black yeast paste."

"Yech! And people in Britain like that?"

"No," the reporter said. "But they're too polite to tell anyone."

Something about what she'd said rang true. I said, "Okay, so your Ringman and my Ghost Mob are in cahoots, but maybe two different goals."

"Don't say 'cahoots.'"

"Oh, hush."

We rocked into the city, coming up the Navy Pier full of vim and vigor, ready to take on the baddies. Then I remembered that the last time I'd been in Chicago, I'd gotten shanghaied and put into a mind-bending, soul-sucking, energy-leeching power matrix that screwed with my perception so entirely that Timothy Leary would have said, "Dude, I'm trippin' balls... way too much. Let's crank this down a few notches, 'K?"

So I dimmed the vim and ball-gagged the vigor a little, deciding stealth mode would be the best approach.

For a few minutes, we hung out near the coastline as she scanned the city. Wherever we were headed, she'd have the best idea. This was her town, and she knew it well.

"I have no idea where to go," the dead reporter said.

"Okay, that might stall our plans a little."

"It's just... I mean, it's not even the city I knew anymore, right? There's now a whole new layer on it, your InBetween—"

"Yours too now, babe."

She wrinkled her nose at me. "Jeez, don't call me babe."

"I was trying to sound cool."

"You didn't."

"Yeah, it's not my thing."

We stood on the shoreline of the lake. "You know the secret to being cool?"

"Hit me."

"Not caring if you look cool."

"Sure," I said. "Helps if you're already, you know, cool. Right?"

She shrugged. "Doesn't hurt."

She was right, of course. Your world changes after you die. Sure, there was less shopping, no grooming, zero updating of the resume, and dating was an exercise in frustration and futility.

The latter, naturally, being no different for many of us than when we were alive.

But there were subtle changes. Rules that were basically learn-as-you-go. They weren't posted anywhere. No textbooks. You had to hope, especially early on, that strangers might be kind enough to share the basics.

Of course, the only danger in the InBetween was other ghosts.

That led me to lay out another of my rules. The first, as established:

Rule #1: Don' want no douchey, don' be no douchey.

But for the living and the dead, you can avoid a lot of misery with this second one.

Rule #2: Steer clear of bad people, including those who just might be bad for you

And lately in the InBetween, the bad people were getting more organized and stronger. I'd seen the rise of the Ghost Mob in recent months, and it scared me.

There's no government. No authority. No police. But the worst spooks in the world were getting organized? There soon would be no one to stop them. But why would you even make plans in the InBetween? There's nothing to gain. Sure, you can drain juice from other spooks, but to what end? Why bother?

Maybe shitty people just really dug being shitty. Perhaps that was enough.

Yeah. That didn't feel right. They were planning something.

"Do you think they know you're out of that power thingy?"

I shook my head. "Don't know, but... how many of us were there? Between the two power stations the Mob has, given the numbers, Chicago seems like it might have been built after the one in the Twin Cities. As you described it to me, it was maybe twenty or thirty in there? Still, that's enough to get lost in the crowd. I can't imagine my absence would be noticed."

"Except they'd been looking for you."

Forgot that bit. "Right."

"Maybe they had other plans for you after the power station, and they were just stashing you for a while."

I laughed. "Well, I'm a hell of a singer."

"You are?"

"No."

Brenda huffed. "That sucks, because man, I really miss music. I listened all day when I was alive. The car, at work, at home. Plug into my jams at the gym."

"Yeah, it's a total heartbreak for nearly every spook I know. Gary will bore you to death about 'One wish, man, one wish: Guns N' Roses' Appetite… on repeat!' But I suppose some work it out. Lonnie did in that old warehouse. It's just the one song, but maybe that's enough. You wonder how often he's listened to that old Bobby Darin tune, sitting in the dead kids' car."

The reporter stared off for a moment then asked me, "What do you miss most?"

"I miss the grit you get in your teeth after you've eaten the perfect oyster. I miss the headache you get when you eat ice cream too fast. I miss reading a book you've already read, the feel of cold lake water on your body just as the sun breaks the horizon, and the comfort of a pair of jeans that you've had so long you don't remember buying them."

She smiled. "Those are nice things." She smiled again. "You ever had a ghost boner?"

"Jesus, what? No. Aw man," I said, feigning disgust. "You ruined such a lovely moment with your lurid designs on my body!"

"I have zero designs on you and, obviously, zero body. I was just wondering."

My friend started walking across a perfectly manicured expanse of land that butted up to a path adjacent to a city block of massive buildings. They were huge steel and glass structures that from my angle, that of a tiny ant on ground level, looked like something out of a futuristic comic book.

Impressively, Brenda was picking up the walking thing pretty well, too. Of course, our feet didn't really pull at the ground to propel us forward—and some ghosts just glided from place to place—but there was something oddly comforting and familiar about the motion. And if there were any other spooks around, we wouldn't stand out so much.

I followed in a similar fashion but frankly not much better than she was already doing.

"I think the South Side is a little off limits," she said. "That's where The Grind is and where you got nabbed by the guys Lonnie led to you."

Anger boiled back up into me. "That prick. He has no idea—"

"Well, hold on," she said. "To be fair, at one point he was helping us out. Maybe they threatened him."

The old barfly had apologized and looked sincere when he'd done so. But I wasn't about to forgive him for putting me through that. If he was just saving his skin? Well, that's fine. I get it, but I'll tuck that little note card in my mental file for later. I run into the guy again? Me and him were going to be different.

Rule #2: Steer clear of bad people, including those who just might be bad for you

We did a swing past where the reporter had been killed, and she took me up to the floor that had been under construction and where Jorgensen had driven rebar up under her chin, through the soft palate, and into her brain. She hadn't died instantly but had bled out as her mind drifted away.

She rubbed her hand, fingers tumbling over a thin gold band that wrapped around a finger on her slightly illuminated right hand.

"I remember now that he stole my mom's ring," she said. "Me there, helpless on the floor, I was so scared because I realized I was dying."

"Jesus, sorry, Brenda."

She nodded and bit her lip. "But the fact he'd take something so precious to me. My life, sure, but that ring was all I had left of Mom." The reporter laughed, then habitually sniffed away tears. "Isn't that weird? The guy killed me, and I felt more violated by him stripping my mother's ring off my finger."

I pointed toward her hand, where she'd been rubbing.

"Is that it?"

"Yeah," she said, and a real smile returned to her face. "My perception of reality, right? Or memory."

"So in that way, you've still got it. She's still with you."

She nodded, her mascara-stained eyes moistening, and she said softly. "So's he."

We circled downtown Chicago a couple times, crisscrossing and weaving through one-way streets, service lanes, and overpasses and in and out of coffee shops, pubs, and restaurants. It was like a game of hot-cold.

Brenda would get a feeling—"This way"—and we'd follow the scent for a little while until it seemed to vaporize for her. She said, "It's fainter than before."

"Well," I suggested, still mulling over the trinket-link idea, "that could be a good thing, too, I would guess. If you can feel him, maybe he can feel you?"

That thought played across her face for a moment. "I don't think so. When we were in that pub, he was up there trying to get the barman's attention. He never even turned my way."

Nor had he sensed me creeping up on him, and I was sure that if I looked closely enough, my aunt's necklace would be around his neck along with several others.

Following Brenda, I'd noticed that our turns were getting sharper, more frequent, but I didn't say anything. It seemed that she was narrowing her search.

We were getting closer.

Finally, as we swung past a city park, she put out her hand and held me back then shuffled in reverse near an area of road construction, shuttered up for the night. We stood in a small garden of circular, flashing lights atop sawhorse barriers painted in red and white stripes.

Without a word, she pointed toward the far edge of the park.

In a cluttered parking lot were three food trucks. On the far edge was a scattered group of homeless people—some sitting in the grass, some leaning against freshly planted saplings, others standing and waiting as if at the post office, listening for their number to be called.

The trucks were still doing business, it seemed, a handful of people from the neighborhood grabbing an ice cream from one vendor that sold mostly frozen desserts and various oversized pastries that would have looked more at home in some low-rent carnival.

The other two—now a fourth pulling in—were mostly calling it a day.

Every few minutes, a vendor would hold up a paper sack or what looked like some variation of butcher paper. One of the homeless would come forward, grab what was being offered, then retreat to the darkness of the park with the night's dinner—or possibly the day's only dinner—held covetously in their dirty hands.

Brenda whispered to me as we hung back in the shadows. "We had a story about this on the late news a few months back."

"What are they doing?"

"It's leftover product from the day. Usually, whatever's still on the grill—the trucks come into this spot, and instead of tossing it out, they give it to people that don't mind if the food's been sitting on a spit the last couple hours."

It sounded a little demeaning to me, but I guess I'd never been near starving.

"Why would they even bother?" I asked. "Not to sound cold—"

"No, no," she said and waved away whatever lame apology I had not yet been able to craft. "Fair point. It could easily be argued that health codes might preclude a three-hour-old corndog or enchilada from being handed over the counter. The park's kind of an amnesty zone for that."

"Really?"

"Yeah. Those folks on the grass waiting, they know it's not always going to be top notch, but hell, some of them dig through trash behind restaurants for dinner. This, at least, comes off a grill not out of a Dumpster."

I nodded, and a sense of shame, even as a ghost, warmed my cheeks.

She continued, "And like you said, it's not all about having a big heart. While the truck vendors could normally write off the spoilage, this way it becomes a charitable donation. In the end, that could mean thousands of dollars of tax credits."

I got it. "Real money."

"Yep," she said. "A junior congressman heard about it in some other city, out west from what I remember, and he put it into play here. As long as the Health Department turns a blind eye—and nobody ends up in the emergency room with food poisoning—then it's pretty much a win-win."

Looking over, I saw a man in layers of coats shuffle toward a food truck with the words Taco Time! splayed across its belly. The collection of jackets made his arms a bit stiff. As he walked, something about him reminded me a little of Julius and his penchant for multiple coats. Had it not been for the home, would Julius have ended up on the street?

The homeless guy grabbed what was offered to him and nodded. The park was quiet, and the cold night air carried his voice as he thanked the guy in the truck.

Brenda pointed to a man hanging out near the curb. Much better dressed than the others, he was in stark contrast to many who directed their eyes toward the ground or their hands.

It was Jorgensen.

He seemed almost fixed in position, leaning forward slightly, staring at the two men under the awning, inside a truck with faded red lettering shouting Curry Up. One of the guys behind the counter was wearing basically what all the other vendors were— white cap tight to his head, apron strapped around his ample waist. It seemed the only variation in dress was whatever the T-shirt under the apron read.

The curry truck guy's was stained in several places, looking a little like he'd been shot. It read, 2016 World Champions!

The man next to him, incongruously, was in a suit with a loosened tie.

We both recognized him at the same time. The young congressman. Stephen Lee.

"I don't think the Ringman is here for a curry."

Brenda shook her head. "He's got the congressman in his sights again."

I started to move forward. "Jesus, he's going to kill him."

Brenda tugged me back, and I felt my juice meter tick down a notch. I spun around and flicked her ear to get it back. She frowned at me, playfully waggled her finger, then got back to business.

"He's not going to kill a congressman."

"Why not?"

"Too many people around. Wait a minute, look!"

We both tensed as Jorgensen strode up to the food truck as one of the homeless walked away with the night's dinner. Lee looked up, wiping his hands on his apron, as this new customer approached. From this distance, we couldn't hear their words, but what started as a practiced smile from Lee changed. The tone of their conversation turned aggressive very quickly.

"He can't do anything now," Brenda said then relaxed slightly. "As long as all those people are around, no way he tries anything. And Lee's up in the food truck, out of reach anyhow."

After an exchange that lasted nearly a minute, another hungry person stepped up. Lee's partner in the truck went to help, but then the congressman waved him off. An excuse to get away from the confrontation.

Jorgensen took a few steps back and turned, shouting something as he walked toward the nearby park.

"Okay," the reporter said. "Whew. Wonder what that was about?"

"Doesn't matter. We've got to follow Jorgensen and see what he's up to, what his plans are. From the little bit I saw in the power station, it ain't go—"

"Whoa, whoa, whoa!"

I turned back to look, feeling my heart begin to thump as if it were slamming a big wooden door at the top of my esophagus, making it hard to catch my breath.

Congressman Lee slipped out the side door of the curry truck, rolled down the short staircase, and began walking into the dimly lit park. He was walking right toward Jorgensen. Also, strangely, it looked like something was coming through the tops of the trees downward. A very, very faint discoloration. It warbled a bit, and I could see that it was… long? Hard to tell. Like some incredibly long glass flagpole, sticking out of the treetops at an angle. Not glass. There was a very subtle shimmer to it. Not a pole either, more like—

"Okay, I was afraid of that," Brenda said as Lee was swallowed by the darkness of the park. "Looks like he is planning to kill the congressman."

If I'd had a stomach, any meal I'd had that day would have been spewed all across the grass. Brenda glided through the darkened park a few paces behind me, watching our backs, because while livies could sneak through the dark clandestinely, for the dead, lit up by our sole possession—energy—it's not clandestine but Saturday night, neon-strapped, downtown-porn-shop style.

We walked past a homeless guy eating the dregs of what may have been a couple tacos at one point. Sitting on a wooden bench bowed with rot, he was pinching bits of white lettuce—red sauce dripping down his wrist, which he slurped with is tongue—and dropping them into his mouth six inches above his face. Like he was sprinkling fairy dust. But you know, instead of magical power, cascading into his mouth was wilted lettuce, wax-like cheese, and strips of onion that had likely been frozen so long they had all the taste of unseasoned wheat noodles.

But hell, I'd been there on a few occasions when I'd tried my hand at screenwriting in Los Angeles many years earlier. When all your dough is going into just not getting kicked out of your apartment, there's not a lot left over for luxuries like food. At that point, a shitty burrito can taste like ambrosia.

We slipped past the happy, less-hungry hobo unnoticed because, of course, to the living, we'd have nothing to worry about. Brenda could have done a lap dance on the guy, and he would have just sat there, picking taco bits out of his teeth.

Not trying to be sexist. I suppose yours truly also could have performed said lap dance, but it's not beyond the realm of possibility that some ethereal revulsion would have passed over both me and the hobo. And, you know, he'd just eaten, so...

However, to any spooks in the area, we would have glowed in the dark. Not wholly. It was more like thin icing on a gingerbread man, an outline where our energy ended, the terminus of our "bodies."

Whatever Jorgensen was—livie, spook, or some combo of both—it seemed that he was in partnership with folks in the InBetween. For what still wasn't clear.

But if he had any ghostly hooligans around, they might spot us in an instant.

So Brenda and I hung near the streetlamps, bathing in the bright spotlights.

If Ringman Jorgensen was somehow part of the Ghost Mob, he could have others nearby. Still, if we were going to save Lee, we couldn't hide in the light all night.

Stealth-mode stalking prevents really swift reconnaissance, I've learned, and it took us a bit too long to find them. Still, had we come upon Jorgensen throttling the guy or jamming a letter opener into his ribs, I wasn't entirely sure what we could have done.

It turned out that wasn't Jorgensen's plan.

"... -king lunatic, I'm going back," the congressman said but made no move away from Jorgensen.

The two men were sitting on a bench between two tall streetlights. Just behind them was a large fountain with strips of UNDER MAINTENANCE KEEP OFF tape to explain why there wasn't any water in it.

Brenda and I slid around the back of it and tried to listen in. To my left, I could see their long shadows cast in the amber glow of the park's tall lamps.

"You made a promise to me, remember?" Jorgensen said, a shadow finger pointing at the congressman. Strangely, the homicidal killer looked... sad. Emotionally wrecked. "Doesn't that mean anything to you?"

Lee stood, spun around the bench, and slipped into the darkness behind them. Then he returned, arms in the air.

"Nope, no way! I'm not buying this. This is not how the world works!"

"Stephen, there's a lot you don't know." Jorgensen stood. He took a few steps closer. "We don't have to be over. We can pick up where we left off! But I need you to tell me—"

"No, no. It's not possible," the congressman said. "What you're doing is cruel. My Chandra is dead!"

"I died waiting to get back to you, Stephen." Jorgensen reached out to Lee. When the congressman flinched, the Ringman pulled his arm back. "But I'm back. I just need her addres—"

The congressman's hands went to his head, and he began tugging at his hair in two fistfuls. "This is crazy."

Jorgensen leaned in and smiled, but there was no smile in his voice. "I know a secret that's about to change this world. For now, I'm inside this man, but we can fix that. We can be together again. You pick out any pretty girl you see. Anyone you want. Model. Movie star. I'll break her will, and she won't even know it. Takes a bit of time, but… I'll enter her, and I will be her."

"What?" I said reflexively, which was a bad move, actually, because then the shadow–serial killer turned his head toward us.

Busted! We weren't going to hang around. We jumped up and made a beeline out of the park.

Only once did I look back over my shoulder. Jorgensen was still trying to convince the congressman, but his eyes burned into us, locked on me and Brenda as we sprinted out of the park.

The one thing we had going for us was that if he had anyone from the Mob around, he wasn't in a place to call out and tell them to chase down two ghosts in the park. It seemed he was already having a tough job of convincing the congressman of his sanity, and shouting "Get those ghosts" would not have helped him make his case.

The two of us whipped through the park, ignoring the paths and instead making a beeline for the bright city lights. My vision filled with stone monuments, metal casings, leaves, bark, and, at one point, maybe a nest of baby birds, innards and all, very blechy, until we finally reached the park's skirting.

Brenda didn't even slow, crossing the street and launching down the first alley. She then made another four or five turns in quick succession—I was losing count—until she slowed and we glided to a halt near an empty bus stop. She went to sit down and, naturally, fell right through the bench, landing on her ass.

"Ow! Mothershitting dammit!"

When I offered to help her up, she shot me a scowl. In truth, she wouldn't need it—her body no longer had any weight—but sometimes, you know, it's just the gesture that can help make a woman not so mad at you.

"Goddamn, Painter."

Sometimes.

"You know, for a private investigator, you don't really have that coy-in-the-shadows thing nailed down."

"I'm working on it," I said.

Brenda kept an eye on the street. "Jorgensen's real name must be Chandra. Somehow stole his identity. That could be how, with all the blood on his hands, he's been able to stay under the police's radar."

"That explanation might have made more sense to you a few days ago, when you were alive, but not anymore," I said. "The congressman said whoever this Chandra is, they're dead."

She nodded. "Which explains why when you yelped like a little girl, Jorgensen, a livie, could hear the dead. Us. Or you. I was completely quiet."

"You're going to hang onto that for a while, aren't you?"

"Absolutely," she said and finally smiled. "So there's a dead Chandra inside a live Jorgensen. That's certainly in line with your livie–spook theory."

"Right," I said. "But why didn't the congressman just split when this weird dude started talking about running away and making ghost babies?"

The reporter leaped in place and punched the air. "Booyah! The congressman's fiancé was killed in prison. Murdered. The killer, unknown."

I nodded. "Damn. Chandra is the dead fiancé."

"She wants to find her killer."

For a moment, I mulled that over. "If she exposed her killer, she'd clear. But Chandra is looking for someone."

"She said, 'I need her address.'"

"Exactly. She plans on staying. She even told Stephen to pick a girl for her to overtake."

"Hell, I can't even grab a bench," Brenda said, giving the ground a swipe with her foot. "How much juice would you have to put into grabbing a body? Moving it, controlling it?"

"For a little while, maybe. But you would drain so fast." I shrugged, frustrated. "Even at one hundred percent, you wouldn't have energy to…"

"What?"

Ahead, I spotted another clearing and waved for her to follow me as I headed toward it. As I did, I traced my eyes up to the sky. Searching.

Brenda looked at me strangely, then her face lit up. She reached for my arm but didn't grab it, which would have tapped a bit of juice out of me. Looking up, she said, "There was that shimmer above Jorgensen. Do you think we can track him by that?"

"Yeah, I hadn't thought of that. Maybe. Harder to see under the city lights, but in the park, it looked like really long rope."

"Right. It's like a rail-thin cloud or something. It moves and twists a little. Really hard to see from where we were."

Brenda shrugged. "Maybe that's part of Chandra. Like a part of her, uh, spook body."

"Maybe."

She whispered hoarsely, "Where are we going?"

"Up to this clearing. Need to see something."

"What?"

"Come on."

We were moving quickly but being cautious. If Chandra had a line to the Mob, they'd be on us fast. I was already on their radar.

"Everything Jorgensen-Chandra has done up to this point—"

"Let's just go with Chandra."

"Fine," I said. "She's got some bad spooks on her side. And right now…" I said, craning my neck up to better see the sky. "…their full-time job seems to be getting ghosts for their two power stations."

Once we hit the middle of the park, I lay down on the grass and looked up to the heavens. It gave me a clear panoramic view of the sky, with the city buildings just at the edges. A moment later, Brenda did the same.

"Whatever Chandra's grand plan is, her endgame is to be with Stephen. She can only do that with a body, and any sort of permanent plan would require enormous amounts of energy. So that cloud or rope or whatever we saw above her? I think that's more like a cable. An electric feed."

"The power plants. They're giving her a shit-ton of juice. Enough to hold onto a living body."

The ice lightning pulsed and flowed, but every now, and then the surges would leave a dark spot. It was in those spots that I searched. After a few minutes, I saw what I was looking for.

"There," I said. "When the luminous sheets move to where it goes dark in that area over there—watch."

She did, and it took nearly a minute, but eventually she saw what I did. Against the backdrop of the dark sky was a pulsing, slowly twitching filament of energy. Tracing it patiently, we both saw that it arced down toward the park where we'd seen Chandra and the congressman.

Brenda went into reporter mode. "Wait, we still don't know why Chandra is on this killing spree."

"She's angry, I suppose."

"She's a chick with a plan, though. How does killing people fit into the plan?"

"It fits into the Ghost Mob's plan," I said slowly. "They want spooks to power their machines. Maybe it's like some sort of payment to them for all that juice they give to her." Looking over at Brenda, I saw she was slowly twisting a ring on her finger. A habit from when she was alive. Maybe it helped her concentrate. Then I remembered something the Professor had said to me. "You said Jorgensen had taken your ring."

"Douche."

"Right. My lady on the mountain told me something physical like that, something special, will have a link to you even now. Like a very thin wire."

"Yeah, that could be why I could sort of track the guy in Chicago. He still had my mom's ring, so I was picking up on that."

"Sure, but if you were supposed to be in the machine like the mailman, that link, that very thin wire, could be like a conduit. That hooks her back to the power station, and she gets plugged into the juice of maybe sixty or eighty ghosts. Once that link is established, anyone who's thrown in, they're feeding her."

I convulsed in a brief shiver, remembering what that had been like, even just the short time I'd been plugged in.

"But if this is a trade with the Mob, what do they get?" the reporter asked. "They've got plans for those power stations, and I don't think it's just so she can make ghost babies with Stephen."

"I don't know."

Brenda shifted in the grass, turning toward me. "How could you torture all those spooks and not care at all? What drives someone to put innocent people through that kind of hell? Love? Love doesn't do that."

I said, "Only one reason someone goes through all of that to come back from the dead. Only one reason some spook is that driven. The Professor once called it the most powerful force in the InBetween."

Brenda looked at me, the mascara marks streaking from her eyes glittering in the dark. She said, "What?"

I shrugged. "Revenge."

Chapter Twenty-Eight

I moved through the city with Brenda close behind me. This was her town, something she'd made clear several times in the previous minutes, but I knew where I needed to go.

However, that didn't mean I knew the streets I needed to take.

But looking at the sky like some ancient mariner guided by the stars, I headed toward my destination. For as much as it terrified me, I knew it was the only way forward.

"Okay, where are we going?"

I said, "We're playing catch-up but too slowly. We know Chandra will kill again. And remember she said there's something coming. Something that will change the world. I don't think she means everyone will be getting free glitter nails."

"But you said being in that power thing was tortuous. Soul crushing."

I shrugged. "I exaggerate. Part of my charm."

"Not buying that," she said. "We can track Chandra now. Let's just go do that!"

"She's way too powerful for us. But if we can find out her plan, maybe we can get ahead of her. Work out a way to pull the plug. Some of the images I saw when I was plugged into the power station didn't belong to me. I think they belonged to her. But to get a glimpse at that..." I said and pointed toward the sky. "I gotta ride the lightning."

"Don't do this."

"It's the fastest way," I said. "And we're running out of time."

Brenda looked at me with watery eyes, which complimented the mascara streaks down her face. She shook her head but knew I was right.

We snaked through Chicago, ending up just southeast of the city.

And we found what we were looking for.

Brenda had helped me get plugged into the power station on the outskirts of Chicago, which was in the gymnasium of a high school that had been shuttered, all the doors chained and the windows that hadn't been reinforced with security wire boarded up. At first, it seemed as if the school had likely lost funding in some redistricting scheme or there just weren't enough students in the area to necessitate it.

There were still remnants of student life on the walls. The random display of some themed homework project for all the world to see (that is, if the world could get through the chained doors). A trophy case with most trophies now gone. A few photos. And folded bits of masking tape that suggested items too personal to leave behind in the dying school.

We moved slowly through the dark halls, because if we were seen by one of the Mobsters, we'd both end up in the power station with no way out. We took each corner after first looking through the masonry to the other side.

It was sensible to take that precaution, but admittedly, I felt like a bit of a pussy. We were the good guys. We should be able to confidently stride through enemy territory and, if we saw some bad spook, take them out.

Me? Not so much a take-them-out kinda guy. I'd love to be, just never really developed that skill. Brenda told me the closest she'd come to combat training was cardio-boxing class.

"You sure you really want to do this?"

"No," I said. "I'm a bit freaked the fuck out, actually, but I need to see more of what's behind the curtain."

We crossed to a long hallway that passed by some administrative offices and a set of chained double doors that led into the front parking lot, which was slowly being overtaken by weeds.

At the far end, light pulsed through a pair of long, vertical windows.

"How do you know this'll give us anything? You told me you didn't really see much last time."

"I felt anger there, no question, and it wasn't mine," I said. "And there was more just under the surface, but I wasn't really of a mind to concentrate on it."

"Are you sure you can this time?"

I shrugged. "It's worth a try."

We agreed that I would stay plugged in for about a half hour. None of the clocks worked in the school, naturally—all frozen to the same time—so she was going to guess.

Entering the school, we'd spotted some houses and a nearby community center that was all lit up. Brenda was going to head over and try to slip into a group of people in case Chandra or any of the ghost mob was looking around for us.

No question, they'd be looking. But it seemed that anywhere near a torture chamber like one of their power stations would be the last place they'd think we would go.

We moved slowly down the dark hall, her hand gripping my shoulder. She squeezed me a bit tight, which wasn't unpleasant but did trickle some of my energy away. That reminded me.

"Oh, hey, when you pull me out, I'm going to be drained, remember."

"Right."

"So we need a place we can lie low for a few hours afterward."

The reporter looked at me with a strained face, blinking slowly, and murmured her agreement. We each stepped into a rectangular spill of light, farther away from the double doors to the gym at first, then slowly eased closer.

The sight of the power station was sickening. Similar to the one back home, it pulsed with light. There were probably a third as many ghosts connected to this one as to the other, which led me to believe it was newer.

The realization of that only solidified my plan to get plugged in and learn more about what they were planning. Chandra appeared to have all the juice she needed to keep suspended in the livie–spook form.

So why would they need more spooks? More power?

The answer seemed to be that Chandra wasn't going to be the only one straddling both worlds. Was that why she'd gone to see the congressman? Would he be the next? Or were there even bigger plans in place, and Congressman Lee was a means to make that happen?

The light from the power installation was overwhelming, but we didn't want to risk being seen coming in by anyone who might be guarding it. Whispering to each other, we agreed that Brenda would hang in the wall, going clockwise around the room, while I went counter-clockwise.

When we met on the other side, we both shook our heads.

No baddies around.

Not yet.

She turned to me. "One last chance to back out."

"Okay, you're right," I said. "This is a bad idea."

"Really?"

"No!" I waved my arms in big loops, like stretching before getting off the bench and heading into the game. "Don't freak me out more than I already am, 'K?"

"Okay," she said then gave my shoulder a squeeze. "I'll be nearby. I promise. Whatever you go through in there, know that it'll be over in no time."

I nodded, her pep talk having the reverse effect, but I tried not to show it.

A moment later, she walked with me to within a few feet of the power plant and watched me step between two poor souls who were gesticulating in a wash of electric light.

I crouched low, slipped between them, and gave Brenda one last look.

Then the world fell away from me.

My head was swimming instantly, and it was as if I'd fallen deeply asleep, fighting to regain consciousness. Swirls of dark colors (and darker thoughts) filled my eyes and ears, punctuated every (second? minute? day? week?) by the ionized cobra that stuck its teeth deep into my back every time I got just within grasp of yet another fleeting moment of cognition.

wait.

there is a plan i am here for a reason.

i chose to be here.

what the fuck was i thin—?

thwak! goes the snake.

Beyond the lash of pain and light so intense it left my ears ringing, there was a deep sorrow, a totality of anger so complete that it constituted itself in my mind as a separate entity, a fully forme...d other being that wandered arrogantly through my mind.

Some of the sorrow I felt was mine, mingling with this other being as if its physical presence in my head was, as a result, bathed in a dark-hued light of my own creation. But all that anger? That wasn't mine.

not mine.

follow that, that's why you're here

I reached out to this wandering beast, a malevolent creature loping through the halls of my mind, trying to get my fingertips c-l-o-s-e-r.

Each time I reached, lunged for it, the creature would twitch its flank away from me. I tried again and, not bothering to turn out of its lumbering gait, it again pulled its thick arm forward, its shoulder passing just out of my reach.

Finally, one last attempt—at the moment the snakebite stole my mind—it was as if the creature could not then sense me, and I grabbed on, clutching at the muscles in the valley between its shoulder and neck.

Pulling forward, I misjudged, couldn't stop, and then entered the beast, the intruder. But instead of passing through it, I was trapped inside. A passenger.

Hot eddies of rage swirled around me, shooting dark electric light down my body, through my bones, twisting my muscles then snapping at nerve endings, passing some sort of energy back into the creature I was now a part of.

My stomach heaved, nauseous, as consciousness slipped in and out of my grasp, just along for the ride as the creature navigated the world in front of it, clomp-clomp-clomp, me like a sweaty, naked infant unable to keep its head up.

the world passing by.

everything passing by me.

My head flew back, and color and shapes began to fold out of the darkness. Terror pierced my heart as I felt punishment for some unnamed infraction was coming, due to me. Squeezing my eyes shut made no difference. The visual assaults flowed over me like brackish water.

force it to make sense dont let it take control

okay its got control check youre being carried along like in a kangaroo pouch but look look thats why youre here

Staring into the terrifying swirl of shapes and colors, I compelled solid imagery to birth from it, fold into substantial form, something tangible—

dont create your own reality steal theirs steal theirs see you are here to see

—and before me grew what at first looked like a sports arena, then no, with its corner towers, high walls, and razor-wire fencing, searchlights crisscrossing, crisscrossing, it became a prison, a dark keep.

My vision surged with the imagery of the outside wall, thick and impenetrable, as it raced toward me, and I burst through it, smashing a succession of barriers, ending up trapped inside a cell, a small room I hated, two beds, the other filled by a fat, slovenly form that sat hulking, brooding, waiting for me to let my guard down.

no, not me

not me

chandra

this is why youre here look look look this is why youre here

The light in the room strobed like the dance floor of a German disco, and I saw the inmates whipping around me at incredible speeds, their feet not even moving as they crossed the floor, in and out of cells, in and out of the cell block.

not a strobe light.

days.

Each burst of light was the entire sunburst of a single day then night then another day, and I endured dozens, hundreds, thousands of them.

years.

In the back of my brain was this worming, something trying to wiggle into my consciousness, and it felt alien. Unreal.

Although I willed it to take form, it could only appear as gossamer thread, undulating as if in a light, pleasant breeze.

this is hope there is hope and there is shame because it doesnt belong but here it is and with it there is joy an—

Around me, the flicker of light—the days—became a long, violent river of fire and screams, fists flying, the flash of blades, a knife with a dragon hilt, then gunfire from above.

My vision flickered, dulled, then sharpened, and I saw a shimmering wooden stump, strange leaves splayed out across it, walls of dusty concrete with menacing and rusted bars cruelly piercing the floor and ceiling.

wait

Then darkness, total darkness.

The world oozed back up from below, from the dark, but it looked different. Like a world on top of the world. Some film that lay across it.

i know this place this is the inbetween i remember it looking so strange like this unnatural unreal

Fear shot through me as if I'd put a fork in an electrical outlet just to see what would happen.

I turned, just my head.

Fear stared back at me, a look on the man's face that was at once defeated and pleading. I recognized him.

"Please help me," Jan Jorgensen whimpered.

Then were my own thoughts mixing in? I suddenly saw Katie's father Hank. His face was cut with lines of rage, gun pointed at me. Bursts of light. Then another—the stepdad Boyd. But back when he'd been alive.

Then more faces. I saw the congressman lying next to me, my hand reaching for his face. Then someone else. A woman. Distorted, bent.

Then whoosh! those images were sucked away from me.

When I looked up, the sky of the dream world InBetween flickered through purples, blues, and deep reds and then began moving, coursing past my eyes, the buildings, the street, everything around me passing so fast nausea rose again, and I started tumbling forward until resting, hovering in the air above a slowly spinning cube.

Not just a cube.

A luminous cube spinning within a ring, the ring moving in the opposite direction of the cube. Of all the images, this was the queerest, the most strange. The rest seemed to have some… substance to it, but this was like a thought expressed in bad modern art.

The cube then began to transform. At first, it looked like a sphere, but the sphere was instead the early formation of a head. A face was starting to appear, the ring speeding up now. I tried to look—

Around me, the world went dark, and I felt as though I'd died. Again. My body was cold, but I could feel my sweat making me colder. My knees and wrists ached, and my hands were going one past the other as I slowly crawled forward.

Brenda released the grip she'd had on my head and helped me to my feet.

Exhausted, I felt like a drunk, leaning up against my unfortunate date. She lifted my chin, and I nearly wept when I saw the concern on her face.

She whispered, "You okay?"

I could only nod the once, my eyes still refusing to focus. My energy had nearly bottomed out. She had to drag me.

Outside the door, the reporter put a finger to her lips.

"Had to pull you out," she whispered again. "We've got a bit of help, just up the road. And I found some stuff out."

"Me too," I drawled as we passed through a chained door. "I know who Chandra's going after. The revenge she's looking for."

"Who?"

Fireworks burst around my eyes as my vision began to flicker. I wanted to tell her more but for now just said, "Woman."

Chapter Twenty-Nine

As the blurred colors and shapes slowly got their shit together and started properly forming things like chairs and beds and darkened televisions lurking up in the high corners, I slowly sat up.

"Why'd you put me on the floor?"

"You want me to carry you everywhere? I'm not a pack mule, Painter."

"Is your friend here now?" another voice, female and airy, said, "Will I be able to hear him, too?"

Brenda turned to me and held a hand out, lifting me to my feet.

We were in a hospital room. Outside, the halls were bathed in a half light. My eyes hurt despite, of course, my not really having eyes anymore. The Professor explained this sort of thing to me once. "While you're bound by the physics of the InBetween, you don't really have a physical form. So matter is a matter of perspective. What your mind dictates."

Unfortunately, "what your mind dictates" doesn't mean willing free ice cream and baby kittens for everybody. It's more like a part of the brain's autonomous system, like breathing or your heart beating or the troubling reflex of wanting to punch Ed Sheehan in the face.

A bit wobbly on my feet, I lifted my head to see Brenda standing at the foot of the hospital bed of a frail woman with a smile that seemed too big for her face. Her eyes shifted from corner to corner.

"Painter's to your right," Brenda said, her hand hovering just over the woman's blanket-covered foot. "Mostly to the right. He's a bit unsteady right now."

The frail woman's face wrinkled into a frown. "Is he okay?"

"I'm fine." I spoke softly because it seemed louder words might snap her bones. "Is it all right that we are here?"

The woman nodded, and Brenda introduced her to me as Mrs. Weathers.

"Alice, please," she said, half extending her hand, then recalling it with a smile, shaking her head slightly. "I don't suppose you shake."

"Not without a tasty treat and a belly rub, certainly," I said with a smile in my voice.

Alice laughed. "I can tell you're trouble."

Brenda said, "While you were playing around in the machine, I came here. I knew there was a hospital in this area, just took a moment to find it."

"It's not really a full hospital," Alice said. "Some call it a comfort clinic. It's basically for end-of-life patients." The woman sat straighter in bed, reached her fingers up to her short-cropped hair, and rubbed absentmindedly at a small spot. "No one here's getting better."

"I'm sorry about that."

Alice said, "Painter, you're dead, for cryin' out loud! Between the three of us, I'm in the best shape."

It was my turn to laugh. I liked her.

Brenda told me that she'd come down the halls calling out, and Alice had responded. It had taken a few minutes to convince the dying woman that she wasn't losing her mind.

"All the drugs leave you kind of sick, exhausted," she said. "But nobody tells you about the hallucinations. At first, I thought you were just one of those." Her eyes misted slightly. "But I remember

Brenda Matthews when your newspaper would put you on the TV. She was the prettiest reporter. You know, locally."

"Aw, thanks," Brenda said. "I think."

For the next few minutes, I told them what I'd seen inside the power station. A lot of it, obviously, I didn't understand, so we spent a little time going over some of the visuals to see if maybe they could work it out.

Alice had an iPad out and was tapping away as I spoke.

"Chandra died in prison." I remembered the image of the knife, recalling that it looked like a dagger. "Stabbed."

"Yikes," Alice said.

"You said she might be after a woman."

I shrugged, slowly shaking my head.

"Congressman Lee's fiancée Chandra Withy—" Alice said, tapping away on her tablet, "—was killed during a small prison riot last year." She continued thumping. "Caught in the crossfire of some gang-related scuffle."

I came around the side of the bed to see the screen, but she was holding it at an odd angle. Drifting into the bed frame gave me a better vantage point.

"You see an update? Is there any more?"

Alice reached over and plugged a charger into the device. "I don't see much more about it. Wait—"

"What?"

"Oh, I remember this. So sad," the frail woman said then cleared her throat, which started her coughing. After she stopped, she continued. "First trial was a hung jury. The congressman's live-in girlfriend was waiting for her second trial in prison."

"Okay," I said. "What'd she do?"

Brenda said, "Maybe it was the start of this killing spree? Hold on." The reporter slowly shook her head. "Yeah, a junior congressman gets caught up in a scandal over his fiancée. It wasn't huge news, but I can't believe I forgot that case."

Watching as Alice tapped away on the tablet, I said to Brenda, "It's just this place. Your memory goes like a damp patch of concrete drying in the sun. Bits and pieces of it, here and there, just start to go."

Alice read from a couple of articles she'd pulled up, while the reporter filled in the gaps.

"Chandra was a drunk, it seems. She got into a car and killed a kid. Her lawyer was good and got a shred of doubt into the that first case. Hung jury."

The second trial had garnered less interest than the first. As it dragged on, some jurors from the first trial had spoken out in paid interviews about how contentious the first had been. Arguing, swearing in their chambers.

Alice said, "Then, before trial two wrapped up, she was killed in the riot." She turned the screen to where I'd been standing. The Professor once told me livies only think they hear us. Not sure exactly what that meant (as with most things she says), but it seems that our voices appear in their heads and aren't actually cast across the room.

The woman in bed said, "It looks like for the second trial, Congressman Lee had agreed to appear at the trial for the defense. He was going to take the stand as a character witness."

On the screen, I recognized a face. "I know who she's after." Pointing, I said, "That's the woman I saw in the machine. "

The reporter looked down at the screen. "Right. Her lawyer."

Chapter Thirty

I spent the next hour trying to gin up some energy but then realized I could do that better across a long stretch of water. Even better, several long stretches of water.

"We should go see the Professor, find out if there's a way to take apart those power stations. Without that, Chandra can't hold on. The killings stop."

"She'll know how to dismantle the power stations?"

"If not, she'll give us something that'll help us work out how to do it."

Brenda wasn't convinced. "We can track Chandra now just by looking up and searching for the twin streams. She's after her old lawyer. Maybe she blames the woman." The reporter put her hands on her hips. "I'm going to stop her. The congressman apparently knows where this lawyer is."

Alice's head perked up. "I'll help, Brenda. I'll go."

Brenda moved toward the woman, who looked like no more than skin and bones beneath the thin sheets. "You have to stay here."

"No, I don't," the woman said and confidently slid out of her bed and walked to the small closet. "Sure, I can't hit the clubs with you…"

Brenda smiled at me. "I think my club days are behind me."

"…but if you need information, Brenda Matthews, you're going to need someone like me to help you out."

"Someone like you?"

"Someone not dead," Alice said and pulled a pair of jeans over her thin pajama pants. "At least, not yet."

We decided to split up, me going back to Stone Mountain to find out what I could from the Professor while they tried to stop the lawyer from being Chandra's next victim. We'd meet back in Alice's room.

This time I headed southwest and caught the Mississippi near Davenport, Iowa. The time across land slowed me down, and for a while, I was forced to take a couple back roads and interstates at top speed.

It wasn't terribly risky in these parts, not too densely populated, so odds were I wouldn't smack into any ghosts along the way. Unless, of course, I was drawn toward them. Still, I didn't have time to dawdle.

At Nashville, I headed southeast, rolling the case over in my head. Chandra was planning revenge, but was Jorgensen a part of it? Maybe they were partners.

Then I remembered what I'd seen in the power station. Jorgensen with his arms wrapped around his knees, begging for help, pleading to be let go. It seemed most likely that Chandra had somehow taken control of him to go after the lawyer and had made a deal with the Mob to get the juice to do it.

What would they get in return?

"Whoa, Professor?"

I slowed quickly, having caught sight of her, a glow emanating from her ribcage, coming across a large plot of grass near the north face of Stone Mountain, Georgia. From what I could tell, this was an area that often hosted festivals, carnivals.

Flashes of memories associated with the area crackled into my mind briefly, and I saw a crowd of thousands all sitting quietly, families gathered on blankets and in circles of lawn chairs, watching a giant screen at the end closest to the mountain. A war film had been playing against the white, billowing screen.

"Painter," The Professor said, and she smiled. "To what do I owe the pleasure?"

"I had a couple of questions it seemed you might know something about," I said, coming up beside her. "First off—"

She held a hand up. "Wait, wait. Not here. Ears are everywhere." The Professor then pointed up to the mountain. It was the first time I'd ever seen her outside of her sky-high perch, at least as far as I could remember, and it was clear the "Guru Is In" sign was only hung up there. It seemed the mountain wasn't just some silly role-play. She was worried about being overheard and, up top, you would see literally anyone and everyone coming from a mile away.

Who was she afraid of?

Why was I asking myself so many questions? The whole asking questions-in-my-head thing wasn't coming up with any answers. Maybe I should stop?

We traveled without speaking, side by side, and when we arrived at the bottom of the mountain, we headed for its summit. I stumbled a few times, still a bit low on energy from the power station drain, and she deftly reached out and nabbed my wrist—gently, so as to not drain a single drop of energy—and pulled me right again.

That was what she did for me any time I'd come to see her. She pulled me right again. My rock on a rock.

But something odd had flashed in my brain when she'd reached out. As her hand wrapped around my wrist, I saw the flash of... something from an old textbook or maybe that old movie out on the Stone Mountain lawn?

A farm. Fields planted with barley. A tiny house with horses. Uh, a barn, maybe, then (I'm not exactly the farming type, you may have guessed).

Then in the next instant, it was gone, and we'd arrived at the top of a massive slab of rock.

The Professor took a few moments to get herself settled, sat down in the lotus position (which did actually feel as if it was for show) and looked up to me, waiting.

I was about to ask her my questions when suddenly another popped into my head.

"What were you doing off the mountain?"

She blinked once. "I'm not a prisoner here."

"But I've never known you to leave here," I said. "Am I wrong?"

"Yes, of course you are," she said and spun slowly in place, head cocked and looking down slightly. "You've seen me leave. You just don't remember. It's flitted away, Painter."

"Sure, but you're in the same boat as me, right? Are you saying your memory doesn't degenerate?"

"What good would I be to you if I couldn't remember the things you sought to know?"

"That doesn't answer my question."

The Professor slowly moved her head to the other side, still spinning. "I have taught myself ways to retain information."

"How?"

She looked up at me and smiled. "I don't give away trade secrets, kid. Then suddenly there's prophets on mountaintops from here to the sea. What is it you wanted to know?"

I told her about getting plugged into the power station in the Cities after getting jumped by the spooks Lonnie had led to his dead-car music room in Chicago. The pain in her eyes touched me.

"I got out, obviously."

"How?"

"A friend," I said. "She's probably a bit braver than me and has been a big help recently."

The Professor's spinning came to a stop then moved in the other direction. "Dangerous. Your friend risked getting caught and put into the hell herself."

"I know. But we've been careful."

"You were lucky."

I nodded and left that part of the discussion behind. "This Ringman is really a woman spook inside a live man. I think this Chandra person is using the energy from the power station to hold onto the livie."

She nodded.

"Can those two power stations be stopped? Take away that power?"

The Professor's eyes went wide, and her mouth started moving, but then she stopped, composed herself, and started again. "I'm sorry, that is outside my knowledge. I don't understand how the apparatus they've created works. I've seen similar things on a far, far smaller scale. But those had been benign, created to help souls that had suffered a trauma gain some energy back," she said then bit her lip. "But this... this is something entirely different."

"So can they be destroyed?"

She slowly shook her head. "I don't know. But I expect you'll work it out."

I waited for more from her, but she didn't give it and resumed her slow spin, hands resting on her knees. I told her about my vision of Jorgensen, tempered with my concerns that I might have projected the man myself into the hallucinatory experience.

"How would that be possible, though?" I asked. "How would this Chandra be able to use Jorgensen's body?"

"I'm still not convinced it's entirely real," she said. "There have been plenty of spirits who have bragged about possessing a living person or simply claimed to witness someone else do it. It's the ultimate revenge. Taking over someone else's body, someone who wronged them, and committing the most severe self-harm. Debasing things. But the claims? It's always been bluster. Bravado."

"Always?"

She blinked a few times. "Except once."

I waited for her to speak again, but she instead just sat quietly in thought. Just as I was about to ask her more about it, she continued.

"From the little I know of it, the instant the livie dies, in that split second, the spirit can take over. There can be no break. Almost like one relay racer handing the next a baton. No gap. And despite how improbable this occurrence is, while the body is in effect dead, with the spirit's energy, it's not completely so. However, it will begin to decay, albeit far more slowly than it might normally."

"Except I saw Jorgensen. He's not dead. He's still in there, begging to be set free."

The Professor looked at me for a long time. She looked away for a moment, to the west. Conflicted. Then, finally, she said, "What I'm about to tell you is the most dangerous piece of information on Earth."

I looked at her. "You know who killed Kennedy?"

It was hard to make her laugh, but this time she smiled. "No. John knows who did it. He told me."

"Wait? What?"

"That's not important right now. This is," she said and relaxed her body. "There has to be some complicity. The will to give up the shell, the body. That is a doorway for the dead."

She sucked in a deep breath and let it out slowly. Cleansing, calming. Then the Professor explained a concept of the InBetween she'd never spoken about before.

It was called a "cab ride."

"This requires the surrender of a living being to a soul in the InBetween. Of course, it is only those close to death who can hear spooks, as you're fond of calling us. But for the spirit's bond to be strong enough to hold the body, this can't be an afterthought. Active." She looked at me. "A choice to leave."

I pictured the elderly residents of Shady Hills. None of them had a choice; it was coming whether they wanted it or not. Then it clicked. "Wait. A suicide? Are you saying Jorgensen was a suicide and Chandra was able to jump in?"

She shrugged. "If the ephemeral spirit can inhabit the body at the exact moment the host exits, the body remains alive. In the first case I mentioned, the person has chosen to leave and throws the keys to the vehicle to the spirit on their way out, as it were. The body slowly rots, a process that can take weeks but can be slowed further."

"What about a cab ride?"

"Staying with the analogy, the living mind hops into the back seat. Still present but relinquishing control. Cognizant of all that is happening around them. I can't imagine they fully understand what they've agreed to."

"So Chandra convinced Jorgensen to do that?"

"It's an unbalanced partnership. And the timing must be perfect for either process to work at all. A body cannot live, not for a fraction of a second, without a mind to will it to do so. But thankfully, a cab ride is virtually impossible. The energy it would take to pull it off is more than a spirit can generate. A few seconds, maybe, but more than that, no."

Unless, of course, they had an outside power source.

I looked at the Professor and knew she was holding something back. I called her on it. "What aren't you telling me?"

A sad smile. "Coercion."

"How?"

"The power of whispers. A susceptible mind. Someone lost, confused, hurting. Then an idea begins to form in their head. A tiny seedling whose roots begin to grow and grip the mind, but it's not one the livie planted." She spun for a moment and looked at the dull-white latticework of the sky. "Ghost whispers. Over time, a person can be nudged toward leaving the light. Their impending death can crack open a door like it does in the old and infirm, allowing them to hear our plane. A malevolent spirit can take advantage of that. Speaking through the crack, muttering poisonous words over days, weeks, maybe more. The living person has no idea these thoughts are not their own. They are the will of another. And that will can be absorbed by the living without them knowing it. Over time, if the whispers are persistent enough, they are compelled to give themselves over to whoever wants in."

"Compelled?"

I saw something on her face that was my second big shock of the visit. Her lips slightly trembling, the Professor used the back of her index finger and brushed her face. She'd wiped away a real tear.

"Such a banal term, 'cab ride.' But the very concept is a violation," she said then realized I was staring. She hardened her expression. "More than that, if it's possible, it is a threat to both the dead and the living worlds."

Then I knew I wasn't working on two cases—Katie's stepdad and the killing spree of Chandra Withy. They were the same case. Boyd had been increasingly depressed in those weeks before Hank had shot him. Officially, the cops' report said Boyd had popped enough pills to make his heart stop beating.

When Hank had shot the "dead" man—"Whatever was behind those eyes, that wasn't the accountant"—he had been right: it wasn't Boyd. He'd shot Chandra, who'd likely been ghost whispering Boyd into taking his own life. He was susceptible, likely someone who struggled with depression all his life. But once she'd finally taken hold of the man's body, all that work was down the tubes. Here came drunk Hank to fill him full of slugs. The body was now shot up to hell, rotting like any other corpse would.

So she fled, left the body, and sought someone else out. After all the patience she'd wasted with Boyd, this second time, she took the shortcut—a cab ride. But it would require more juice than one spook had. That was why she'd needed the Ghost Mob's power station: to hold onto Jorgensen's body and pin the man in the "back seat."

Images from the power station's fever dreams came back to me. Now it was all beginning to make sense. She was desperate. Jorgensen hadn't been a part of her original plan. A young man looking miserable holding... what? He wasn't yet committed to going through with it. Maybe hoping someone might stop him. Hoping someone might care.

Instead, he got her.

Jorgensen hadn't been groomed for days and weeks. His commitment was more tenuous. He'd been only contemplating a leap, but Chandra had used that to slip in. The power stations let her keep control. The killings I didn't quite understand yet, but they were a part of the fuel or connection back to the grid.

But somehow, Chandra knew how all this worked when no one else did.

"It's her secret," I said, and the realization hit me like a truck.

The Professor looked at me, her head tilted slightly. She said, "After you told me about this creature, I sought Chandra out and watched as she moved. She's constantly being tugged back toward the InBetween."

"So that's where you went."

The prophet smiled.

Looking up, I said, "Chandra needs that extension cord in the sky to power the cab ride. Somehow she's linked to the power stations, dragging the cord along."

She nodded. "There are just the two streams of light powering her. The Ghost Mob's leader is keeping her on a short leash, trying to work out how she does it. But she's keeping her distance to prevent that."

"That's why there was no one to snap up Bernard or Brenda right away. Calkin and his crew didn't know until after the fact." The fever-dream images flashed across my mind. Slices of light, metal, charms. Rings. "Maybe Jorgensen's fighting back now, so she needs that extra hit of juice from a fresh kill. But it's the charms, that's what connects her back to the power stations—that extension cord is all those necklaces and rings. The spook who owned that stuff goes into the machine, and the possessions direct their and the rest of the station's energy to whoever has those trinkets."

"Probably a piercing or two."

"Blechy," I said and put my hand on my stomach. "Secondhand piercings. That's an image I did not need."

"Thank heavens you've got a continuously dissolving memory."

I laughed. Yes, I supposed there were some advantages to having a mind that would turn to Swiss cheese over weeks and months. Which always made me wonder how the Professor knew what she knew and didn't lose it.

We all have our gifts, I thought, then I looked at her frail body, wrapped in a thin sheet. Or curses.

The Professor tilted her head and waited as if she were expecting me to say more. She then looked up to the warbling night sky.

She said, "Painter, don't you remember the sky before this all began? Don't you remember how clear it was?"

"Yes," I said, looking upward. "I know that I should say yes to that. So I'm saying yes."

The Professor looked back to me. "The stars shone to us, visions from the past, even in death. Many of them were suns that had long since gone dark but stood as reminders that not all that is dead is forgotten. Not all that has died is without light."

Despite a memory of looking at stars, the darkness above us was more like a thin, dark eggshell with myriad veins.

"The crisscross of shimmering light you see above, like some luminescent film on a picture window, all of that was not here before. That is the energy generated from the Mob's power cells. They've been at it for decades, and now they're close. Their grid is nearly complete. Look up."

She stood up slowly, spread her arms, and began to speak, but then no words came. Looking toward me, the Professor motioned me to stand next to her. Most of the time I've ever been atop Stone Mountain, I've been laser focused on talking with the smartest person I know. As I stood next to her, she drew her hand toward the horizon, encouraging me to look more closely.

She whispered, "They have swallowed the stars, foretelling the darkness that is to come."

Then I saw it.

"From the ground, mostly it's a vast ocean of light threads," she said. We turned and looked to the west, the slowly writhing fabric of light dulling the closer it got to the horizon, the farther away from where we were standing.

For the first time, the sky terrified me.

"There aren't only two of those monstrosities," I said. "Those power stations are everywhere. All over the world. Thousands of them."

"Maybe more."

From this vantage point, high above the ground, you could see what looked like long, skinny trees made of fungal spores, wrapped into thick, twisted tornadoes of energy. All around us, in every direction, as far as the eye could see, these energy twisters writhed and pulsed, pumping power into the gossamer lace that had become our sky.

"What is it?" My mouth felt dry. I struggled to find the right words. "What is all this for?"

She smiled sweetly to me, like a doctor who'd just given me a terminal diagnosis. "You know, there was one before. Before this Chandra of yours. One other nearly, gosh, fifty years back. I'd hoped he was just some anomaly. Because the power to go back? There's nothing more dangerous to our world—" She looked down at the groups of people in the park. "—or theirs."

Despite the magnitude of the threat we faced, I suddenly was very worried about Brenda.

"The lawyer you mentioned." The Professor nodded slowly. "It's troubling how powerful vengeance is here. Sometimes, I wonder if that's what tore the space between life and death to create the InBetween." She turned her head to me slightly. "We shouldn't be here. None of us should. But we are."

I didn't have time for philosophical discussions. All that brash light in the sky told me the stakes were much, much higher than I'd realized. Because it was clear why the Ghost Mob was giving Chandra all that power.

"They want the secret, don't they? That's the trade. The Mob has the power, but they don't know the secret to pulling off a cab ride."

"Chandra's the only one to learn how to do it in a half century. Very, very few even know how it works."

"How few?"

She blinked. "Including Chandra? Far as I know, just three."

"Well, you just told me, so…"

"Right. Like I said: three."

I realized how grave things were if she was entrusting me with the most powerful secret in the world.

"I need to get back to Chicago," I said. "So what do you think the Ghost Mob is planning."

"An army of the dead."

I stopped then turned back. "Wait. What?"

"Okay, that is a bit dramatic," she said. "But fairly accurate. It's been their plan since the start. Members of the Ghost Mob all came here individually, and they were recruited. Those who didn't join the plan were plugged into the power cells. Those recruited, all of them, are angry, hateful, bent on the one thing we have left here. The one thing the InBetween was created for."

"Revenge."

She nodded. "If Chandra gives Calkin the secret, he will finally be able to cross over. A mob of lunatics both alive and dead. Powerful. Unstoppable. Kill one, and with all that power, they jump into another body and keep moving.

"The armies of the living will fall. And as they do, they will either join the march of the Ghost Army, or they will be its fuel." She turned to me and placed a hand on each of my shoulders without taking the smallest amount of energy from me. I now knew why she had entrusted me with the secret.

I said, "You want me to stop the rise of a ghost army."

She said, an urgent tone in her voice I'd never heard, "It can't happen. It's a corruption that would twist both of our worlds into something vile. Life on Earth would be Hell for the dead and the living."

The Professor started to slide away from me, as she does, but more slowly than usual.

"So you kind of buried the lede, right? Maybe you should have started with 'you need to stop a ghost army from destroying the world'?"

She kept sliding but turned to me. "It's a big ask, I know."

"Nah. You just want me to save the world. Both of them. Me."

Her slide stopped. "There are the paths we choose and the paths that choose us."

"I just wanted to be a ghost P.I. This is Armageddon-level shit," I said but then already knew what I had to do. "Okay, fine. I'll go stop Chandra."

"She's too strong, Painter. Those machines make her the most powerful entity on the planet right now."

"Then I suppose," I said, crossing my arms high on my chest, "I'll need to even the playing field."

Chapter Thirty-One

The tall, thin man at the tiny desk looked up as the door slowly settled back on its jamb behind the graying woman. Alice thought she caught the hint of a frown.

"Can I help you, ma'am?"

"Of course, that's what you're for, right?" Alice's voice was thin and a little harsh around the edges. But pleasant all the same. "I need to speak with the Congressman."

There was no hint this time, just a frown.

"Great," the young man said, reaching into a drawer and pulling out a ringed notebook. "What is your name?"

"He won't know my name, actually. If I could just—"

"He's not available today, ma'am. But I can put you down on the list, and when an opportunity—"

"No, that won't work for me," Alice said with a smile. But sometimes a smile can be far more intimidating than any other expression. "It will have to be today." The middle-aged woman's head tilted for a moment. "Actually, it will have to be right now."

A smile with the same warmth as the frown before it. "I'm sorry, that is not—"

Alice turned from the desk, shuffling her feet across the linoleum floor. When the Congressman's aide looked at them, she appeared to be wearing hospital slippers.

He tried again. "Ma'am, I appreciate your tenacity, but it—"

"Tell Congressman Lee my name is Alice Weathers," she said as she sat down, making a grunting sound as her bottom hit the plastic chair. "And that I'm here to talk about Chandra, his fiancée." The young man started to talk, and she added. "She's dead, by the way."

"Yes."

"Just not enough, it turns out," Alice said and chuckled softly. The young man simply stared at her for a moment. "You need to call him now, because I'm dying, on a raft of drugs that make me terribly incontinent. If I were you, I wouldn't make me wait."

Five minutes later, she had been shown into an adjoining room and was sitting in a large wingback chair, one of two, across from Congressman Lee. He'd been on the phone when she'd entered, so she sat quietly and waited.

Alice knew he wasn't speaking to anyone. He'd been thrown by what she'd told the aide and was taking the opportunity to size her up.

Brenda said, "He's not talking to anyone."

"I know," Alice said and shrugged. "Let him have his fun."

The Congressman looked at Alice, then to the empty chair next to her. He said, "Are… are you talking to me?"

"That's why I'm here," Alice said. "Time's a-wastin', Steve. I could drop dead right here, and you'd be up poop creek."

The Congressman sat down and, watching the woman, said "I'll call you back." He pocketed the phone and placed both hands on the desk, palms down.

She waited, a genuine smile coming to her face.

"You're enjoying this," Brenda said and laughed.

"I'll admit, it is fun to watch the man squirm."

The Congressman looked into the corners of the room then back to the frail woman sitting in the big leather chair. "Did you know Chandra? A relative? I don't remember seeing you at the funeral."

"No, but I've been conversing with the dead over the last few hours or so, and they've made me aware that there's some serious shit going on, and you're caught up in it. So is your Chandra. She's bad news, Stephen. Bad news."

His eyes fell closed briefly, and he began to stand. "Ma'am, I appreciate you coming by, but I don't really have time for this."

She smiled. "Make the time."

"Listen—"

"You would think after your visit from Chandra last night, you would be brimming with questions."

"How do you kn—" The Congressman's face darkened. "Are you two working together? Is this some sort of racket? Are you looking for money, because I can ass—"

"No, nothing like that, I assure you," Alice said, stifling a cough. "My friend Brenda says you may be in some serious danger. Chandra is unhinged. Angry. She's killed countless people."

"What are you talking about? My fiancée is dead! She was killed in prison!"

"And now she's in a man named Jan Jorgensen. And using his body, she's been on a killing spree." Alice cocked her head slightly, then continued. "Brenda says they thought, at first, she was looking to kill you for some reason. Probably a cheater. All men are, you know. At least all the ones I—" Alice shifted slightly, pulling a few inches away from the empty chair next to her. "All right, all right. Brenda says you may need to find somewhere safe for a while."

Another long blink. "And I assume this is a dead woman, right? Talking to you right now."

"And she'd really appreciate any info you might have on where your fiancée may be heading."

Stephen tried to laugh, to look casual, but his face betrayed him. "This is nuts."

"But true."

"So says you're dead friend sitting in my empty chair, I suppose."

"She's not in the chair."

"Good."

"She's behind you."

Like a shot, Stephen jumped up and slid out from behind the desk, staring into the empty space there. He sighed and wiped his mouth. "Okay. Funny."

"Brenda says the room behind you is a small bathroom. There's a small sink and toilet. A toothbrush. A blue one. Boring. A prescription for Lisinopril, 20 milligrams. A cloth robe that looks like it was stolen from a hotel."

"I paid for that!" he said and caught himself. "All of that you could have found out in some article written about me. I've given dozens of interviews—"

"Oh, one more thing, wait... really? That's exciting. Did the articles also say you've got a .45 caliber pistol in the toilet tank? Wrapped in plastic."

He eyeballed her for a moment, sitting back down behind the desk, nearly missing the chair at first, righting himself then settling into place.

"It's a dangerous part of town. And it's registered. All legal," he said then shook his head. "And you probably broke in and saw it."

Alice stood up and loosened the belt on her pants. She wasn't used to all the moving around. It had been months since she'd had this much exertion, and it was taking its toll. "Do I look like someone who could break in anywhere? I'll have a bugger of a time just walking out!"

As she sat back down, he began to speak, but she put her hand up. "Okay, we've got to get down to business. Brenda says you've got a bottle of whiskey in the drawer, bottom right, next to another cell phone. Why do you need two?"

"Who are you?"

"And that you've got on two different socks, same color but different, an undershirt with a coffee stain that looks like it's been there a while. Oh, and red jockeys. Uh, rather tiny, she says."

Stephen leaned back in his leather chair, and the harshness on his face fell. He exhaled.

"It's a trick."

"No trick. I promise you," she said and coughed dramatically. "Swear on my life."

"You're talking to ghosts. That's insane. You can't expect me to beli—"

"We don't have time for this, Stephen," Alice said. "For now, just take it on faith. Chandra is still here. And she's dangerous."

He stared off for a moment, then his eyes went glassy. "Red jockeys. You know, Chandra actually bought these for me. She thought it was funny. I'm supposed to be proper. Presentable. She thought it was a kick that underneath, I'd be wearing these red speedo-type undies." He laughed.

Alice furrowed her brow. "You still love her?"

"I always will," he said and dropped his head for a moment. When he looked up, he said, "So you're saying that was really her? In the park the other night? That just... that can't be true. But he—she—knew things about us—intimate moments—no one else would. But this can't be real."

Alice leaned forward slightly, which took a bit of effort. "She's dangerous now. The person you knew, your fiancée, maybe there's something about the next world that can change people. I don't know anything about it. That's where Brenda is."

Stephen looked just past Alice's shoulder. "Is it... Hell? Or something?"

"No, not hell, but sort of a stopover. Like taking a connecting flight into whatever's next. They're just sorta stuck in the terminal."

His eyes went back to the window, and he spoke more to himself than to the frail woman sitting in front of him. "You know, my advisers, they warned me off from her."

"She's bad news, Stephen."

"No, the Chandra I knew was lovely. Determined, focused, and ruthless when she went after something, but she wasn't unkind. Just the opposite. She had a good mother. Raised right."

Alice simply listened. She resisted closing her eyes for fear she might fall asleep. Or never open them again.

"Her father," Stephen said and chuckled. "That was another story. He was crazy. I mean sociopath crazy. Brilliant guy, I'd heard, but if you want to talk about a killer, that's him. Worked for organized crime or something. But to hear Chandra tell it, he liked killing."

"There are very broken people out there."

"But not Chandra. In fact, her father's father had been a really dark guy, too. Did some horrible shit, I believe. I never looked into it too much, but there's a file around here somewhere that my people put together. That's why they'd told me to back off. A lot of baggage in the past. Could hurt me, maybe down the road."

"Brenda says she would like to see that file if you do have it. Might help."

"I'll look. I probably burned it," he said, chuckling. Then he grew serious again. "You say she killed a lot of people? I just can't imagine that."

"Who knows? I've heard of people having killer traits, psychos like her dad and grandad, but without the triggers, you don't go on killing sprees. Good at business. CEOs and things like that. In fact, apparently, a huge percentage of CEOs are borderline sociopaths. They just kill competition instead of people."

Stephen came around and sat in the empty chair next to Alice.

"So why are you involved? Alice, is it?"

"I'm waiting to die," she said and shrugged. "But I can do good before I go. And it passes the time. Brenda says you're in danger." She sighed and asked again, "Do you know where Chandra was going? Did she say anything?"

"Listen, I'm not sure I really believe all this. It's, I mean, it's so much to take in," he said, searching her face for some tell that this was all some game. "But if I take you at your word... last night, that man asked about Chandra's old defense attorney. Wanted to know where she was."

"Why is she mad at her? Does Chandra blame her for dying in prison? Did she screw up the trial or something?"

"No, in fact, Bron was one of her biggest advocates. She fought hard for my fiancée. She always held out hope. Even went door knocking herself, canvassing the neighborhood looking for any other evidence to prove my Chandra was innocent."

"Did she find anything?"

"No. And she'd spent days out there, I understand. It was her passion about it, that's why she'd gotten a hung jury that first time. She was convincing."

"What do you think happened?"

Stephen looked away and, a moment later, wiped his eyes. "I ran out that night after I saw Chandra pull in. I'd been waiting at the window of our apartment. We'd been at a restaurant and had a fight. I'd taken a cab home. I guess she stayed and tried to forget about the fight. Or me. We know what happened. If she hadn't died in that riot, she was going to spend a long time in prison. That's the truth."

Alice leaned toward the man and put a frail hand on his knee. "She feels wronged somehow. And in the InBetween place, something triggered her. So much rage, she's found a way to come back, and it's not for anything good."

"So your friend thinks I need to lie low? How long?"

A tilt of the head. "Until she's stopped. Could be days. Weeks. Who knows. But she's hurt a lot of people. Killed people, Stephen." Alice coughed, and her body shook for a moment. The congressman got up and poured a glass of water from a small table by the wall. He returned with it, and she took a small sip, cradling the glass in her hands.

"Do you have any idea why she might be angry at her old attorney—what was her name?"

"Bron. Bronwyn Redding. She lives at some place off River North, near downtown, last I heard."

"What did she do to Chandra? Why is she a target?"

Stephen looked out the dirty window of his office, a view of mostly gray buildings. He turned back. "I honestly have no idea."

Chapter Thirty-Two

Chandra was frustrated.

While speaking with her Stephen, just a few lovely moments, had been wonderful—I never thought I would touch him again!—he hadn't given her much to go on. But he didn't know. He knew nothing about Bronwyn's treachery.

Why had she kept the dash cam video secret? Even if it confirmed what everyone knew, it would at least be an end.

Why did she never tell me? Why didn't she tell anyone?

The biggest reason why Chandra hadn't spent more than a few minutes with Stephen was the same that was draining her now. Jorgensen was fighting her. This sack of meat she was running around in, who'd been sitting in his apartment with a gun in his lap—his choice; he'd been ready to check out—was now having second thoughts. Trying to climb out of the back seat of the cab.

It was a struggle she didn't need right now. She had to find Bronwyn and settle a score. Her "friend" knew Stephen had been the only really good thing in her life. And she'd seduced him, got him drunk! Then fucked him write on the dining room table.

Right in front of me! I was in the room, shoved aside, forgotten!

Chandra trolled the area around River North. She'd killed a homeless guy in an alley for a boost, but he'd been old. Wasted. Barely a snack. However, he'd had a cell phone on him. It looked dead, but in the end, it turned out, the idiot just hadn't known how to turn it on after he'd likely stolen it from some schmuck.

She'd used the smartphone to search out Bronwyn. An office phone number, cell, Skype address, and handles for Twitter, Facebook, the 'gram… but the home address of the defense lawyer wasn't listed anywhere. That seemed to be on purpose.

Over the years, it seemed Chandra might not have been her only unsatisfied customer.

After asking around at a few bars, a diner, she'd finally struck gold in an unlikely place.

Her former friend used to brag that she hit the gym every day. Probably just to prance around in the latest lululemon abomination. Chandra sought out the swankiest gym in the area, on the seventh floor of the Guardian Trust building.

The inside had the air of a nightclub, pumping music, low ceilings, and the lighting only marginally brighter than some late-night hangout. As she approached the desk, she came up with a story she'd hoped would convince the bottle blond at the counter to give her an address, a solid story, involving a handb—

"Sir?" the woman said, and Chandra smiled as she approached. It took a moment to realize the receptionist had been talking to her.

Right. I'm this sack of shit, not me.

"Uh, hi." Chandra forced a smile onto the man's face. "I was hoping—"

"I'm sorry," the greeter said in a singsong voice. "This is a women-only facility."

"Well, I'm transitioning," Jan Jorgensen's face said. Then he broke into a smile. "Oh my, that was only a joke. I'm sorry."

"Wow," the woman laughed. "No, no. That was good. I had no answer. Ha."

"Actually," Chandra said, thinking fast, "I shouldn't be joking around. I am desperate. Running out of time."

"Oh?"

Buying a moment to think, she looked up and pointed toward the clock. "Twenty-three before seven? Christ, too close to the wire. It's a court thing."

The woman got serious, straightened up. "Court? What does that—?"

"No, nothing to do with you guys," Chandra said, forming a plan. "You've got a great lawyer that comes in here, opposing counsel, but she's incredible. Anyway, she says how she works out in your club and, wow, this is embarrassing… but I've got an offer for her client and, you know, the damn thing expires at seven."

"Oh no!"

"Yeah, woman killed her husband. But you know, he was an abuser. I'm with the prosecuting attorney's team, just a paralegal, but between you and me, the guy got what he deserved."

"Oh wow."

"Yeah, well, it took forever to get the documents collated and printed up—you don't want to hear all of this—but I've got to find Ms. Redding before seven. That's when the offer expires. It's the best deal she'll see. I pushed for it, you know, but this could all fall apar—"

"Did you try her office?" the woman said, sitting up, straightening her shoulders. "She works really late. Sometimes she's in there at two, three in the morning."

"Did that. Nada," Chandra said then gave it a shot. "You don't happen to know her home address, do you? I'm desperate."

The woman's shoulders fell slightly, and her lips thinned. "No. I mean, we've got that but… of course, I just can't give that out."

"I get it, it's just this is the best deal Donna's going to get, and—"

"Sure, I understand."

"It's a tragedy, the whole thing. She suffered at that fucker's hands for years, then when she sets things right, she's looking at hard time. Twenty years minimum. This deal, and there's no telling whether she'll take it, but this cuts that by a third."

"Oh, you're making my heart hurt," she said.

"I'm already there. Been there this whole case."

The blond said, "Well, of course you know I can't give you the address. But really, you've already got it. I'm surprised she never mentioned it to you."

"Well, opposite sides of the fence, right? Not so much time for girl chat," Chandra said then blinked Jan Jorgensen's eyes slowly.

The gym bunny shrugged. "Her apartment is her office."

"What?"

"I mean, you were there! She's got some swanky setup at the office. Not on the same floor; she showed us all some pics one day. Cool spiral staircase and all that. But you already know where her office is, so I guess I'm not really telling you anything you don't already know." The woman winked.

Chandra turned away with a quick look back over her shoulder. "You are a godsend."

Before the woman could even respond, Chandra hit the button for the elevator. Come on, come on!

"Hey, you've got twenty-one minutes, counselor! Take the stairs. It's only seven floors. Hopefully you've kept up with your cardio."

The woman in the man's body flipped her a thumbs-up and hit the door to the stairs, taking the first three steps at full stride. She stopped when, below, she saw a sudden spot on the wall growing into a large blister. Moments later, a familiar spook slid through it. Casually, he looked up at her.

"What are you doing here?" she growled.

Calkin theatrically glanced down the stairs then up. No human within earshot could have heard him. No one making the low-tech trip to the top would have seen him. He was letting her know, with his slow, deliberate moves, that he was the boss. He was in control.

It had taken far too long for him to wrest that control from the former leader of the Ghost Mob to not enjoy a bit of swagger every now and again. But this wasn't a pleasure trip.

"You know, we've been at our little private venture for a long time," he said. While her question had bounced off the concrete walls, echoing in an unpleasant timbre, the sound of a man's voice generated by something that wasn't supposed to inhabit his body, Calkin's voice was clear and sharp. The walls didn't know he'd come. "It isn't easy starting up private enterprise in the InBetween."

Chandra was anxious to get to Bronwyn Redding. Hungry for it. But her benefactor—at least in some part—was standing in front of her. She'd always knew he'd be coming to check in. She'd learned about these plans, this "private venture," in her cell on the same day she'd been told about how the dead could inhabit the body of the living.

"We just don't have the same VC structure as Silicon Valley, yeah?" he said and finally looked up toward her. "So we're anxious to go public, as it were. Turn on the lights."

"Ha," she said, taking a few steps down from the top and stopping. "You act like you have been working this. That you came up with your grand plan, worked out the mechanisms that could power an army of the dead." She chuckled. "That kind of stuff is genius level. Seeing through the fabric of the InBetween while everyone around you is flopping on the beach gasping for breath. That takes an Einstein. You ain't Einstein."

Calkin came off the wall and drifted up toward Chandra slowly, not using his feet, just sliding up the stairs. "Yeah, your old man was a genius, so what? His time has come and gone." His dark face smiled, a gap between his two front teeth. "What? You gonna do some little-girl vengeance thing?"

"Don't be an idiot," she said but was losing the edge in her voice. She knew she needed this man and his crew—his power at least—for a little while longer. "He was a monster, and I'm glad you took him out. "

The smile went wider. "Well, I had help."

"Hey, all I did was talk to him. What of it? Fair trade. You got what you needed."

He shrugged. "So did you. But whereas I'll always keep up my end of the bargain—"

She looked up and saw two veins of light, thick cables of white that snapped and twisted above her, helping keep Jan Jorgensen at bay. Calkin was peering intently, trying to search for it himself. Maybe if he was just close enough, he might work it out? Not likely. But if by some chance he did, that would leave her powerless. Literally.

"I appreciate what you're doing, our arrangement. And it's helping me."

"How does it do that, by the way?" He smiled.

She ignored it. "But you're getting something in return. Hell, you're winning the Olympics, Eurovision, and the Oscars all in one day with me."

"When you finally deliver!" he bellowed, his hands flexing into fists.

"And I will," Chandra said and walked through the ghost on the stairs, knowing he'd be treated to a visual display of blood and bone and sinew and tendon as she did. "Once I get what I came for."

"When will that be?"

She stopped and looked back over her shoulder, up at Calkin, the leader of the Ghost Mob. "Tonight." Moving down the stairs again, she said, "You'll get it tonight. I'm doing what I came to do. Then I'm going to find somewhere quiet while you wage your war. I don't want any part of it. I'm done with this fucking world."

Chapter Thirty-Three

"You okay?" Alice couldn't see the concern on Brenda's face, but she heard it.

The frail woman nodded, smiled. "No, I'm dying. You didn't hear?"

"Dark," the ex-reporter said. "You know what I mean. You look a bit drained, hon."

"It's the most I've done in more than a year," she said, closing her eyes for a moment and leaning her head back against the wall behind her chair. Above their heads, a brass logo read Chicago Post.

"Maybe we should take you back. I'm sorry, Alice."

"Don't be," she said, looking at the row of hard plastic chairs next to her. "It's also the most fun I've had all year. In years, actually."

Brenda looked around the large, imposing waiting room of her former employer.

"You know," the ghost said, "you would have been a good reporter."

Alice smiled.

The two women behind the desk exchanged a few words but then did their best to avoid looking at the one person sitting in the reception area, an older woman having a conversation with herself.

Brenda watched, her heart aching a little, as Alice drifted off to sleep.

It was better to focus on her new friend than on everything around her. This was what she'd lost. As a teen, when she'd first realized she loved the thrill of the hunt, the pursuit of truth, knocking down shitheads who take advantage of others… she'd wanted to be a reporter. The Post had always been that icon, that beacon.

Many of her university friends had given her grief for going to work for a newspaper. Sure, they were the height of journalism, but like the thin, pale woman on the plastic chair, they were dying. Holding on to a world that was moving two mediums on from there—radio newsrooms had begun to collapse, while TV was barely doing news at all anymore. To keep the eyeballs on the tube, the definition of news was becoming increasingly more open to interpretation.

Brenda looked up at the large rectangular display window that she'd seen guests' faces pressed up against when she'd been on the other side. People were still impressed by the machine, the desks piled with papers, coffee cups stacked askew, phones to ears, arms waving, reporters and everyone else moving through the newsroom. The animals behind the glass.

She watched the grace, the beauty of this dance from this window as she had done her first day on the job. She'd waited to get the nickel tour, then been shown to her desk, which was so close to the copier that she'd had to wear sunglasses because of the flickering of the light when someone was making reams of copies.

She missed it.

No. She missed what it was supposed to be. What she was supposed to have. That had been stolen by a vengeful woman named Chandra. Someone she'd never met, never knew.

Pushing that thought from her mind, she looked for her former managing editor. Pete Davis had been brutal. Like something out of Central Casting, the guy never smiled, had little tolerance of other people, and seemed to be doing his job after all these years merely out of spite. Despite cigarette-stained fingers and a sunken chest, the man had a booming voice.

He had this favorite way of starting conversations: "Why am I talking to you?"

Brenda jumped and spun toward the door. The man hadn't even bothered coming into the reception area, instead calling out from the door, one hand on the jamb, so that he might close it and leave whoever it was on the other side of it without notice.

"Ma'am? Ma'am?"

After a few moments, Alice opened her eyes slowly. She cleared her throat, tilted her head strangely as if noticing something on the other side of the room, then said, "I'm here because a friend asked me to come. Brenda Matthews."

* * *

Pete motioned to a well-worn but expensive couch along the wall next to the window. Alice pointed at a chair next to his desk.

"If I sit down in that, I won't get back up." She forced a smile, realizing, with the wheeze in her voice, it sounded a bit too like a dismissal. Not a great way to win someone over. Especially some guy running a newsroom. A guy like that likely had ego issues. She righted herself and said, "Thank you, though."

As the editor rounded the desk, in front of her he placed a glass of water he'd poured from a decanter on a table near the wall. She took a small sip and returned it to the desk.

Despite the mention of the murdered reporter's name, it still had taken some persuasion in the reception room to get a few minutes of Pete Davis's time. But Alice had always had a gift for convincing people.

Declaring that she was carrying out Brenda Matthews's final wish, of course, had been a good sell. Even Brenda thought so. The dead woman had given her an "Ooh, nice play!" when she'd first said it.

"Okay. I only got a few minutes." He looked at his watch and said to it more than to her, "I don't have a few minutes." He looked back up, his chin coming off his chest more slowly than it had gone down. "I don't get it. Why did she even care about some prison riot?" Instead of sitting, he propped his butt up on the windowsill. Crossed his arms. "She didn't do crime. Some court stuff, but most of that was probate, some petty procedural shit."

After a moment, she answered, "It was a passion project."

"A time waster, you ask me."

Alice lifted a shoulder. "I didn't."

Pete started to say something, but his words got snagged in his teeth. Brenda had rarely seen him speechless, even briefly. Somewhere in the InBetween, for a moment, there were peals of laughter.

When he'd found his tongue again, he said, "How'd you know her? You like an aunt?"

"Right. I'm like an aunt," Alice said and then added, "Listen, I'm sorry, but Brenda says you're a busy man—"

"Says?"

"She once told me you're very busy, being a newspaper editor and all, so I will get right to the point. And, not to sound too dramatic here, but this is actually very important. Not just to me. Not just to Brenda." She was quiet for a moment as a series of words failed at her lips, tumbling back down her throat. "I wish I could explain, but it's really so critical. To everyone."

He huffed, pulled his arms tighter. "This is about a prisoner who died in a low-boil riot—barely a disturbance, it was done almost before it started—from last year?"

"So you do remember it?"

"Sure, looked into it," he said and walked to his chair and leaned an elbow on its back. She wondered if he ever sat in it. "Congressman's girl, right? She got drunk, got in a car, and hit some kid. Killed it. The trial ended because after the prison thing, you know, no defendant. I'm not sure—"

"We don't want to know about the trial."

"We?"

"I'm speaking in the royal 'we,'" she said and smiled. "But it would help—more than you can imagine—if the name of the person who had killed her was… known."

Pete stared at her for a moment. "Really? Why would you want to know that?" He was momentarily lost in thought. "Why did Brenda even care, make this her passion project?"

"Indulge me," Alice said. "It was her final wish for me to find out."

"Well, you won't," Pete said, sighed, and leaned back on the wall now, arms outstretched along the back of the chair. "It was during midday mess, there must have been thirty or forty other women in there. Could have been anyone. And despite it being, you know, a bit of a nothing riot, as these things go, it was still chaotic. From what I remember, after everything calmed down, this woman was there, bleeding out from the neck under one of the tables. No one knows who put the blade in her."

"I suppose you could just look around for the nearest murderer sitting nearby? Maybe someone who hadn't finished their cling peaches, other things on their agenda."

Pete smiled at her, surprised for the second time. "I can see why you were friends. Brenda was a smart-ass too. She thought it was endearing."

"It still is, Mr. Davis."

He nodded, squinted in thought, spun the chair slightly, then returned to his perch at the window.

"The Congressman's running a campaign right now. He's doing all right, and to his credit, he didn't turn his fiancée's drama into an election platform despite how hard, no question, his D.C. advisers pushed him. He'd have gotten some easy points off." Pete softened his face, theatrically clutched a fist to his chest. "'Hi, I'm Congressman Fucktard, and I'm launching a drunk driving awareness campaign in memory of my fiancée and… that little boy.'"

Alice nodded. "That must be the newsroom gallows humor Brenda told me about."

A shrug. "If the average person knew what we said, what we joked about, in newsrooms around the country? They would burn our buildings to the ground. But if you don't, it gets too much. You'd lose your everlovin' mind." He nodded slowly. "I've seen it."

The frail woman took another sip of her water, slid over some paper as a coaster, then set it back down on the desk. She looked through the window's office into the newsroom. "The horror that must come through here daily."

"Yeah. We also got a cooking section," he said, smiling. "Truth is, it's pretty horrific, too. Who the hell eats beetroot?"

Alice chuckled, the first time in a long time. Pete gave her a warm smile. She was quiet for a moment then gave a small nod.

"It's funny, you know? You said to pick the nearest murderer around, and odds are they're the doer."

"Doer?"

"Yeah, ain't that what the cop shows and detective novels say?"

"Probably. I'm sorry, I interrupted you. You were saying?"

"Well, this was a lunchroom full of violent women," he said, talking faster now. "Sure, some were domestics, maybe set a shitty boyfriend or husband on fire. Who could blame them, right?" She nodded slowly. "But some of these ladies, you read their sheets, and it'll make your short hairs curl." He then thought about what he'd just said and added, "Curl more, I suppose."

"So there were a lot of suspects?"

"Ma'am, everyone there, every woman with a metal cafeteria tray and a plastic spork, would have been a possible killer."

Alice leaned forward and slowly stood up to stretch her legs. Watching Pete move around the room made sitting difficult. She exhaled a deep breath and walked to the window, where the light was giving up its fight against the night.

"So too many suspects. A glen full of wolves, each baring blood-stained teeth. Impossible to know which had made the killing blow." Alice nodded and extended her hand with a weak smile.

Pete nodded and jutted his lip out in what he tried to pass off as a smile. "I'm sorry," he said, looking at his scuffed brown shoes. "I know that's not what you hoped to hear. Not what you wanted to leave with."

With effort, the thin woman with the rounded shoulders offered him another smile. Nodding, she turned, reached for the door, and opened it. Then she stopped.

Pete watched the dying woman, who seemed momentarily frozen in thought.

It was clear she wouldn't see the end of the year. Possibly not the month. Out of respect, he just waited. He watched as she, strangely and ever so slightly, nodded a few times, each several seconds apart. As if... as if remembering some list? Or instruction?

Then she turned toward the managing editor and stiffened her back and squared her shoulders.

"You know something more, don't you?

He shook his head slowly. "I'm sorry, Ms. Weathers, I do not. Hand on heart."

Again, she paused. Nodded again, only slightly. "But something doesn't sit right with you, then? This case gives you an, um, itch in your brain."

Pete's mouth hung open for a moment, his eyebrows raised. "Where'd you hear that expression?"

"Who do you think?"

He smiled. "Sure, Brenda. She would have been a good reporter. Smart. Pain in the ass. But she could smell blood, that one. I admit I miss her."

The editor watched the strangest expression come to the woman's face. It suddenly flushed with warmth and sadness, and tears quickly pooled on her eyelids. One hand went to the thin skin of her chest, while the other hung in the air, outstretched toward empty space.

She righted herself, sniffed, cleared her throat, and asked again, "What's your gut tell you? Something about this case bothe—"

"I told you!" Pete barked then softened and put his hands up. "I already said it. You missed it."

"I'm sorry, I'm not a journalist. I was a dancer, and a very good one for a while. But while I won't ask you to pirouette, I would hope you would do me the same professional courtesy, Mr. Davis. Explain."

"Too many suspects. She was in a mess hall with dozens of murderers."

"You said that."

"Right," he said, rounding to her quickly and pushing the door closed again. They stood at the threshold face to face. His voice quieter but strained, he continued, "She was accused of vehicular manslaughter. The first jury, they weren't entirely convinced she even did it. Hell, she didn't even know if she did it. She wasn't like the others."

"The others?"

"Killers, murderers, attempted murderers. Violent gang members. Ex-military that couldn't quite shake the bloodlust. Psychotics, lunatics…" Alice's gaze was momentarily pulled to a spot on the opposite side of the room, then her eyes met the editor's again. He finally said, "Why the fuck was a woman awaiting trial, no prior violent offenses, no violent tendencies as far as anyone could see… locked in a cage full of killers?"

Alice nodded slowly. "She shouldn't have been there. Maybe minimum security or whatever the middle level is."

"Medium security, right," he said, eyes darting toward the tiny window of his office door. "Makes more sense. Who knows, courts mighta known something the rest of us didn't. Flight risk, maybe. But maximum security? That don't make sense."

The woman put her hand on the handle of the door, propping herself up. Her jaw tightened, and she said, "What aren't you telling me? Brenda says—"

Pete burst away from the door, throwing his hands up. "Brenda says. You're batshit crazy, you know that? Losing your grip on reality. You need to get back to the home or the hospital or whoever helped you into those shoes this morning! I don't need you dying in my office."

He walked back to the wall, to the other side of the desk. Alice took slow, deliberate steps, rounded the chair, and put both hands on the desktop. She looked up and waited for a moment. Then she spoke slowly but deliberately.

"Brenda would have been your best reporter," she said, her voice shaking. "Better than you'd ever seen. Maybe better than you."

He laughed with flat eyes, crossing his arms.

"She was so strong, so tenacious, so dogged as you said, maybe she wasn't ready to give this last story up. Just this last one. Her passion project." Alice rounded the desk and stood before the newspaper editor. "Maybe that strength means, despite her death, she wasn't ready to go yet. So she didn't and convinced a sick woman to get up from her hospital bed and put on her own damn shoes, thank you very much, and for the first time in nearly a year leave the care home, catch the number 17 bus downtown to ask a man she trusted and respected for some help in her last story."

The tall, thin man blinked then blinked again. His arms fell to his sides.

"This is it, Pete," Alice said. "Give her one more shot."

For nearly a minute, Pete Davis stared out the window, and Alice could see the reflection of the dimming sun off his eye. Finally, he turned and spoke in a soft voice.

"Like I said, the congressman, he did well. After this woman, his fiancée, was gone? He did all right. But he wasn't doing all right. A killer fiancée? That was killing his chances." He pulled in a deep, deep breath and blew it out. "She dies in prison, she dies at that point as an innocent woman in prison, and not only is this scandal not weighing him down, but who knows, the guy lost his fiancée. Sympathy vote, maybe. Either way, Congressman Lee benefited." He turned to the woman and gently placed his hands on her shoulders. "My crime guys have been doing this since back when they locked guys in bell towers, for chrissakes. They say she should have never been in that prison. Not maximum security, no way. And that riot? It wasn't any riot, that was cover."

"Cover for what?"

"To murder Chandra Withy. Someone put her in there and put a hit out on her so she'd go away. Someone needed her to go away."

Alice did that quick bird look to a corner, smiled, then began to once again walk for the door. Then she stopped and gave Pete Davis a hug, her thin arms barely able to get around his body. He could hardly tell she was hugging him, but it was the sweetest thing he'd felt in as long as he could remember.

The frail woman began to walk to the door, labored. Pete huffed dramatically, then held her arm gently, helping her.

She said, "Thank you."

"You got it."

When they got to the door, she took a couple breaths and said, "I don't really want to take the number 17 back. I'm told there's something called a taxi chit that I should ask for. You got 'em in your desk."

Pete just stared at her with a smile. "You're told. I think," he said as he walked to his desk and pulled open a drawer, "that you knew my reporter far better than you're letting on."

Alice grinned. "I just met her, but we're fast becoming friends."

Chapter Thirty-Four

Why had I gone to precisely the last place I wanted to be in the world?

Sure, my plan sounded so brave when I ran it past the Professor. I thought it sounded brave, despite her saying, "Painter, that's stupid. You're going to get hurt. Or worse."

I knew what worse was. I'd been there already in the very building I was now looking at. Inside, there were at least one hundred spooks were doing worse.

The Minnesota State Fairgrounds.

Minnesota doesn't sound scary, but if you ever saw Garrison Keillor coming at you down a dark alley gnawing on a deep-fried Snickers, you'd be shitting kittens.

Brenda was tracking down Chandra and, since she was a reporter, she'd probably found her. If there hadn't been yet, there would be a confrontation. That was why I was standing in front of the building that housed the Twin Cities branch of the Ghost Mob's power grid.

Our dead-livie's arrangement with the Mob gave her juice from here and Chicago. Thick tendrils of light, ethereal extension cords. Enough to give her the strength to move around in a living person's body! That was not power we could hope to combat. Not both of us. Hell, probably not twenty spooks. So I had to weaken her by taking this power station offline.

Down to just the one in Chicago, she'd still be the most powerful creature in the world, but she would be half as powerful.

That might help.

And if my short time with Brenda was any indication, the reporter wasn't waiting for me. She had that sense of right and morality that young journalists have. A righteousness that could trump rationality.

No question, she was going to try to take on Chandra without me.

So I knew I had to take one of the asshole's legs out from under her before that happened. And time was running out.

A quick glance left, then right, then behind, and I drifted across the street toward the Gass Station. The homeless guy I'd seen earlier was leaning against the wall. The night had turned a bit crisp, so he piled clothes on either side to block the wind. In front of him, he was eating something out of a tin. A can of Sterno sat between the heels of his well-worn sneakers, lashing ribbons of light across his haggard face.

"Hey, man, some bizarre shit's about to go down. You might wanna keep low," I said, although any real dangers there were in the spirit world would not affect this man, who had already taken the brunt of the living world. No, between the two of us, there was only one that was way out of his depth. And it wasn't the guy wearing the horrifically stained Red Lobster bib.

He nodded to himself slowly, as if he'd found a nice tasty bit, and I turned away.

After another quick glance to each side, I again moved toward the wall and pushed my face inside.

The machine of light was even larger than before, pulsing and surging, fat ribbons of light moving up and down the spooks trapped in rows like spiders' legs.

Before I'd come here, I'd spoken with Sergeant Peterson to see if he could spare a few of his zoo people to lend a hand. He'd reiterated his "we keep to ourselves" mantra, which I had to respect. It was my Rule #1: Don' want no douchey, don' be no douchey with a Monroe Doctrine. However, I'd explained the circumstances, and he'd said he would run it by his people. Maybe a small win could help convince them.

As still as a mask, I scanned the room for any of the Mob but saw no one. No patrols, no lookouts. It seemed I was free and clear, but after my last experience, the worst moments I'd ever spent in the InBetween, I was cautious. If I got caught now, the pains delivered to me by the hideous machine before me wouldn't be able to hold a candle to what the Ghost Mob was planning to bring to the world.

Quickly, I wove through the hunched-over men and women, almost indiscernible from one another, grist for the mill, each bobbing slightly in perfect rhythm to a song played only for those in the grasp of the machine.

It took me a few minutes, but I finally found Bernard. Emblazoned on the back of his blue coveralls was the stylized rectangle and eagle's head. Reaching down to grab his shoulders, I instantly felt sick, weakened, and as if my head was going to burst off my body.

I pulled up and then back, unsure of what unseen chains might hold him in place. It was energy, so it seemed if I could just break the field...

"Come on, man. It's Painter. Let's go, little brother," I said, straining, my mind feeling as if I'd dropped acid while smoking crack and downing tequila shooters. "You gotta help me, man, come on."

Slowly, I felt he was lifting away, but it was hard to tell. Up was becoming indistinguishable from down. The only difference seemed to be that my arms were straining less.

"That's it, man," I said, grunting.

Then, as if someone had momentarily shut down the stadium lights, the rush of panicked energy was gone. I held the man as he got reoriented to his feet and saw the tiniest flicker in the hulking power station. It was down by one. It would barely register, but it was at least movement in the right direction.

Bernie lifted his head, eyes a bit crossed, but after a moment, a look of realization passed over his face.

"Heyyy, is that you, Painter?"

"Yeah, man. Sorry I took so long."

"Did you? I… I don't remember much. What the hell was all that? I feel kinda oozy. I think I might throw up."

"You can't throw up, man," I said. "You're still dead, dude."

He looked to the ceiling and took a breath. "Oh, yeah. That's right. That sucks. I wish I weren't dead."

"Well, if wishes were kisses…"

"What?"

"Never mind."

Then, as if he'd snapped awake, he reached out and gave me a hug. Hugging wasn't really a thing in the InBetween because it could drain your energy into another person a little bit. Hell, it'd been a long time since anyone had hugged me.

My memories of the past, the living part of my life, were all just wisps of smoke now. I couldn't remember the last time—

"Hey, Paint?" Bernie said as he let go of me and looked to the wall I'd just come through.

"Yeah?"

"I don't think we're safe."

Chapter Thirty-Five

Brenda was moving quickly through the dark city, eyes trained on the sky.

Above her was the crisscrossed latticework of energy she'd seen since Day One, but if she looked closely, she could see two distinct lines arching down toward the ground, coming to an intersection.

That's where he would be.

Jan Jorgensen, the man who'd killer her.

Or, actually, the murdered, back-from-the-dead sociopath named Chandra.

"No problem." Brenda swallowed, looking left and right as she crossed a street, blinking quickly.

She knew that she was tracking the most powerful creature on Earth, the most dangerous in the realms of both Before and After. And, of course, she had no idea what she would do when she found him.

Her.

Whatever.

The ex-reporter looked up and spread her arms, palms splayed as she slowed for a moment.

Jorgensen looked as if he'd stopped moving. Wherever he was headed, he seemed to be there. And as she traced her eyes up and down the skyline, that looked like about where the congressman had said an attorney named Bronwyn Redding lived. Chandra's old attorney. The one she was going to kill tonight.

Brenda started moving, more quickly now, still without a real plan of what she'd do when she arrived.

She took some small solace in the knowledge that Alice—the Amazing Alice!—was now heading back to the Post. Pete Davis would make sure she was okay. Their quick return trip to the congressman's office had been productive.

Twenty minutes earlier, Lee had put up a strong front, but it collapsed quickly. The congressman, like any successful diplomat or politician, was good at convincing people of the story he was selling.

But in the past few hours, since meeting this frail woman named Alice in the hospital shoes, the world had changed. He'd always been quick to adapt. But this had cracked that resolve. Evidence of something called "the InBetween" had turned everything upside down. And he was still reeling.

When he'd first emerged into his office, she'd been sitting, arms in her lap. Stephen Lee had stepped out of his bathroom, wiping his face with a towel. His eyes looked red. He'd spent a minute denying it, but with Brenda's help, Alice reminded the congressman that, in the space of an hour, everything had become different.

He was in danger.

After a long, long stare out to the city skyline, he'd caved.

"I'm not a bad person," he said. "I just… I feel you need to know that."

Alice's bony shoulders moved slightly. "How did this happen? You couldn't have snuck in there yourself."

Lee looked at her for a moment, eyes suddenly wide, and nearly laughed. Then his face returned to a soft, dark expression. "I've actually been around this part of town most my life. My family moved around a fair bit; my dad had trouble holding a job back then. But some of my earliest memories were growing up on these streets, not far from here." He looked outside again. "It was different back then."

"Stephen, you understand we are perilously low on time."

He grinned weakly. "I don't think I've heard anyone actually use the word perilously out loud."

"You're stalling. Please stop."

The congressman nodded. "I know some guys, right? You can't get anywhere in this business without coming across some pretty… intense people. At various times, they're the ones in control of the neighborhood, they—"

"Stephen!" Alice said, hiding her exhaustion with deep, heaving breaths. "This isn't a game. Some clever word duel, a bit of play. You are out of time. Right now!"

He was startled by her voice and saw the anger on her sweet face. "I'm… I am so ashamed."

"I know."

Suddenly, he froze. "Christ, you aren't recording this, are you?"

Alice glared at him then spread her hands theatrically, glancing down at her dress. It looked less like fashion and more like a hospice housecoat. Which, of course, it was.

"I'm sorry," he said, nodding quickly, and sat in his office chair. He lowered his head, putting both hands on his scalp. "I put six thousand dollars in a mailbox. An address in the warehouse district, nobody around, not a camera in sight, and of course, I was dressed like I was going on an Arctic expedition. No one would have recognized me even if they had seen me."

"Six thousand dollars? That's it?"

He lifted his head, eyes still closed. "Yeah. Turns out, life's cheap."

"Go on."

"And within a week of dropping the package off, a small bundle, she was—I mean, that was it. I'd heard about the small riot and that someone had been killed. I knew what had happened." His lips trembled. "I got drunk that night, cried a lot. Woke up on the floor, still in my clothes."

Alice's head tilted, and she nodded. Then nodded again. "Yes, yes. Brenda says we need a name, Stephen. We need the name of the person you hired to kill your fiancée in prison."

He opened his eyes. "I didn't, I mean—"

"We need a name. Once we have that, no time to get into it, but she goes away. You're safe. Chandra is no danger to you anymore, and your life goes back to what it was before I walked in your door today."

"What does that mean? Danger."

Once again, Alice nodded then waved her hand downward slightly. "I know, I know, Brenda. Your harping isn't going to help here."

The congressman inched his chair toward the wall—and away from the woman in the housecoat—slowly, as his eyes darted around the room.

"As you know, Chandra has taken over the body of some man named Jan Jorgensen."

"Yes, I met him." Any resistance from Stephen Lee to this new, bizarre reality was now gone. He'd moved from disbelief to concern at an impressive pace.

"You met him before you knew you were looking at the eyes of your dead fiancée," she said, scolding. "While in Mr. Jorgensen, Chandra has killed countless people. Ten, surely, maybe twenty. It somehow gives her the strength to hold onto the body of the man she's in."

"Are you fucking serious? What if this Jan Jorg—"

"No, no, by all accounts, this is the girl you wanted to marry. Turns out, she had the heart of a serial killer. I suppose you dodged a bullet, Stephen. So to speak."

He nodded, blinked once. "You'll be surprised to hear me say it, but that maybe doesn't entirely come as a shock." The frail woman only raised her eyebrows, listening. "Her father. I don't know all the details. She never talked about him much. But he'd been the worst. Worse than you can imagine. Terrorized this city for a time. And others. Many others. Killed a lot of people. Channy's mother kept her away from him. But he'd find them sometimes."

"You don't inherit 'serial killer,' far as I know."

"But you do inherit traits, right? Hell, you can inherit mannerisms and what your pick for favorite color might be. So the same designs that made him a serial killer made Chandra a brilliant businesswoman. She'd gotten a half dozen start-ups off the ground. Each made it there fueled by her unbridled tenacity. She was ruthless. No one could stand in her way." He sighed. "The difference, from what I've read, comes from the triggers. Those traits in her, nurtured by her mom, she becomes a small-business genius. In her dad, different triggers, tough upbringing and all that, he becomes a killer." He locked his eyes on the far wall. "Something, finally, must have triggered that in her."

Alice shrugged. "Maybe it was being beaten in prison for months—and who knows what else, we've all heard stories—then eventually stabbed in a riot, paid for by her boyfriend, and stuffed under a metal cafeteria table, her life draining out of her, and left to die utterly alone." Alice smiled weakly. "You think that might have been distressing for her?"

He nodded slowly, and his head dropped again. Large hands covered the top, a small circle where the hair was beginning to recede.

"Congressman, let's be clear. Your girl, your fiancée—the one you had killed with a bundle of cash—is now angry, vengeful, and the most powerful thing alive or dead on the planet. My vocabulary isn't a robust as it once had been—all the chemo drugs over the years—but if there is a word that means 'totally safe and won't be killed in a horrible way that will make headlines around the world and eventually turned into a blockbuster movie'… you are the opposite of that word."

She smiled.

"I don't have a name," he said. "But I can get it."

"Then get it."

"It will take time."

"We don't have time. You don't have time."

Stephen moved quickly. This was a moment he knew—plan of action, act swiftly, surely, only steps that take you to your intended goal. He knew his goal now. The woman in the chair had explained it succinctly.

He pulled out a set of keys, which jingled in his fingers for a moment then tumbled to the floor. He cursed under his breath, reached for them again, and then pushed on with a grinding sound into a drawer on the other side of his desk. Then he used another key for yet another lock within that drawer.

With one hand, he leaned forward and put a bulky plastic sandwich bag on the desk in front of him. His other hand stuffed something unseen into the back of his waistband, hidden under his suit coat.

"I've got to go."

"Call whoev—"

"Ms. Weathers, these are conversations you have in a secure room face to face," he said, his voice warbling. He stood, donning a long coat, and began stuffing items into its pockets. He took one of the plastic sandwich bags. Left pocket. In his right, his pricey cell phone, his keys, and a handful of things Alice couldn't see. As he worked, he motioned to the other plastic bag with his head. "Take that."

"What is it?"

"Phone. It's got fifty bucks' credit on it, and there's a battery pack in there in case the battery gets low."

"Burner phone," Alice said, one eyebrow raised.

"Yes, burner phone," he said and shook his head slowly. "Once I have a name, I'll call you."

"Don't dawdle, Stephen," Alice said. "She may be headed here right now."

The congressman stiffened briefly then grabbed his desk phone, muttered a few quick words, and hung it back up. "She's not after me. At least not yet. She's headed to her old attorney's office. I think she plans to kill the woman."

"You need to warn her!"

"I can't call her!" For the first time, Stephen shouted. "I can't be connected to any of that! If you want to call her and warn her, that's fine, but say nothing about me, understand? Don't say my name on the phone."

Alice bristled, disliking this side of the man immensely.

He gave her a name and said she had an office downtown that doubled as an apartment.

"Bronwyn. Sounds Irish."

"Welsh," Stephen said, grabbing the door to his bathroom. "Turn that phone on, and I'll call you the moment I've got a name. Then thank you for everything, but... I never want to see you again."

He opened the door at the back of his office, and Alice said, "You put on a coat to go to the toilet?"

The congressman smiled. "Like I said, I've lived in this part of town a long time. Not everyone here is my friend. So I had an extra way out put in. Dumps down to the street. You go back the way you came."

"Time is running out, Stephen."

"You'll get your name," he said, disappearing into the dark room. "Then please get the fuck out of my life."

* * *

After the congressman had left, Alice nearly collapsed on the couch. She was clutching the burner phone through its plastic wrapping. It crinkled under her fingers.

"Alice, are you okay?"

"I'm fine, Brenda. Just tired," she said and sat up on her second try. "Woo, this is an adventure, huh?"

"I think I'm killing you."

"No, dear," she said. "You're not the sort. I'm fine. Just sick and dying."

"I think I'm speeding that up."

Alice stood, and she smiled, eyes watering. "You have given me such a gift. I haven't had anything to do in, well, years actually. Not really. And haven't had a purpose since, well, since I was quite young."

"But I'm asking too much."

"You're a reporter, Brenda."

"Was a reporter," the dead woman said and sat down next to her friend. It took a moment and a tiny bit of juice, but she balanced on the cushions, getting the hang of her new world.

"You still are." Alice smiled and turned toward her, which startled Brenda. "No, I can't see you. But… there is a sort of shimmer. I see it now." She reached out, putting her hand somewhere near where she thought the dead woman's head might be. "You still exist, so you are still a reporter. The truth drives you. A purpose. You don't know what a gift that is. And you've helped me find one, too. My final purpose."

Brenda laughed joyfully. "What's that?"

Alice rolled her eyes and slowly stood up. "To save the world, of course."

"Of course."

"But," Alice said ambling toward the door, "I will need to nap first." She then stopped and turned around. "Aw, hell, no use in going back to the home. I'll lie down here."

"Here?"

"Sure," she said and returned to the couch, gingerly lying down and pulling the phone from the plastic. She put the bag on a small coffee table next to her. "There's water and a small fridge. Might be a sandwich in there. If not, I'll order something and put it on the congressman's bill."

"I'll stay here to make sure—"

Fiddling with the phone, she quickly raised a hand, then went back to the device. "You know you can't do that. I know you know that. We'll google the lawyer, and if she picks up the office phone this time of night, that may be enough. But odds are you'll have to go there and warn the woman yourself."

Brenda had had just the one thought: It was time to stop the killing spree.

It would end tonight.

"At least, I hope it ends tonight," Brenda said as she zeroed in on the two streams, closer now, snapping in the sky. Painter had told her about skating. She'd never been terribly athletic and had never learned how to skate.

"No time like the present, right?"

Unsteady, she began pushing her feet out in gliding motions, which did little other than destabilize her. If anyone had been nearby to see her, they'd have probably tried to shove a wallet into her mouth to prevent her from biting off her tongue.

"Maybe I'll try running instead. Or jogging. I liked jogging," she said, and then, pumping her legs, she did indeed begin to pick up speed."

The apartment above the office was like its owner—sleek, stylish, and expensive. The slick, smooth lines, brushed metal, and enormous bay windows told anyone who came into it that this was a woman who'd done well. She'd succeeded and would continue to do so.

However, it was now utterly wrecked. Like its owner.

A small wraparound bar—a quaint little thing that had cost its owner upward of $40,000, imported from Hong Kong—had been toppled. Its engraved mirror now lay in thousands of pieces among smashed bottles.

The bar had been where the rampage had begun. Bronwyn had been enjoying a drink, alone, while reading a legal brief. She'd only just caught sight of the man in the moment before he'd picked her up and thrown her at the mirror.

From there, he'd used her body as an implement—swinging her around with a strength that was more than a man his size should possess—to smash, break, and crack the possessions she'd spent years collecting.

Much of the furniture was upturned, some broken.

Some was splashed red, the stains already beginning to darken.

Now Jan Jorgensen sat on the only piece in the room that hadn't been attacked, the barstool where Bronwyn had been sitting. He began sipping her brandy, ice tinkling against the glass.

On the floor, she was breathing heavily.

At first, she'd tried to fight him off. After her face had been slammed into a brass lamp, the flattened ring around the bulb piercing her cheek and tearing it, she simply pulled her limbs inward and tried not to die.

Now she was splayed on the floor, her head at a queer angle against part of a busted brushed-pine cabinet she'd recently acquired at an estate sale.

She bled from the mouth and ear. One eye was purple, swollen. Her little black dress was torn off the shoulder, and beneath the now-jagged hem, the wood of a split table leg pierced her left thigh.

Terrified to fully meet his gaze, she stole small glances at him, waiting for what could come next. When she did look up finally, he was squinting slightly. Then he began scowling.

She quickly looked away.

"Fuck," he said sharply. "That's my goddamn cabinet, isn't it? Stephen gave you my cabinet? I got that in—"

"No, no!" the attorney said. Her own voice sounded odd to her. With the soft tissue of her mouth swelling, several teeth cracked and bleeding, her cheek pierced and split to where she was sure she could put two fingers through it, it was hard to talk. "That is from… I bought that… after a friend died."

"You bitch," Chandra said, kicking a foot into her stomach without standing from the barstool. "My mother had that made for my first apartment in New York."

"What?"

The man took another pull from the drink and winced. "That's right. I remember now. You said something to me one time. Something about the wood, how it—"

"It is New Zealand kauri," Bronwyn said, staring at the man now. "Rare. Harvesting any new wood is forbid… what do you mean you 'remember'? I said that to someone else. I don't know you."

"Yes you do," the Ringman said and casually threw the empty glass at the downed woman's head. A quick-moving hand deflected it, but it hit hard, likely cracking several fingers. The attorney yelped then stifled a sob.

The man stood, dug through the remains of the bar, and returned with another glass and a bottle of Chivas 18. He poured himself a large glass, then hurled the bottle at the far wall. When it hit, the glass exploded, raining its pieces down upon the woman on the floor.

Through the man's mouth, Chandra took another sip. She then said, "I want to see what you hid from me. What you hid from the court. Show me the tape."

The attorney's eyes widened, and she blinked several times in quick succession. "Tape? Is this about a tape? You can have whatever you want. I don't care. Please take whatever you need."

"Yes. That's the plan, Bron."

The woman balked slightly at the familiarity of the way he'd said her name. Then she added, "There's nothing here that can't be fixed. I don't want any more... I'll give you whatever you want."

He stood and crept toward her. She flinched as glass crunched under his expensive shoes. Each slow, deliberate step seemed to double Bronwyn's heart rate.

"Please! I'm sorry for—"

"The dash cam footage," he said, standing over her. "I want to see the footage you hid from me. Hid from Stephen. Hid from the courtroom."

He then began to yell. But his voice did not sound like a man's anymore. "I don't care if I'm on it! I don't care if you've lied to yourself, believing you hid it to protect me! You should have shown me! You should have given me peace!"

Bronwyn recognized the voice, but she did not understand.

"This isn't possible. I don't... how do you know these things? My friend is dead, she—"

Another kick, this one harder, and the attorney felt her breath explode out of her lungs, ribs cracking. She lay convulsing for a moment, like a fish landed on a boat's hot deck, struggling to breathe.

"You were never my friend!" The man lifted his shoe once more and held it over the broken woman's face. "I don't want to hear another word from you. Now, show me the tape."

Tears were streaming from Bronwyn's eyes, the salt stinging the cuts and gashes in her face. She started to say something, but when she saw the shoe lifted, menacing, she stopped.

With her left hand, she motioned toward the far side of the room. Unable to point with three of her fingers, as they were now bent and misshapen, she used her pinky. In such a horrific scene, it looked almost comical.

The man strode quickly over to the wall and looked for what she'd been pointing to. When he looked back, she motioned downward. He saw the laptop, bent down, grabbed it, and then placed it in front of her.

"Find it," he said and went back to his barstool, sat down, and took a long pull of the amber liquid.

The man intently watched each painful tap she made as she maneuvered around the file system. Bronwyn flashed her eyes momentarily at him then quickly back to the screen and made a few jerky twists of the computer's mouse.

"Don't bother deleting the tape of you and Stephen fucking," he said, but again Chandra's voice was now coming from his lips. It sent shivers through the attorney's entire body. "I saw it already. You make such noises. Such loud, loud noises when you make love to my fiancé." The man looked around the apartment with a strange expression on his face. "Maybe we find a broom after the tape. What do you think? Or a wire brush, maybe, and see if we can make you make those noises again. What do you think? Or a cheese grater? A fireplace poker?"

The woman's breathing quickened, another sob escaped her lips, and a few moments later, she spun the computer around. When Chandra saw it, she became transfixed. She took a few steps then sat slowly in front of the dark screen.

Again, the scene played out.

She watched as the young boy once again left the safety of the convenience store's light and crossed through the abyss of night, head bobbing to music. When his sneaker hit the pavement, that first step, Chandra didn't even realize she was holding her breath.

Another step.

Then another.

The boy almost looked up, a starburst of light to his right, and then the moment she had come to see. This is what had driven her to this attorney's apartment. This was why after she finally saw it, she would kill the woman who'd hidden it. Well, that and the fact that she'd slept with Chandra's fiancé with her remains, her ashes, just ten feet away.

The Audi moved across the screen so swiftly, left to right, with such force—even without the sound—Chandra could almost feel the impact.

One moment the boy was there in the street.

Then he was gone.

The tape continued to play. The world through the lens showed little concern for what had just happened.

Chandra felt dizzy and began to convulse slightly. It was Jan. He was—then she realized it. She'd been holding her breath. His breath. And he was suffocating. She sucked in some air and could feel a burning in his lungs. After a few more breaths, it settled, and she went back to the tape. She hit the space bar to stop it. Then reversed, watching the scene play out in reverse.

The boy reappeared.

Forward again. She hit pause right at the same moment that Bronwyn had before. When had that been? Days ago? Weeks? Months? She couldn't tell anymore. But it didn't matter. All that mattered was right now.

Chandra discovered that the arrow keys would let her nudge the tape forward frame by frame. After a few seconds of tapping, the car came clearly into view. Chandra finally saw it and rolled back slowly on her heels.

Her Audi. Shiny, beautiful black car.

The dent, the burnt hair, the dried blood? That hadn't been a dog after all. It was this boy. She had indeed hit this boy.

But seeing it now, she felt… nothing for him. No remorse. No regret.

"He shouldn't have been in the road," the person at the computer said flatly, this time with a mix of Chandra's voice and a man's. "As much at fault as I wa—"

The voice trailed off as something drew her attention.

On the screen, the image showed the car, her Audi, in a partial blur. The kid was bent at an unnatural angle, head arched over the hood now, the feet disappearing under the car. But the light from the street, from above, caught the inside of the car.

She had been leaning down. Maybe grabbing something off the car's floor? Just one hand on the wheel, it looked like. The reason why the car never slowed was that the boy had never been seen.

But what caught her eye was the one hand still on the steering wheel.

There was a red-yellow spot on it.

"Wait." Chandra's voice was back. "Wait, that's not right. Hold on." She looked over at the attorney, who was trembling, arms pulled in close as if shirking a blow that was bound to come. "That's—hey, on the tape, that's—"

"A cigarette, yeah," Bronwyn said, nodding. Chandra stared at her, waiting for more. But the woman's mouth only moved in small jerks.

"But… I don't smoke," Chandra said, her voice quiet. "I can't. I'm allergic to smoke. I was always getting on Stephen about—"

Wait.

Wait.

No. No, that can't…

"It wasn't my idea," Bronwyn finally said, her voice phlegmy but coming quickly, flecks of blood and spittle flying. "When I showed Stephen—"

"You showed Stephen? He never—that's not true!"

"Yes, of course it is," the bleeding woman said, almost pleading. "He was torn. Really upset about it, but… I don't know, someone on his team said it was the only way. He had a lot more good to do or something. That this would have ruined him."

Chandra blinked, her mind racing. Then she said it out loud. "Stephen. He's driving."

Bronwyn nodded quickly, eyes spilling more tears that had welled at her lids.

"Wait. No," Chandra said, standing.

"Chandra," the attorney said, sniffling. "How are you in there? This isn't possible. Christ, what is happening?"

The man with her dead client's voice ignored the question, vexed by what the dash cam video had shown. "But I was driving. The CCTV footage at the apartment... That doesn't make sense."

"It was Stephen," the attorney said, unsure of the words she needed to offer to avoid being killed. Then she just decided on the easiest path. The truth. Or part of it, at least. "He put you in the driver's seat. The tape at the apartment was from only after he'd switched places with you."

The dead woman uttered, "How?" But as she did, chaotic images began to flood back to her. The night out at the restaurant. It was supposed to be just the two of them. An anniversary of something. Of their first date maybe?

But then there were others. Three men, maybe four. His old college buddies or colleagues. Or possible political backers? It hadn't mattered."

Chandra sat down in the chair again, eyes focusing at middle distance. "He invited them to stay for drinks," she spoke as the images came back to her as if calling the play-by-play. "But it was our dinner. Our night."

Bronwyn sat up on her elbows and said, "You were playing the politician's wife. Smiling and acting out the role. The role you would soon have."

There'd been shots. Stephen occasionally caressing Chandra' arm as if it was some sort of appeasement for ruining their night. More shots. Loud, cackling, laughing too hard at jokes that weren't funny.

Bronwyn watched the man in the chair, eyeballing the part of the table leg that wasn't embedded in her body. If she could just get to it...

The attorney said, "You got pissed and left. Said you'd take a cab. But instead, you crawled into the back of your car, puked then passed out. Two hours later, Stephen came out after calling you a dozen times, saw you in the back, and got in the driver's seat."

Chandra grew angrier and angrier, and then it occurred to her. "How do you know all of that?"

"It was Stephen, Chan," the defense attorney said, pleading. "He threatened me. Gave me some money—"

"You were paid off? How do you let an innocent person rot in jail—"

"I was trying to free you! I was working day and night, not sleeping."

"But the one piece of evidence that would have gotten me out you hid from everyone! How could you ev—" Chandra stood and walked over to the woman on the floor. "That time on the dining room table with my ashes right there in the room, your old house, that wasn't the first time. Was it?"

"Wait… you were… there? How…?"

"WAS IT?"

Bronwyn leaped for the table leg, fingers grazing it for just a moment, but Chandra was too quick. A succession of three quick kicks to the head and chest and the woman on the floor curled into a ball, whimpering.

"I'm sorry, I'm sorry, I'm sorry."

Chandra laughed and leaned down, picking up the long, jagged piece of table from the floor.

Bronwyn Redding watched as the man swung it through the air as if he was hitting a home run. She knew what was coming next but was too weak to move anymore. Hopefully, it would be quick.

"It's got a good heft to it," Chandra said, grinning from ear to ear, the smile too big for the man's face. "I think, after, I'm going to keep this. It'd be poetic if I killed both of you with the same thing, right? Or maybe romantic. Yes, the two lovers killed with the leg of the table they fucked on with the remains of the woman they let die in prison nearby."

"Please, please, I tried—"

Chandra raised the long piece of wood over her head. "No more lies from you, friend. The rest of your life, which ends tonight, will be filled only with pain. Just pain."

"No, no…"

Bronwyn saw the man bring the club down, his face contorted in a horrifying grimace. She heard him grunt as he struck her with all his strength, her knees pulled close to her chest, but her body was already so broken that she didn't feel the impact.

Then the man above her swayed, unsteady, and stumbled a few steps backward.

"Uhhh, what…" Chandra's voice said, almost slurring. "What just… who are you?"

Bronwyn opened her eyes to see the man looking to the far side of the room, but she saw no one.

"Wait, I remember you." The anger returned to her voice as she regained her footing. "The reporter. You're that reporter I killed."

* * *

One minute earlier, Brenda had discovered Bronwyn Redding's name in the directory on the ground floor of the multipurpose building. Still unable to break physical rules that no longer applied to her—something she instinctively knew came down to her own perception—she'd taken the stairs up the seven flights.

In a lighter mood, she would have laughed. It was the easiest she'd ever taken a flight of stairs, and she wasn't even tired when she'd reached the top.

But Brenda was terrified.

He was up there, the last face she'd ever seen while alive. And she was inside of him, whatever that meant. Brenda had never heard stories of ghosts taking over people's bodies. That was the work of demons. Possession.

In her mind, that fit. This person was evil and deadly and angry.

Those thoughts were in her head as she crossed the threshold and heard a woman's harsh voice, unnatural, scream out, "WAS

IT?" Then there'd been the sound of a frantic, violent beating, and after that crying. Sobbing.

Don't think, just go!

Brenda took a moment to psych herself up and then jogged around the corner, turned that into a brief sprint, and leaped at the man standing with a table leg over his head, connecting with the woman inside him with a crack! That felt electric. She tumbled to the floor but quickly got to her feet again.

All things aside, she actually felt kind of good. Then she realized that was due to the energy she'd stolen off Chandra, who was now wobbling slightly. In an odd sight, as the man struggled to stay on his feet, the woman inside wasn't entirely in sync. For a brief moment, it looked like she might split from him entirely.

But the brilliant white tendrils of light thickened for a moment, and she was restored. Full control once again.

The woman-man was talking to her, grinning, but she ignored it, and once back on her feet, she charged again. As she leaped this second time, a hand—both alive and ethereal—reached out and grabbed her by the neck.

Brenda's own hands reached up, trying to break Chandra's grasp. But the killer held her the way someone might hold up a kitten. Or dirty linen. The reporter struggled and quickly felt the energy she'd stolen deplete. Then, despite not having a body, she was overtaken with a tiredness that could only be described as bone weary.

"You can't hurt me," Chandra said and laughed, squeezing tighter. "Ha, pitiful! Have you been hunting me this entire time?"

Brenda's arms dropped, and she wished she could spit. "Screw you, prick."

The supercharged spook laughed again, then shook her hand, and the reporter's head lolled from side to side. Brenda's vision swirled and darkened at the edges. She then felt herself flying through the air and landing on the ground hard. Face down, she couldn't even lift her head but turned it to face Chandra.

"I can't kill you again, but even if I could, where would the fun be in that? You wait there though. I've got just the place for you.

Some associates of mine are taking volunteers, so I'll take you along to your new home." Chandra laughed. "Man, eternity is going to be a bitch for you. First, though, I've got to even a score."

The man picked up the table leg once again and moved toward the defense attorney, who was again curled into a ball, begging.

"Leave… her."

Chandra looked over her shoulder at the reporter. The woman on the floor spoke again. "Leave her alone."

"Shut up. Why do you even—"

"Your fiancé, he… it was him."

"I know, idiot. This traitor told me. He knew about the tape."

"No," Brenda said, trying to make eye contact with the other woman on the floor. Chandra was too strong, but maybe if the lawyer were to strike the living man and she the dead woman at the same time..?

Then she realized the problem with the plan. Of course, she can't see me. Damn. All she could do was try to distract her killer and hope the other woman could get a blow in.

"In prison," the reporter continued. "He ordered the hit. On you. Your fiancé had… you killed."

Suddenly, the table leg in Chandra's hand dropped a few inches, her eyes focused elsewhere.

From the floor, the attorney took one last shot, swinging a busted lamp toward her attacker, but the table leg quickly came down on her skull, ending any last rebellion from Bronwyn. She was close to passing out

Something passed over Chandra's face. She shrugged the man's shoulders. "Doesn't change a thing. It'll just be more satisfying to kill 'em, I suppose."

Then she lifted the hard wood of the table leg over her head once more.

But the leg stopped at the top of its arc and wobbled. Then the fingers holding it went stiff, the grip so tight that they turned bloodless, white. Brenda watched as Chandra convulsed for just a moment. And one of the streams feeding her, fueling her with energy, flickered, thinned, and crackled for just a moment. Then it disappeared altogether.

Chapter Thirty-Six

There was a loud crack! as the stream that had been flowing from the top of the ghostly power station was snuffed out like a match in a hurricane. The air was dense and filled with an ozone smell. Electricity fried the air around me.

I was moving quickly. I'd been lucky so far, working without being noticed. But now, with Minneapolis taken off their grid, they'd be coming.

"Bernie, we gotta move fast," I called across the room to where the mailman was pulling spooks from their ethereal bindings, easing each of them up to their feet and walking the dazed men and women to the back wall.

"Going fast as I can, Paint."

"Good," I said. "Because they'll be coming very soon."

Bernie paused and looked at me then looked up to the dimmed power station and then to the wall nearest the street. "Uh, going faster now."

There were now at least fifty of them sitting, recovering. Some were crying, some chuckling, happy to be free. One of the women I'd pulled from near the center of the power station had wearily asked something about President Reagan.

I wasn't exactly sure how the ethereal machine worked, but the power station hadn't stopped spinning entirely. It just no longer had the power to broadcast the energy into the Ghost Mob's grid. I thought of how thrilled Nikola Tesla would have been to see such a machine.

There were still at least thirty spooks still strapped into the machine.

I'd freed Bernard Grimsby first because owed him. I'd promised to help the guy out, and instead, he'd ended up in the nightmare of the machine. It took a moment to get him the energy he needed, first by having to take it directly from me, then we both recharged from the stream.

We'd done the same for the first of them, helping each regain a bit of strength, but were reluctant to take full charges because it was still the people trapped that were being drained of that energy to provide it.

Now that the stream had gone dark—which had been the plan in the first place—it would be harder to get the remaining ones recovered and on their feet again.

"Damn," I said, lifting a young man with the back of his head missing. The man was massive, wobbly, a rag doll, so I dropped his hand onto my shoulder a few times to collect a bit of juice, and he stiffened his legs and began walking with my help.

Moving slowly toward the wall, I looked up at where the stream had been. The room was now much darker than before, the only illumination the spinning, weakened power station. I could only hope I'd weakened Chandra Whatever-her-name-was in time to help Brenda.

A moment later, I realized I was worried about the wrong spook.

"What the hell? What did you do to my beautiful machine?" I recognized the voice. He'd been standing over me the last time I'd had a run-in with these guys. Calkin. The Mob's leader.

He didn't sound happy.

"Motherfucker!"

Nope. Not happy.

I whispered to the young man who'd slung his arm over my shoulder that he'd have to make it to the wall without me. He gave me a nod and said, "Hey, thanks. Thank you."

Smiling, I said, "No problem."

"Painter?" Calkin snarled. "Of course it would be you. Goddammit, do you know how long that took to build?" He looked over at the wall. "Ah well, at least I got all the raw material I need here."

Calkin was flanked by his boys again, the tall guy and the other with the dumb-ass hat. What is it with dudes that can't go anywhere without other dudes?

The spook lieutenants began to head toward the wall where the newly freed group was sitting, just behind me. I spread my arms.

"Nah, man," I said, hoping the terror that was spinning my ghost stomach wasn't bleeding into my voice. "You got clubhouses all around the country. This one's closed for business."

"Yeah," Bernie said coming around the other side of the machine. I waited for him to stand next to me so the two of us could take on these assholes together. He didn't slide up next to me. I glanced over my shoulder. Bernard looked very content hanging back, crossing his chubby arms. "Out of business. So you know, git."

I mouthed at Bernie, Git?

He shrugged and gave me a faltering smile.

"No, it ain't," Calkin said and glided toward me. "Just needs a few repairs. We'll be back up and running in an hour. And I'll plug you back in, Painter, so you don't give me any more trouble!"

From the wall, I heard a voice. It was the young man I'd walked there moments earlier.

He'd gotten back up to his feet, putting a hand on the wall to steady himself. "That's not going to happen, man." Next to him, those with the energy to stand slowly did. Two or three dozen people. They weren't strong, but that many against three?

The odds were in our favor.

Calkin wasn't feeling the same as me and laughed a big hearty gut laugh, all bent over and hands on his knees and shit. So I squared off and kicked the prick straight in the face, which sent him flying back. Momentarily disappearing in the darkened space, he tumbled a few times then stopped. Slowly he got back to his feet.

I'd weakened him somewhat, but I'd also taken a big gulp of juice from the guy. I was nearly full strength. Ready for a fight. That was when the walls came alight with spooks. At least thirty, maybe forty members of the Ghost Mob slid into the room. Calkin had come prepared.

I was suddenly marginally less ready for a fight.

"Boys, I want you to beat the ever-living shit out of all those gangly spooks hanging out on the wall back there to where they can't even blink." His two dudes were back at his side. Not even looking at them, he threw a punch through both of them. They barely flinched.

And with that, Calkin was all juiced up once again.

"Damn and shit," I muttered.

Behind me, my wingman was right there. "Damn!" Bernard said, recrossing his arms. "And shit!"

I don't think my boy got out much back when he was alive. But he was trying. And right now, he was in the line of fire as much as I was, standing his ground. So he was all good with me.

Calkin pointed at me. "This guy, I got." He came at me, slow and menacing.

The mob began to close in on the spooks on the wall, nearly all of them on their feet now, fists raised. In their weakened state, it wasn't anywhere near a fair fight. At least not yet.

I held a hand up to Calkin and asked, "Do you remember laughter?"

He slowed to a stop, blinked once, seeming unsure of what I'd said. He cocked his head then looked back at me, an annoyed look plastered on his face. "What?"

I said calmly, "Do you remember laughter?"

He blinked again, slowly, then began moving toward me again. "What the fuck is that supposed to mean?"

Behind me, I heard Bernie whimper slightly. "Painter? Come on, man."

"It's a code word. Or code phrase, I guess. Technically, it's a phrase," I said, putting my hands on my hips. "Right, I'll give you that. Not a word, totally a phrase."

"You losin' your marbles, and I ain't even hit you yet?" he said, raising his fists and grinning wildly. "Code word for what?"

"Ah," I said, raising a finger in the air. "Code phrase."

"Whatever. I'm done with you. So get read—"

In an admittedly disappointing attempt at a rock singer's voice, I wailed, "Do you remember laughterrrrr?"

The walls exploded with light, and ghosts poured in from every direction. At the sight of them, the crew who'd been bearing down on the weakened spooks on the wall spun and recalibrated for these new intruders.

The room began to shake with the screams and yells and calls of two armies about to clash in battle. Over the din, I yelled, "Ghost Mob, this is the Zoo Crew!"

Calkin spun in a circle, mouth hanging open as he watched the melee begin.

"Zoo Crew, these are the assholes who've been hurting your people!"

Then the Mob's leader locked back onto me—

I added, "Time to return the favor."

—and it was on.

Chapter Thirty-Seven

Chandra stumbled as she fought to keep control. Brenda was still far too weak to take a swing and began yelling at the defense attorney, willing her to take up the fight.

"Hit him! Hit him with anything!"

Bronwyn was moving, slowly scooting herself back toward the overturned couch. Chandra caught sight of her and took a few steps closer, then struggled again, flexing, twisting. Exasperated breaths were coming from the man in bursts.

The attorney grew bolder, moving faster, scuttling across the floor.

All the while, Brenda was rocking back and forth, trying to generate enough juice to get moving. One blow directed at Chandra and she would have the strength she needed to possibly finish this.

Chandra saw Brenda was gaining strength again and took a half step toward her but then changed tacks.

"I just need a boost, that's all," Chandra said, gritting the teeth of the man she'd hijacked. "I snuff you out, friend, and I'm good. No time to draw it out, though. Shame. Would have been fun." She yelled, almost roared, and began to charge but then stopped.

At first, Brenda wondered if the man, Jan Jorgensen, was regaining control. Taking his life back inch by inch, tripping up the killer inside.

But then she saw what had stopped Chandra in her tracks.

The lawyer—her body busted and bleeding, her ankle so horribly twisted now it would never again be right, the other leg skewered by shards of jagged wood—was now pointing a silver pistol at the man standing in her living room.

"Stay back!"

Chandra balked for a moment then said, "You can't kill me! I'm already dead!"

Bronwyn found the safety and switched it off. "I beg to differ. But let's see what a couple slugs in your chest does. See who's right."

The voice of her dead friend burst into a laugh. "Ha, yeah, you'll kill this slob, but I won't be going anywhere. Maybe," Chandra took a half step closer, "maybe, I'll slip into your body? That would be sweet! Oh, the horrors I could put you through. I wonder what wearing nothing but a slip down a few dark alleys downtown might bring you?"

"Stay back, or I will shoot," Bronwyn said, her hands shaking. "You were going to kill me!"

Chandra, frozen in midstep, smiled, "I was angry. You slept with my fiancé. With me still in the room."

"You were DEAD!"

A nod from the man. "Fine, shoot the guy. Then I slip out of this meat and then into you. Maybe I'll see what it feels like to put your hand in the garbage disposal? Or pull an eye out with a ballpoint pen. Or get you arrested for messing with some kid. The girls in prison told me all about what they do with those ones."

Brenda called out, but only Chandra could hear her. "Don't. You'll kill him, not her. He didn't do anything! You can't!"

There was hesitation on Bronwyn's face. Then, as if she'd argued the case in her head, the judgment was handed down.

Bronwyn Redding scowled. "I'll take my chances," she said, and her finger went to the trigger.

From her right there was a shimmer, a quick swirl in the air. Then a sound erupted, an unearthly "nnnnnooooOOOOO!" As she fired the gun, something hit it, shifting the trajectory, and the bullet only clipped the shoulder of Jan Jorgensen, lodging in a framed portrait of some family member.

Brenda had no idea where she'd gotten the strength, maybe from the pure emotion of it. As she tapped the gun, she rolled, losing her footing, but then popped back up and charged at Chandra again. She clocked the woman, who'd already begun to make a run for it.

"Bitch!" Chandra shouted, smashing into the overturned bar, half bent over it. As she pushed off, the reporter came down again, this time with both hands, and Chandra tumbled against the wall.

Jan Jorgensen did not.

Chandra went to stand, but, weakened, fell back to the ground.

Another shot rang out.

For the first time, Bronwyn heard Jan's voice, his real voice. Taking in gulps of air, he pleaded, "Don't. Please, don't. She's... not in me anymore. Oh, Christ, she's finally out of me."

The defense attorney wasn't yet convinced. "How would I know that? I can't trust you—"

"My name is Jan Jorgensen. I'm sorry for what she did, but that wasn't me."

The barrel of the gun lowered. "Where is she then? Gone?"

"No," he said and looked across the room. "I can still see her. She's by the wall. Drained. she won't be going far, I don't think. Not for a while."

"What was... the other thing? What hit me?"

Jan looked up at Brenda and began to weep. "Thank you. Brenda, isn't it? Thank you," he said and choked on tears. "I'm so sorry for what happened to you."

Brenda smiled and then realized something. "Wait, you can see me?"

Jan nodded. "I suppose it's some type of hangover from... whatever that was." He put his face in his hands and sobbed. "Oh, Christ, all those people."

Chandra was back on her feet, sliding toward the door. Brenda began to move for her but then realized that even if she had incapacitated her, she had no idea what to do with the woman.

"Don't worry, old friend! I'll wait for my moment, and then me and you—"

Jan spat in her direction. "She can't hear you, you idiot. You're dead!"

"Fine," Chandra said before she slipped away. "Oh, it's going to…"

Brenda and Jan watched as the woman's expression changed. Her image wavered for a moment, like a weak television signal.

She looked up but not at either of them. "That's not ri—"

Then she was gone.

Jan waited for a moment for someone to explain. When no one did, he asked, "What happened?"

* * *

Across town, Pete David was rubbing his mouth with the back of his fist. He'd finally sat down. Seated opposite him was Alice, grinning from ear to ear.

"I'm still not entirely comfortable with this," he said. "We should do a full investigation before publishing. Dammit. I should pull that back to drafts."

"No, leave it. The investigation, yes. You can do all of that. There's plenty of time for that."

"I don't know how you talked me into this. It's borderline irresponsible. There's no real evidence."

"Are you joking? You heard the congressman on the phone. Hell, you recorded the conversation."

Pete nodded.

Publishing the name of Chandra Withy's jailhouse killer, even in a small web story just a few paragraphs long, was about to set off a firestorm. Reporters would soon be circling the congressman's office. Within the hour.

"You know, hate to say it, but part of me doesn't want to get lapped by any of the other news guys. Everyone will be on this. I need to get a reporter up to speed ASAP—"

"You've got a reporter on it already," Alice said and smiled. "I suppose I can type it up and she'll be, well, the ghostwriter. As it were."

The newspaper man nodded and stared out at his city once again.

"The world is a lot weirder than we ever imagined."

"I dunno," Alice said and shrugged. "I always had my suspicions about it."

* * *

Jan stared at the space where Chandra had been as if she might wink back into the room, and the horror would begin all over again.

"Is she gone?"

"Looks like it."

The man stared down at the rings on his fingers, several chains around his neck, a half dozen broaches pinned on the inside of his shirt.

"All of these people," he said. "What do I do now?"

Bronwyn fired her gun into the ceiling, and Jan yelped, clutching at his chest. The attorney shouted, "Who are you talking to?"

"A woman named Brenda. Can you give me—"

"No, I can't give you anything," Bronwyn said, lowering the gun but not yet putting it down. "I'm still not convinced I shouldn't give you a bullet. But for now, can you call an ambulance so I don't bleed to death on my living room floor?"

Brenda moved toward Jan and said, "Um, you may want to delay that just by a moment."

He glanced at Bronwyn, who glared at him. "She does look terrible."

"Yeah, but you did kill all those people."

"Not me!"

"The world won't see it that way."

His face sank. "Oh. Oh wow. That's… you're right. Oh my God."

"And, just being honest, you're going to be named as the killer of—" she pointed at the jewelry on his hands and neck and body "—all those people in a newspaper article in a few hours."

"How do you know that?"

"Because I'm going to write it."

He started to say something but stopped. He then nodded. "What do I do?"

Bronwyn offered, "You'll need a good defense lawyer. I could maybe argue insanity? I don't know. I'll come up with something."

Jan thought about it for a moment, then said, "You don't have the best track record, actually."

"One time," she said and shrugged. "One slip-up."

Brenda stared at the lawyer for a long moment and then instructed Jan to ask her why she'd kept the tape secret. The question made Bronwyn chuckle through blood-stained teeth.

"I know, it would have freed her, sure, but I wasn't kidding about the threats. Not Stephen directly, his people, but he knew. If I'd turned it over to the police, I'd be dead. And as long as I had it tucked away, they couldn't touch me."

"So your client rots in jail, then?" Jan Jorgensen said.

"I knew she was innocent. I would have made sure she never got convicted," the lawyer said, her lip quivering slightly. "Never knew about the prison hit." She then added: "And don't judge me, you're a serial killer! You don't want my help, fine. But first thing you do is call an ambulance."

Jorgensen turned to the ghost reporter. "I'm going to have to run, aren't I?"

Brenda nodded. "But I need you to do something first."

"I know, call an ambulance."

"Uh, right. Hold that thought," Brenda said, and Jan Jorgensen laughed. Then he let out a shuddering sob. The reporter added, "Chandra lost half her power because my friend knocked out a power station back in Minneapolis. And if he did that, he's got a bull's-eye on his back as big as the moon. There's this type of mob of dead people, and they—"

"Listen, I can't take any more revelations. It's freaking me out. But I owe you. Tell me what I need to do."

"We're going to the pub."

"Good, I need a drink."

"No time for that," she said. "A friend of mine is trying to stop all the really scary bits of the bible from happening. Basically, Revelations rewritten by Stephen King."

"I'm not... prepared for all this. I can't process it."

"You don't have to." She thought for a moment. "Okay, I also need this weird guy. Well, sometimes he's a guy, other times he's a terrifying thing, actually. Do you have a phone?"

* * *

The staff was stumped. They would have to call a locksmith to get into the room at this rate. Also, after a thorough search of the basement of the facility, it seemed the bingo room of the Shady Hills retirement home was on a localized circuit, somewhere in the room.

Which meant they couldn't turn the music system off from anywhere but behind the door.

When the song began to play once again, the volume so loud it shook the walls, the glass, and even some fillings, the director could only shout hoping to be heard.

"What triggered this? Off his meds?"

"No, Bethany thinks he got a call from someone. Three-one-two area code."

"Chicago?

He doesn't know anyone in Chicago far as I know," the director said to the staffer.

"What did the guy say to him?"

"Who knows? But Mr. Wilner has been in there blasting that godforsaken song for the better part of twenty minutes now! If he wasn't already half deaf—"

"Get Andy, the locksmith. Not the other guy with the weird teeth. He tears the doors up too much." The orderly ran away, hands over his ears. The director tried again, pounding on the door. "Mr. Wilner! Julius! Julius, you must turn that god-awful racket down!"

The director had been hoping to end the week quietly. And now, he was fighting with a senile, near-dead octogenarian who'd suddenly developed a late-eighties rock-and-roll fetish.

He sighed. "Welcome to the jungle, indeed."

Inside, Julius was posting notes on an online cloud account but then heard it. Someone was singing along with the music.

Took you long enough. Julius smiled then yelled over the music. "Gary? How fast can you get to Chicago and back?"

Chapter Thirty-Eight

I spun in place several times, struck hard by the hulking leader of the Ghost Mob. However, as I'd been hit, I'd thrown both arms outward—a spook version of Christ the Redeemer—so that when I spun, the fists of both my hands clubbed Calkin's chest and shoulders, the concussions sending a thump-thump-thump through both of us.

He'd really done a number on me with that hit, a right cross crashing into my left cheekbone, but I'd picked the juice I needed right back up again with the spinning-fists-of-doom move I'd come up with moments earlier.

Calkin stumbled backward, his hands momentarily too heavy for his thick arms, and they dropped slightly from the sides of his head. Obviously, this guy had done a bit of fighting—he'd taken up a classic boxing stance. Left foot forward, right back, and both fists usually planted somewhere in my face.

But actual strength doesn't mean anything in the InBetween. It's about two things and two things only: how much juice you've got and how strong you think you are. It goes beyond just convincing yourself you're stronger; you have to know it. Even if, you know, it's not actually true. Much harder than it sounds. But it helps to have led a life of misleading yourself a great deal.

Check.

"Shit, it would be so satisfying to kill you, Painter," Calkin said, fists clenched, waving them in circles and building up a small charge. "Look around you. All you are doing is bringing all of these people to me!" He laughed, a bit too loudly, it seemed. "Look up. You've seen the sky. This, all this? It's done. The only one who doesn't get it is you."

The zoo people were doing all right at the start despite their hesitation to join the fray. The mobsters had been in scraps before, but they were fighting for gain. A goal. The folks from the zoo were people with something to lose. They were fighting to keep their home, their friends, which made them stronger.

When the sergeant and I had thought up the basic plan, we hadn't counted on one thing. Once the power station at the fairgrounds went dark, it had become a hole in the sky. Sure, you couldn't see it from, say, Belgium, but it seemed Mob members from all over the Midwest began flooding in.

At first, it was just a few, but the sheer number of people from the zoo kept them busy. Over several minutes, the few became dozens, and the dozens became hundreds.

In between trading belts with Calkin—at one point, I'd actually laid him out on the floor for a few moments—I could see that some of these newcomers were now just watching the fight. Entertainment. Like this was the Colosseum.

At the Minnesota State Fairgrounds. So a colosseum with corn dogs.

As some of the Mob's crew, swirling like thick black ants around my friends from the zoo, were dispatching innocent people one by one, others hung in the wings, some comfortably leaning back on their elbows on the floor, watching, cheering, laughing.

I said, "What have I done?"

Calkin saw my expression and smiled, so self-satisfied that it turned my stomach.

"This plan has been in place since long before you were here, Painter," Calkin said. He saw an opening, ducked low, and straightened with a punch, clocking my chin. Stars filled my head, and I swam in the air, trying to keep my footing. "Long before I

was here. You heard of inertia? You can't stop this. Wheel's in motion. You can either be in the tank or under its tracks."

Around us, the Ghost Mob was just cleaning up now. Their yelling and screaming, the sounds of armies clashing, had abated. I had some thought that if I could take their leader out, maybe that would change the playing field.

Seeming to sense my intentions, Calkin smiled and dropped his fists. He pointed to his chin.

"Come on, then. Why don't you take yourself a poke? See what you got?"

He was baiting me, but if I could get a shot in—

Calkin then spread his feet slightly and put both hands behind his back. I realized the Mob had grown quiet. They only watched us now. We were the show. He thought knew how this fight was going to go. It could make him overconfident. Or, in the end, just… correct.

The next few moments were all that mattered. Arguably, there were the only things that mattered on the planet.

So I ran right for him. Straight at the guy.

He cocked an eyebrow, shifting his weight back and forth.

The thing with fighters, especially those who think they've already won, is that they can get big-headed, theatrical, like he was now. So when I saw the heel on his left foot rise slowly, I knew what he was about to do. He'd already laid two wicked kicks into me earlier.

But this time I was ready.

Just a few feet away from him, I raised my right fist high in the air, and that was when he launched his leg at me, with all his strength. I fell.

Instead of striking him, I dropped my fist down as fast as I could, as if punching the floor. This set me into a quick roll, and I went under the leg he was using to strike his final blow. I slid past him on my left knee and extended fist, feet first, and when I put them down, I was moving.

I was back up and going fast. Skating and picking up speed. This guy looked at me as he spun in place,. I circled again and again, faster and faster, crossing foot over foot like I'd learned when I'd been a pee-wee or bantam skater in South Minneapolis.

My circles were growing smaller. He tried to take a swipe at me, but I had the momentum, and each time he reached out, I tagged his arm. At my speed, each thump weakened him. The third put him on his knees.

Behind me, the voices rang out. Jeering, yelling. If there were actual words, I couldn't hear them. I made a quick cut, losing a bit of speed, but my angle changed so fast he didn't see it coming. I cut behind the leader of the Ghost Mob, elbow to the head.

"Fucker! Shit," he barked, then went to one knee.

I picked up speed once again, sizing him up. The guy had both fists on the ground, trying not to collapse. One more circle, and with that speed—

Some of the shouting, I realized only too late, was my name. Someone was calling my name. When I finally picked it out, turning, I saw the mailman. Bernard was waving his arms, pointing, shouting my name.

Then he covered his mouth.

That was when the blows came. Calkin's two lieutenants had slid in on either side of me suddenly, a reverse of the energy transfer move they'd done with their boss when first arriving. Each man put a fist into my stomach, and I went down in a heap and slid to a stop.

The world around me was pitch black. I couldn't see Bernard anymore. I couldn't see the wall people, huddled together, captive. I couldn't see the dull glow of the crippled power station. I couldn't see Calkin and his two thugs.

But I felt them.

One swift kick flipped me over. I'd been facing down and now was staring up at the ceiling. Another kick to my side and my head filled with stars.

"I never saw shit like that, man," Calkin said, taking shots at me, draining my energy into himself. "You worked out how to skate in the InBetween? Ha, that's amazing. Once we put you back in the machine, we gotta get into your head and see how that's done. A skating army? What a sight that will be!"

Another kick to the side of the head. Boot heel to the face.

I looked up at him. "You can't do this."

"We are doing this, man. It's over." Calkin lifted his arm high then came down onto my chest, draining me to a critical level. "You put up a fight, but the fight is done. Time for the army to rise." Then something passed over his face. A smile grew, and he bent down and lifted me to a sitting position.

"Hear all that racket? That crazy bitch is coming here with my ticket. Our ticket," he said and let me fall back again. He stood and shouted, "Tonight, the Ghost Army rises on the world of the living!"

Around us, the room burst into cheering, a roar that only sent my head on more of a spin.

I cracked open an eye, my vision darkened at the edges, and caught the leader's face. He was smiling so widely, it was obscene. This spook hated the world. You could see it. If you're around long enough in the InBetween, you see more than just the shell. This guy wanted to hurt millions, billions. I'd had a chance to stop him but had failed.

My head lolled toward the wall, and if I could have wept for the world, I would have. And at the wall, all those people, stuck in the horrific machine for years—some for decades! And they'd stood their ground, trusting in me, and I'd failed. They were going right back in for, well, forever.

And so was I.

But then I heard something. Not heard so much but felt. The slight tug, the pull of something familiar.

I said, "Ha, amazing."

"Don't even," Calkin said.

"I got rules, man."

"Whatever. So what."

"Rules that, you know, work for the living and dead. Just the three."

Calkin raised his arms in the air, thumping his hands together. "I got only one. I'm going to deliver you more pain than anyone has ever felt."

I said, "So the last rule is Rule #3. And," I said as the wall across the room began to shimmer. "It's a biggie. You ready?"

"Fuck you."

"No, that's not it. Rule #3: Find good people and make them friends..."

Calkin smiled a menacing grin. "No friend can help you, man."

"Ah," I said and tried to lean up on my elbows. I simply collapsed, too drained. "One caveat. Call it 3a, maybe: Make friends with good people... who are big. Very, very big."

Calkin's face started with a belly laugh, but then it changed. Time for me turned slow and inky, and he began yelling at some of his crew. The leader of the Ghost Mob had his arms pointing in two different directions, gesturing wildly. His face was still contorted in anger, but there was something else there now.

Panic.

That was when I felt the tremors, the concussive beat that felt almost like a baseline getting louder and louder. Coming closer.

Then I saw it.

Calkin had spun toward it and looked undecided whether to run or charge. But who could have run at that?

This was a nightmare. Five legs, hulking, part insect, part bear, part wolf, part dragon.

This was a killing machine with two heads, one lizard-like, the other the head of a barracuda spitting fire.

This was a monster. Its three arms were muscular and flexed, claws dripping with darkened gore as if from countless victims.

This was Gary.

Gary 2.0.

"Raarrrrh! Eat all of you, shit out your bones!" the horrible creature said, running straight for Calkin. "You!" He pointed at the mob leader. "You! Prepare yourself!"

Calkin looked at the Gary-monster, still shouting at his Mob, waving wildly. He was calling for them to take down this creature.

The Mob hesitated, unsure about the power of the terrifying new enemy. Was it as deadly as it seemed?

Of course… there were all dead already.

After a few of the braver agents moved toward it, the rest seemed to grow some spines, and they began to charge Gary. Gary continued his beeline for me and the Mob leader.

Thomp, thomp, thomp!

"You! Prepare!"

Calkin squared his shoulders, standing his ground. If nothing else, he needed to show his crew he wasn't afraid. His feet, pointing in two different directions, told a different story. The Mob leader roared back at the creature, then called to his men to attack with everything.

Again, Gary pointed. "Get ready!"

It was, frankly, a lot of chatter from a horrific, scary, bloodthirsty monster.

When the creature was about ten feet from Calkin, it raised its three arms high and roared with such an unholy quake the world of the living would have felt it, and I was sure the windows had rattled.

That was enough to make the Mob leader move, and he began running toward the largest group of his men, who were running toward the two of them. Twenty men and women, all in black, homing in on Gary, with more than a hundred, one-hundred fifty coming from the other side.

My heart had leaped when I'd seen him. We had a chance! But against this many, he just couldn't. The first wave would mean hundreds of blows. No one could stand that.

Looking back to Gary, I was puzzled. He was running, his bulk undulating up and down as I could only watch, barely able to move, but he was still heading toward where Calkin had been. Had he not seen the Mob man bolt from his path?

Then I realized, as usual… I'd misread the scene.

"Prepare yourself!" Gary shouted again. He hadn't been shouting at the Mob leader. "Ready yourself, Painter Mann!"

Right!

If I could take a swipe at my friend, I might be enough to be able to stand again. He was running right for me. I'd have to time it just right—I would have to hit him, not the other way around. As weak as I was, it would be hard to pull off, but we could do it.

With all of my strength, everything I had, I struggled, shaking, raising my arm slowly, opening my fingers.

The timing would have to be just right.

When he was just one stride away, I would move my hand forward in a slow strike. That should give me the juice I needed. My mind momentarily went dark, the exertion too much. Then he was right there!

The light in the room was eclipsed by this colossal beast. I moved my hand and struck! But no. No burst of energy. No surge of juice. Gary leaped over my head to avoid bashing into me but was now still running full tilt away from me. Too far away for me to try and take another swing.

But I couldn't anyhow. The little effort I'd made had took the last of everything I had. My arm fell and felt heavier than I could ever remember.

Gary would have to take them on his own. And I knew that he couldn't. It would only be a matter of time.

The Mob was closing in on him quickly now, racing past me like black fire ants, all of them yelling and screaming again, and it made my head spin, my stomach turn.

It seemed Gary knew that we'd failed and was running hard for the far wall. Through the two streams of mob agents, I caught a bleary sight. Calkin was smiling again. Laughing. This was his time.

Soon, the Ghost Mob would reign.

Through all the shouting and calling and yelling, I once again heard Gary roar, "Painter Mann! Ready yourself. It is coming!"

What is he talking about? We're finished.

"Prepare!"

Darkness had closed in even more on my vision… so weak… but the weight of my arm didn't seem right. Slowly, I willed my head to turn, and when my eyes fell on my hand, it looked wrong. Too big. It even, just slightly… sparkled?

Then I knew. Gary hadn't been trying to rejuice me by letting me take a swipe. He'd handed me something. That was what had made my arm so heavy. In my hand was the bat from the Chicago pub. The bat that had first taken out spooks in 1974, the only thing I'd ever seen a ghost hold in its hands in all the time I'd been in the InBetween.

But Gary was crazy if he thought I could—the sparkle. Why was it twinkling like that?

Squinting, I could see things embedded in the bat. When I'd seen it in the bar, it hadn't looked like that. In the long crack, there were bits of metal, strands of silver and yellow and even what looked like—but couldn't be—a milk bottle charm.

And rings. Lots of rings.

Stuffed in the crack were dozens of rings, necklaces, pendants. Like the sort of bat someone like Liberace might have swung.

Gary was right. I had to prepare. I centered my mind and gripped the bat with weak fingers.

Because Gary wasn't running away.

Gary was running for the machine. The power station.

This anomaly, this creature who was never totally full of juice, never totally empty, was about to insert himself into the power station. And I was holding the other end of the plug.

Calkin's expression faltered when he caught the weak smile on my face. When he saw what was in my hand, his head snapped up and worked it out.

"NO!" he shouted to the bloodthirsty crew, who simply couldn't hear him. "Don't let him go into the mach—"

There was a roar. Then an impact as if a meteorite had crashed through the ceiling silenced the room. The Mob stopped in its tracks, no longer shouting.

Calkin began running to me, full speed.

Back behind my head somewhere, I heard a quickening thrum-thrum-thrum as the light in the room turn from dusk to dawn to midday sun in a matter of seconds.

The bat began to glow. As those first drips of energy passed through the bat into my hand then my arm, I didn't feel so exhausted anymore. In fact, I began to feel better than I'd ever felt in the InBetween.

As I got to my feet, Calkin's pace faltered, but he kept coming.

My arms, my legs, my fingers, my toes, everything in my ghost body felt electric, light and powerful! I looked up and saw a steady stream of juice flowing from the power station directly to me. I now had the strength of a power station coursing through my body.

Calkin stopped and cursed then called for his men to change tacks. "Attack Painter! Take him down!"

I was stronger than I'd ever been, but with two hundred of these angry creatures coming at me, it would be close. But I hadn't thought it all the way through. But that was okay, because my friend Gary had.

Even plugged into the machine, on all fours and immobile, writhing in what I knew would be the worst pain he'd ever endured, Gary once again roared out, "Paint-Painter! Prepare yourself! It's coming!"

I'd already had more energy than ever and, it seemed, an unlimited supply, as long as Gary could hold out. I wasn't sure—

Then the machine began to spark and snap. The fat tendril of light arcing toward me twisted and writhed like a fire hose on full blast. It seemed to be damaging the machine!

But it wasn't hurting the device. It was breaking—not itself, but whatever bonds had been put on Chandra's connection to it. I wasn't sure how it worked, but it had seemed that the Mob had restricted her two to the two power stations, Minneapolis and Chicago.

But inside Jan Jorgensen, Chandra had carried out a killing spree that had taken her through the Midwest, the Pacific Northwest, and southern California.

Time froze, and my chest began to swell, a burning that turned into an inferno, an inferno that turned into an angry, dying star. Gary's unlimited energy was snapping the ethereal bindings the

Ghost Mob had put on this station. After that the power from chains and lockets and rings of all those poor souls did the rest.

The glinting objects embedded in the bat had come from countless victims from all across the country. This wasn't just two groups feeding me now.

It was all of them.

Within me, everything was on fire, surging with electricity, and outside of time, my ghostly body exploded, then reconstituted itself. It was now stronger, more powerful.

I gripped the bat tighter in my hands. The world around me froze.

The spinning of the power station slowed to a barely discernible crawl. The arms and legs of the charging Ghost Mob were static. Calkin's face, shouting, angry, strained...

... scared.

Above me, I saw the one stream turn to two. I convulsed, and two became three. Another tremor turned three to four, four to five, five to six, until I could no longer count them. This thick conduit of energy carried the might and strength of hundreds, thousands of lost souls who were now not powering some grid.

They were powering me.

And I could feel this. These innocents, trapped inside against their will—from all across the country, the continent, and maybe the world—they knew something had changed. And while they'd fought their machines for years now, this was a new game. This was their chance. This was their vengeance.

And they no longer fought the machines.

They gave me all of it. Everything they had.

I caught sight of the mailman who'd been held down earlier by the boot of some thug. He was back on his feet, arms raised. He was the only one to speak.

He said, "Painter? Fuck these guys up."

The army charged me, and I pulled the glowing bat back and could hear it move through the air, leaving trails of energy. When I connected with the first group, there was a burst of electricity and thunder-crack, and a dozen mob members flew back past the walls at a high angle, rocketed through the ceiling, and showed no signs of stopping.

Another swing, zttt-crack! And another dozen exploded with light and were gone, moving almost too fast to see, up and up, and gone.

The others were now not so sure.

So I skated in big, full circles, using the ringed bat almost like a hockey stick, smacking Mob agents as I went. To the left—that one he wouldn't stop until Boston. Crack! Those three would end up in San Paulo. Crack! I'd leaned into that one a bit, and that half dozen looked like they'd land somewhere in a very cold part of the world.

Slicing across the floor, swinging the bat faster than even I could see, I sent Mob members flying from the room in every direction, some going vertical. They likely would one day be the first to leave the solar system, and they would spend a very, very long time alone in the deep recesses of empty space.

After less than a minute of cleaning up, I looked around.

No Calkin.

Bernard came up to me and, strangely, I had to look down to see him. He seemed so small. My arms and legs and chest pulsed with light. It was intoxicating! This powerful, I could be more than a lowly private investigator. I could be a superhero!

A god!

The mailman read my face. "You can't keep it, right? You know that."

"With this power, we can track down Calkin! End this," I said, and my voice rattled the windows. I was now affecting the living world, not only the dead. "This terrible power can do so much good."

"Too much," Bernie mumbled, avoiding my eyes. I realized he was scared of me. I felt sick. "And all of that power comes from people, right? Innocent people. Time to let them go, man."

But what did he know? To use such strength—such thrilling, amazing power—for good instead of bad?

"Painter," Bernie said and placed a hand on my leg. Then he began to shake a bit and snapped back. "Whoa. I think... I think I've got a chubby."

"Jesus, man," I said and winced. "Never tell me stuff like that."

Bernie's face fell. "If I know anything about history, absolute power isn't good for anyone. It always goes bad."

"History? I thought you were a mailman."

"Well, you know, comic books."

"What?"

"And graphic novels. And just novels. A lot of fantasy and sci-fi—"

But Bernie hadn't seen what I'd seen! The pain the Ghost Mob had caused! The pain they'd given me by putting me in that machine! I could end it all!

Strength flowed through me, and I couldn't ever remember feeling better than that very moment. However, I'd need every bit of power I could get.

I looked at the mailman and the others around me, the ones I'd freed. If I got them back in the machine, this one would be functional too. Then, in a matter of hours, I could clean up the Blind Spots of the world! Make things right!

"Power like this?" Bernard said has he took a few steps backward. "It can turn Good to Bad, man."

"IT DOESN'T HAVE TO!" I roared and the ghosts around me buckled. I softened my tone and explained, "If a good person had this power—"

My mind suddenly drifted back to what Brenda told me at the capitol building.

"Lincoln said 'If you want to test a man's character, give him power'," she said. "Problem with that though is by the time you find out their dangerous, they're already powerful."

I was the InBetween's best private detective. But I was also its worst. Before that, I don't really remember.

Bernie was right. Smiling, I nodded and patted him on the shoulder, and he collapsed in a heap.

"Shit, sorry." Leaning down, I grabbed his hand and made it swipe me a few times until he was okay again. He stumbled to his feet and laughed. He shrugged and said, "Do it."

As I walked, each of my steps left behind a glowing print, juice oozing from my every ghostly pore. When I looked back, my footprints looked massive. Once at the machine, I gently lifted my friend Gary, who was no longer a monster.

Just a Gary.

He was limp but okay. He'd never been drained like this before. I gave him a bit of energy and then did what I had to do.

"Grab him," I said to some of the people at the wall. "And get out of here. Everyone clear out."

Before I did the deed, I looked to the wall and saw my friends watching. Gary and Bernie had pushed their faces through the wall like I had done the first time I'd been here.

Bernie said, "We just want to make sure you're okay."

Gary said, "And I gotta see this!"

I waved, and huge trails of light filled the air. My hand looked impossibly big.

Turning, I knelt and went back into the machine.

Above me, the light thickened and swirled, the machine taking too much power now, draining it from me in a feedback loop that moved faster and faster until there was nothing left in the room but light and the hum and buzz of electricity.

Then the machine exploded, sending a shock wave through the ceiling, and all went dark.

*   *   *

I wasn't sure how long I'd been lying on the road just outside the fair pavilion.

Gary and Bernie were there.

At first, none of us spoke. We were all just enjoying the sky. The beautiful dark sky riddled with pinpricks of light. In the distance we spied a comet. I quietly wondered if that was someone I'd sent up there. Something told me that if I looked a little closer,

I'd have seen that shooting star was actually wearing a stovepipe hat.

"I missed the sky," Gary said, and I agreed with him. "Never knew how much I did. I'm glad it's back."

Up on my elbows, I said, "Where's Calkin?"

Bernie shrugged. "High-tailed it out of here. Had a few of his guys with him, but the power grid is down. They're done."

I felt tired but not drained. In fact, I was full of energy. I shook my head. "He'll try again."

The mailman looked at me and smiled slightly. "How do you feel?"

I shrugged. "I think I've got a chubby."

Gary stood up and said he'd had enough fun for the night. I stopped him and asked him how he'd gotten there, and he told me how Brenda had come up with the plan. They'd gotten Gary to Chicago to pick up the bat from the pub called The Grind.

That move—cranking Guns N' Roses in the bingo hall—had put Julius in rest home detention, and I laughed and said I'd find a way to make it up to him.

Gary shifted his feet for a moment. "You can't, Painter. He's, you know, passed."

"What? Did all of that—?"

"Nah," Gary said with a look on his face that was the most content I'd ever seen him. "It was just his time. But I can tell you when he went, he had a smile on his face."

My heart broke, and if I could have cried, I would have. He had been an excellent Temp. A good man. A good person.

I was very lucky to know these people.

Gary finished by telling me Brenda had worked out that the rings and necklaces and baubles were the bridge to the power, had had Jan Jorgensen stuff them into the bat, and had had Gary run back with it.

"Jan Jorgensen?" I said, then realized it. "Chandra's gone."

"Yep," Gary said then began walking back to wherever he goes.

Sergeant Peterson came by for a moment, and I shook his hand gently and thanked him and his people, telling him they had been the heroes tonight. They had taken back the InBetween for the rest of us. He smiled, nodded, and said there was a big barbecue planned the night after next at the zoo.

"What? Who's cooking?"

"Livies. It's some corporate thing. But we can watch. Next best thing."

I told him I'd be there. He hugged me and went to go be with his people. Bernie stood up, taking a sudden interest in his hands.

"Long night," he said. "I feel woozy."

Getting up slowly, I agreed. "You and me both."

"What was that like? Being, you know, like that?"

I shrugged. "You were right. Too much power for one person."

"Well, Thor had power like that, and he did mostly good. So maybe it would have been okay."

"What?"

"But probably not."

Smiling, I nodded. I'd liked it too much. Like no drug I'd ever felt. It was, regrettably, good that it was gone from me.

Bernie smiled and shifted for a moment then leaned into me, startling me slightly, giving me a guy hug. He broke away, looking a bit sheepish.

"Hey, I wanted to say thanks, Painter. You said you'd take care of me, and you came back."

"You were great, man. Don't sell yourself short."

"Oh, hey," he said then put his hand to his head, wincing. "I worked something out about you. I wanted to tell you—"

Then he was gone.

I blinked. "Bernie? Hey, man…"

Then I realized it.

With a small smile, I mumbled to myself, "Prepare yourself, Painter…"

I braced for what was coming. Brenda had written her final story, and she would be remembered for being a great reporter. The victims of Jan Jorgenson would finally rest.

I said, "Way to go, kid," looking at the sky one last time.

Chapter Thirty-Nine

"Is she gone?" Pete Davis said, rubbing his eyes. Alice could only nod.

They both stood in his office at the Chicago Post, neither saying a word. The newspaper's managing editor had hit Publish himself and was now looking at the article online. It had detailed the end of a killing spree by a man named Jan Jorgensen.

In the coming weeks, Pete Davis had promised to track all the victims down. Not himself, of course. He'd have some junior editor on it.

But like the article he stared at now, the stories would all carry the same byline.

By Brenda Matthews.

Pete told Alice he was already working on a believable story about notes left behind by the dead reporter. And that from those notes, she would also be publishing a series of stories about how a junior congressman had, in a moment of panic and stupidity and greed, framed his fiancée for the death of a young boy.

The stories about how he'd ordered the hit would have to go through a team of lawyers, but those would come too.

Before he'd published, Brenda had hugged both of them, which of course neither felt. But there was something. Something warm. They knew.

For his part, Jan Jorgensen had disappeared. He'd apologized for his role in the killings, detailing each as best he could. Where he couldn't remember names, he did his best to recall dates and cities. While he hadn't been the cab "driver," he had let Chandra in—a story no one would ever believe. And he was a good man. He agreed with Brenda, Alice, and Pete: the families of the victims might find a little peace knowing a small part of what had happened.

Brenda had given him an hour to hide, get away. Maybe get to Canada. Just go. He'd begged for more time, but all of those souls had waited long enough.

He couldn't deny that, in some way, he'd been complicit. He had agreed initially to the idea of letting Chandra take over, unsure really what he'd agreed to in a moment of weakness as he'd sat in his bedroom rolling a .38 revolver between his hands.

Everything had changed when Chandra began her reign of terror, but by then it was too late.

Through Alice, Brenda had made one final request.

A follow-up to this first article listing the fourteen names of Jan Jorgensen's victims would list the others. These were the ones that Jan could remember.

"But today, we need to add one," she'd told the frail woman. It had been a very long day, and both were tired, albeit in different ways. A good tired. "Without him, none of this would be possible."

Alice nodded. "Painter."

"Who's Painter?" Pete said. "Odd name."

"Painter Mann is a private investigator," Alice said and smiled. "The best dead private investigator in the world."

Pete Davis sighed. "I am not putting that in the article."

"No, but he was one of Jan Jorgensen's victims, too. He's earned a rest."

Using some program called Trace Tools, they searched for details about the life of the private detective but came up with nothing. As Painter had said to Brenda during their long trip to the capital days earlier, he'd made no mark when alive.

354

He'd done nothing of note. The world did not miss Painter Mann.

Alice said, "That's why he loved being the world's only dead P.I. He was doing good and was good at it. The best."

Epilogue

The Professor took a deep, cleansing breath and stared at the sky.

Well, as deep and cleansing as she could with the rock concerts blaring below her at the north face of Stone Mountain.

Other than the rock concert, it was quiet. The electric hum of the sky no longer poisoned the night. The stars had returned once more. She knew that the leader of the Ghost Mob was out there. He wouldn't give up. He would try again.

But he wasn't the only threat. There was another. The first.

The man who'd been Chandra's father had disappeared years earlier. For a while, the Professor had convinced herself the world had solved his murder. He'd cleared. But she knew better. And now, with the sky quieted, she could feel him again.

Out there.

Waiting.

"Do you know who that is?" A voice came up the rock, sending pebbles into her lake of calm. "Man, that's Lynyrd Skynyrd!"

The Professor sighed. Her peaceful respite would have to wait a moment. "No, I don't. Should I?"

"Come on, 'Simple Man'? 'Sweet Home Alabama'?"

"Doesn't ring a bell."

"Seriously? 'Free Bird,' for chrissakes?"

The Professor started to speak, stopped, then went again. "Wait. Yes, 'Free Bird.' With the lighters and all that."

"Well, not anymore. But yeah."

"Painter, you know I was really enjoying my quiet there for a moment," the Professor said, despite a small smile escaping her lips.

"Not during 'Gimme Three Steps,' man. That's a toe-tapper!"

The Professor turned north, inhaled and exhaled, closed her eyes. After a half minute, she said, "It's not an unpleasant beat. Catchy."

"Toe-tapper, yeah."

The Professor swayed slightly then opened her eyes and looked at him. "The mailman? The reporter?"

The dead private investigator smiled and nodded. "Yep. They're clear. Along with a bunch more. And more to come." Then he started humming along with the music.

The guru nodded. "And the little girl? The one who put you on her stepfather's case? Any explanation on how she could see you?"

Painter sighed. "I don't know how she knew I was there. Hearing me and seeing. But I'll work it out."

Another nod from the Professor. "A successful case, then."

"Yeah, not bad. So maybe I earned a rock concert sitting with my friend."

The Professor opened her mouth to say something but then thought better of it. She asked, "What about you? I saw the article. I saw your name. But here you are."

"Nah, I'm good. I'm as solid as a spook can be," Painter said. He lolled his head back and listened. "Maybe my time ain't done yet."

"Maybe." A shrug.

"You know, I was thinking about it," he said, turning and leaning on an elbow. "I don't know if when I looked at Chandra I got that entirely right. Yeah, it looked like my killer, but when I think about it, really concentrate… the features were similar."

"Okay."

"But I musta got it wrong. Maybe it was someone who just looked like her."

A nod. "Like a relative. A parent?"

"Yeah. Or a brother. Or sister."

"A father?"

"Right," he said and closed his eyes again.

The Professor smiled. This type of thinking, reasoning, might be why he was actually a good investigator. At least a good dead one.

Painter indeed did have a talent for sniffing out—or at least sniffing toward—the truth.

But she knew something about the man sitting next to her that he didn't. He'd forgotten. A stark truth that would one day shake Painter to his core.

Another time, she thought. And the Professor mimicked the private investigator's position and just listened to music, with a friend, under the stars.

They were up there.

Both of them in one place!

The parking lot was full of cars, but not a person was in sight. Only him.

That old bitch who had stood in his way so many times before. And him. He'd ruined plans for their army.

They had been so close!

Time to rebuild.

But in time, soon, before the army marched on this world, those two would have to go.

He caught a glimpse of his face in the side mirror. Well, not his face. Not the one he'd been born with. Not the one he'd died with.

When alive, this man had been a genius. A homicidal genius, sure, but brilliant nonetheless. He'd worked out the physics of the InBetween like no one had before. One part Einstein, one part John Wayne Gacy. Maybe two parts John Wayne Gacy.

The "cab ride"? That was just one of the hidden secrets of this world. There were others.

The young man took another drag of his cigarette and then threw it through the open window of a nearby car. On its bumper: a faded sticker of the rebel flag.

He slowly pulled from the lot toward the exit.

He knew of a place to throw these two who were now sitting up on that mountain so smug. He had once discovered a place that was not life.

Not death.

Not afterlife.

An infinite prison.

Before the army would rise again, that was where these two were headed.

Into the eternal pain and madness of being fully conscious within an envelope of pure nothing.

ACKNOWLEGEMENTS

The author wishes to thank the masochists who agreed to read early drafts of The InBetween like Leah Pasnin, Jeremy Elwood, and Nicola McHaffie. The New Zealand health system offers four free psychiatric counselling sessions for those who need it. You'd be wise to take advantage of that. And extra thanks to Jack Roach, who is the Alpha Beta and helped me not look like an ass (He's also a terrific writer, so go check his stuff out). And of course, my wife. Thank you for being a sounding board, a comforting voice in the dark, and my very best friend.

DEAR LOVELY, GOOD-LOOKING READER...

If you liked The InBetween, please take a moment to leave a review on Amazon, iTunes, or wherever you might have picked it up (and thank you for that!). This allows other readers to find the novel and, no matter how short, reviews help book sales.

Enjoyed The InBetween?
Pick up Dick Wybrow's "laugh out loud" thriller
available now….

Hell, inc.

Chapter One

The wind gust hit me like a drunk stepfather, and I fell forward.

On all fours and exhausted, I struggled to keep from collapsing into the pools of rain in the long, shallow trenches time had clawed out of the dirt road beneath me.

The hidden beasts beyond the clouds were still tossing their electric balls to one another like some threat. I knew somewhere in my head it was just lightning, however, they now seemed content to limit their play to the part of the sky behind the dark man.

Naturally I couldn't see his face, which was probably the point. Asshole probably thought it made him look cool or something, all backlit and spooky.

And I dunno… it kinda did.

Craning my neck up to look at him, I tried to pull his face, an expression, out of the darkness but didn't try too hard. His was a face you weren't supposed to see unless everything went real bad. Thankfully, when the sky flashed, all I could make out was the brim of his hat.

He may have spoken by that point. I don't remember.

"Either way," I answered. "I don't…" I collapsed into a coughing fit. He waited until I was done, mainly because it seemed like he enjoyed watching me experience this very basic discomfort.

Maybe it reminded him of old times or early days. The simple pleasures.

Because it doesn't seem like the Devil on Day One was all about burning souls for all eternity and all that. First morning on the job, he probably drummed up a couple hay-fever attacks, maybe someone got popcorn stuck in their teeth with no floss handy, a couple of light bruisings.

I lifted myself back off the road.

The only things that moved were his hands as they slowly manipulated the top of his walking stick. Where the stick met the road, there was some meshing or a bumper that stopped it from digging too deep into the Mississippi mud.

Then, I tried again: "I don't know how it... works."

Pitiful as it was, this made him laugh—an awful sound that trailed off into the sky, folding itself into a roll of thunder. This made the damp, dead grass tremble, and for a brief moment individual blades shed fat drops of rain; the ground on either side of the road appeared to burst with starlight.

Then, dark again.

"Seriously, man—" I said.

"Of course, you know how it works," he said. "That's why you came." Silent for a moment, I could feel his eyes on me, taking me in. "What's your name, boy?"

"I dunno... I thought you'd know that."

With a twitch of his hand, he lifted his walking stick, and through the torrent of rain, I felt a dull throb of pain where my neck met my skull. It rose like a fever and then washed over me.

"Don't fuck with me," he said flatly, as if he'd just ordered a cheese sandwich or something. "Me, I know your real name. The names you had before you were born to this shithole, that is. Hell, y'all don't even know that much. What do they call you 'round here, is what I was asking. What is your name?"

"Raz," I said. "My mother called me Rasputin. Named after some—"

"Shut up. Don't care."

"Got it."

"Raz," he said, a smile in his voice. "Ha! That is one fucked-up name you got. Goes well with your fucked-up life, I suppose. And your fucked-up wife."

My fists turned to balls, and this time I looked up at him, caught his eyes. I wanted to hit him. But I knew better. At least, I knew now was not the time. Not when I needed something from the prick.

That aside, who throws a punch at the Devil?

That seemed like a lose-lose scenario to me, so I kept my knuckles buried deep into the Mississippi muck.

The dark man let out a big breath of air, like he'd been holding it for a long while. It stank like he'd been licking a dog's ass half the day, then ate a corndog found in the back of a refrigerator three months past its sell-by date and washed it down with some warm Clamato.

Couldn't hit the guy, but I could at least rag on him. If only in my mind.

"Okay, so, me I'm not an accountant or anything," he said, his words tumbling down onto my head, "but... I don't have to be. Got a fuckload of accountants. Christ, we're up to our collective assholes in accountants, truth be told. And lawyers. And more recently, corporate 'brand ambassadors.'"

By the way, no joke, the Dark Lord of the Underworld, Satan himself, actually used air quotes with his long fingers when he said that last bit.

"Whatever," I said. "Like I care about your overcrowding issues. Just tell me: What do I have to do?"

The stick went up again, but he didn't strike me. Instead he said: "If you'd just— Damn it, your kind does not listen! That's your big problem. Everything's about you, you, and you."

My arms were weakening, so I locked them to prevent myself from collapsing, but I couldn't hold my head up any longer. Dropping it, my chin hit my chest, and I closed my eyes and listened as the rain poured down my face.

"Gotta check what it's worth," he said. "What you're puttin' up here—barter, right? That's the plan?"

He stood up to leave, and I snapped my head to where he'd been sitting earlier. He was gone from the stump.

"Right," I said. "Yes, that's the plan."

"You'll know," he said, standing next to me now. "We'll have one of our people reach out."

I nodded, then nodded harder so he was sure. "Yes, yes. Whatever, yes!"

He chuckled, the laugh dry and heartless. "You don't even know the deal yet, but you're already saying yes to some accord?"

"Yes, yes," I said, spitting out water and snot. Raising my head, I still couldn't see his face. My eyes wide, I said again: "Yes."

He took a few steps, but I couldn't tell which direction.

"Don't work that way, Raz. Wish it did, but there are rules," he said. "But let's say you and me, we've got a tentative agreement. You gotta sign off on the final still."

My chest began heaving. I was sobbing. "Yes! Christ, yes! I'll do it."

For the first time, I saw a part of his face. Just his mouth, really. He smiled wide. "Not yet. But real, real soon. It will all come together real soon."

I yelled with what little strength I had left. "You... but you promise to do your part? That's how it works, right?"

"Sure, of course. As long as you meet the terms. Need to run the numbers, and then—"

"Just save her," I screamed at the smug prick. "It's eating her up from the inside, and you fucking probably put it there in the first place."

"You lookin' to blame someone for your wife dying, you gotta look up, not down, little brother. Not my thing, Raz."

Leaning on an elbow, I cocked my finger and pointed at him. "This is exactly your thing!"

"There are concentric circles, sure, but... nah. I don't get into that line of work. Me, I'm more of a global mover."

He was gone again, slipping away from my sight, my outstretched hand just hanging out there in the rain. A moment later, I felt his breath on my neck.

"Listen, you know what they say about pointing fingers?" he said, grabbing mine with a hand that was both ice cold and warm. His other hand, bone white, appeared in front of my face.

With that hand he merely pointed at my forehead as if it were a gun, then pulled back his thumb, cocking the hammer. "When you point a finger at somethin', you got three pointing back... and one at God."

The rain stopped as if a spigot had been twisted shut. There was a final low rumble off in the sky somewhere, but the lightning was gone.

Then everything turned black as a deep, deep hole in every direction.

Finally collapsing, wet gravel dug into my cheek but before I passed out, his voice drifting toward me one last time.

"My people... they'll reach out sometime tomorrow. Then the clock will be ticking, Raz. You better get your rest."

And with that, I was seconds away from passing out in the middle of a lonely, rain-soaked dirt highway in bumfuck Mississippi.

Some "Crossroads."

Not that it mattered. I had already proven them wrong! They said she couldn't be saved.

They said "say goodbye to her" and things like "it's just her time."

They said there was nothing that could be done, and they were wrong.

Wrong!

At least... shit.

I damn well hope they were wrong.

Upon brief reflection, as I passed out shivering and coughing, it occurred to me that I may not have thoroughly considered the totality of my actions before green-lighting my plan.

I had just made a deal with the Devil to save my dying wife.

Me.

Damn.

Chapter Two

The next morning, I woke up slowly, frying under the Mississippi sun and caked with Mississippi dirt.

Given the circumstances—that is, if evolutionary forces had been aligned in my favor—one might have guessed that, sensing imminent danger, I'd have instantly sprung up, crouching like a tiger dragon, ready to test my fight-or-flight instincts.

But no.

I'd fallen asleep, lying facedown on a muddy highway in rural Mississippi, and my mind was slowly drifting back into my skull as if I had no cares in the world.

As if there was nothing that should concern me. Nothing at all.

Like the fact that I was lying facedown on a muddy highway in rural Mississippi.

Ultimately, it wasn't the sun beating down hard that finally woke me. A deplorably early riser, the sun had already been up for hours.

I wasn't even stirred by the binaural hum in my left ear, which turned out to be two small black flies that had found a dark place to express their forbidden love.

And it wasn't the choking dust, which had risen up again after the sun had burnt away last night's rain. That put the humidity somewhere around what you might expect to find if you tested the gap between the plastic seat and the taint of a 350-pound NASCAR fan during the final lap of the Daytona 500.

No, what actually pulled me from sleep's embrace was the sensation that my balls were being jiggled.

And it seemed, for the first time in months, I wasn't the jiggler.

It took me a full ten seconds to finally process all this, but when I did, my body instinctively flipped over.

"What the fu—?"

Then I was on my feet, unsteady and momentarily blinded by the sun.

I ached everywhere but managed to swing my arms in the air, hoping whoever had been digging in the front pockets of my shorts would feel the wrath of my fists.

They did not, in fact, feel my fists' wrath.

I stood there, eyes like slits, swinging my arms like an angry drunken orchestra conductor.

A gravelly voice tumbled toward me. "Aww, you ain't dead."

"What?" I said. "No!"

"Shit, I thought you was dead."

Cracking one eye a little farther open and shielding my vision with a dirty hand, I saw an old woman, heavy and sweating, baking in the sun where she stood. Thick, bulky clothes despite the punishing heat.

She looked disappointed.

"Gross," I said. "Weirdo. You normally go around jiggling the balls of seemingly dead men?"

She didn't answer.

Stumbling a few steps out of the road, I found the stump the Dark Man had been sitting on the night before.

"I know this is a bit of a flash judgment on my part," I said to her as she continued staring at me, "but if that's your thing—ball-jiggling dead guys—you've got some deep-seated, emotional fucked-upness that you should probably address with a trained professional."

She didn't answer.

I plunked down onto the stump, and my sore legs briefly loved me as if for the first time. For a man of thirty-two, it didn't seem like I should feel this old yet.

Could be that the previous night's accommodations had been rather lacking.

Could be that many of my thirty-two were "hard-livin' years" as George Jones had once put it. Or maybe that was George Thorogood. Possibly George Michael.

"I thought you was dead," she said again. She started walking away, slowly and wobbly, in a way only old women can.

"You already established that little fun fact, ma'am."

"Was looking to see if you had anything... worth having."

"Wait," I said, letting out a deep breath. "You were robbing me?"

Nice. That'd make it the second time in twenty-four hours.

"I thought you was dead."

"That... you know, every time you say those particular words, my thoughts turn a little more violent. I'm not normally, but... you know—"

"You don't got nothing anyhow worth taking," she said, still wobbling away, but she hadn't yet traveled more than a few feet. It must have taken her weeks to make it down the road to get to my balls.

"But you thought digging through my pockets, stealing from me, would be a good way to kick off your morning, huh?"

"Well, I thought you wa—" She cleared her throat. I stood up from the stump to follow her. She was slow, but my best guess was she at least knew the way back toward town. She continued: "You seemed like you wouldn't miss whatever somebody else might find."

The old woman ambled down the middle of the dirt highway. The sun at our backs, I matched her pace but still clung toward the edge of the road.

"I'm just trying to get a feel for the locals," I said, my voice frayed at the edges. "So when you find a guy facedown, instead of, I don't know, calling the police or a doctor... you fine folks jiggle the man's balls."

The buzzing in my ear had suddenly reached a crescendo, and realizing there were two insects having sex in my skull, I violently shook my head back and forth, trying to forcibly evict them from their love nest.

Not the wisest choice. This became clear when I found myself flat on my back, down on the dirt highway again.

Thankfully, in the torrent, the bug lovers had quickly checked out. For a brief moment, I felt a little cheap and used.

I made it back up to my feet, slower this time. The old woman was now about thirty yards ahead of me.

Crazy old bat can move when she wants to, damn.

When I finally caught back up to her, the effort it took drained any last bit of anger from me. We walked silently for a few minutes.

I thought about the previous night. As much as I could say that it seemed like a dream, I knew it was real enough. Having exhausted every effort to save my Carissa, as she'd saved me time and time again, I found I'd had no options left.

In fact, that very scenario had been explained to me in detailed medical terms. But still, when it came to my wife, that wasn't good enough. So I'd ended up at the famed Crossroads to make a deal with the Devil.

And it seemed a deal had been struck.

Or a tentative deal.

My part, which was easily established, was wagering my soul. Whatever. Frankly, without Carissa, it didn't seem worth very much anyhow.

The deal—or "accord" as he'd called it, all fancy-like—still wasn't clear. He'd said something about his people getting back to me. Odd.

So in essence, I was only vaguely sure that I'd put my everlasting soul on the line, hoping to save my wife from her deadly disease.

Sure, it was selfish, in part. I just didn't see the point of being here if she wasn't around. As I said, she'd saved my life countless times—nearly every precious day we'd had together.

And she was—if you pardon the mushiness and potential irony, given my present circumstances—my soul mate.

If she were gone, I was essentially dead anyhow. It had taken me years to finally realize a humiliating fact about myself: I'm no good on my own.

Seriously.

If it had been me on that deserted island instead of Tom Hanks, I would have died within twenty-four hours. And fuck Wilson because a) he didn't have any hands or anything, so he was no help at all, and b) he was a critical and bitchy little leather asshole. Total downer.

I freely admit the shortcoming, but at least realize my own Achilles heel. Most people never do.

And now the only partner I wanted in the whole world was dying in a hospital bed as I trudged along, frying in the late morning sun, next to an old woman who moments earlier was trying to rob my not-dead body.

Things were not going terribly well.

"How far is it back to town?"

The old woman sighed. "What town you trying to get to?"

"I don't know... any town."

Then she stopped and slowly turned toward me. Staring intently for a moment, she then twisted her head back to where I'd been lying, where she'd found me not dead. She looked back at me. "What the hell was you doin' out here, then? You fall out your car?"

"I don't own a goddamn car, haven't for... It doesn't matter."

Walking again, she said, "And you say I got the deep-seated, emotional fucked-upness. I ain't the one who falls asleep on dirt highways."

"That's not... those aren't my usual accommodations. I passed out," I said. "It was... You wouldn't understand."

"Oh, nah, dumb ol' woman like me wouldn't get you and yo'r big thinkin' ways," she said, all syrup and sass.

"I don't mean it like that. It's just... it's kind of unbelievable."

The old woman chuckled, deep and throaty. "Oh, I understand all right. Didn't realize it at first. Don't get so many out here no mo'," she said and pointed a thumb back over her shoulder. "You thought you was at the Crossroads down here to make a deal with Lucifer hisself, right?"

My mouth opened, and my jaw hung there for a moment, then I closed it and said nothing.

"Boy, they ain't no Crossroads," she said in a manner better suited if she were rocking in an old chair on an old, dilapidated porch. And maybe smoking a pipe. Or whittling. Maybe whittl pipe. Or smoking a whittle. She added: "That's just a dumb ol' legend some record company made up to sell blues records."

"Okay, whatever."

"Fine, believe whatchu want."

She hadn't been there the night before. This woman was someone who attempted to rob not-dead bodies for chrissake! What did she know?

Ahead, through the dust and haze coming off the hot road, I saw the first signs of several buildings. Shops.

Still, my fists were banging off my thighs at how quickly she'd dismissed my incredible, mind-boggling metaphysical experience from the night before.

"So, I talked to the guy," I said. "Not that you'd buy that."

"Talked to who?"

"The guy. The Dark Man. I came out here, damn right, to the Crossroads. And he was there, had this wide-brimmed hat. Waiting right there for me."

She was quiet for a moment. "That was probably Randall."

"No, it wasn't a guy named Randall!"

"Fine. What'd he look like?"

"What? It was dark. And he's, you know, the guy... so you can't see his face. I think."

"You didn't see the man's face?"

"No... 'cause, you can't, right? It's just black."

She shot me a look.

"I mean, it's dark. No light. You can't see."

She nodded slowly. "Sound like Randall."

"No, no, and NO! Of all the things that could possibly be anyone 'led Randall, this guy was none of those things!"

"Uh-huh. So I'm guessin' you came up on a guy in the middle of ⁓hway you didn't know, a face you couldn't see, and you ⁓d said you'd sell him your soul."

"⁓'s way, way more complicated than that."

⁓id. "He had this... stick."

"A walking stick. Very powerful. One tap, it sent these… bolts of pain right through me!"

"Right. A stick."

"With… uh, I think it may have, sort of, had a tennis ball on the end of it. For the mud."

"Uh-huh," she said, looking toward me with a mocking, wide-eyed expression. "You right. Stick with a tennis ball on it? That sounds like some serious Old Testament shit right there."

"Whatever."

"So spooky!" She put her hands to either side of her mouth very theatrically, and I asked myself if I could live with having punched an old lady. "Boy, sounds like you met the Devil hisself!"

And all signs were pointing to yes.

"Stop talking," I said. "Now. Okay? Please?"

Kicking up little swirls of dirt as we walked in silence, I watched the buildings form before us. One looked to be a diner, and the thought made my stomach growl.

I was hungry and so thirsty it was hard to swallow. Curling the toes of my right foot, I could feel my ID and credit card were still there. Hopefully the card hadn't gotten too wet from last night's storm.

"That there's Wardoff. Sort of, uh, in between spots out here. Not a big place," she said, nodding ahead. "Got a Kmart, though. Hardware store. Diner."

"Great," I said. Then: "Thank you."

She nodded, and with that, we'd made some sort of unspoken peace.

I offered to buy her lunch at the diner—after all, she'd led me back to town— but she said she'd just stick to the road, whatever that meant.

With about ten minutes left of walking before we'd reach town, she coughed something up and spit it out. Cleared her throat.

"So, why would you come all the way out here, risk expirin' in this heat? You obviously ain't used to it. Just to offer up your sou to Randall?"

"It wasn't any guy named Randall."

A small smile bent her lips, and she raised her hands as if surrendering.

"Fine, not Randall," she said, then paused and stopped. Her breathing was a little labored. I guess nobody really gets used to that kind of heat. "Well, hold on, now. You really wanted to make a deal with the Devil, din't you?"

I nodded, eyes closed.

"Boy, why would you even consider that? You talking about your everlasting soul, now, ya hear? For what? For a chance to be a better guitar player or to discover the unified theory or something?"

"No, nothing like th— Wait, what was that last thing?"

"I read the science magazines at the dentist's office. Not much else to do out in these parts."

"Except rob dead guys," I muttered.

She shrugged. "Certainly better than jigglin' their balls."

I laughed, and she gave me a smile. As we walked the final few minutes into town, I explained to her why I was willing to risk my eternal soul.

Don't let the adventure stop there! Pick up *Hell, inc.* now on Amazon, iTunes, Kobo, Barnes & Noble and others.